CAUTION to the WIND

USA TODAY & WSJ BESTSELLING AUTHOR
giana darling

Published by Giana Darling

Edited by Jenny Sims @ Editing 4 Indies

Proofed by Erica Russikoff @ Erica Edits

Cover Design by Najla Qamber

Cover Model Josh Mario John

Cover Photographer Lane Dorsey

To my readers for making my dreams come true.

"The dragon teaches you that if you want to climb high you have to do it against the wind."

– *Chinese proverb*

A note to my readers

This is a dark romance. Axe-Man and Mei's story features graphic violence, kinky sex, and sensitive subject matter such as death of a loved one and violence against women. Additionally, it contains important spoilers for *Dead Man Walking* (The Fallen Men, #6) and the rest of the series. I urge you to consider reading those beforehand, but *Caution to the Wind* can be read as a standalone as well.
If you have a problem with any of these topics, please do not proceed.

Also, please note The Fallen Men books are written in Canadian English, and the Cantonese translations are in Jyutping.

PLAYLIST

You can listen to the full playlist on Spotify.

"Under The Big Top"––Cris Jacobs
"The Night We Met"––Lord Huron
"For My Crimes"––Marissa Nadler
"Never Gonna Be The Same"––Mia Wray
"Nothing Else Matters"––Miley Cyrus, WATT, Elton John, Yo-Yo Ma
"I Did Something Bad"––Taylor Swift
"Consequences"––Camila Cabello
"Blame"––Grace Carter, Jacob Banks
"Broken Bones"––KALEO
"Leave Like That"––SYML, Jenn Champion
"After You"––Meghan Trainor
"Starting Over"––Niykee Heaton
"Straw in the Wind"––The Steel Woods
"me without you"––Morgan
"I Found"––Amber Run
"Midnight City"––M83
"Hurt"––Johnny Cash
"Waking Up Without You"––Rhys Lewis

"Sorry"--Halsey
"Unconditional"--Richard Walters
"Dodged A Bullet"--Greg Laswell
"Let You Go"--WILDES
"Bad Habits"--Ed Sheeran
"Still Don't Know My Name"--Labrinth
"New Person, Old Place"--Madi Diaz
"Hunger of the Pine"--alt-J
"Riot"--Camino
"Bridges Burn"--NEEDTOBREATHE
"Hoping"--X Ambassadors
"Where The Wind Blows"--Blacktop Mojo
"Trouble I'm In"--The Unfaithful Ways
"Run To You"--Ocie Elliott
"To Build a Home"--The Cinematic Orchestra, Patrick Watson
"Bitter Sweet Symphony"--The Verve

CHAPTER ONE

Mei

THE DAY EVERYTHING CHANGED FOR ME STARTED WITH A CARNIVAL game.

The Country Fair was an annual summer attraction that appeared suddenly at the end of spring in a wide, wild field outside of the city and disappeared just as jarringly as soon as the cool autumn winds blew in from the east. The air was thick with prairie heat, hot with the scent of grease from all the fried foods and a hint of almost acrid sugar from the cotton candy motes floating on the heavy currents. A constant cacophony of fairground sounds rang across the field: the mechanical heave and whoosh of the large rides, the whoops and cries of excited children, and the errant screams of heat-induced, sugar-exasperated tantrums, the tinny jingle of canned carnival music and the spit and rattle of balls in slots, pellets hitting empty bottles, and horseshoes swinging around metal pegs. Calgary was a cosmopolitan oil and gas town, but even the wealthy wore cowboy hats and tooled leather boots. There was a sea of them that day, from white to black and every shade in between, making everyone look the same under the shadows cast by the wide brims. When I tried to remember the faces of the men in the dark, I always remembered those hats, obscuring everything from gender to race. A question mark in a cap.

My memories of that day were bright and jarring, collected pieces of a shattered funhouse mirror that didn't make much sense, no matter how hard I tried to fit them back together.

But I remembered him.

I always remembered him.

He seemed like some kind of heathen god, big enough to kill a man with his bare hands, so broad through the shoulders it seemed like he could carry the weight of the world. The flashing lights of the carnival carved his strong features out of blue, red, and gold. His eyes shone in the shadows beneath his heavy brow, a blue-green as bright as oxidized copper. I watched as his massive hands, threaded through with prominent veins and tight cords of muscle, flexed on the rough wooden handle of the axe. He was one of the only men not wearing a cowboy hat, his burnished gold hair bright even in the deepening gloom of twilight, slightly over long and curling like ribbon ends over his ears and around his square jaw.

"Come on," my best friend, Cleo, encouraged as she tugged at his bulky arm. "I've got to have the stuffed bear."

Henning Axelsen turned his head slowly to look down at her, his stern-featured face cracking slightly around the mouth to give her that small smile he reserved only for her.

"Don't you think you've got enough, Glory?"

Cleo and I looked at the prizes she struggled to carry in both arms. The head of a plushy giraffe tangled with her long brown hair, and a stuffed snake wrapped around her neck. In her arms, she carried a gorilla, a bumble bee, and a giant rabbit with pink fur.

Cleo blinked at her new friends and bit her lip as she considered his question. Even though they weren't related, Henning and Cleo shared that same kind of thoughtfulness. They weren't loud people or very chatty, either. They meant what they said when they spoke, so sometimes it took them a little longer to respond.

Cleo cast me a sidelong glance, noting that I only had a small doll I'd won at the bottle toss earlier. We were almost too old to go to the carnival with our parents, and we'd sworn to each other this was our last year going to the fair as kids, so I understood her desire to milk it for all it was worth.

Henning caught her gaze, then looked over her head at me with sparkling eyes. "You think maybe I should win this one for Rocky, instead?"

Glory and Rocky.

Henning had nicknames for everyone, even his stepdaughter's best friend. Hearing it from his lips always made something inside me squiggle and squirm.

Rocky because I was scrappy and loyal. He said people were prone to underestimate me due to my slight and dainty build, but they'd inevitably find out some day that I was a champion.

Glory because Cleo's full name was Cleopatra, which meant "glory of the father," and Cleo was his pride and joy.

Cleo instantly nodded, grinning at her stepfather, then at me. "Definitely."

"You're so damn sweet." Cleo's mum, Kate, bumped Henning with her shoulder, then pressed a kiss there. "You know that?"

In response, he pressed a kiss to her brunette head.

"What do you want, Mei?" Cleo asked me, wiggling her

hand through the stuffed animals to grab my own in a tight squeeze.

I stared up at the prizes hanging between two poles at the side of the axe-throwing game and knew immediately which one I wanted. It wasn't the largest or boldest prize, but it meant something to me because it was a dragon.

My Chinese last name was Lung, which meant "dragon" in Cantonese. Everyone called my grandfather Old Dragon, and the symbol of one had protected my family for centuries. Even though I addressed him as *Gung Gung*, the Cantonese title for my maternal grandfather, I always thought Old Dragon suited him perfectly. He was the wisest person I knew.

When I pointed at the small red animal with gold wings, Cleo protested because it was too small, but Henning only gave me that tiny, mysterious smile and stepped up to pay the carnie to take his turn at the bullseye.

"It's a long way," I muttered to Cleo as we stood with her mum to one side to watch him.

The target was at least thirty paces away from where he stood, and it wasn't very big.

Cleo giggled softly, her hand still in mine, sticky with the refuse of cotton candy. "He'll win. Didn't I ever tell you his daddy was a builder? Hen's been using an axe since he was younger than us."

I didn't think using an axe and throwing one were quite the same thing, but I didn't say another word because Henning was getting ready to throw.

Through my twelve-year-old eyes, he seemed as big and mythical as a Viking, his thick muscles rippling under the tight white tee shirt plastered slightly to his torso by the humid summer air. He raised the axe with only one hand, back over his blond head, and then with a hard flick of his wrist, he released it with his elbow extended toward the target. I watched with my mouth hanging open as it wheeled end over end across the length of the grass until it embedded itself just to the left of the centre target.

Before I could recover my shock, Henning had picked up the second axe and sent it spinning after the first.

Thud.

It landed in the red bullseye so hard, the entire target vibrated on its legs, rocked back far enough to seem it would inevitably fall, and then tremulously righted itself again.

The three of us let out a series of whoops as we rushed Henning, hugging any part of him we could find. His soft, almost silent chuckle vibrated through my hands as I fit them around his hard waist. Kate's soft, sweet scent was in my nose, and Cleo's sticky hand was still glued to mine. It was such a simple moment; it felt silly to be sentimental about it, but I was. Both then, engulfed in a family hug, and now, so many years later, looking back on it.

I had my own family and traditions, my own parents and loved ones, but the moment I met Kate and Cleo, then Henning years later, I'd united with them. A *click* of connection I felt in my stomach like two mechanical parts fitting together to create something more.

I loved the Axelsen family, and they loved me.

It was sweet and uncomplicated.

Kate would pick Cleo and me both up after school every day and take us back to her tiny, meticulously clean bungalow so we could play and study while my parents worked. We had a routine, a unity forged by time together that meant everything to me.

Because before Cleo, I was a loner.

Kids made fun of me early on. I was different, which wasn't really enough to tap into the human fear of and prejudice against the unknown. But I was different and *loud* about it. Unlike the other few non-white kids in my class, I always made a point of sitting with the other kids. I was curious about them, and when they proved not to be curious about me, I clung to my uniqueness as if it were both a weapon and a shield. I begged Old Dragon to make me smoked carp's head so I could eat the eye in front of my peers with relish while they gagged and groaned. Sometimes, I wore traditional dress to school even when people asked me why I wore a costume.

It wasn't that I wanted my whole identity to be Chinese. To be defined by the culture of my mother and not the place I was being raised. But I found solace in the richness of my mother and grandfather's customs. I found community there outside of those school walls. A Chinese child was taught from an early age about the importance of history, of ancestors. That we were all linked through time and space. It was comforting for me to imagine them at that cafeteria table with me, two long lines on either side of geishas and fishmongers, of warriors and dark-eyed comrades. It helped to not feel so alone.

And then, when I was in second grade, Cleo arrived in my classroom one day. She was too thin, almost gaunt, with ashen smudges beneath her haunted eyes. There were scabs on her hands and blood on her fingernails because she picked at them nervously while she sat huddled in her seat.

At lunch that day, I knew what would happen because it had happened to me.

Ray D'Angelo and his crew of stupid boys crowded around Cleo when she sat alone at one of the tables in the cafeteria. He pushed her tray off the table, her food splattering to the linoleum, the red apple rolling and rolling until it stopped at the toe of my shoe.

To this day, I wasn't sure if it was the red of the apple, a deeply symbolic colour, my favourite colour, or the look of shame on Cleo's face that made me do it.

It didn't really matter.

One moment, I sat alone at my table doing my mathematics homework and the next, I was striding over to the bullies. I bent mid-step to retrieve the red plastic tray from the ground and swung it at Ray D'Angelo's stupid, pretty face a moment before he could turn fully to face me.

He went down like a barrel of apples.

His friends gaped at me until I raised the tray and bared my teeth at them in warning. Then, they scattered. Ray moaned on the ground for a moment, clutching the side of his head.

"Get lost, D'Angelo," I suggested casually, pressing the toe of my sneaker into his back to give him a gentle nudge.

He cursed under his breath at me, but he did as I suggested and scrambled to his feet, red-faced with humiliation, before running out the cafeteria doors.

One of the teachers came for me then, hauling me to the principal's office, but before they did, Cleo reached out and ran her fingers down my arm until she could squeeze my fingers in her own.

And that was it.

That little moment was the moment we became best friends.

I thought of it then, secure in this little bubble with the Axelsen family in the middle of carnival chaos. And I made myself a promise little girls often made to themselves that I would love Cleo and her family for the rest of my life.

"Here," the carnie ambled over with a discontented expression, the red dragon in his arms. "And if you give a damn about my business, you'll get that bleeding axe out of the target. Can't budge the damn thing."

Kate laughed brightly, squeezing us all once more before stepping away with an arm around both Cleo and me. Henning moved forward to take the dragon and then crouched in front of me.

He studied the fierce-eyed toy closely, then offered it to me. "I've noticed you have an affinity for dragons."

I nodded, mute suddenly under the powerful force of his full attention.

"Mei Zhen," he murmured as if suddenly realizing something.

I didn't really know much about Henning. He'd just appeared one day after school on the back of an enormous motorcycle to pick Cleo up two years ago and never left. He worked most of the time as a resident at Rockyview Hospital, but he was also a reservist in the military, which paid for his schooling, so I rarely saw him after school at their house. But I did know he spoke at least a bit of Cantonese because sometimes, he seemed to understand me when I was talking to my parents on the phone. When I asked Cleo about it, she told me his stepmum was originally from Hong Kong just like my ma and grandfather. "Your name means elegant pearl, doesn't it? Like the pearl seen beneath the Chinese dragon's chin or clutched in its talon."

I beamed at him. "That's why Grandfather and my parents chose it. Because he wanted me to carry on his legacy and become a dragon."

A slow smile curved that firm, serious mouth into a crescent moon. He reached up to clasp me warmly on the shoulder and pressed the dragon into my chest. "I have no doubt you will, Mei."

"What's that mean?" Cleo asked. "Becoming a dragon."

"*Mong zi sing lung*," I murmured to her. "Parents hope their children will become a dragon among men. That we'll be special."

"Exceptional," Henning echoed, squeezing my shoulder before he stretched out of his crouch to his full, immense height.

Cleo nodded sagely. "Well, okay. Mei's definitely a dragon, then."

"Definitely," Kate echoed, smoothing her hand down my

head. My slippery straight hair was falling out of the ponytail, so she stepped closer to fix it gently for me.

"Can I be a dragon too?" Cleo asked, cocking her head to the side as she considered it. "Or is it only Chinese girls who can be dragons?"

"Girls *and* boys," Kate corrected even though Cleo made a face because we both hadn't yet developed an affinity for boys.

"I think you can be a dragon," I told my best friend, and even though I wasn't usually demonstrative, I reached out to take her sticky hand again. "We're best friends. Whatever I am, you are, right?"

"Right," she agreed with that bright, pretty smile she'd inherited from her mum. "Of course."

It was so easy back then, the ties between us all so innocent and bright.

I had no idea that only two hours later, everything would change, and nothing would ever be so simple again.

CHAPTER TWO

Mei

IT WAS PITCH DARK AROUND THE PERIPHERY OF THE FAIRGROUND. The multi-hued, flashing lights of the carnival seemed all the brighter against the starkness, my vision haunted by coloured streaks even when I squeezed my lids shut. We'd been at the fair for hours, and I was weary, but Cleo was still having fun. Everyone liked Cleo now that she wasn't so sickly and too shy to speak, so when we ran into kids in our class near the roller coaster, they'd been happy to include her in the group, even with me dragging behind.

I didn't like them, but then, I didn't like many people.

So, when Cleo was distracted with a flirtatious Ray D'Angelo, the same idiot who had once bullied her, I drifted away from the ring toss booth and meandered through the crowd to get a lemonade from one of the food carts. I'd just paid for my sweating plastic cup when I noticed the small red tent at the edge of that sucking darkness.

My feet drew me closer without conscious direction, my mind drawn to the colour in the way of a bull. I'd always been like that, driven by instinct without the filter of my brain or the softening of a voice from my heart. If I was moved by something elementally, I let it move me.

It drove my parents crazy.

It was quieter near the tent, as if it occupied its own bubble of tranquility on the chaotic carnival grounds. A small sign was stapled to a post by the entrance.

Madame Cheung's Palmistry & Face Reading.

I knew the Chinese practice only vaguely. Old Dragon had told me that there were people in China who could read your face as easily as a picture book. People who could discern from a single palm whether you would bear two children or none, if you'd rise to great success and fortune or die young.

It seemed like a terrifying science, a looking glass into a future that humans weren't meant to see.

A wise soul, I figured, would turn their back on the tent and make their way back into the present.

Of course, I'd never been particularly wise.

So I followed the scent of myrrh incense between the flaps in the red canvas tent and stepped into the darkly lit interior.

It was larger inside than I would have thought, a vast emptiness surrounding the round centre table made it seem important, majestic, the high-backed chair before it like a throne.

But it was the woman seated facing me behind the table who ensnared my attention. She was old, as in *old*, seemingly ancient. The silken, pale skin of her face was creased into precise folds like some ornate origami. The loose drapery curtained her unsmiling red-painted mouth and cast shadows over her long, dark eyes. Her red silk garments mimicked the same textile, billowing around her slight form.

She looked magnificent.

Instantly, I went to her, my feet moving fast over the carpets strewn on the ground until I reached the chair before her.

Even though I'd been born in the flat plains of Alberta, Canada, I'd been enchanted by the culture of my mother's family since before I could remember. There was so much history and culture, a richness and a magic so tangible I imagined I could literally feel it on my skin when I wore my traditional dress at Lunar New Year, when I walked down the streets of Calgary's tiny Chinatown, when Ma wove bedtime stories about her childhood in Hong Kong. So, the small pocket of Chinese magic at the carnival seemed meant for me.

"May I?" I murmured because my parents had taught me well.

She tipped her head only slightly.

I sat, my palms offered up on the black tablecloth for her to study.

"Eager," she murmured in a deeper voice than I would have thought her slight body capable of. "Caution to the child too eager to race into the future."

"My father always says knowledge is power," I countered, voice soft with respect even though I disagreed with her.

Her lips twitched slightly as she raised her arms to shake the silk sleeves back from her hands. They were small and knurled with age, but dexterous as they collected mine. Her fingers were cold as they lifted my right hand closer to her face under the single light hanging from a lantern attached to the ceiling.

"Ah," she said, and the one word was worth an essay of interpretation. "You see this?"

I leaned forward to see where her nail traced the long line curving away from my thumb.

"This is the lifeline. It is big and clear. This means a vibrant life, a bold one. You do not shy away into the shadows."

This was true, but then again, anyone who'd met me could have told me that.

"This, this is interesting," Madame Cheung murmured, almost to herself as she twisted my hand closer in a way that ached. "A long love line all the way across your palm. This is unusual. It means a big love. But this, here and here?" Her nail slashed across my palm in two places, the same locations where small lines cut into my love line. "This is bad. This is tragedy."

An ominous chill moved through the tent, biting into my shoulders. It was not an icy summer night, and the tent was closed and warm. But the cold settled under my skin and moved deep.

"The marriage line is too long," she added. "Your reputation or theirs will be affected by this union. You are not very lucky, daughter. Not in love."

I wasn't the kind of girl to dream of ending up married with four children and a golden retriever, but I liked the idea of love. Of what Kate and Henning had and my ma and dad.

The idea that I might not ever have that left me feeling oddly hollow, filled only with the chill of her words.

"This is the money line," she continued easily, as if she hadn't just dropped a bomb on a twelve-year-old girl. "You have two. They run together." The tickle of her fingers over my palm made me shiver. "Two different jobs that intersect."

"I'm going to be a doctor," I told her because my parents wanted me to have a good career, but more, Henning was a doctor, and he was as close to a real-life superhero as I'd ever known.

Madame Cheung's sagging chin folds tightened as she

pursed her lips, but she didn't argue with me. Her eyes were narrowed as she traced the straight line beneath my heart line.

"Clear and thin. Clever and focused," she praised. "Love is your weakness, but success will be yours however you seek it."

My lips twisted unconsciously, fingers flexing in her hold.

"You do not accept this balance," she intuited, dropping my hand to grab my chin tightly. My head was pushed back into the light by her clasp, my eyes dropping to continue to hold her intense gaze. "There are mountains"—she traced my brow ridge and jaw—"and rivers in all faces." Her cool skin slid like silk down my nose to brush over my mouth. "The eyes, the nose, the mouth. All full, smooth, glossy. This is a lucky face, you have, daughter. But this sharp chin and stern brow, this is unlucky."

She smoothed the crease that appeared between my eyebrows at her words and clucked her tongue. "This is *balance.* Too much of any one thing is no good. Not even luck. For those whose life comes easy, their character can be weak."

"I'm not weak," I whispered, half statement, half question.

I was strong.

I was Cleo's defender.

Henning's Rocky.

Ma and Old Dragon's *bou lik neoi,* the girl who fights better than any of the boys in town.

But I was old enough to realize strength was found in more than just the body.

The most precious kind was sourced from the heart.

"No," Madame Cheung agreed. "But there is an imbalance in you. It is stamped into your face. You must not be too hard and unyielding, too focused on death and the dark."

"Because I'm a girl?" I countered, bristling against the idea that women had to be all yin, all soft and yielding, summer and birth and new beginnings.

"No." Madame Cheung shoved my face back disdainfully

and folded her hands back beneath her silk sleeves before clasping them beneath the fabric. Her eyes were barely visible beneath the folds of her silken skin, but they burned into me like twin suns. "Because there is strength in softness too. There is purity, success, and happiness in finding balance between yin *and* yang. If you don't learn this, the tragedies of your life will overtake you."

I opened my mouth to say something, I don't remember what, but it was probably to argue because I didn't believe in soft for myself. Not when I had to protect Cleo's big heart from bullies.

But a familiar voice cut through the still air in the tent and set it to buzzing.

"Don't you dare!"

My head swivelled as I sought out Kate through the slightly transparent red walls of the tent. She sounded strange, edgy with panic. I'd always known her to be soft, almost dreamy and a little forgetful. Even when she was having one of her bad days, she was languid and soft-spoken.

"I mean it." I could only hear her next words because I was straining. "Don't do this. I've done everything I was supposed to. Please, I'm here w-with my daughter."

A deep voice, the bass of it lost beneath the murmur of crowd noises outside.

"Thank you," I murmured to Madame Cheung, fishing money out of my jean shorts to hand to her.

She caught my wrist in a punishing hold when I tried to empty the contents into her hand. Her gaze was narrowed and burning when I met it with my own.

"Do not follow trouble," she warned ominously. "You are a child. Stay one for as long as you are able."

I ignored her, my stomach clenching around the acid building in my gut.

Something was wrong.

Kate's voice echoed between my ears. The hairs on the back of my neck stood on end and I shivered in the warm air, chilled deep in my bones as I wrenched away from Madame Cheung and stumbled away from the table.

"I didn't do anything," Kate's voice pierced through the tent again, drifting farther away but growing even more frightful. "I mean, I did, I did do exactly as you asked––" A strangled noise like someone was hurting her.

I turned on my sneakered heel and raced out of the tent.

The air outside was even more humid, sticky and thick. It took effort to run through it, around the crowd of bodies surging through the lanes between carnival games and attractions. She had to be close because I'd heard her as if she was shouting in my ear, but even after I circled the tent twice on a pant-inducing sprint, there was no sign of Kate.

I bent double, hands on my knees as I caught my breath, the taste of stale popcorn on my tongue, and surveyed the scene. It was dark and late, the families mostly gone to give way to couples holding hands, kissing under neon lights, men faking bravado as they won gifts for their girls. A group of teenage boys drank from a communal paper-bag-covered bottle of liquor, shouting and shoving each other as they made bets on a shooting game to my right.

To the left, nearly swallowed in shadows, the massive mouth of a clown yawned open menacingly. It was the entrance to the House of Horrors, the name dripping down the sign over the tunnel like blood from a fresh wound.

I hugged myself, staring into that dark mouth I desperately did *not* want to enter, and I made a choice.

Fear or love?

Cowardice or Kate?

If she needed help, how could I act like a baby and refuse to offer it just because some stupid carnival attraction gave me the heebie-jeebies?

I wished I had the dragon Henning won for me in my care, but he held it along with Cleo's bounty so we could have fun with our friends.

I wished even more I had Henning there to help Kate with me.

Someone bumped into me, jostling me toward the cavern.

I let the momentum propel me forward.

My first step onto the tongue that rolled out of the mouth like a perverted red carpet prompted a series of mechanical prompts to go off. A tinny maniacal laugh echoed around me and bats attached to clear wires dropped down from the ceiling, one of them falling low enough to brush my hair. I squeaked and dashed forward, racing deeper into the dark heart of the house of terrors like a demon chased back into hell.

Inside, it was dimly lit, the scent musky and damp like it was dug straight out of the earth.

I shivered, holding myself like my arms were a shield and a cloak of invisibility.

"It's just an illusion," I murmured to myself because it made me feel better to hear it said aloud.

The first room was an asylum, a woman shackled to a table rocking back and forth like she was possessed. When I tried to cross the room, she flew at me, a flurry of dark tangled hair and eyes that were pure white. I screamed as her fingers brushed my arm, curling into talons as she tried to grab me.

I ran.

Through the next corridor where a man with a chainsaw burst from some unseen corner and chased me up a rickety staircase, through a retro-style children's room where hands shot out from under the bed to grasp at me, a low wailing cry sounding from its depths, into another room built like a science lab where it seemed a doctor was cutting open a man lying writhing and crying on a metal tabletop.

I screamed and I ran, a continuous cycle of both that made

me nearly mindless with fear. It was enough for my twelve-year-old brain to almost short-circuit and forget why I'd subjected myself to these horrors at all.

Finally, I made it to the attic, a vast space littered with gross and terrifying displays like a collection of heads floating in jars and old surgeon's equipment rusty with dried blood. I moved through the shelves trying to modulate the sound of my heaving breath and failing. It was too loud, every breath, every step, and I couldn't shake the feeling that I was being hunted even though I tried to soothe myself with the knowledge that all of this was *fake*.

Only, the sound of Kate's voice, raised in an indecipherable shout, was absolutely *real*.

Fear speared me through the heart, the force of it making me stagger forward into a shelf. I dislodged a jar of something that smashed and splashed against the old wooden floorboards.

"Please!"

Kate's voice again, thin and high with stress and, I thought, excruciating pain.

"Kate!" I called as I started to run again, winding my way through the bookcases until I reached the other side of the attic space.

A narrow staircase descended into pitch darkness.

I stared down it, knowing that Kate was in there, in that blackness, and she needed me. My foot hovered over the first tread. I still remembered how the shadows seemed to swallow it whole.

And then from behind me, a whisper of sound that was really only a displacement of air. But I knew with utter certainty someone was behind me.

I started to swing around to face them, an image snapped from the corner of my left eye as I made it halfway around. Someone, not too tall, wearing a wide brimmed cowboy hat with only a burning ember like a cigarette butt in the dark mask of their shadowed face.

And then, nothing.

Because two hands curled around my shoulders, squeezing so hard I whimpered.

"Should have listened to Madame Cheung," a voice--male?--hissed.

Right before those two hands shoved me forward over the edge of the staircase into the voracious dark.

My shoulder hit the stairs first, jarring me so brutally my entire body was thrown into the wall, one of my fingers, raised to brace myself, broke with a sharp *crack* at the impact. Gravity took me down again, rolling end over end down the steep stairs, hitting every bone like a child banging on a xylophone until I finally landed with a *splat* at the bottom. My entire body vibrated with pain, even my teeth, the edge of my front right eye tooth broken off, the sharp tip actually hooked through my lower lip, a caught fish bleeding and flapping for release. There was a severe pain in my right arm, and when I tried to fix my blurry vision on it, I noticed almost numbly that a shard of white bone had split my pale skin.

And the blood, the scent of it, all around me.

People said blood didn't have a scent, but they were wrong.

It smelled like old pennies picked out of the bottom of a fountain, like rust and metal, like something struggling to return to the earth.

And that scent, it closed in on me, stuffing my nostrils, sliding over my tongue down my throat to suffocate me.

It was worse than the pain because I knew, no way, all that blood was coming from me.

Using my good arm, the one with the broken finger, I pushed myself into an upright seated position, closed my eyes against the dizziness, and then forced myself to take in my surroundings.

And immediately, I wished I had not.
Because I'd found Kate.
After all of that, I'd found her.
And immediately, it was clear...
I was too late.

CHAPTER THREE

Mei

THE ROOM I'D FALLEN INTO WAS DESIGNED TO LOOK LIKE A dungeon.

Wallpaper made the walls look like stone, and a single window with iron bars was high enough to make it look like we were mostly below ground. Torture equipment hung from racks—axes, spears, huge shears, and multitudes of knives.

But some of it, I thought, was already in use.

Because Kate Axelsen, a woman who had been like a mother to me for most of my life, hung suspended from iron chains in the middle of the room. A prone form just behind her lay crumpled, and I'd realize later that it was the actress who had been paid to play the role someone had forced Kate into in real life.

She swayed like some macabre ornament, her face a mask of horror as she laid eyes on me in the dim light.

"Mei, no—" She started to moan, but the words cut off with a whimper as men appeared around the room, stepping in from hidden doors that swung out of the walls.

The seven men were dressed like anyone else at the carnival, Stetsons in an array of colours, cowboy boots, and denim. The shadows obscured their faces, but then my gaze was distracted by the long, curved blades each of them held in one hand.

"No, no," Kate begged, sobbing so hoarsely she gagged. "Please, not here. My daughter is out there. A-and not in front of a child. Please!"

They didn't seem to hear her.

One of them detached from the circle and stalked over to me, boots clicking. I tried to stand, only to realize that something bad had happened to my right foot, and it wouldn't hold my weight. I collapsed to the ground, but didn't let that stop me from getting to Kate. As if somehow, I could disarm those men and save her. I rolled to my knees and crawled with one hand along the packed earth floor toward her even though my body screamed in agony.

When the armed man reached me, his booted foot swiftly reared back and kicked me right in the face. The force snapped my head back, spit and blood flying, pain so bright I almost didn't feel it explode through my skull.

My vision shifted in and out, but I was vaguely aware the man looming over me pinned me to the ground with the tip of the blade digging between my shoulder blades and his other foot pressing my hand to the ground. My broken finger throbbed, my foot ached, my brain wheeled madly, and the bone shooting out of my arm dug excruciatingly into the dirty floor.

But none of that mattered as I struggled to stay conscious.

Because the men had started to move in a strange kind of dance.

First one slid across the ground, almost weightless he was so graceful, and arched the blade through the air at a sobbing Kate. He struck her so quickly, I couldn't map where the blow landed until a red line opened up across her torso, cutting through her blouse into her chest. It was shallow, but long and deep enough to bleed.

Then a second man did the same.

Each time they struck her, she cried out with less force.

A scream, a shout, a sob, a whimper.

And finally, when the fifth man sliced her open from stem to stern, only a faint, fragile *hiss*.

It was that sound that urged me to gather the last of my strength. I didn't waste it fighting off any of the men who were certainly older and stronger than me.

I used it to scream.

Louder than Kate had.

More fiercely than I had ever done anything in my life, I gathered air into my lungs, tensed my belly, and *bellowed* for help.

It didn't last long.

After three seconds of shock, the man above me delivered a swift kick to my temple, and I passed into cold, dark relief.

When I opened my eyes again, panic already surged through me. I scrambled to my knees, already crawling toward Kate again before I was conscious I was doing it. Tears dripped from my eyes, and my body howled with pain, but all I could think was *Kate, Kate, Kate.*

The men had gone.

Only imprints in the dirt and blood splatter remained.

And Kate, head dropped like a wilted flower over her bloodied torso. The blades her attackers had used to slice her up now protruded from her body like macabre needles from a red pin cushion.

"Kate?" I whispered, my own pain forgotten, my eyes so round in my face they burned the surrounding skin. "Kate?"

Somehow, she managed to lift her head woozily and attempt a smile, a tremulous thing that barely moved her lips. "Rocky," she breathed, the sound gurgled as blood seeped from the edge of her mouth. "Rocky girl, I-I-I'm so sorry."

"Kate," I said. "Kate, Kate, what's happening?" I couldn't stop saying her name. As if saying it would break this horrible scene in the House of Horrors. As if saying it would wake us both up from this nightmare. "H-how can I help?"

I was close enough to see she trembled violently. The chains rattled with her movement, masking the frequent drip of blood to the floor as it sluiced down her body and pooled beneath her feet. The force of her shivering made the blades wobble precariously. One slid out of her body with a smooth, slick sound that made bile rise to the back of my throat. It clanged against the bloody ground as it fell out of her followed by a gushing torrent of red down her left side.

"Oh my God," I whispered as my fingertips met cool, viscous red pooling in an ever-increasing puddle around her. "Kate! Who did this to you?"

Her lids fluttered, eyes rolling and black with pain. "I did it to myself."

She was clearly delirious and speaking nonsense. I opened my mouth to ask her again, but a drop of her blood fell warmly against my cheek and shocked me into silence.

"Can you get help, baby?" she asked, still shaking, eyes drooping.

Blood dripped from her steadily.

Splat, splat, splat.

I reached up gingerly, grasping the handle of a sword.

"No!" she whisper-yelled, then groaned in immeasurable pain. "No, Rocky, please. Get Henning."

"I don't want to leave you." I didn't have the courage to even consciously think it, but I knew deep down in the well of my gut that these were the last minutes Kate Axelsen would remain on this earth, and I couldn't bear the thought of leaving her alone in them.

"I don't want to leave," she echoed, her lids dropping closed, her lips moving thickly as if they were numb. "My sweet Cleo. My baby girl."

My chest seized at the thought of Cleo without her mum. My fragile friend, so beautiful and kind with a heart as tender as a budded rose, would not survive this death. Which meant if Kate died, I'd lose them both.

"Just wait," I pled to her, unleashing my grip on the sword so I could carefully reach up to take her hand.

She was too weak to squeeze me back, but I saw the way her lashes trembled around a tear slinking through her closed lids and knew she appreciated the contact.

"Promise," she whispered, barely audible. Blood leaked from the side of her mouth, so dark it was almost black. "Promise you'll take care of them. 'S not fair to ask you. B-but please."

"Always." The word was harsh with severity.

I wrote it in the air between us like a contract signed in our shared spilled blood.

It was the moment I shed my girlhood forever.

A thud drew my attention to the dark hole at the top of the stairs. Fear skittered through me, momentarily erasing the sorrow eating at my heart. I got to my feet, whimpering at the sharp agony in my foot, struggling to find my balance as my head ached and roiled. I bent to grasp the bloody handle of the curved sword that had fallen out of Kate's torso.

My hands trembled as I raised it in front of me, but I refused to let anyone come back and hurt Kate further.

I refused to die alongside her in a fake dungeon at a Calgarian fairground.

Another series of thuds at the door. Obviously, whoever had pushed me down the stairs had barricaded the entrance afterward. It explained why no one had wandered down and found us yet.

Another thud and then a crashing, ear-splitting roar as the door caved in and sailed into the wall before falling loudly down the stairs the same way I had.

"Kate?" a familiar voice boomed through the room. "Mei?"

Seconds later, Henning descended the steps at a run with one of the carnie's axes in one hand, his thick thighs eating up the steep stairs in short order. He caught sight of us before he reached the floor, eyes blown wide, face a mask of shocked horror, and then he jumped the remaining six steps to land heavily at the bottom.

Another man was behind him, a big man dressed in leather who I barely noticed in my relief at seeing Henning and my overall shock.

"Henning," I murmured, suddenly shaking so hard I couldn't lift the sword anymore, and it went clanking to the ground again. My knees caved in after that, and I fell with a short cry to the ground. "K-Kate, she's hurt so badly."

Henning was already moving toward us, his long legs eating up the space in seconds. His big hand found my head, threading through my hair to hold it, to anchor me, even as he addressed Kate first.

"Katie Kay," he murmured, his voice filled with heartbreak and barely bottled rage. I watched as his free hand fluttered over her, heavy palm and thick fingers helpless against her many wounds. I knew he was taking stock, his doctor's mind searching for where to start saving her. Only, even I could see there was too much blood spilling out of her. Fountains of it. "Fuck. What the fuck happened?"

"H-h-Henning." She was barely conscious now, her head lolling back between her shoulders, an unsteady smile on her face. "The white knight come to save me."

"I will," he said viciously, releasing my hair so he could rip off the bottom of his tee before wrapping it tight around Kate's left thigh where a deep slice had opened an artery.

I pressed closer to his feet, sprawled slightly over one of them as he worked. Pain blurred time and the edges of my vision as I watched him talk to Kate, reassure her, love her as she slowly, drip by drip, died.

The other man was in front of me, crouched, shoulder pinning a cell to his ear. He was speaking to the authorities, I thought. With his free hands, he gently moved his tattooed fingers over my body, cataloguing my wounds.

"Help Kate," I pleaded, but the words were thick in my mouth, and my vision was tunnelling narrower and narrower like a scope.

"Hush," he ordered me before returning to the phone.

I tried to get up, to help Kate and Henning myself, but the stranger pushed me back to the ground gently but firmly with one hand.

"Still."

"Help Kate," I repeated, an edge of hysteria bubbling up my throat along with a surge of bile. I gagged, then turned my head and lost the cotton candy and corn dog I'd had for dinner.

The man held my hair back with one hand.

When I was finished, I heard Henning muttering fiercely to Kate, begging her to stay with him, cajoling her to keep breathing as if she had a choice.

"Bat, hold her still," Henning barked to the man beside me, who immediately stood to gently clasp Kate's hips.

Hen raised his axe and brought it down with a harsh

metallic clatter on the joint of the locked chains. After two firm strikes, one side fell to the floor with a muted clamour. Bat caught Kate as she swayed unbalanced to one side, but as soon as the other chain was broken, Henning quickly but reverently swung her into his arms.

"Hold on, Kate," he murmured, adjusting her gently before he stared across the ground to the staircase. "Bat, take care of Mei. Kate, come on, love. Stay with me."

But I could tell the moment I swung my bleary gaze toward her that Kate's last choice was being taken from her. Her head lolled against Henning's massive chest, limbs dangling, soaked in blood and dripping to the ground.

She was gone.

But Henning sprinted up the stairs like Atlas used to carrying the weight of the world on his shoulders, and seconds later, they disappeared.

CHAPTER FOUR

Henning

The first time I saw Katherine Kay, she was lyin' in a hospital bed in the emergency room of Rockyview Hospital. It was my second day in residency, and I was doin' my first six-month rotation in the ER after finishing two other rotations in internal medicine and orthopaedics. After a few more weeks, maybe I wouldn't have felt the sight of her as acutely as I did. Maybe I would've been better steeled for the sight of a young, beautiful woman broken down by the brutality of a deviant customer and an unforgivin' pimp.

I was old for med school, old for residency. My peers were all early twentysomethings with fresh, dewy-eyed optimism, but I was twenty-six, and after a tour in the Middle East when

I'd first enlisted in the military when I was eighteen, I thought I'd seen it all.

So I was unprepared for Kate.

As Dr. Pandey checked her chart and issued orders to the rest of us, I couldn't stop starin' at her.

"How old?" I asked low as I instinctively obeyed her instruction and took over for the paramedic holdin' the compress to the wet mess between her legs. "How old is she?" I bit out again when no one answered me.

"Twenty-three."

Just a kid, really.

"Christ," I muttered to a fellow resident as he started to intubate her.

"Get her into surgery," Dr. Pandey demanded, all efficiency, her face a mask of professionalism. "Fast."

We worked on her for hours.

A brain hemorrhage from blunt force trauma.

Brutal tears in delicate places that had to be sewn up carefully so she'd have a hope of regainin' sensation.

A broken clavicle and fractured eye socket.

By the time we finished, I had a vicious ache in my spine from hunchin' over as I assisted Dr. Pandey and a headache that beat a strong tattoo behind both eyes. I'd been on shift for twenty hours straight but didn't go to the bunk room like the others. I knew the moment I closed my eyes, all I'd see were visions of Baghdad overlaid by that young girl twisted apart by male cruelty.

It shouldn't've been so much worse, this one girl broken open by a cruel pimp compared to the dozens of soldiers and insurgents I'd seen in combat blown to bits by bombs, bullets, and shrapnel, but somehow it was. I'd been driven to join the army 'cause I needed the structure and some kind of greater purpose to my life, 'cause I couldn't afford university without their fundin', 'cause I'd craved a sense of belongin'.

What had driven this girl to prostitution?

Whatever the reason, she hadn't signed up for violence like I had. She hadn't gone to work each day worryin' it might be her last.

"You're too soft," Dr. Pandey said when she caught me with my head in my hands in the cafeteria, starin' blankly at my uneaten tray of food. "You won't make it as a doctor if you don't toughen up."

"I'm a vet in the Medical Services Training Program," I explained woodenly, redundantly 'cause she already knew. "I've seen worse."

"Have you?" she countered mildly, stabbin' a straw into her apple juice box. "That woman in there didn't sign up for pain or danger. The circumstances of her life bought that for her because it was all she could afford." She paused, sucked on the straw, and cocked her head to contemplate me. "In real life, Dr. Axelsen, white knights rarely get happy endings. Only broken hearts."

I didn't have a response for that, so I sat there in silence while she ate and chatted away about hospital routines. It wasn't 'til she was standin' up to leave that she put a long-fingered brown hand on my arm and smiled softly down into my face.

"She's got a child," she said. "Waiting with a neighbour in the ER if you want to check on the patient and give them an update."

I told myself not to do it. They taught you about professional detachment in medical school. They basically pounded it into your brain so even those with the thickest skulls would brand it into their grey matter.

My dad had always told me my skull was thicker than most.

'Cause I went to check on Katherine Kay, tiny and fragile as a broken doll in the hospital bed, and then I went to the ER to update her family.

Twenty-three years old, a prostitute, and she had a kid.

Not a young one either, I noted as Nurse Watson pointed them out to me, but an eight or nine-year-old little girl with straggly brown hair and a red-tipped nose. She sat in an elderly woman's lap, snifflin' like she was at the ragged end of a cryin' jag. The moment she saw me, she froze, then curled into an even smaller ball in the lady's lap.

"I'm Dr. Axelsen," I introduced and learned their names were Shelby Yikkers and tiny Cleopatra Kay.

"You scared about your mama?" I crouched down to address the kid.

She stared at me for a long moment with enormous, spiky-lashed pale eyes before noddin'.

"Yeah, that's fair. She got hurt pretty bad, but she arrived here just in time, and Dr. Pandey is the best at what she does. Your mama is gonna be just fine." It was a lie, probably. Sure, she'd recover from this, slowly and brutally, but I knew she'd go back to her pimp, and the whole thing would likely happen again.

I didn't know the stats around that kinda thing, but I vowed to look them up when I had a spare minute.

"Are you a real doctor?" Cleopatra asked in a tired, croaky voice.

"You bet I am."

"You don't look like a doctor," she accused with a frown.

Despite everythin', I almost laughed. She was right, and it wasn't the first time I'd heard such a thing. At six foot four, two hundred and forty pounds of military-grown muscle, and hair I hadn't cut professionally short since I'd returned from tour at nineteen, I looked more like a savage than a doctor. The tattoos didn't help much either, but most of those were covered up by my scrubs.

"Are you a princess?"

Her small mouth fell into a pink "O" of shock. "No!"

"You sure?"

She nodded empathetically as if she was worried about my intelligence.

"Huh, well, you look like one," I told her, smilin' at her little hiccoughed giggle. "Sometimes people look different than who they actually are, huh?"

"I guess," she agreed, her small shoulders relaxin' slightly. She turned into Shelby Yikkers' chest with a yawn and snuggled closer.

Shelby cupped the back of her head, her wrinkled face lax with sorrow. "She's just a kid. I try to take care of her as much as I can, Kate too, but Jimmie Page is a dangerous man, and I can only do so much..."

"You found her?" I asked softly, 'cause Cleopatra's eyes were closed, and a soft snore soon followed.

Shelby dipped her chin to the little girl. "I look after her sometimes when her mum is...busy. She came to get me. Hid in the bathtub while the bastard and his friends did that to Kate."

Fuck.

How did other people do this? See sufferin' and endure without excruciatin' empathy.

"I'll keep an eye on Ms. Kay and let you know when she wakes," I promised as if that would do this family any good.

Shelby stared at me with weathered eyes, worn smooth by years of toil and tragedy. "You new here?"

I nodded.

"Ah, well, I suspect we'll be seeing you again soon."

And I did.

Katherine Kay was admitted to the hospital six more times over the next eighteen months, and that last time required surgery for the removal of her ruptured uterus, a surgery that made her sterile at the age of twenty-five.

The day after she was discharged, I made her my wife.

"HENNING?"

I exploded from sleep like a swimmer from icy waters, gaspin' and alert the moment I opened my eyes.

"Yeah?"

Dr. Pandey stared down at me with that soft, tragic smile she seemed to wear so often in my presence.

"Mei Zhen Marchand is out of surgery. Her parents have been alerted, and they're on their way, but I thought you and Cleo…you might like to see her."

My hand instinctively stroked Cleo's hair where her head lay on my shoulder, a puddle of cold drool beneath her slack mouth on my tee.

"Yeah, yeah, that'd be good." My voice was rough as gravel and just as painful passin' through my throat. "She's gonna be okay?"

"She is, physically." Becky Pandey sighed as she looked at Cleo. "But mentally? She watched a woman get murdered, Hen. I doubt she'll ever recover from that."

"Yeah," I grunted, rememberin' the way she'd clung to Kate's hand as she lay awkwardly on her broken body at her feet.

Mei was twelve years old, and she'd witnessed a murder.

Cleo was twelve years old, and she'd lost her mother, the

only permanent fixture in her crazy, fucked-up life so far.

I pressed a kiss to my daughter's fragrant hair and wished for the millionth time that I could trade places with my dead wife.

"Henning?" Becky Pandey prompted. "The parents will be here shortly, and I'm not sure they'll want you to see her after that."

'Cause I'd dropped the ball protectin' their daughter.

I was too saturated with my own guilt to deal with any more bein' doled out by the Marchands when they barely made time for their own daughter as it was.

"Glory," I murmured, gently shakin' her shoulder. "My girl, wake up."

She stirred, clingin' to me like I was a life raft. She was a heavy sleeper, and it took her a couple moments to wake. "Dad?" A shudderin' breath as she fully woke but didn't open her eyes. "It was a nightmare, right?"

My throat closed up so tight I thought I'd never breathe again. "No, sweetheart. Mum's still gone."

A whimper that shot me straight through the heart. My head thunked against the wall behind the plastic chair back as I squeezed my eyes shut and fought for control.

War had taught me a pivotal survival technique.

One minute at a time.

Thinkin' any further than that was a death sentence to productivity, and I couldn't afford to lose that. I had a daughter to take care of and a girl who counted on me in a hospital bed down the hall.

"Glory, Rocky's awake," I told her, pausin' when she tensed with shock, then sagged in relief against me. "You wanna go see her?"

"Can we?" she pleaded, eyes glazed with tears as she pulled away enough to look into my face. "She's okay?"

"She's gonna take a while to recover, but we'll be there for her," I promised.

And even after everythin' that had happened in the last twenty-nine hours, Kate's greatest gift to me looked up into my eyes like I was her hero.

"Okay, Dad, let's go."

She stood up on coltishly long legs she hadn't grown into yet and immediately tagged my arm to throw over her shoulder when I stood too. I clasped my hand around the ball of her shoulder and tugged her close. It was awkward 'cause of our significant height difference, but we walked like that down the linoleum hall to Mei's room.

Cleo stopped before the closed door, peerin' up at me from beneath her bangs. Even red-eyed and swollen from sobbin' too long and too hard, her sweet, trustin' face reminded me I still had so much to live for, even without Kate. "I'm scared."

"She's gonna be okay," I promised, but I wondered if she knew I would've promised her anythin' then and meant it.

"I…" Tears sprang into those rainwater eyes and sluiced down her cheeks. Her voice was a ravaged whisper as if her throat was too tight to talk when she spoke. "I don't think I can survive losing them both."

"She's gonna be fine––" I started to say, but then I remembered that my daughter was smart, and she'd seen more in her short life than most adults. She knew there was a possibility that Mei would recover from her physical injuries but not her spiritual ones. That she might rise from this day of death like a zombie, alive but not whole. And my sweet, tender-hearted Cleo couldn't stand to lose her mother and her best friend at the same time.

With sudden, acute misery I realized that I'd never have Kate to turn to for parentin' conversations again. She'd always steered the ship 'cause I was just the stepfather, but now, I was all Cleo had. The gravity of that responsibility pressed against my shoulders 'til I thought they'd buckle.

But the look in those wide eyes reminded me that Cleo believed in me.

All I had to do was give her a reason to continue doin' that.

I dropped my arm from her shoulder so I could take her face in my hands and bent my knees so we were closer to eye level with each other. I wanted her to read the sincerity in every inch of me.

"It's just you and me now, Glory." The words ached in my throat and tasted bitter on my tongue. Cleo choked on a sob and reached up to latch onto my wrists. "But nothin' is ever gonna tear us apart. You hear me? We don't share blood, but I don't give a damn. Someone tries to take us from each other, I'll kill them. Does that scare you?"

"No," she said instantly, remindin' me that this was a girl raised by a prostitute who'd seen darker things than most twelve-year-old kids ever had. "I know you will."

"Those people that did what they did to your mum? I'll find out who they are and make them pay for it," I vowed 'cause I wasn't the dad Cleo should've been born to, a suburban guy with a minivan and a degree in accountancy. I was a trained killer tryin' to atone for his sins by savin' lives now as a doctor, and this was exactly the kinda dad I had to be.

"Okay," she breathed, her shoulders straightenin' slightly. "I believe you."

"And Mei? She's a part of our family, now. She was before, in a way, but tragedy bonds people. You know Uncle Bat and Uncle Cedar? They're my brothers 'cause of what we went through durin' the war, and now, Mei and you are like sisters 'cause of what you've been through today. Nothin' will take that from you two. Nothin' forged in fire like iron can be so easily broken."

"You think?" she whispered, eyes dartin' to the closed door of Mei's room.

"I know so."

"You'll help her too, right?" she asked, clutchin' at my wrists, beggin' me with those big green-grey eyes she'd shared with her mum. "Just like you helped Mum and me."

"I promise," I said, and I would have written that promise in blood let from my own vein if Cleo had handed me a knife. There was nothin' in the world I wouldn't do for this slip of a girl that Kate had trusted me to love and care for. I could still remember the day I'd married Kate at the courthouse, the awe and trust shinin' from the eyes of both mother and daughter. The memory was bittersweet now, but I kept it at the forefront of my mind just the same. "You won't be losin' any more family on my watch, okay?"

"Okay, Dad," she murmured, and relief suffused her expression as if her prayers to God had been answered.

Her belief in me made it hard to breathe for one long, hard moment. Only two other people had ever believed in me like that. Kate and my stepmum, Lin, who taught me everythin' I needed to know about family bein' thicker than blood.

"You ready?" I asked my whole world.

Cleo searched my face one last time, then nodded before turnin' to push open the door.

Mei looked tiny in that white hospital bed in that white room, her black hair the only spot of colour like an ink spill over the pillow. Metal plates obscured part of her face to fix her shattered nose so you couldn't see the faint freckles she had from the summer sun or the dimple that popped out when she smiled. She was a pretty kid, but she looked next to death in that bed, one step away from a much too early grave.

Cleo burst into silent tears, wet racin' down her cheeks into the tee she'd worn for well over a full day now. She let go of me to rush to Mei's side, her face a pastiche of agony and guilt. Her hand shook as she extended it to push a lock of hair back from her friend's ashen face, and she looked to me as if for permission.

"You can touch her, Glory," I whispered as I dragged two chairs to her bedside and sat in one.

"When will she wake up?" Cleo whispered back as she stroked Mei's hair, then leaned over to kiss her forehead. One of her tears fell to Mei's cheek and rolled off her jaw.

"When she's ready."

"Can we wait?"

Anythin' for you, I thought, studyin' how fragile she was. "Of course, 'til her parents come."

So we did.

When Cleo got too tired to do anythin' but sleep, she carefully crawled into bed with Mei, a curved shield at her side. A lump the size of Alberta lodged in my throat when she gently twined their fingers together and then immediately fell asleep.

I studied the two vulnerable young girls in that bed and finally let myself have a moment of pure anguish. Clutchin' my weddin' ring between my palms, I bent over it and started prayin'. I had no fuckin' idea how to pray, seein' how I didn't much believe in God, but I sent my wishes for goodness in those two young lives out and up as far as I could.

I dragged my chair to the other side of the bed closest to the door to protect them from whoever might enter.

I prayed they'd have a future filled with only love, joy, and success.

I prayed I'd be strong enough to give that to them, the way I had failed to give that to Kate. Not just Cleo but this poor girl so forgotten by her busy parents that she'd become a second daughter to Kate.

I prayed the worst had come and gone for them, and honestly, a weary part of my soul prayed the same for me.

And when I finished prayin', I lay my head on the bed for a second, one hand on each of those thin shins, and let the agony of grief drag me into a restless sleep.

CHAPTER FIVE

Mei

The first thing I felt when I woke up was pain. It was a dull drumbeat under the muffled coating of drugs in my system, but it was still uncomfortable enough to set my teeth on edge.

The second thing was Cleo.

Her Vera Wang Princess perfume in my nose, her soft hair tickling my cheek, and the sweet tangle of her fingers in mine.

I opened my eyes to see a white ceiling, white walls, and two Axelsens.

Cleo was curled at my side, salt tracks crusted on her cheeks but otherwise blissfully peaceful in sleep.

Henning lay across my feet, his hand on my shin, the other curled around Cleo's. He had to be uncomfortable with his big body bent in half like that, but I was grateful he was close.

I wondered if I'd ever feel safe without him again.

It was hard for my twelve-year-old mind not to tangle him up in the role of hero. I'd heard the story of how he'd saved Kate from her troubled past and Cleo from a childhood of dangers, and now, he'd saved me, even if he hadn't been able to save Kate.

Looking back, that was the start of it for me.

Falling in love with him.

Ruining his life.

They would become one and the same, but right then, it was pure and simple.

I loved him the way a child loved a superhero.

As my mind raced through the horrors of Kate's death, I felt an overwhelming panic that I'd ever have to leave this room and these people. My hand tightened so fiercely in Cleo's that she protested in her sleep. I reached out to touch Henning's overlong, wavy hair, curling a piece around my finger so I could anchor myself with both of them, but it was enough to wake him up.

One turquoise eye, bloodshot and heavy-lidded, opened to stare at me.

"Hey, Rocky," he muttered, hand flexing on my shin.

"Hey, Henning."

"How're you feelin'? Let me call for the doctor."

"No!" I whisper-shouted, wincing as my ribs protested. "In a minute, okay?"

Henning straightened slowly, so I had time to disentangle my hand from his hair, but he compensated me by reaching out to give it a squeeze. "We aren't goin' anywhere 'til your parents get here, yeah?"

I nodded. Dad and Ma were in Toronto for a conference on oil and gas, which explained why they were taking so long to return. I'd been meant to stay the weekend with the Axelsens.

"She's gone, isn't she?"

Henning's face spasmed with hurt so profound he looked eighty years old instead of twenty-eight. "Yeah, Rocky, she's gone."

"Why did those people do that to her?" The words were chewed up in the garburator of my swollen throat.

His lips thinned. "I have no clue. The police don't seem to have any leads right now either."

"Could it have been one of those bad guys from before?" I asked hesitantly.

I knew, even though I shouldn't have, that Kate had been a prostitute when she met Henning. She had loads of scars on her beautiful body from her old pimp, Jimmie Page, and the jerks he sent to her as clients.

"Maybe," he conceded, but his jaw was hard-edged as a knife, and he didn't seem like he wanted to speak any more about it. "I'm sorry you got hurt."

"I'm sorry I couldn't save her," I told him baldly, somehow too sad to even cry.

His head went limp on his neck like it was suddenly impossible to carry the weight of his thoughts. "Yeah," he said, rough as a cough. "Yeah, I'm sorry I couldn't save either of ya."

"You saved me," I argued vehemently. "I think I could have died if you didn't come soon. How did you find us?"

"Was keepin' an eye on Cleo when I noticed you weren't with her crew anymore. I'd met up with some buddies, and one of them stayed with them while the two of us searched for you." He paused, eyes shuttering. "Heard you scream from the mouth of that House of Horrors and knew in my bones it was you."

Silence for a long moment as we both considered how

lucky I'd been and how *unlucky* Kate had been that Henning hadn't found us just a few minutes earlier.

"How bad is it?" I asked, jerking my chin at my casted arm and leg.

"Broken arm, broken foot, a severe concussion, a few broken ribs, shattered nose, and a ruptured spleen," he catalogued for me. "You've got a broken tooth the dentist will have to fix for you when you're feelin' better, too."

"Not so bad," I murmured, thinking of Kate.

"No," he agreed slowly, one thick finger tracing the line of my cast. "You can get your friends to sign this."

My laugh was a hollow bark. "What friends?"

Henning's mouth thinned. He knew Cleo was it for me.

I wasn't sure if something was deficient in my personality or something was wrong with my heart, but I couldn't seem to connect with people easily. It was all or nothing in games of the heart, and the only people I'd ever trusted with mine outside of my family were Cleo, Kate, and Henning.

"Here," he muttered, patting his jean pocket until he found one of the felt-tipped pens he always kept on his person. "I'll start you off."

He bent over my arm, flaxen hair a wavy curtain on either side of his craggy face. His brow was furrowed with concentration as he started to pen a design onto the pristine cast.

"What are you drawing?" I asked after a minute.

The soft sound of the pen scratching over the rough plaster was strangely soothing. I didn't care what Henning drew; he'd always been a good artist, so good that Cleo and I used to beg him to sketch for us so we could colour them in instead of using generic colouring books.

"Koi fish."

My numb heart prickled painfully, coming alive after a long frost.

"Why?" I whispered.

"You tell me," he countered without taking his attention from the drawing.

"In my culture, the koi fish is a sign of strength," I said softly. "It swims against the currents and when it reaches the end of the long, hard journey upstream, it becomes a dragon."

A very small smile hid in the hard edges of Henning's face. It didn't curve his lips or brighten his eyes, but it was there, a coded message written just for me.

"You want to be a dragon one day," he reminded me of our conversation from the carnival, a conversation that felt years ago instead of hours.

"So why didn't you draw a dragon?"

He looked up then, capping the pen with his thumb as he studied the finished design, then looked up at me with eyes that seemed to know all the secrets of the world.

"Everyone has to start somewhere. But today you proved that you are already an exceptional kid, Rocky." His words were rough, unpolished gems that meant everything to me. "You might just be the bravest girl I've ever known."

I swallowed thickly, trying not to dissolve in a whirlpool of tears that waited just at the back of my eyes. Two black outlined koi fish swam in the centre of my cast, head to tail so they formed a kind of yin and yang. They were so beautiful and their meaning so profound, my nose itched with the need to cry.

"Kate told me to take care of you and Cleo." I wasn't sure why I shared that with him. I'd meant to keep it a sacred secret, but he looked so lonely and broken sitting there hunched over that I couldn't resist the urge to comfort him.

He made a noise in the back of his throat. "No, Rocky, kids don't worry about stuff like that. You leave that to me."

I was shaking my head before he was done. "I don't care what you say." I spoke in Cantonese and then roughly translated for him even though I knew he could probably understand. "*During difficult times, it's your family that supports you.*"

I was so caught up in the wide, almost startled look on Henning's face that I didn't hear the door creak open or notice the people who entered until one of them spoke.

"The Axelsens are not your family," Florent Marchand scolded from the doorway, his arm around his wife, Daiyu.

I stared at my parents and felt conflict tug at my heart like a rope in a children's camp competition. It was so good to see them, but it was also good to see them because they were away all the time. Dad was the CEO of one of the top oil and gas companies in Canada, and Ma was one of the top heart surgeons in the country. They were the ultimate power couple, and even at twelve, I admired them so much that I almost feared them and the long shadow they cast over me. They looked beautifully put together even after a four-hour flight, even with faces creased with strain and worry.

On the other hand, resentment festered in me, lit to high flame by the trauma of the carnival and losing Kate. Of course, they wouldn't understand that Kate was almost as much my mum as Daiyu was. That she was the person who picked me up from school and listened to the daily drama of a preteen girl. That she was the one who hugged me after a bad day and teased me lovingly for my idiosyncrasies. Losing her hurt so badly, I couldn't even begin to explain it to them, and it infuriated me that their lack of intrinsic understanding deepened the void that already existed between us.

Of course, I couldn't articulate all that at twelve, but years later, it was all obvious to me.

I just wished it had been obvious to *them*.

"Florent, Daiyu..." Henning rose to his feet to address them. "I'm so goddamn sorry Mei was hurt under my care."

"You should be," Dad lashed out with all the powerful fury of a man used to being revered.

Ma ignored the men and darted around Henning to get to

me. The soft scent of her jasmine perfume wafted over me, and inexplicably, I wanted to cry.

"My baby," she cooed in Cantonese, touching my face with those surgically careful fingers. "My sweet pearl. Oh, baby, I'm so sorry."

Over the lullaby of her voice, Dad's angry words rose like a tidal swell. "I told Daiyu you weren't fit to take care of our Mei, but she assured me you were a doctor and well-respected." His eyes cast over Henning with obvious suspicion, eyeing the overlong hair, the tattoo on the inside of his wrist revealed by his rolled-up cuffs. "Mei even mentioned you have a connection to that godawful Fallen Motorcycle Club."

"Brothers," he corrected automatically, too weary to be caught up in Dad's passion. "Men I met in the sandbox."

Dad bristled. "Where was your training last night, then? How could you have let this happen to our little girl? Have you considered your affiliation with them could be the reason my daughter was *attacked*?"

"Dad!" The shout tore from me with more force than I'd known I could muster. My ribs ached fiercely, and for a moment after, I thought I'd throw up from the pain. Beside me, Cleo finally jerked into wakefulness, curling into me instinctively. "Don't you dare!"

My voice was hysterical, thready with panic and fury so formidable I felt it steam up my throat from the inferno in my belly. It made my ribs and belly ache, my blood pounding too hard in the broken bones in my finger and foot, but I was glad for the drug-muted pain. It reminded me I was alive when Kate was not.

"How dare you talk to him like that? How dare you make this about me when Henning and Cleo just lost Kate. Wh-when I just lost Kate too. None of this happened to *you* so just shut. Up! And leave all of us alone."

Silence followed in the wake of my outburst like a mushroom cloud after an atomic hit. My dad looked shaken and pale, his normal unflappability disturbed by my uncharacteristic outburst. Ma shot him a disappointed glower as she sat on the edge of my hospital bed and gathered me carefully in her arms, kissing me on the brow.

Henning just looked shell-shocked, but I think that had more to do with losing Kate than anything else.

"If you want to stay," I continued, voice shaking now but chin held high as I locked eyes with my father. Talking back to your elders wasn't done in Chinese households. Even though my dad was French-Canadian, it was almost exactly the same in his culture, and in the Marchand household, Ma and Old Dragon ran the roost. Still, this was too important not to make clear. "You have to be nice to Henning and Cleo. I don't know why I have to tell you that when they just lost Kate, but I guess I have to." I paused, mouth curling under in a pout I was embarrassed to display. "You should be happy I'm *alive,* and you have Henning to thank for that."

"We're staying," Ma said immediately, settling back against the pillows and reaching one arm over to place on Cleo's head. "Florent, take a seat."

Dad hesitated, his dark eyes flashing to Henning with blatant hostility.

"Now," Ma suggested mildly, but there was iron backing the words.

Dad took Henning's abandoned chair, but he sat.

And all of them stayed in that room until I fell back asleep.

Unfortunately, it meant I didn't hear my dad make a promise to Henning he would prove capable of keeping.

"If my daughter ever comes to harm in your presence again, Axelsen," he warned without taking his eyes off my sleeping body. "I'll end you."

Florent Marchand wasn't like Henning. He didn't know how

to kill a man in forty-five different ways or how to save him in just as many.

But he did know how to end a man's life without ever spilling a drop of blood.

And five years later, he did exactly what he promised.

CHAPTER SIX

Henning

Five Years Later

2015

My kid was too old to be picked up from school by her dad, but she didn't say a thing when I still insisted at the start of her grade twelve year that I'd be there every fuckin' day to get her. Cleo was smart in the ways of people, quiet and keenly observant. She didn't need me spellin' out why I felt the overwhelmin' need to protect her from anythin', even somethin' as innocuous as walkin' the ten miles home each day.

Doctors and nurses who had the tough jobs, on the front

line of life and death, didn't have the luxury of pickin' up their daughters from school.

Which was why I was no longer a doctor.

Technically, I still had the designation. I did my time at school, made the grade, passed the exams, and spent three years in residency.

But then, Kate died.

She died and left me with her twelve-year-old grievin' daughter whose one constant her entire life had been her mother.

How could I be a single parent to her when I worked all hours at the hospital? When I made crap money 'cause yeah, doctors made serious cake, but not 'til they'd finished their residencies and specialties, and I was still two years off from that. I'd already used my dad's life insurance policy to pay off Kate's debt after I married her, buy our cookie-cutter house on the city's outskirts, and pay for Kate's GED and real estate courses.

So, I said goodbye to being a doctor and a reservist in the military.

I'd had to buy out the rest of my contract with the army to pay them back for subsidisin' my tuition without fulfillin' my obligation to them as a military doctor after I finished, but Lin and I'd been able to scrape together the money to do it. Takin' care of Cleo, bein' there for her in a real way, was a helluva lot more important than my savings.

It wasn't as hard a choice as you'd think, given all I'd wanted to be my entire fuckin' life was a doctor. It wasn't hard 'cause tragedy makes a man feel helpless, especially when that tragedy takes a good woman from him and leaves him the sole caregiver of a preteen girl. Lookin' into Cleo's tearstained, gaunt face in the weeks followin' Kate's murder, the decision came to me as easily as the tears that came at night when I lay unsleepin' and alone in bed.

So, I gave up medicine and exchanged it for somethin' I'd

always loved but never thought was practical enough to make into a career 'til I was searchin' for a job with flexible hours and decent pay.

Art.

Sure, I wasn't some fancy painter with shows in galleries and multi-thousand-dollar price tags on shit only the insanely rich could afford. But I was an artist peddlin' my wares, and it surprised me, more than Cleo, Lin, and Mei, that I wasn't just good at this new gig as a tattoo artist at Battle Scars Ink.

I fuckin' loved it.

Turnin' someone into livin', breathin', walkin' art. The way a design flexed and reformed on the flesh, how pigments changed on different skin tones and evolved with the body through age. Any vainglorious artist would love it, the way their work could be paraded through the world for all to see and admire. Any empath would love the look in a client's eyes when you pulled somethin' outta their heart and worked it onto their sleeve.

It was beautiful, but more, for me, it was a kinda therapy.

A marriage of the healin' I'd loved seein' as a doctor with the freedom and expression that had always drawn me to art.

Even more, I liked drivin' Cleo to school and pickin' her up in the afternoon. I liked havin' time to raise her as well as I fuckin' could. I was no Kate. No mother. When Cleo got her period and called me cryin' from a fuckin' pool party 'cause that shit had happened to her in front of her friends in a white bikini, I'd nearly beaten the boys who made fun of her to a pulp, and it was Mei who'd gone into the pharmacy with me while Cleo waited in the car to help me pick out the supplies she would need. I was probably too strict (no fuckin' way was Cleo allowed to date), and conversely too mellow (my girl was a good kid, what the hell did I care if she didn't get all A's and didn't like to eat broccoli, neither did I). I made so many mistakes sometimes at night they haunted me 'til I couldn't fuckin' breathe.

But I did what I could.

Not just 'cause I had to as Cleo's legal guardian.

'Cause I wanted to.

Cleo was my daughter in all ways except for blood, and I was the first guy to admit, blood meant shit all if it wasn't backed by heart. Lin had been the one to teach me that.

And all the heart I had left after Kate's death was owned by my cherub-faced, grey-green-eyed girl.

"Dad," she cried as she appeared between the crowd of teenagers spillin' from the doors of the main buildin' after the final bell rang.

She always cried this when she saw me.

Once, some punk kid had made fun of her, but before I'd had to take care of him, Mei had stepped up and hit him in the side of his head with a binder.

No one bothered Cleo about it again.

I grinned at my girl and opened my arms, where I stood with my ass against the side of my Harley in the pickup line. On cue, Cleo dashed through the students and lunged into my arms, squeezin' me tight. I held her to me, peerin' down at her closed-eye smile and the look of peace on her face as she pressed her cheek to my leather-covered chest.

This.

Fuckin' *this*.

This was the reason parents sacrificed again and again for their kids. Why those sacrifices felt halved instead of enormous. Why I woke up every mornin' and fought hard to be the best man I could.

So this girl, my girl, could have some peace after a lifetime of pain.

"Hey, Glory," I murmured as I palmed the back of her skull and stroked her long, wavy brown hair.

She hummed a response and kept huggin' me.

I knew this meant she'd had a rough day, and this was further solidified when I spotted Mei in the dispersin' crowd.

She stood still in the surgin' bodies watchin' us with a sort of pained smile on her face. Dressed all in black, one dark lipstick application away from full-blown goth, Cleo's best friend watched over her as she always did. It was a kind of hand-off we had. I had Cleo before and after school, and Mei had her durin' the daytime hours.

In ways that might have been unhealthy but explainable given the tragedy we'd lived through together, we were fiercely bonded together. Mei and I parentheses around Cleo and her tender heart. Between the two of us, we wouldn't let anythin' bad happen to our girl ever again.

We'd never spoken of it, but we didn't have to.

Cleo was smart about people, but Mei was plain fuckin' *smart.*

Kid was the brightest in her year with an early acceptance to some of the top universities in the country.

Beyond that, Mei and me, we got each other.

We always had.

She was tough as nails but built like a slip of a fairy-tale creature. All big, luminous eyes, small red mouth and slim, short build. She could've been a model or an actress, at the very least, the most popular girl in her class.

Instead, she was our Rocky.

The girl with chipped black polish on her nails and bruises on her knuckles from almost daily bouts at the martial arts gym downtown. The girl who, since Kate's death, only wore black as if she was in perpetual mournin'. The girl who had been suspended for bad behaviour three times in the past two years for beatin' up bullies even though they were young men with probably a head of height and at least fifty pounds on her.

Our fighter.

Somethin' in my chest constricted watchin' Mei standin' alone in that group of happily oblivious students. She didn't fit in, and she didn't want to. I got that. She was content bein' Cleo's watchdog, but what did that leave her?

I knew she was waitin' for Cleo to figure out what she wanted to do after high school 'til she made her own decision about university, much to her father's disappointment. Selfishly, I was glad. If Cleo decided to move away, I'd only be able to see her off knowin' Mei was there to look out for her.

But I knew it wasn't healthy. The friendship these two had. They were as codependent as conjoined twins. There was nothin' but love and kindness between them. Even when puberty started, and boys hit the scene, I'd never seen the two of them fight over anythin' more significant than which movie to watch. Still, Mei was seventeen years old. She should be out makin' her own mistakes, kissin' boys, and focusin' on her future.

Not focusin' on the Axelsen family.

From ten yards away, Mei tipped her little chin up at me the way men did to acknowledge a silent communication. I bit off the edge of a grin and tipped mine right back at her.

A second later, she disappeared into the crowd.

"You ready to go home, Glory?" I asked.

Cleo worried her lower lip. "Mei's got detention again, and her dad's in Montreal. Principal Rice asked if he could speak with you instead."

Anger flared in my belly at the mention of Florent Marchand, Mei's father in name only. At least in my opinion. The bastard never made time for his daughter, even now that his wife and her mother, Daiyu, was diagnosed with stage four brain cancer.

Helplessness fanned the flames of my anger.

I'd prayed so fuckin' hard the day after Kate died that both

Cleo and Mei wouldn't experience another day of tragedy in their lives, and as per usual, God had ignored me.

Daiyu was dyin', and Mei was gonna lose another mother.

It was no wonder she was actin' out. She'd already lost so much; how could she pretend to be anythin' other than angry with the bad hand she'd been dealt?

"Yeah," I said gruffly, smoothin' a hand down her hair before pressin' a kiss to her forehead. "You gonna wait for me right here?"

"Is it okay if I go shopping with Emma? I can meet you at home in an hour."

"Emma a good driver?" I asked with narrowed eyes 'cause Emma wasn't the smartest of Cleo's friends.

"Dad," she protested in that way teenagers had of draggin' out one syllable into fourteen. "She's fine. Please? I want to have a good dress for prom, and you know how much Mei hates shopping."

"Okay, fine. But home in one hour," I allowed.

It was hard not to wrap Cleo in bubble wrap and keep her locked up at home, but I got that she was eighteen and technically an adult with her own autonomy now.

She rewarded me with a megawatt grin and a smackin' kiss on the cheek before she pushed off my chest to skip away. She'd only gone a few steps when she looked back over her shoulder, brown hair flyin', looking so much like Kate it made me ache, and called, "Take it easy on Mei, okay?"

I rolled my eyes, which made her laugh, and then I waited 'til she'd ducked into Emma's idlin' silver sedan and they'd slowly pulled out of the lot before I headed for the doors to the school.

This wasn't the first time I'd been called in to speak with Principal Rice 'cause the motherfucker Florent couldn't be bothered to care for his kid. I didn't mind lookin' out for her, but that didn't mean I cut Florent any slack. He had more money than sense. How could he ever think work was more important than his wife dyin' in the hospital and his girl strugglin' to make sense of it all?

My heavy bootsteps rang through the halls of the already empty school. Teenagers didn't loiter long after the bell, and only a few stragglers remained in the hall. I was just down the corridor from the principal's office when a pair shootin' the shit at an open locker caught my attention.

"You make it worth my while, maybe I'll tell you." A snot-nosed teen was leerin' down at a dark-haired girl, his expression filled with teenage lecherous intent. One of his hands was perched on the girl's ass, squeezin' like he'd never touched a woman before.

"I can do that." The purr was practiced, breathy and filled with sexual promise.

It surprised me a teenager knew how to talk like that.

"Just tell me I can finally meet him," she continued in that husky voice. "You've been keeping me on the line for months. I want to meet him."

The guy laughed, his dark eyes dartin' to me as I drew closer so the next time he spoke, it was in a whisper, "What's a girl like you doing dealing anyway, huh?"

"Maybe I need to make some extra cash."

He snorted. "Your daddy's CEO of Barrington Grouse Oil. You don't need shit."

Shock skittered down my spine.

That breathy little bimbo was *Mei*.

Before I could curb my baser instincts, I stalked toward the kid and moved her away from him with one palm curled around her shoulder. She spun into me, a snarl marrin' her small red mouth 'til she saw it was me.

And then she went white as a ghost.

Which was fittin' 'cause I was about to *kill* her.

"Get lost," I bit out at the startled, pimply-faced teen who thought he was some hot shit drug dealer.

He tripped on his own feet in his haste and banged into the open locker. I watched as he fell, then popped to his feet, looked back at me in panic, and broke into a sprint only to trip again 'cause his fuckin' pants were ridin' too low.

Only when he'd finally flown out the doors to the back field did I train my furious gaze back on the reason I was even in the school in the first place.

Mei stared back at me, her composure gathered enough that she had the audacity to jerk her chin in the air righteously.

"You shouldn't scare students like that, Henning."

Flames of molten fury licked at my heels. My teeth ground so hard pain radiated through my jaw.

Usin' the hand still curled around her shoulder, I pushed her with controlled force up against the lockers and planted my other hand just under her throat between her delicate clavicles. She was so slight, I could've pinned her entire body there for hours without tirin'. Realizin' that just made me even angrier.

She was so delicate, so young. Didn't she understand how fragile that was? How fuckin' precious?

"I'll scare *you* whenever I damn well please," I growled, usin' all of my six-foot-four height as a tool to overwhelm her. "What the fuck do you think you're doin' with some lowlife drug dealer, Mei Zhen? Please fuckin' tell you me you aren't involved in that shit."

I only used her full first name when she'd pissed me off. I didn't even do that with Cleo, but then again, my daughter was a golden child, and she rarely did anythin' worse than misplacin' the remote control.

It was Mei and Mei alone who seemed able to rattle my legendary calm.

"It's none of your business," she had the gall to say to me.

"You wanna look me in the eye and say that one more time?

You wanna pretend we're not family when it suits you to do so, Mei, then we aren't really family."

"Well." She bared her small, straight teeth at me. "You're not my dad."

"For fuck's sake, did I ever say I was?" I countered. "Florent is an asshole, but he's your dad."

"So what are you?" she demanded, and suddenly, I felt as if I'd lost sight of the argument. There was vulnerability in her large, hooded eyes that panged at my heartstrings like an ill-struck chord.

"Your friend," I said, but there wasn't much muster behind it 'cause I couldn't stop wonderin' why she looked sad beneath the anger.

"Yeah," she scoffed. "What you really are is a man with a white knight complex. I don't need saving, Henning, so why don't you back off?"

"Like hell you don't."

"I can handle Brian."

"You need savin' from your own damn self," I snapped, my hand flexin' on her chest so she was plastered to the lockers for a moment before I let her go and stepped back to drag both my hands through my hair. "I've never met someone more self-destructive. What the fuck are you doin' hangin' around with someone like that?"

"Someone could say the same thing about *you*," she pointed out with an arched brow, takin' in my leather jacket and motorcycle boots, the tattoo sneakin' out the end of my jacket sleeve.

Everyone wanted to pretend they were above judgin' books by their covers, but the truth was, we were raised to judge, and judge we all did. The difference between one person and another was what their definition of normal was to judge others against.

At Cleo and Mei's wealthy high school, I was *not* the norm.

Hell, even when I'd worked at the hospital, before joinin'

The Fallen, I'd been too different to fit in with my fellow residents who drove compact sedans instead of Harleys and wore wrinkled polos on their rare days off instead of old denim and cracked leather.

"Don't try to talk your way around this one," I warned. "I'm serious, Mei. First, Cleo says you got detention again, and then this? What is goin' on with you?"

She canted her chin higher in the air, crossed her arms, and stared at me mulishly. She could be as stubborn as a goat when she set her mind to it, and it was clear she didn't want to share anythin' with me.

This was new.

After Kate passed away, Mei transferred all her love for my wife onto me. She told me about her hopes and dreams, those few things that dared to scare her. She shared her quick wit, funny sense of humour, generous spirit, and carin' nature.

But in the past six months, somethin' had changed.

Daiyu's doctors had declared she wasn't gonna get better.

And the Mei I'd known was slowly dyin' along with her.

The recklessness in her had ratcheted up, a vibration under her skin that made her twitchy, too eager to displease, too ready to dive into a fight head first.

"Hey," I said, softenin' like butter in a pan, reachin' out to cup the back of Mei's head and shake it a little. "You used to talk to me. I'm still here. What's goin' on in that madly brilliant brain?"

Her lips twitched, eyes scourin' my face for a long moment. When she finally spoke, the words were so soft I had to read her lips to understand them. "Nothing I can do to help Ma, but I can still help figure out who killed Kate."

Contrary emotions attacked me simultaneously. A reluctant sense of pride in her, that this young woman would be so loyal to Kate, to Cleo and me, that she'd risk herself in the pursuit of justice. And an overwhelmin', helpless kinda fury that made my tongue numb in my mouth as poison spilled over it and onto her.

"You listen to me, Mei Zhen. There is nothin' you can do to bring Kate back, and I'm sorrier than you'll ever fuckin' know that you gotta lose two mothers at the age of seventeen. But under absolutely no fuckin' circumstances are you gettin' involved in anythin' to do with Kate's death. The sheer stupidity of you thinkin' you can take on a group of murderers makes me seriously rethink your IQ. Do you get me?"

Another stubborn look.

I shifted my hand on her head to grasp the back of her neck tightly. "You get me?"

"I told you I remembered that Kate spoke Cantonese in the end," she said all in a rush, eyes eager as she beseeched me to understand. "But I think I also remember there was a tattoo on the ankle of the man who kicked me. I woke up from this dream a few months ago, and I knew exactly what it looked like! It was a series of circles within circles. I looked it up and—"

"Enough!" The word barked out of me, and Mei flinched, not with fear, but somethin' that was somehow worse.

Rejection.

I ignored the way that burned inside me and fixed her with my unhappy stare. "You are not gonna do this. Those people who killed Kate were criminals, and if they were a Chinese gang, they are *serious* criminals. You don't fuck with people like that."

"You used The Fallen MC to help you get information about Kate and about some of the women who showed up at the hospital abused and broken," she pointed out. "Now you're *one* of them. Should I avoid you, using that very same logic?"

"That's completely different. I'm a grown man and a trained one at that. I can take care of myself."

"So can I! You know I just got my gold belt in Shaolin kung fu, and I've been taking MMA for five years."

"You're seventeen years old," I shouted, my voice ringin' through the empty hall. My hands were suddenly bracketin' her shoulders, shakin' her lightly before I lifted her clean off her feet so she was raised to my eye level. "You're just a kid. You wanna get yourself killed too?"

"No one would even care!" she cried, that sadness lurkin' in her eyes suffusin' her entire face 'til it was almost grotesque with agony. "Ma is dying, and Dad doesn't give a flying fuck I'm alive."

"What about Old Dragon?" I demanded, but the heat had gone out of me, leavin' a mess of smolderin' ash in my chest. Fuck, but this girl had so much tragedy in her small frame, so much poison. A part of me wanted to suck it out of every one of her wounds, ingestin' it myself so she didn't have to. "You think that old geezer wouldn't miss you like crazy? What about Cleo? That girl loves you more than she loves anyone else in this world apart from me. She wouldn't know how to live without you."

Mei blinked at me, her slim nose wrinkled with the effort not to cry.

"You think I wouldn't care?" I asked softly, the words scourin' up my throat like knives. "What do I have to do to prove to you that you're loved, Mei?"

Unbidden, her gaze dropped to my right bicep where, beneath my leather jacket and tee, Cleo's and Kate's names were tattooed in a ring of fire.

"Mei…" I said 'cause I didn't know what else I was supposed to do.

There was no way I was gonna tattoo a seventeen-year-old's name on my body when she wasn't my kin.

Mei read my mind, and her expression shuttered completely, iron doors slammin' shut over those expressive dark eyes and that mobile mouth. She struggled in my arms 'til I dropped her, and she turned to pick up her discarded backpack without lookin' at me.

"I get it." Her words were quiet, tender like bruised flesh, and it killed me to hear that 'cause Mei never spoke that way. "But Kate loved me, and I loved her. That's between me and her memory whether you like it or not."

When she set off down the hall toward the principal's office for detention, I was still standin' there like a bastard tryin' to figure out how to love a girl who desperately needed love when it was socially unacceptable for me to love her any more than I already did.

CHAPTER SEVEN

Henning

I TOLD MEI TO QUIT LOOKIN' FOR KATE'S KILLERS, BUT THAT didn't mean I'd stopped or that I ever would.

The police found fuck all in their investigation. As in, they found enough to assume a local Chinese triad was involved in the murder, and discoverin' this, they decided to turn tail and run as far from the murder of a former prostitute as possible. It was easier for them to blame her death on the sins of her past--a disgruntled or psychotic former john or an affiliate of Jimmie Page, the Chinese-Canadian pimp who'd been released from his latest stint in jail just months before Kate's murder--than it was to sink into the swampy, treacherous waters of Chinese-affiliated gangs.

But the connection to them was obvious.

There was shit all known about Chinese gangs compared to the usual organized crime outfits. Enough movies and books were written about the Italian, Irish, and Russian Mafias to fill the entire city of Calgary. Even motorcycle gangs, Mexican and Latin American Cartels, and backwoods American drug dealers were researched enough to produce a metric shit ton of books and fuckin' TV shows and movies.

But not the Chinese triad system.

Those motherfuckers were shrouded in so much mystery, the only information I could find disappeared almost as soon as it was uttered in the wind.

One thing was certain, though, the way they'd killed Kate was ritualistic. The punishment for betrayal based on the concept of the triad's oath of five thunderbolts. A public, symbolic murder of death by a "thousand" cuts, known as *Lingchi*, to serve as a warnin' to others not to fuck up the same way she had.

Five years on, and I still didn't know how my wife had fucked up.

Probably 'cause I'd never had any goddamn clue my Katie Kay was involved with a Chinese triad. The only reason I knew that much was, indirectly, 'cause of Mei.

Almost a year after her murder, I'd been porin' over everythin' I had on the investigation I'd been able to cajole outta the police, secure from my connection with The Fallen MC in Calgary, and find out myself through a few lengthy conversations with some witnesses from the fairground that day that involved my fists.

It was nothing. A whole fuckin' pile of nothin'.

I had my elbows to the desk, fingers tunnelin' through my hair when Old Dragon had wandered into my office, obviously havin' arrived to pick up Mei from her hang out with Cleo. I didn't shift away from the old man when he shuffled up beside me and peered over my shoulder.

There was a rapport between us that had never been confirmed with words.

The demons in his eyes matched the demons in my own.

We'd done things, the two of us, our families would never know about, and we carried that burden with stoic grace.

So, when Old Dragon's surprisingly strong hand clamped over my shoulder, I was instantly alert to the change in his energy.

He recognized somethin'.

Or, it would seem, someone.

"This man," he murmured, crushin' the tip of his index finger into the photo of Kate with her arm wrapped around a client in front of a Sold sign. His fingernail cut a half-moon into the neck of a man carefully lingerin' in the background of the shot, as if he didn't want to be documented. "This man is Kasper Kuan of the Hong Kong Kuans."

I unearthed the partially buried photo and held it up to the lamplight to see the image more clearly. "Why does that name ring a bell?"

Old Dragon snorted. "Everyone in Hong Kong has heard this name. Everyone in Canada with ties back home knows this name. Anyone in business. Take your pick."

"Why would he be in a photo with Kate?" I murmured as I studied the pixelated face of the Chinese business tycoon. His face was cast carefully away from the photographer, ostensibly on a phone call. A wide sparklin' watch on his wrist and a tailored suit were enough to brand him as highly successful.

"It is not enough to own land in China," Old Dragon explained wearily, movin' around my desk to lower himself into a chair. He smoothed a hand stippled with age spots over his baldin' crown and then down across his face. It took me a minute to get the expression he was tryin' to hide behind that hand was *fear*. "Powerful men *expand*, you understand? For themselves and for China."

"And he's expandin' into Canada," I concluded. "Usin' proxies to buy up real estate."

Old Dragon blinked as he folded his hands loosely in his lap, a casual pose from a shrewd man. "This is not so uncommon."

"And not so legal," I pointed out, already swivelin' to the computer to check the files I'd transferred from Kate's computer after she died.

She'd kept logs and addresses for everyone she'd ever worked with like any good real estate agent, sendin' Christmas cards and check-ins to keep her forefront in their minds in case they needed to buy or sell again.

"You won't find Kasper Kuan or his brother, Jiang Kuan, among the names," Old Dragon said dismissively. "These brothers are tigers, Henning, not sheep easily led to slaughter."

"No," I agreed. "But Kate spoke decent enough Cantonese 'cause of Mei and me. It's reasonable he would have sent multiple people to her. Not a lot of Chinese-speakin' real estate agents in Calgary."

Mei's grandfather hummed in agreement as I clicked through file after file. Finally, I found evidence of what I'd started to assume.

"Look at this." I turned the computer screen to him, my finger runnin' down the list of names I'd collected. "Kate sold twenty homes last year, fifteen of which were to buyers with Chinese surnames."

"Coincidence?" he quipped, but I had the sense he was testin' me, proddin' me further along the right path.

"In Vancouver, maybe, where the population of Chinese Canadians and Chinese immigrants is somethin' like twenty percent of the community. Here? No, I don't think so."

My heart was beatin' fast and hard, pumpin' adrenaline through my system.

A lead.

A fuckin' *lead* after a year of nothin'.

"Do you think she figured out what was going on?" Old Dragon asked, touchin' his steepled fingers to his mouth.

"She wasn't dumb, my Kate," I murmured, thinkin' about her bright-eyed inquisitive nature. When I'd started showin' up at her house, bringin' her food and standin' guard at her door so her pimp would get the message she was fuckin' done with him, Kate had been too afraid to question anythin'. By the time she died, in her late twenties and safe enough to flourish in my care, she'd questioned everythin'. Why was the sky blue? She'd google it, explainin' to Cleo and me what she found. Who invented the first car? A documentary would be waitin' cued up in the DVD player ready for us to watch that night.

She would have found out what Kasper Kuan was doin'. The real question was, why hadn't she turned him in to the real estate board or the police?

"Don't much like the look in your eye," Old Dragon murmured, leanin' forward with sudden agility and grace that belied his eighty-two years. "This isn't a low-level thug you can rough up with your white man bulk. This is Kasper Kuan. He is part of something much bigger than one man."

"You mean China will back him up?"

"I mean," he said slowly, eyes dark and glitterin' in the low light, "there is more to fear in the shadows than the light. The triads can do what the government cannot."

"He's triad," I confirmed, a chill racin' down my spine, a cold luge of fear.

"Seven Song," Old Dragon confirmed. "Not the group you mess with, hmm? They've existed in some iteration for two hundred years. This is not a rival bike club or even a cartel, Henning. This is a long-established gang based on savagery and smarts. A lethal combination. You will die if you pursue this alone."

"I won't be alone, then," I said easily, already flippin' open my phone to call the president of the Calgary chapter of The Fallen MC.

"Henning," Rooster Cavendish barked into the phone after a single ring.

"Evenin', Rooster," I responded respectfully 'cause that was the only way to address an outlaw with his kinda record, but also 'cause he was the kinda man who demanded it. "Gotta lead on Kate's killers."

A long silence followed.

"This is startin' to become a pattern with you, Axelsen." Rooster had one of those voices, smooth and low, somethin' fluid and bendable that could wrap you up tight as a noose in one of his traps before you were even aware of it. "You know, I don't give without gettin' in return, and our ledger here's already damn unbalanced."

I gritted my teeth. "I do what I can for you."

I'd risked my medical license more than once to go to the aid of the club when one of their brothers was hurt in a skirmish.

"Yeah, well, that's not enough anymore," he said simply. "Kinda support you want, that's club shit. Far's I see it, you're a hangaround. Not a member cut into the leather. Not a real brother."

"I fought with some of your men," I countered, tryin' to keep the fury from my voice.

"Not me, you didn't. You want favours, you try that shit out on Zeus Garro." His laugh was a hideous, slitherin' thing. "That man's tough as nails, but he's got a soft spot for that Sergeant at Arms'a his you were on tour with. Maybe he'll throw a stray dog a bone."

Anyone with an ear to the underground had heard of the mother chapter of The Fallen MC's president, Zeus Garro. He'd killed his own fuckin' uncle to get that status and purged a shit ton of members in the club doin' it.

Rooster hated the man.

Said he ran the club like a pussy, but only in earshot of people he knew wouldn't snitch to Zeus. He didn't have near enough balls to say that shit to the man's face. The president in Entrance, BC, was known to kill men with his bare goddamn hands.

But Rooster was right, even though he was tauntin' me with somethin' he thought would never happen. Zeus had a soft spot for Bat Stephens, my former brother at arms, one of the few friends I'd expended the effort to keep from my combat days. The same man who'd been visitin' town the day Kate was killed.

I'd even met Zeus years ago on a trip out to visit Bat in Entrance and met a few of the men in their club. Each of them had seemed like stand-up men despite the connotation of the 1%er on their leather vests. Hell, I'd even watched Zeus take a teenage misfit under his wing just to keep him from windin' up in jail. For a man who looked like he could rip a grown-ass adult apart with his bare hands, he treated the men in his club like family instead of underlings.

Bat and I'd talked about the possibility of me joinin' the club, but we both had zero faith in Rooster as a prez, and there was no way I was gonna uproot Cleo and move her to another province just to get access to The Fallen's resources to find Kate's killer.

So really, my only choice was the devil I knew.

I nearly gagged on my sigh of frustration. "You want me to patch in."

"It's due time," Rooster confirmed.

Fuck. It wasn't that I was against the idea of joinin' the club, exactly. It was more that as soon as anyone saw you in the patch of The Fallen, they knew you were a criminal. My picture would be added to some bulletin board in the local precinct. I'd be expected to participate in illegal shit without my say so just 'cause the club asked it of me.

Bat's dad had been a member, and his childhood best friend, Zeus, had patched up when we'd been overseas, so it made sense for him to follow suit when he returned from war. Besides, ten years as a soldier, a sniper no less, had crafted Bat into the kinda man that needed a certain amount of danger to function.

Rick "Hazard" Elsher was the only man I'd served with who got out before I did after one tour of Afghanistan. He'd lost a foot in a car bombin' and been honourably discharged. But he'd lost somethin' more than his foot. Somethin' a lot like his fuckin' humanity. I barely recognized him now in his role as VP for the Calgary Fallen MC. He was angry, belligerent, and brash, and he seemed to relish his new life as a hardened criminal. Last I knew, he was servin' eighteen months for distribution of cocaine, and it wasn't his first stint behind bars.

Johnny Hopper, known as "Cedar" to The Fallen in Calgary, had been in our unit too. He told me the club gave him brotherhood outside of the military, organization and somethin' to believe in after bein' disillusioned and tossed out by the army. It gave him family where he otherwise wouldn't have shit. He'd also been there the night Kate died, takin' care of Cleo and her friends while I descended into hell to get Kate and Mei.

My real family.

Kate might've been gone, but I still had Cleo and my stepmum, Lin.

Even Mei.

From what I understood, The Fallen were a fuckin' mess under Rooster's leadership. More brothers were in lock-up than out on the streets. They got into stupid brawls in bars that resulted in civilians bein' hurt, some of the men were rumoured to be rapists, and the reputation of the club as a whole was so infamous most people flinched and ran away the moment they were confronted with the flamin' skull and wings motorcycle patch.

But...

They had the connections I needed, eyes in the underworld of normal civilian life. They'd know how to get to this Kasper Kuan, and they'd have my back if I was one of them and I wanted to *end* him.

And I had to believe if Cedar and Bat were involved in the organization, it couldn't be all bad.

Twin points burned into my cheek. I looked up from my desk to see Old Dragon glarin' at me, his wispy brows tangled into a knot.

No, he mouthed with a slow shake of his head. "Not like this. The only way this ends is in death."

I ignored him.

It was ridiculously easy to ignore him, one of the smartest men I knew, when temptation was danglin' so close to me, a ripe and dangerous fruit.

As a soldier, you were taught that evil could be eliminated piece by piece. First in one region with one target and then another and another.

Maybe that was why I was so fuckin' convinced the evil tragedy of Kate's death could be made better by eliminatin' the man responsible for it.

Simple thinkin'.

A soldier's thinkin' and not a general's.

But I'd never been raised to lead, and back then, dumb with grief and in over my head raisin' a girl on the cusp of womanhood, I made a deal with the only devil I knew.

"Fine," I told Prez Rooster Cavendish. "You want me, you got me. The only condition is you help me find my wife's murderer."

When Rooster's laughter came over the phone, it clawed through me like talons. "Done."

FOUR YEARS LATER, IT WAS HARD TO REMEMBER WHY I'D BEEN SO fuckin' foolish.

It'd started innocently enough. The year of prospectin' was borin' work, fetchin' things like a dog for the patched-in brothers, fixin' what was broke, and mostly keepin' outta the way. I wasn't allowed in church with the rest of them to make or listen to decisions, and I couldn't ride out with them when they went on drug runs. It was easy to dupe myself into believin' nothin' really had to change. Not my lifestyle.

Not me.

But then the year was up, and I was made a member of The Fallen.

Of course, everythin' changed, especially me.

I hadn't joined a jolly club of pleasure-ridin' bikers. I'd joined with an urban-type of militia with its own missions and agendas. Its own myriad of enemies, most of them accrued durin' Rooster's tenure.

We had more of those than allies, and it'd only worsened over the years.

The city of Calgary became a battlefield the way Afghanistan had. The impulses I'd tried to curb to assimilate back to civilian life swelled to the surface and drowned whatever remnants I'd clung to of my own pre-war mentality. I couldn't go to the fuckin' grocery store with Cleo without my head on a swivel, searchin' for assailants in the cereal aisle. Average citizens looked at me in my cut like I was a villain, and it was funny how their censure seemed to stitch itself into my skin. The grief I harboured since Kate died merged with the hardness of outlaw life and welded me into a newer, weaponized version of myself. It got harder to argue with Rooster's orders, to keep distance between my two lives as Henning and Axe. And as the gap shrunk, I started to feel trapped, a claustrophobia that strangled my throat in the dead of night.

How the fuck was I ever gonna get out?

Especially when the club had started an all-out war with one of the scariest motherfuckin' gangs in town.

"Load 'em up," Rooster ordered, thumpin' a meaty hand on my back as he moved by each of his brothers on the way to his bike.

The ten men lined up beside their bikes grumbled in agreement as they finished securin' the bricks of heroin to their saddlebags. The other half of our crew had already peeled off with the first load, bike lights off, Harleys carvin' through the dirt paths between rows of barley so they could avoid the major highways leadin' back into Calgary.

When you were stealin' and transportin' illegal shit, it paid to be cautious.

The rest of us would take a different route, cuttin' east before circlin' back through backroads into town. We had our own secured warehouse south of the city where we'd keep the contraband 'til we could get it dispersed out of town to our dealers safely.

"Shrap's gotta stop drinkin' so much damn Red Bull, and we'd make better time," Hazard grumbled from beside me where he straddled his bike and adjusted his gloves. "Man pees like a pregnant woman."

"Can't get your little bitch pregnant yet," Shrapnel countered cruelly. "Don't take your unused testosterone out on me."

Anger rolled off Hazard in waves, buffettin' me so strongly I felt nauseated. His wife was a fuckin' child bride, given as a gift to him by Rooster himself. She'd been sixteen when they got hitched just last year, and she was only seventeen now. The same age as Cleo and Mei. Too young to have kids unless she had a yearnin' for them, and I knew she didn't.

I knew 'cause I was the one who gave her a birth control shot every three months in secret out in the parkin' lot behind my stepmum's beauty salon.

It was a risk. Hazard and Rooster would kill me for interferin', but there was no way I could stand by as a man who'd been trained as a doctor and watch a woman be forced into carryin' a child by her backward dad and husband.

No fuckin' way.

Joinin' The Fallen had irrevocably stained my soul, but I still had remnants of decency. I refused to lose them, even if it meant losin' my life. The irony of it hit me at weird times, sittin' on the john, crackin' a beer in the backyard, when Mei and Cleo giggled like the carefree girls they were not. Sellin' my soul to the devil and carryin' out their immoral deeds made me foolishly attached to what remained of my honour. It was a surefire way to get killed in this life I'd chosen, but I found there was nothin' I could do to change it.

I'd patched in to find Kate's killers, and I wouldn't leave 'til I'd accomplished exactly that.

I'd compromised my soul to do it, but I'd also die defendin' what remained of my honour to ensure Cleo wasn't raised by a total fuckin' monster.

"Axe," Rooster barked, and I knew by his tone he'd been tryin' to talk to me for a while. "You'll drop the shit with the boys, then go home and see to that paper cut. Still can't believe that fucker got the jump on you." His laughter was a harsh bark. The "paper cut" was a shallow stab wound to my left side. The bleedin' had slowed after Cedar tied my torso off with his tee wrapped up under my cut, but it stung like a son of a bitch. "Need you to visit Pryor tomorrow. Remind him he owes us some serious cake. If we got the fuckin' Seven Song encroachin' on our territory, we need to be flush to fight 'em."

A sigh rattled around in my lungs, but I kept it from leakin' through my lips. Rooster wasn't a dumb man. No leader of an outlaw MC could be without bein' imprisoned right fuckin' quick. But he was an obvious one. Everythin' was black and white, his way or the highway. So, when Rooster looked at me, all six foot, four inches and two hundred forty pounds of muscle, he saw a perfect example of brawn.

He used me anytime someone needed to be shaken down, frightened, and intimidated into capitulatin' to the club.

In some ways, it was the same way the military had used me.

Canada's boogeyman.

The Fallen's weapon.

Hence my biker name.

Axe.

A man whose sole purpose was to cleave people in two.

Rooster swung onto his own bike, not requirin' any assurance from me that I'd follow out my orders. Not 'cause he trusted me--he didn't--but 'cause if you disobeyed Rooster, he'd fuckin' gut you.

Last year, when I'd refused to steal drugs from the hospital or use my old scripts to get illegal pharmaceutical drugs, Rooster'd doubled my dues, decreased my cut from jobs like this, and, worst of all, he'd taken to makin' casual threats about the women in my life. I knew that if I ever seriously questioned him, he wouldn't hesitate for a fuckin' second to hurt Cleo, Lin, or maybe even Mei.

Rooster begrudged me my life outside of The Fallen. Only Rooster was allowed to have his family, his son, Red, and daughter, Faith, and even they were being forced into places in the club at Rooster's orders. Red was only fifteen, but he was already hangin' around the club more than at school, and Faith...well, she'd been forced to marry Hazard. Rooster wanted his boys locked up tight to the club, beholden to its president for every cent and ounce of companionship in their life. The MC tradition of takin' Old Ladies was heavily discouraged and only three brothers had wives who were always kept at home. One of them, Cotton, had a kid he didn't give a fuck about, so I was the only brother headin' home at the end of each day instead of stickin' around the clubhouse to shoot the shit and cater to all of Rooster's needs.

He hated me, my president, and I hated him right back.

But I was too valuable to him to excommunicate, and he had too much on me now for me to break away clean.

I took half a second, straddlin' my bike, feelin' the purr of power beneath my body, to squeeze my eyes shut and wish an impossible wish to wipe my soul clean and feel for once like the hero I'd grown up wantin' to be and not the villain I'd somehow ended up as.

A cacophony of revved Harleys ripped through the cold night air, echoin' across the empty parkin' lot that ran alongside the industrial-sized silos where the local Chinese triad, Seven Song, stashed their heroin.

The silos we'd just raided and fuckin' looted.

"War," Cedar murmured to me under the low hum of bike pipes as the men in front of us peeled out of the lot. "Mark this, brother. Rooster just bought war for us all."

I rolled my lips between my teeth but didn't answer the only man I happened to like in the club. Not because I disagreed, but 'cause he'd stated somethin' so obvious it didn't need acknowledgment.

When I'd tried to voice my objections earlier, Rooster'd claimed he was doin' this *for me.*

Takin' down those motherfuckers who took down your wife. Just like you wanted.

But no.

This didn't have shit all to do with me. Rooster was startin' this war because Seven Song was gettin' bigger and stronger. In another two years, they'd be runnin' shit in Calgary, and Rooster, bigoted and prideful as he was, couldn't fuckin' stand that. They'd already started to monopolize the meth and heroin market, importin' shit tons of product from their production facilities deep in the jungles of Myanmar. There was no way we could ever produce that level of product, but Rooster didn't care about logic.

He cared about being the biggest cock in the hen house.

I knew Kate's murder was linked to the triad, but that didn't mean I wanted to start a fuckin' war over her. Even though I didn't spend much time with my brothers in the club, I didn't want to see all of them die either.

"You think we should do somethin'?" he muttered low, just for me.

"Like what?" I asked, the words sharp enough to cut my tongue. "We signed up for this, man. You know what kinda prez Rooster is. You wanna be the one to stand up to him?"

My old friend went quiet and white as a sheet.

Maybe in other clubs and other chapters of The Fallen there was some semblance of democracy, but in the Calgary outfit of The Fallen, Rooster's word was fuckin' law. The last time a brother had spoken out against him, he'd been excommunicated, his club tatt seared off his skin with a fuckin' cattle brand.

I'd always known that joinin' up with this crew could mean incarceration or death so I'd already taken precautions for Cleo. I'd buried a small fortune in cash beneath the shed in the backyard, and if anythin' happened to me, Lin was supposed to take Cleo with her to Vancouver where she had some family they could stay with while they settled in.

I hoped it would never come to that, but I'd seen too much in my life not to have a backup plan.

Rooster swung onto his bike at the front of our formation and let out a low, growlin' whoop of joy as he gunned the engine and darted out into the night. He was a vet, too. But unlike Cedar and me, he wasn't the kinda man who could leave war behind. He'd always thirst for the next battle, yearn for the blood of another man sprayin' across his cheeks, wet against his hands.

Violence was his language and he refused to be muted.

"I don't like this, brother," Cedar said as he put on his night goggles. "I didn't sign up for this shit. When Bat used to talk about MC life, it wasn't like this."

"What're you gonna do?" I demanded. "The only way outta this life is through death or excommunication. You want your tatt cut outta your flesh?"

"Maybe," he snapped back. "I'd rather have an ugly scar than a Chinese bullet through my fuckin' skull. Maybe we should go above Rooster's head. Zeus is the president of the mother chapter. What do you think he would say about a club war against a fuckin' nationwide triad?"

Nothin' good. But goin' over Rooster's head would mean losin' ours if he ever found out.

"Let me talk to Old Dragon before we do anythin' crazy. He's got old connections with the triad. Maybe we can broker some kinda sit-down," I grunted and kicked my bike into gear to follow the trail of dust into the rows of crops. "If not, I'll call Zeus Garro. We're dead if this war comes to a head anyway. I'd rather be dead for tryin' to keep the peace than by divin' into the chaos."

I had a kid to feed and love. Unlike some MCs, Rooster hadn't taken a vote from the brothers before throwin' down tonight. He'd set a club war into motion I had no fuckin' interest in. I was a part of the club for one reason and one reason only.

Revenge against Kate's murderer.

Yet somehow, over the last four years, my mission had become muddled by the everyday chores and challenges of club life. Sure, they had their connections in the underworld, but it seemed the Seven Song triad was smarter than most, as elusive as mist dispersin' as soon as I got close. It was gettin' harder and harder to remember why retribution was worth the price of the soul I was slowly losin' to the club.

CHAPTER EIGHT

Henning

THE HOUSE WAS LIT UP WHEN I PULLED INTO THE CRACKED asphalt driveway and cut the engine, but it was quiet when I unlocked the door and stepped into the small front hall. It was late, and Cleo was an early-to-bed, early-to-rise kinda girl. She'd be asleep.

But there was a quality to the silence, a hoverin' wakefulness that alerted me to the fact that someone was sittin' up for me. Lin lived close by, but she didn't live with us, and she wouldn't be waitin' up for me this late.

I sighed heavily in resignation and walked into the kitchen off the hallway.

As expected, Mei sat curled in an uncomfortable wooden

chair at our Formica dinner table wedged into the corner of the small space. Knees to her chin, hair curtainin' her black jeans, she had her head tilted toward the sketchbook clutched in one black-fingered hand. Her pencil hovered over the page, the tip attached to a heavily shaded face that looked remarkably like Cleo mid-laughter. Her eyes rose to me as I entered, darker than the midnight shadows beyond the window.

"You're bleeding," she said immediately, eyes trackin' me, sharp as a mother's fingers pluckin' at her child's unruly clothes.

It was her turn to sigh as she unfurled, the sketchbook thumpin' forgotten to the tabletop, and walked across the cold laminate on the balls of her feet to my side. She'd always walked like that, not quite the gait of a dancer, but somethin' like it, a ready grace that came from years of practicin' martial arts and gymnastics. When she reached for my side, I swiped her hands away with one sweep of my palm and grunted. Her lips rolled beneath her teeth to keep the sharp words she wanted to say in her mouth. Instead, she watched me hiss as I took off my cut, tossin' it on the table. An offer to help was there stamped on her face, but I ignored it. I was a grown man and the one who'd got myself into this mess in the first place. I'd deal with the consequences myself.

"'Mei Zhen Marchand displays reckless independence,'" she quoted softly as she planted her hands on the countertop and hopped up to sit there, feet drummin' softly against the cabinets beneath her. "'When she disagrees with her superiors and her peers, nothing will curb her tongue. She speaks up loudly for what she believes is the truth or what she believes is right. Even if she is wrong, even if it would be kinder and smarter to stay silent.'"

"You been goin' to those fortune tellers again?" I asked dryly. The makeshift bandage, an old army tee that was once black and now grey, was stuck to the wound, and it hurt like a bitch to rip it free.

"You oaf," Mei hissed, jumpin' down from the counter to shove me into the chair opposite the one she'd been occupyin'. As soon as I was down, she turned on her heel and went into the hall bathroom to grab the large first aid kit I kept under the sink. "It was one of the comments in my last report card," she finally explained her earlier comment. "They make it sound like a bad thing. Seeking the truth. But you and I both know few things are nobler than that."

I snorted. "I'm hardly noble, Rocky."

The dimple in her left cheek popped into view as she smiled, head ducked to partially cover the expression from me as she reentered the kitchen. "You might drive a Harley instead of riding a white horse, but that doesn't make you any less noble. I don't know many men who would raise another man's daughter better than his own. Who would sacrifice everything again and again to give her the best life he could." Her lips thinned in self-mockery. "A man who'd put up with his step-daughter's best friend, too."

She plunked the kit on the table beside me and retrieved what she needed with the efficiency of a military doctor.

My hand landed heavily on top of hers, so much bigger I could have swallowed her entire hand in one palm. She seemed startled by the contact before settling. I made sure she was lookin' me in the eye before I told her the truth, "Cleo and I couldn't have survived losin' Kate without you. Don't sell yourself short."

She didn't have a response for that, but I wasn't surprised. Mei didn't like talkin' about her own emotional shit, she preferred to pry it out of others instead. I squeezed her hand, frustrated with my lack of eloquence and her lack of perceptiveness. Lately, I couldn't shake the feelin' that I was lettin' her down, disappointin' her somehow. She'd become more and more withdrawn as Daiyu grew sicker, and nothin' I did seemed to bring her the solace she needed.

She claimed scissors from the metal box and proceeded to cut my tee from collar to hem in order to get at my wound. The pieces of the shirt fell to the floor around us when she was done. Luckily, Cleo always ran cold, so it was toasty warm in the kitchen even at this time of night.

"I can stitch it myself," I told her mildly, but the fight had gone outta me.

I was fuckin' tired.

The years since Kate died seemed to drag, dark but for the presence of Cleo and Mei constantly pullin' smiles out of my dried-up heart. The truth was, Kate wasn't the love of my life. It was no secret. I'd married her to save her, and in doin' so, she'd saved me. Given me a family worth livin' for when the only one I'd ever really known was ripped away from me after I left the military. We weren't a relationship built on physicality and passion, but did that really matter? We'd chosen each other. *Saved* each other.

'Til I'd fallen down on the job and failed to save her that night at the carnival.

Slim fingers pinched my stubbled chin, wrenchin' my gaze to dark, fathomless eyes ringed in thick, straight lashes. "Stop that."

I cocked a brow in question.

"Brooding," she clarified, releasing me to focus on her task. "I don't know why girls think it's hot. I think it's just pouty." She peeked at my expression and laughed at my scowl. "There we go, that's much better."

"You're a brat."

She shrugged one shoulder and fell to her knees in the bracket of my spread thighs to get close to the stab wound. It leaked blood down my left side into the growin' stain at the waistband of my jeans. The sight of her down there made me irrationally irritated.

"I said I can do it," I growled, grabbin' her wrist as she made to stitch me up. "Get up from there."

"No." She wrenched her hand away and flashed me a look so cold with determination it chilled me. "Even big, bad bikers need someone to take care of them sometimes."

I scowled but leaned back to let her proceed, avertin' my eyes so I didn't have to watch her dark, silky head so close to my groin. It made me uncomfortable, edgy, and irascible in a way only Mei could do. The first press of the needle made me stiffen, but I didn't make a noise. A little stab wound was nothin' compared to the shrapnel from an IED in Afghanistan that had nearly ripped my right side to shreds.

"What happened?" she asked softly, noble fingers makin' quick work.

I closed my eyes, head thuddin' back against the wall. "Paper cut."

She made an unimpressed noise at the back of her throat. "You know, I'm not a kid anymore, right? I know more than you think I do."

"Oh yeah? Brian tell you some of that?" I asked darkly.

I knew she shrugged flippantly even though my eyes were shut. "Maybe. I know The Fallen are serious business. Most of it bad."

"You don't know shit."

"I know you," she murmured, softer still. A sudden weight on my right thigh had me stiffenin', eyes flashin' open to see Mei perched on my lap, medical tools abandoned, one hand raised to press lightly against my bare chest where my heart thrummed too strongly. "I know sometimes the ends justify the means."

"You don't know shit," I repeated cruelly, my stomach turnin' over on itself, so I thought I'd be sick with anger and guilt. I pushed her off me none too gently even though it made my fresh stitches pull. "You're not my confidante, Mei, or my daughter. I don't owe you any explanations so stop crowdin' me."

Hurt flared in her expression for a moment before collapsin' into that calm mask she'd been perfectin' for months. "Right, well, I'll get out of here and stop *crowding* you then. Tell Cleo I'll see her at school."

She turned on her heel swiftly, hair archin' out behind her like a short black cape.

Made it three steps before I cursed myself for bein' such an asshole.

"Rocky," I called, on my feet and movin' quickly despite the sharp pain in my side.

She didn't stop, but I caught her anyway, tuggin' her back against me so I could enfold her in a full-body hug. After a second of huggin' a plank of wood, she softened back against me and turned her nose into the crook of my arm. I felt the cool dampness of tears on my skin and cursed myself again.

"I'm an asshole," I told her, restin' my chin on the top of her head.

"Yeah," she agreed easily, but her hands came up to clutch at my arms. "But you're our asshole."

"I am," I said, even though this was dangerous.

I'd stopped huggin' her like this, touchin' her easily and casually the way I did Cleo about the time she started formin' from a girl to a woman. She didn't do anythin' for me that way. She was a kid, Cleo's best friend, a responsibility I felt too acutely to develop any other feelings for her, but it was good practice to distance us a bit.

It hadn't really occurred to me that she might miss this, a simple hug. A gesture to prove she wasn't alone. Daiyu was a hugger, but she was too weak to hold her daughter the way she wanted to, and Florent was too preoccupied with work and his own mad grief to think of comfortin' Mei and she would never, ever ask for it.

Her pride and the scars from losin' Kate wouldn't allow her to.

So, in the kitchen in the middle of the night, blood from my wound wettin' her tee, my entire body an oversized bracket for her slight frame, I hugged her tight and let us both have the moment of connection we craved.

"I trust you," she said softly, so softly I could barely hear the words. "I trust you, even if you don't, Henning. I know you'll always do the right thing. It's what makes you so broody. A hero doesn't mean being a man who never does any wrong. It means being a man who seeks truth and justice no matter the consequences. I know everything you do is to get justice for Kate and to keep Cleo safe."

A pause, pregnant with the weight of the secrets no seventeen-year-old girl should have. Her short, black nails dug into my forearm. "I know because I feel the same way."

"But I'm a man and you're a kid," I corrected, turnin' her in my arms so I could cup her shoulders in my palms and stare down into that obstinate face. "You need to focus on school crushes and prom, on university and, I dunno, makeup or social media or whatever shit kids like these days. Not on revenge and murder, yeah?"

When she only rolled her lips under her teeth, I gave her a vigorous shake. "You hear me, Rocky? Focus on bein' a kid, for Christ's sake."

"I stopped being a kid when I fell down the steps into that hell where Kate died," she shot back, chin angled high in the air. "I'm not normal or safe or dull. I'm not scared of pain or death, Hen. I'm only scared of losing the few people I love." Tears swelled in her ducts and trembled. "I can't afford to lose any more of you when there were so few to start with."

"How do you think Cleo and me feel?" I retorted, but I

wasn't angry, just so tired I felt my bones had turned to sponge. It was hard to carry my own weight. "Don't put yourself at risk for a ghost."

She stared at me, tauntin' me with my own words.

We wouldn't solve anythin' like this, not now, or maybe ever. We were too similar, too stupid to value ourselves more than the ones we loved.

"Don't leave," I said, squeezin' her shoulders before releasin' her to grab a glass of water. Bleedin' always made you thirsty. "Cleo sleeps better with you around and it's late."

"I'm not tired yet," she said after a moment, a thread of stubbornness remainin'.

I bit the edge of my smile before turnin' to face her, leanin' against the counter. "You hungry?"

Her mouth stayed flat, but her eyes warmed. "Yeah, I could eat."

"Good, you cook." I moved to the table and sat down with a groan.

She laughed under her breath but moved to the cupboards to scrounge somethin' for us to eat. While she did that, I pulled her sketchbook over and flipped to the last entry.

The drawin' of Cleo was perfectly rendered, so life-like it was hard to believe a seventeen-year-old girl had done it. She'd only started drawin' a few years ago after watchin' me carefully, studyin' me and the way my fingers moved pen and pencil across the page. Mostly, I liked to work with pens, detailed line drawings I'd started to sketch out as a kid on napkins and restaurant menus 'til my stepmum finally thought to enroll me in art class. My sketchin' lent itself well to tattooin' and my talents had started somethin' of a cult followin' in the province, with people travelin' from out of the city to be inked by me. I'd also converted half the garage into a quasi-art studio where I'd started to dabble with paints.

"This is good shit," I murmured, tracin' a finger over the curve of my daughter's face.

Mei made a dismissive noise, but she didn't wrench the book out of my hands, which was what she usually did when someone tried to look at her artwork.

I flipped the page to see a detailed image of a male hand complete with creases, shadows, veins, shrapnel scars, and corded tendons. There was no mistakin' the hand as anythin' other than my own.

A steamin' cup of instant noodles appeared over the sketchbook and I looked up to see Mei glarin' at me in challenge.

"Hands are tricky," she explained defensively.

"They are," I agreed, takin' the cheap but delicious Nongshim Soon Noodles in one hand so I could put it to the side to cool. "Sit."

Mei pursed her lips, eyein' her sketchbook as if to take it, but ultimately, she sat. Her hand was smooth skinned save for the ridge of faint callus over her knuckles from her martial arts trainin'. She gave a little start when I tugged her hand, then lay it just so over the laminate tabletop.

"Let me?" I asked, already pickin' up her discarded pencil, already tracin' the delicate lines of her extended fingers.

It had been a bad night, a bad week. I was foul-tempered and restless, a sense of forbodin' about the war with the triad and Mei's continued rebellion itchin' under my skin like fire ants I couldn't scratch. But this, the quiet strength and trust of the girl across from me and the opportunity to lose myself in art, was the balm I desperately needed.

In answer, Mei merely settled back in her seat comfortably and watched me with low-lidded eyes.

I finished her hand quickly, fingers almost crampin' with my urgency. Still, I ached with the need to purge the ugliness in my heart with the beauty I could create on the page. So, I started in on her shoulder, the delicate wing of her collarbone where her overlarge tee slipped to reveal pale skin smooth as ivory. She had a lot of fine, silky black hair, falling in straight sheets to the top of her chest. A lock fell over her face, tanglin' with long straight lashes, a perfect comma.

She was beautiful, I realized in a way I hadn't ever let myself before. Not just in the way of pretty girls. No, her beauty was written in her very bones. In the slope of her steeply carved cheeks and the faint hollow beneath. In the full brows arched delicately over large eyes that were dark but warm, vital. Freshly tilled earth instead of a night without stars. She looked almost fragile, but I mapped the strength of her character in that stubborn chin, the knit of her brows, and the flattenin' of a full mouth into a fine line. Slim limbs carved with muscle, sharp nails painted black. A surprisingly strong jawline that had taken more than its fair share of punches.

A livin' contrast, Mei Zhen. Our Rocky.

A girl who was both named for a beautiful pearl and a famous fictional boxer.

We had sat up just like this together many nights before, sketchin' together in our own books, the scratch of lead on paper and the soft gust of our breath the only soundtrack to our shared insomnia. But never like this. Never when my focus and art was all about Mei.

It made me look at her in this new way that made my chest pinch even though I fought to ignore it.

I fell into the hazy pleasure of creation, losin' myself to the craft and dance of pencil over paper, only stallin' to reach for another, sharper pencil Mei offered when the one I was usin' wore down to nothin'. My eyes grew tired, scratchy, and raw, but still, I filled pages of Mei's notebook with images of her, not whole renderings 'cause somethin' about that made my stomach clench, but sections of her litterin' the pages, a corner of her forehead, the edge of her sharp little chin, the exact shape of that little dimple divotin' her left cheek.

When I finally looked up, it was 'cause the garbage truck was groanin' outside, clankin' as they collected our trash.

I blinked once, twice, hungover from the high of creatin'.

The pencil fell from my suddenly numb fingers, thumpin' against the page where I'd drawn Mei's nickname in traditional Chinese, the characters thick as brushstrokes even though I'd only done them with the hard press of a lead pencil.

I blinked again, sluggish and groggy.

Somethin' touched my hand, smoothin' over my fingers with firm strokes, massagin' the tension out of them.

When I looked up at Mei, her face was softer than I'd seen it in years.

"Hey," she whispered into the heavy, velvet silence that had stretched between us.

"Hi," I croaked.

It had been a while since we last spoke.

"Three hours," she supplied as if readin' my mind, pullin' hard at my fingers in a way that made me want to moan. "I think you needed that. For a man like you, I think drawing is as close to therapy as you'll get."

My mouth twisted in a wry grin. "Kept you up late. You should've stopped me."

"No," she said easily. "Usually, you refuse anyone's help. I was glad to be able to do this for you." Her dimple popped. "You stubborn goat."

I laughed rough as a cough. "Go to bed, Mei."

"Go to bed, Henning," she returned, sass creepin' back into her voice. It was never gone for long.

She stood up, reachin' for her sketchbook as she did. "I'm keeping these. The cost for services rendered."

I snorted as I rubbed a hand over my face.

There was a long moment of silence. I dropped my hands to see her arrested mid-step, slightly off-balance, eyes riveted to the page beside the Chinese characters for her name.

I'd run out of pieces of Mei to draw and settled on sketchin' symbols I associated with her instead.

The Chinese dragon took up the entire nine-by-twelve-inch page, corner to corner. It curled as if in midflight 'cause Chinese dragons were wingless and undulated through the air like a serpent through still waters. This one was fierce, yes, but also lovely, a softness in the ridges along its spine, a grace to the flow of its immense, muscled form. The number of claws on a Chinese dragon was contentious throughout its history, but I'd given Mei's dragon five 'cause it was considered the most sacred.

And whatever Rocky was to me, it was sacred.

"Is this how you see me?" she whispered, the words raw as if she'd carved them out of her body and handed them to me still bleedin'.

I swallowed around the stone in my throat, suddenly aware of how vulnerable it was for her to have those sketches. They were mindless in that I hadn't filtered the instincts of my pen. As Lin would have said, they were soul-drawn, and now Mei had a piece of my soul in her hands.

In the end, I didn't say anythin', but I didn't have to 'cause Mei looked up at me finally and read the answer in my reluctant expression. In the hand that had fisted unconsciously on the tabletop.

Her fingers lightly traced the twist of the dragon over the page, her entire face suffused with somethin' that made my chest ache.

"It's strange," she whispered, almost to herself, and I held very still, suddenly afraid to startle her out of revealin' her mysteries. "That you could look at me and see everything I've ever wanted to be." She closed the book and hugged it to her chest, eyes dark and fathomless as they raised to me. "It feels just as good as it does bad. To be seen like that." Her lips flattened. "Like being flayed alive."

"I didn't mean to hurt you."

"No," she agreed. "You didn't, not really. I guess it's one thing to want to be known and another to actually have someone see you even when you try to hide." Her laughter was coarse, but her smile was oddly shy as she lifted the book to her forehead in a mock salute and then turned on her heel to push through the door into the hall.

"Rocky, thank you," I called lightly, though my throat ached. "For seein' me, too."

Only a faint hitch in her stride belayed the fact that she'd heard me at all, and then she was gone down the hall, and I was sittin' in the kitchen with a sore side, a sorer hand, and the biggest ache of all somewhere deep inside my chest.

CHAPTER NINE

Mei

Some people are born with rebellion in their blood.

A genetic anomaly.

A quirk of fate.

However you want to classify it, some people just eat trouble for breakfast and spit out the backbone of societal conventions like they don't know how to digest it.

I know because I was born one of them.

They named me Mei Zhen.

Beautiful pearl.

Something elegant and refined, cultivated under pressure.

When they quickly discovered I was nothing more than grit,

they applied more pressure, hoping I'd slowly alchemize into something more precious.

Into something worthy of the name Marchand.

I never cared much about names or living up to them. And no matter how hard they tried, I never learned how to care about what people thought of me.

Why should perfect strangers have any impact on my life?

It wasn't until I was older that I realized why people cared.

Why people followed the often-archaic rules society had laid out for them.

Because bad things happened when you didn't toe the line.

I didn't care about punishments. My parents tried everything: time-outs, spankings, technology bans, public shaming... nothing worked.

Not until Cleo.

The moment my dad figured out how much she meant to me, he used her as both a threat and a lure. If I wanted to see her, I had to help Ma roll six hundred dumplings for the small fundraiser they were throwing out of the house, get at least a ninety percent on my physics test, apply and get into the top universities in North America and make something of myself for the sake of the family.

It was weird how Dad's and Ma's ideas of family differed even though they both held family higher than anything else.

For Dad, who was from old money Quebec and had moved out west fresh out of university to make something of himself in the oil-rich Albertan economy, family meant obligation and loyalty to a shared family ideal. In his case, it meant keeping the Marchand reputation squeaky clean and classy. It meant filling the communal coffers and making friends with the right people to network. It meant adding another, higher rung to the social ladder his family had been building and climbing for decades.

For Ma and Old Dragon, it meant having dinner together at

least once a week, even when we were busy. It meant sharing a mug of hot water and lemon every morning before we ate breakfast. It meant taking care of each other. With money, yes, and with honour, but also with tender loving care.

It meant doing *anything* to protect your family.

That resonated with me early on.

It was the one and only lesson my parents had instilled in me the way they'd wanted to.

They just didn't expect it to backfire on them.

For me to consider three outsiders without shared blood just as much my family as them.

"Your father loves you, you know?" Ma murmured sleepily over the low voices playing from the laptop I had set up on her tray table that played one of her favourite films.

I blinked at her, startled by the non sequitur.

She grabbed my hand, her skin soft as worn paper against my own. I could count the pale lavender and blue veins beneath the pale flesh, and the knobs of her finger bones were too pronounced. They'd stopped chemo weeks ago when it became obvious she wasn't going to beat the disease. The medicine had made her sick, but the cancer in its final stages was eating her up from the inside out.

I raised her hand in mine to rub my cheek against the back of her hand.

"He loves you," she repeated firmly, then coughed at the effort. "I need you to know this, my lovely daughter. When I am gone, you will only have each other and Old Dragon. You must make nice with your father."

"It's not me with the problem," I quipped.

She closed her eyes for a long moment, and when she opened them, they were warm with love. The chemo had taken her hair, straight down to her eyelashes, but she still had the prettiest, softest gaze I'd ever seen. "Your father is a traditional man. He may be Quebecois, but in some ways, his ideals match the traditions of my culture. He expects a daughter to be kind, poised, demure, successful in a quiet way." Her smile was wide, my favourite of her expressions, a grin meant only for me. "From the moment you were born squalling and kicking so hard he could barely hold you in his arms, Florent didn't know what to do with you."

She sighed, rubbing a thumb over my palm. "Your father doesn't hate you, Mei Zhen, nor is he even disappointed in you. He is fearful for you because he doesn't understand you, and for a smart man, there is nothing to fear more than that which he doesn't know."

"He could sit down and try to get to know me," I suggested blandly, but my heart was beating hard and slow against my ribs like the tick of a grandfather clock. Something inside me knew that if my dad and I didn't reconcile our differences now, with Ma still between us to facilitate things, we never would.

"Ah," she murmured. "Well, one thing you both have in common, the Marchand streak of stubborn pride."

I couldn't argue that, but I also refused to admit we were alike in any way. So, after my beat of silence, Ma let out a shuddery breath. "Come closer."

I swung the tray table out and away so I could perch on the edge of her bed and lean forward toward her open palms. They closed over my cheeks, cool and dry.

My eyes closed to better savour the sensation. Since I was a child, Ma had taken my face in her hands this way when she had to tell me something important.

God, I would miss it.

When I opened them again, her gaunt face was soft and filled with so much love, I imagined I could feel it emanating from her skin.

"I love you, my daughter," she whispered in Cantonese. This wasn't an everyday occurrence, this admittance of love. It was a distinctly Western habit to say "I love you" all the time.

For Old Dragon and Ma, love was spoken daily by taking care of their family in little ways. Reminding me to wear a coat in the cold. Offering me food every five minutes. Sharing my ancestry with me in stories and customs they painstakingly passed on to me. Even though I was used to their unspoken displays, it felt immeasurably good to hear confirmation of her love then when I knew I wouldn't have it with me for much longer.

"I know we have been hard on you. Too hard, maybe. I worked too much and left you alone too often. But the day you were born was the happiest day of my life. I only wish I could stay on earth long enough to see all the ways you will succeed, though I have no doubt your success will be bold, rebellious, colourful, and wild, just like my beautiful daughter herself."

Pins and needles stung the backs of my eyes, producing hot tears that flowed unencumbered down my cheeks between Ma's bony fingers.

I clasped my hands over top of her own and struggled to find my voice through the tight clutch of emotions suffocating my throat.

"One hundred hearts would not be enough to carry the love I have for you," I croaked out in Cantonese.

Ma smiled. "One hundred hearts would never be enough to carry the love *and* pride I have for you, my Mei Zhen. Remember that always."

"I couldn't forget it even when I'm old and grey with dementia," I joked, trying to make light when my chest felt like a mineshaft caved in around my heart.

Ma squeezed my cheeks as hard as she could, which wasn't hard at all, and then let me go, settling with a wince back into her stack of pillows. "Now, go back a few minutes in the film. We missed too much."

I laughed wetly. "Ma, you've seen it about four million times."

"As with enjoying your company, I can never watch it too much," she declared with a sniff.

And even though I knew she did it just to make me laugh, it worked, and I did.

"Where do you think you're going?" Florent asked wearily from the doorway of Ma's hospital room.

It was hours later. I was packing up my schoolwork from where I'd been studying on Ma's hospital bed tray, swung out over my lap where I sat on a chair beside her. I didn't bother looking up at him as I finished my task. It was hospital quiet, especially here in the hospice ward––only the steady beep of monitors, the brush of scrubs and shuffle of cushioned shoes in the hall, the occasional murmur of a television playing in another room or a muffled cry from a grieving loved one. But the air between Florent and me felt especially void, like the air in the Osoyoos desert, flat and muffled.

No matter what Daiyu said, there was an unbroachable chasm between my father and me, and it had existed for so long that I didn't even care to rectify it anymore.

"Ma's exhausted; she's been asleep the last hour, and I just finished studying. I've been here since school let out. I need to go home."

"I'll order food," he said in a way that brokered no argument. "We can eat here together as a family."

"Old Dragon brought me pineapple buns after school, and we ate them with Ma."

Dad was quiet because he was smart enough to hear the way I'd left him out. The way he'd left himself out, yet again.

"I had an important meeting, Mei."

"I bet." I swung my backpack up onto one shoulder and turned to face my mother before leaving.

She was wafer thin, her body barely making an indent in the sheets. Dad had brought in expensive ones, fluffy pillows, and a velvet blanket in Ma's favourite lucky red, but nothing could detract from the horror of her brittle bones so easily seen beneath bruised skin. From the fact that she was dying, and every single hour she breathed was a miracle.

I sucked in a deep breath, but there wasn't enough oxygen to fill the emptiness in my chest.

"I love you more than one hundred hearts, Ma," I whispered to her in Cantonese again before pressing a kiss to the middle of her forehead.

When I pulled back, Dad stared at me with dry, red-rimmed eyes. He startled when I walked around the bed, as if he'd forgotten he was sentient and not watching the scene like a ghost.

"I have *In the Mood for Love* cued up on the laptop if she wakes up," I told him. "We already watched it today, but..."

"It's her favourite movie," he finished on an anguished breath.

I nodded, biting my lip as I stared somewhere over his shoulder. It had been weeks since I could bring myself to look in his eyes. I found I could control the onslaught of rage and abandonment I felt if I didn't make eye contact.

"You know I'm dying inside, too," he whispered, the words constricted and breathy like he could barely speak through a too-tight throat. "You don't know what it's like to watch the love of your life just..." He flapped his hand ineloquently.

He rarely showed emotion. Unfairly, I wondered if the meeting today had gone badly. Rationally, I knew he loved Ma to distraction. It was easy to forget that sometimes when he was so cold and distant with everyone else. Especially me.

My gaze flicked up to his face, the sheen of old sweat on his skin, the mouth tight with pain, and the eyes...the eyes dark with regret.

Fury ignited so deeply inside me, the burn took a moment to reach my lips. "I don't know what it's like to watch the love of my life die? No. No, I guess I don't. Because I'm only seventeen, Dad. But I do know what it's like to watch my mother die. And I sure as hell know what it's like to go through that without a father."

"Mei Zhen Marchand," he snapped, grabbing my arm almost painfully as I made to storm past him. "You do not speak to family so disrespectfully."

"You're right," I agreed, staring up at him with all the defiance I felt bristling across my skin. "I don't speak to Ma like that. To Old Dragon or Henning and Cleo. Just *you*."

Dad's eyes flashed. "Are you going to him now?"

I didn't have to ask who he was talking about. That kind of hatred was reserved for Henning alone.

"No, but really, it's none of your business. You're more of a stranger to me than he is."

I wrenched my arm out of his hold and pushed through the cracked open door into the hall. My black Converse thwacked against the linoleum as I stalked down the corridor, only nodding respectfully at the nurses' station instead of stopping to give them proper thanks the way I usually did.

I didn't have it in me.

All I had was a helpless rage against the insensitivity of my father, against the decline of my mother, against the tragedy that had torn my other mother away from me five years ago.

Only, I wasn't helpless against the latter.

Not really.

Because I had a plan.

And it was beyond time to set it properly into motion.

IT WAS HARDER TO BECOME A CRIMINAL THAN YOU'D THINK.

Trust me, I put some effort into it.

Because it wasn't just about becoming a criminal only to get caught as soon as you broke the law. It was about becoming a wraith, a shade travelling in the shadowed recess between the law-abiding and flagrantly felonious.

In order to enter that slim margin, you basically had to be invited by the right people.

Finding those people, let alone earning their respect enough to elicit an invitation to the dark side was a nearly impossible task. These men and women made their living under the radar, so it wasn't as if I could look them up in the phone book.

The only way to find trouble was to throw caution to the wind and *buy* it.

Which was why I was in the basement of the Golden Door Inn in Calgary's small Chinatown sucking on the end of a cigarette as if I enjoyed the acrid taste while I waited to meet with Kang Li.

After months of networking, starting with Brian, the dead-beat ecstasy and cocaine peddler at school, then to his hook-up Paul Yang, I was finally meeting the head of their youth gang boss, Ashes Li, who would eventually determine if we were worthy of moving from "Blue Lanterns" (the uninitiated members) to 49ers (initiated members) who were trusted foot soldiers for Seven Song. Until that day, we were merely *leng jai*, "little kids" with weapons and drugs in our pockets.

Chinese gangs had a different structure than most.

Adult gangs were often fed by youth gangs, kids who peddled in drug dealing, larceny, and the occasional violence with rivals over territory. If the kids didn't get torn up by the drugs, imprisoned for the thievery, or killed in the turf wars, they were given the opportunity to earn real money as a soldier in the triad. It gave the triads a group of easy scapegoats and also allowed them to indoctrinate kids early.

I was seventeen years old and a girl, so I couldn't get to the Seven Song triad to find out who exactly had put the hit on and then executed Kate. But I could get my foot in the door with the Centre Street Crowd.

"He's late," Paul complained where he lounged on a red chair with his feet up on the table. It was a disrespectful thing to do in an establishment that wasn't his, but I had a feeling Paul was in the gang because he liked to flex his power over any and everything he could.

"He's our *dai lo*," Brian corrected from across the table. "He arrives exactly on time."

I rolled my eyes, but only because the two idiots couldn't see me.

The *dai lo* was a term for "big brother," which meant, in this case, the boss.

"Ashes" Li, nicknamed for his prolific heroin drug dealing, was the only link between the Centre Street Crowd gang and the Seven Song triad. His older brother, Kang Li, was the Red Pole enforcer for the triad and rumoured to be best friends with the youngest Kuan brother. He was my golden ticket.

Brian rolled his head to pin me with his dark eyes. "You know, you want into this shit, you gotta get serious, Mei."

"Do I look anything but?" I questioned sharply, eyebrow raised over my glare.

He looked away quickly because he was a sheep. "No, but serious means getting your hands dirty. You ready for that? I know you say you don't give a shit about your family's reputation." He hesitated, a moment of silence for my sacrilege. "But dealing is dangerous work. You could get sent to juvie."

If Brian hadn't been arrested for his antics yet, I doubted I would be. He wasn't exactly a rocket scientist. But I understood his concern. For Brian, dealing was a necessity. His single mum worked at a local restaurant, but she was also on disability, and they needed the extra cash. He wasn't a natural badass, so he couldn't understand why rich little me would want to engage in illicit activity.

"You let me worry about that," I told him. "I can handle myself."

"Is that right?" a new voice said from the doorway.

My head snapped toward the sound, and I gasped a little, unable to help myself. Because it wasn't just Ashes Li and Kang Li in the doorway.

Jiang Kuan stood there, too.

I knew him instantly. Most people in the criminal community or the business community knew of the twenty-three-year-old and thirty-three-year-old brothers who'd moved to Canada when Jiang was merely a child and amassed their own empire. His brother was *the* Dragon Head of the Seven Song triad in Alberta. The boss. The man who signed your promotion checks or death warrants.

Jiang was his weapon and right-hand man, a position known as the Vanguard.

There was a famous story about how he'd used a chopstick to impale a rival gangster's temple in the middle of a Chinese New Year celebration when Jiang was just twelve years old.

A shiver stabbed like ice picks into my spine.

Not just because he was dangerous but because, shockingly, he was gorgeous.

Tall and leanly muscled with cut glass cheekbones and fine, almost delicate features, he could have been a pop star or an actor. Instead, he was a criminal overlord, his expensive finery punctuated by the bulk of a gun strapped beneath his arm and a watermelon chopper knife affixed to his belt.

Too late, I remembered myself and realized he'd asked me a question. I got to my feet and sent him a little bow of respect before tipping my chin up and offering, "Yes, I can."

He peered at me, blank-faced, while Ashes smirked as he lit a cigarette and took a slouching repose on a stool at the bar. Kang Li didn't move an inch from Jiang's back, a living shadow.

"Sorry about her," Brian hastened to say, standing so abruptly his chair scraped and screeched across the floor. "Her father is white."

I fought the urge to roll my eyes. Being half Chinese didn't make me any less aware of the traditions and culture of my mother's people. I wasn't being rude, I was being confident, and there was a significant difference between the two. I just had to hope that the revered Jiang Kuan knew that too.

He peered at me for a moment, completely ignoring Brian. I

wanted to fidget under his unnerving gaze, but I held meticulously still and let him look his fill.

Finally, he blinked, shattering the strange hold he had over me. I frowned as he slid out of his jacket and unfastened his cuff links.

"Clear some space," he ordered Brian and Paul mildly.

They almost tripped over themselves to do as he bade, bumping shoulders as they pushed tables aside and hauled chairs on top so there was a small, square space of emptiness in the restaurant.

When he was down to his white tank, blazer, and shirt laid carefully on Kang's offered arm, Jiang raised his brows at me and stepped lightly forward.

"You can handle yourself, you say?" When I nodded, he pursed his lips and settled gracefully into the ready position favoured by Wing Chun martial arts practitioners. He raised his right hand in my direction and flicked his fingers back and forth, beckoning me. "Let's see how true that is."

"Mr. Kuan," Brian started to protest, concern etched into every inch of his form. It made me feel a little bad that I thought so poorly of him.

Paul pressed a hand to his chest to silence him, and Brian didn't say another word.

I stared at Jiang Kuan. He wasn't overly tall or muscled like Henning, but there was a whip-like corded power to his physique that spoke of restrained and exacting violence.

He could kill me, I knew. Easily, quickly, and worse, without a qualm.

But I didn't think that was the purpose of this exercise.

Something about me intrigued him—my assertiveness, which could be construed as rude in traditionally minded households, especially toward strangers and elders, or maybe my boldness in seeking out criminal company as a teenager.

Whatever it was, I wasn't going to squander it. This was my

chance, probably my only chance, to get an in with these people.

Slowly, I toed off my black Converse.

A flicker of something––a smile, a sneer––flashed across Kuan's face.

I shrugged out of my black leather jacket and placed it along with my shoes neatly on the chair I'd been sitting on. My skinny jeans had enough stretch in them to allow for a decent range of movement, but my long-sleeved tee was too baggy to wear in a fight. It would be easy to control me with a single grab of the fabric, so after a moment's hesitation, I pulled it over my head and added it to the pile.

Brian let out a low whistle at the sight of me in a black, full-coverage sports bra, but Paul hit him in retribution.

This wasn't about being desirable.

It was about being deadly.

I slapped my hair into a high bun and stepped forward to match Kuan's ready position, sinking into it with an ease that spoke of my many years of training.

Just as I drew in a readying breath, he attacked.

A snake strike straight to my low belly with his far hand. Despite his ready position in the Wing Chun style, Kuan didn't fight like a professional kung fu fighter.

Chinese martial arts were about showmanship over debilitation. Watching two professionally trained kung fu fighters was like watching two dancers, acrobats, their bodies achieving impossible angles and leaps.

If you wanted to learn to defend yourself, many other forms of fighting would better prepare you. Clearly, Kuan knew quite a few of them.

Happily, his street-fighting style didn't throw me off.

I knew I'd never meet a combatant who would know or follow the rules of traditional kung fu. Fighting for your life was different than fighting on the cushioned mats at my kwoon.

Which was why I'd supplemented my traditional Chinese fighting with mixed martial arts.

I lent away from Kuan's fist, twisting to land a kick to the side he'd exposed leaning into the punch. He absorbed the blow, grabbing at my ankle before I could retract it. I braced on his grip, launching off my other leg to land a whip kick on his chin. My tender instep impacted, pain bursting through my foot. I had to twist my body to land the hit, and he took advantage by wrenching my knee until it *popped* with pain. Gritting my teeth, I fumbled and landed on my hands and knees.

There was a little curve to his mean lips, a glimmer in his eyes.

He enjoyed this.

I watched as he smoothed a hand over his chin where I'd landed the powerful kick.

"Interesting," he murmured in Cantonese before flinging himself at me in a flurry of fists and kicks.

One connected with my side, punching the air from me even as I rolled and rolled away from him. My back hit a table leg, and I quickly scrambled beneath it to pop up the other side on my feet.

Kuan wasn't even breathing hard.

I was, but not just from exertion.

This was *fun*.

I hadn't fought a true opponent with real seeming stakes *ever*, and it felt good to flex my muscles and my mind.

With one hand braced against the table, I slid across the surface to scissor kick at Kuan. He evaded it easily, but that was the point. A distraction. As I whirled away, almost as if I was fleeing, I caught sight of him leaning forward to grab me. Quick as I could, I ducked beneath his reaching arm and pummelled him in his right side, directly atop his kidneys.

Breath left him in a grunt, torso bending to shield the tender spot.

I pushed closer, trying to land a series of hits he blocked with one hand before finally connecting a well-aimed chop on the side of his throat. He choked on a breath, and for one clear, vibrating second, I thought I had him.

Silly me.

Just as I relaxed my guard to grin triumphantly, he snapped forward faster than I could blink and swept my legs out from under me. I fell flat on my back, breath expelled from my body like an exorcism. Breathless, I was only able to roll slightly onto my side before he pinned me to the ground, but it was just enough room to work with. If he'd pinned me with both shoulders to my back, it would have been over.

But I'd been training as a woman against men for a long time.

So it wasn't over yet.

I lay there under his crushing weight for a long moment, lulling Kuan into thinking he'd won.

And then, I braced my hands to one side of his body against the left leg that was straddling my torso and used my opposite leg to hook over his left foot. With his weight in his knees, I was able to drag his left foot to the inside of my leg and use my hands to push him off-balance, sliding his left leg off my side to between my legs. I readjusted my position onto my left side, still keeping my legs locked around one of his, and then swept out from under his body to escape.

I scampered to my feet, hair half escaping from its bun, chest heaving, and faced Kuan again in the same ready position we'd started.

He didn't remain on his hands and knees for long, but something was sinuous and slow about the uncoiling of his body as he stood. A dangerous kind of calculation like a predator stalking his prey.

I bit back the bile on the back of my tongue, afraid I'd made a mistake that would cost me my life.

This wasn't just a sparring match at the Calgary Martial Arts Society.

This was a test handed out by one of the most powerful men in the triad system. A man who would not hesitate to put me down.

I pulled on every ounce of bravery I had inside me as he prowled toward me, thinking of Kate and her beautiful face, Cleo and her loss, Henning and his belief in me becoming a dragon.

Miraculously, I didn't vomit when Kuan reached up to rub a lock of my loose hair between his fingers. His gaze was narrow and dark, utterly unfathomable.

"*Who said women cannot compete with men*," he murmured in Cantonese, and I recognized the phrase from the opera *Hua Mulan* because it was one of my mother's favourites.

Slowly, my tension dissipated, and a reckless grin overtook my face.

"You want to be a soldier," he said in a way that should have been a question but wasn't.

I nodded anyway.

"Well then." He dropped my hair, turned on his heel, and collected his things from Kang Li. "So be it."

"But she's a *woman*," Brian said, and he had a point.

There was a popular adage, "men do not fight with women," and traditionally, it was men's duty to protect them. But we weren't in China, and in Canada, equality was practiced almost to the detriment of gentlemanly behaviour and all chivalry.

I wasn't surprised Kuan had adopted some of that Canadian philosophy. It would be good for business. People didn't often suspect girls to be criminals.

Kuan didn't spare him a glance as he redid his diamond cuff links and shrugged on his jacket. "Kang will give you the package. If you can sell the total amount by this time next week, you can consider yourself Centre Street Crowd. If you cannot...don't let me see your face again."

I shivered as he stalked out of the room, leaving Kang to give his lowly teen soldiers the details of our chores, but it wasn't just fear that cut through me like a knife.

It was the dark, sweet joy of revenge finally coming close enough to grasp.

CHAPTER TEN

Mei

"SILLY GOAT," LIN CLUCKED AS SHE FUSSED WITH MY HAIR. "SIT still."

I adjusted one more time in the kitchen chair with a sour grimace that made Cleo giggle in the chair across from me.

It was the evening of our prom, the final dance of our high school careers.

I would rather pluck out my own eyeballs with a hot poker than go, but Cleo had begged me, and of course, I couldn't find the will to tell her no. She was a beautiful girl and popular, but she still had a shyness and an edge of fear from what had happened to her mum, making her hesitate about social situations. If it made her feel better to go with me, I'd happily go as her guard dog.

Lin muttered again under her breath in Cantonese, cursing because my sleek, straight hair just wouldn't hold a curl.

"Just leave it," I told her, batting at her nimble fingers as they tried to coil another lock around a hot barrel. "I'll just wear it down."

Henning's stepmum stepped away to frown down at me, her finely creased face pretty even in its scowl. "You should try to be a girl sometimes, hmm? Maybe then you'd have a boyfriend."

Lin told me the same things nearly every week. I didn't think it was actually about wanting me to have a boyfriend as much as it was her despairing over my lack of femininity. My baggy black clothes and clunky boots were the anthesis of her carefully made-up face, polished fingers and toes, and perpetual high heels. She was a talented aesthetician, and she hated that I wouldn't let her make me beautiful.

Lin's love language was giving people shit, so I laughed. "I don't care about boys, Lin."

Henning entered the kitchen then, drying off his paint-smudged hands on an old rag that he then tucked into the back waistband of his jeans. His hair was collected in a messy knot at the back of his head, streaks of honey, caramel, and gold shining in the red-gold light of sunset spilling through the big window over the sink. There was a smear of vermilion acrylic paint on his cheekbone and some turquoise on his stubbled jaw. The tee stretched too tight over his broad chest was old, thin enough to trace the planes and hollows of dense muscles. My mouth went dry at the sight of him.

"*Boys*, maybe," Lin muttered.

I jerked my gaze away from Henning, but Lin was already puttering with the makeup Cleo had spread out over the dining table.

"At least some lipstick," she encouraged, lifting a tube dramatically.

I rolled my eyes.

"You'd look pretty with some lipstick, I think," Cleo said in that soft, lyrical voice that had provided so much soundtrack through my life. "Not that you don't always look pretty. But this is a special night, Rocky."

Henning emerged from the fridge with a beer, popping the top off on the edge of the counter with one knock of his big fist. He raised a brow at me as he took a sip in a silent challenge.

He didn't think I'd wear the lipstick.

That I could put on a pretty dress and be a kid for one night.

I'd known him long enough to read every word written in his expression, and it made me glare at him.

His lips twitched with a smile around the mouth of the beer bottle.

"Fine," I declared, pursing my lips. "Do your worst, Lin."

Her face lit up with glee. She owned a little salon in Chinatown that did hair, makeup, and nails, and I'd never let her do anything more than my hair before.

The instant she undid the top of the lipstick and a brilliant shade of red appeared, I regretted my decision, but it was too late.

Behind her, Henning chuckled.

Damn manipulative bastard.

"Just tell me when you need a ride to the dance," he told Cleo, already moving out of the room, probably back to his studio in the garage.

"Um, I thought maybe Zander could take us?" Cleo asked hesitantly.

"Fuck no."

"But Dad—"

"No."

"Dad, seriously—"

"Cleopatra," he said, low and leaden, no room for argument. I watched as he went to her and brushed his big hand over her hair before cupping her neck. "*No.* I told you things are goin' down with the club, and we're bein' vigilant, yeah? Not only that, I am not gonna let some punk kid drive two of my girls when he's barely got his license, and I got no doubt he plans to drink tonight, but this is a big night for you. I get your mum can't be here, which kills me, Glory, fuckin' *kills* me. But I'm here, and so's Lin. We wanna be a part of this night, too, 'cause it's important to you. You understand me?"

Cleo tilted her head back into the cradle of his hold, a little move of trust that made my throat close up tight.

"Yeah, okay, Dad," she agreed easily. "I'll text Zander."

"Good." He pressed a kiss to the top of her head.

"Is Brian picking you up?" Cleo asked me, already reaching for her phone to text her date.

Henning stopped mid-step on his way back to the studio.

"You've got a date to this thing?" he asked me, rudely incredulous.

I sniffed, staring down my nose at him. "Is that so hard to believe?"

"You got lipstick on your teeth," he pointed out with a jerk of his chin. "So, yeah, a little. Didn't think you were much interested in that."

"Dad." Cleo laughed, shaking her head. "She's a seventeen-year-old girl. *Of course*, she's interested in that."

But Henning was right. I wasn't. I was "going" to the prom with Brian only because Kang ordered it. I needed supervision for my first drug deal before I was allowed to go solo, and Brian was the obvious choice.

"Besides," Cleo added, unaware of the bombs she was dropping, "Brian's cute."

"Brian?" Henning growled the word, putting his beer down

on the counter slowly. Still, it hit the surface with too much force and frothed over. "That motherfuckin' drug dealer you were with at your locker?"

"Drug dealer?" Cleo asked, eyes comically wide. "No way."

"Yes way," Henning bit out, staring me down with those vivid blue-green eyes. "What the fuck, Mei? Didn't I tell you to stay away from that kid?"

I shrugged casually even though my insides felt like shaken soda, fizzing and overfull.

"Good thing you aren't my father."

Henning's jaw popped with strain. "Yeah, good thing, or I'd tan your ass."

"Dad!" Cleo exclaimed in surprise, then laughed. "You've never spanked me. Not even once."

"Yeah, well, you never deserved it," he muttered darkly, crossing his thick arms over his chest. "What's the angle here, Mei? You doin' shit that's gonna get you in trouble?"

As in, was I poking my nose into Kate's old mess?

Hell yeah.

But I wasn't going to tell Henning that, or else he'd probably lock me up in the basement.

So, I tried to force the expression I'd often seen Cleo have when she talked dreamily about Zander onto my face. My eyes wide, lips soft with a little smile, gaze faraway.

"I just like him," I said on a little sigh. "He's cute."

Cleo beamed at me. "See, Dad, I told you."

Henning wasn't so convinced. He glared at me, a Mexican showdown until it became obvious I wasn't going to cave.

"I'm definitely fuckin' drivin' you," he grunted before stalking out of the room.

The door to the garage slammed behind him.

Cleo turned to me with huge eyes. "Is Brian really a drug dealer? Because if so, I get why Dad's mad, Mei. Why would you want to get caught up in that?" A pause, delicate and shivering with her anxiety and remembered pain. "Didn't Mum's death teach you anything?"

I tried to swallow the stone lodged in my throat to no avail.

Of course, it taught me something, I wanted to confess.

It taught me to protect my loved ones at all costs.

It taught me to seek revenge for injustices.

It taught me that no wrong goes punished unless people are brave enough to risk themselves to see them penalized.

But I didn't say any of it because I didn't want to burden Cleo with my secrets and my shame. Her mother had died, yes, but she hadn't *been there* in that room, swearing on the blood spilling between us that she'd take care of Kate's loved ones no matter what.

I took that responsibility seriously, and tonight, I'd finally be a huge step closer to figuring out why tragedy struck the Axelsen family five years ago.

I just had to sell a little of my soul to get there.

AN HOUR LATER, AFTER CLEO AND I DELICATELY PICKED AT A pizza because we were too nervous––for two very different reasons––to eat much, we were ready to go to prom.

Lin had ushered us out onto the front lawn for a few photos while we waited for Henning to clean up before taking us in his old Ford pickup. She was so tiny that to get the right angle for the photos, Cleo had carried out a small stool for her to stand on.

"I know you'd rather saw off your arm than go to prom," Cleo said through her smile as we posed with our arms around each other.

I laughed under my breath. "I was actually thinking earlier I'd rather pluck out my own eyeballs with a hot poker."

"Wow, points for creativity," she teased, turning us so we were in the typical "date" pose for prom photos, her arms around my middle while she stood behind me. "I just wanted to say thank you. I know you do a lot of things for me you wouldn't usually want to do, and it means a lot to me."

Something funny happened to my heart, a too-tight feeling like it was expanding in my chest.

"You mean a lot to me, so it's no big deal."

"No," she argued, turning me again to take my hands in hers. "That's just the thing, Mei. It is a big deal. The truth is, I don't know how I'd survive without you. You make me feel safe, you know?"

My chest was so full that I could barely draw breath. I took a moment to compose myself and squeezed her hands. "Yeah, I know. Same goes."

She smiled before raising her curled index finger and thumb between us. "Best friends for life."

"Best friends for life," I agreed, adding my curled index and thumb to her half so we formed the shape of a heart with our fingers, a little ritual we'd done since we were kids.

Lin's loud sniffle broke our moment, and we both turned to see her dabbing carefully at her eyes with a handkerchief.

"What?" she snarked. "I'm a grandmother now. I'm allowed to cry when my babies have big moments."

Cleo and I shared a look before moving forward together to hug Lin and pepper her with kisses. She pretended to hate every moment, but she had a hand on each of us like she didn't want to let us go. Once properly smothered, I moved off to one side while she got some shots of Cleo next to the hydrangea bush. I was grateful for the reprieve because I hated getting my photo taken.

It didn't help that I was feeling increasingly nauseated about tonight. I'd never even *done* drugs, so how the hell was I expecting to sell them to students at the after-party tonight?

The only thing that helped to distract me was the joy on Cleo's face. She was thoughtful, reserved, and quiet, but when she smiled, she warmed everyone in the vicinity with her light.

"You look stunning," Lin promised as Cleo fussed with her half-up style, fat locks of golden-brown hair curled into bouncy waves around her chest and back.

She was right. In a sage-green dress that brought out the grey-green of her eyes and the unblemished gold of her skin, Cleo looked radiant and every inch her mother's daughter.

I was glad of my viewpoint when Henning pushed out the door and storm door into the front yard and paused on the top step to stare mutely at his stepdaughter. Surprisingly, he'd changed into an old suit he'd worn while working at the hospital with charcoal-grey trousers and a crisp white button-up that strained slightly across the width of his broad chest. With his hair brushed into gleaming waves around his ears and his tattoos covered up, he looked like the Henning I'd first met years ago before tragedy and circumstance had made him harder, rougher around the edges.

Cleo twirled for him, satin skirt flaring. "What do you think?"

I watched as he swallowed hard, once, twice then shook his head. Cleo's smile faltered a little, confused.

But I knew Henning and his struggle to find the right words

at the right times. He was a man of action more than speech, so it didn't surprise me at all when he shook off his shock and stalked down the steps to her side. He stared down at her for a long minute, the last of the sun's rays penetrating his irises, turning them translucent and green as sea glass.

One hand, huge and scarred, reached up slowly and gently curled around Cleo's cheek.

"You're so beautiful," he said gruffly. "So much like your mum. Fuck, she'd be so proud of the woman you're becomin', Glory. Almost as proud as me."

Tears sprang to my best friend's eyes. "Dad, don't. I'll ruin my makeup."

"There's no ruinin' anythin' about your beauty," he countered easily before gathering her in his arms like she was delicate, breakable.

Lin moved to my side and nudged me with her shoulder as we watched the tender moment between them.

"Never thought he'd have kids," she divulged in a little murmur. "A boy who always wore the weight of the world on his shoulders, I think he thought it'd be too much for him to bear. He always felt so deeply. Drove his dad crazy. He called Henning 'too soft' like that was a crime. I think it's why Hen enlisted, to prove he was the kind of man his dad wanted him to be. It nearly killed him, and not just physically. When he came back...well, studying medicine helped, but saving Kate and Cleo...that made all the difference. Really, they saved him. When we lost Kate, I thought he might break under the strain."

A pause as she captured their embrace on the camera.

"Now, look at him."

I was looking. In fact, I didn't think I could have looked away if a bomb went off next door.

This was what I wanted for myself.

Not from my dad, exactly. I knew that wasn't in the cards for us or Florent's power to give me. I had it with my mum when she made time for me, but...she was too sick to share moments like this with me, now, and probably never again. I had it with Old Dragon, of a sort, though he was of a different generation when effusiveness was rare and a sign of weakness instead of strength.

No, I didn't want that *type* of love, but the magnitude of it.

I wanted a man to tremble as he held back his strength to touch me like I was made of glass, not because he thought I was weak, but because he thought I was precious. I wanted a man to change his career because it would have meant too much time away from me even though I'd never ask him to do so. I wanted a man who'd join a criminal motorcycle gang just to find justice for my murder. I wanted a man who would always try to save me, even when I tried to sabotage myself.

I wanted what Cleo had, but not how she had it.

I wanted Henning.

Not as a father figure.

But as a *man*.

My man.

My breath left my body in a long whoosh until my lungs were compressed in my chest, and I thought I'd never breathe again.

My God, I was in love with Henning Axelsen.

As if sensing the shifting tectonic plates of my reality, Henning looked up from Cleo and straight at me.

I tried to breathe and failed again.

Because he was so beautiful, the most beautiful man I'd ever seen.

Why didn't women talk about men like that? It wasn't only feminine to be so beautiful. It spoke of his goodness, the generosity of his heart, and the power of his kind, keen gaze. It spoke of a man who was confident enough in himself to be soft when needed and strong enough to take on the whole world if someone he loved was at risk.

God, he was beautiful.

And at that moment, I knew I'd never love anyone better than I loved *him*. So much of the kindness I'd experienced in my life had been at the hands of Henning, and what made that all the more poignant was that he had absolutely no obligation to be good to me. I was no one, not tied to him through blood or marriage, but only the relationship I'd forged with his deceased wife and her daughter largely before I'd ever even known him. It was in this way that he made me feel worthy. If I could earn the kindness and love of such a man, I had to be worth something even though I so often felt less than in the eyes of my overachieving family.

It was more than that, though.

His gaze seemed to cut me open like a knife, like I was prone on a metal slab, and he was performing an emotional autopsy. There was nothing I could hide from him, no insecurity, no secret hope or hidden dream. Maybe love was that simple, to see and be seen. So simple and so impossibly complicated because I couldn't bear for Henning to know what I knew now.

That I loved him.

Not tenderly, not softly like a song or a poem.

I loved him in all my dark places. In the way I would die for him, impaling myself on a sword intended for his side. In the way I would kill for him––a happy murder, a giggling death with blood on my teeth that tasted like love and sin.

What cruel, tragic irony that he should be so forbidden to me.

My best friend's dad.

Sixteen years my senior.

We locked eyes with five yards between us that felt like an impossible chasm.

As quickly as I realized I would love him forever, I realized I would never have him.

Henning watched as my heart swelled and broke, a wave against the sheer rock of reality. He frowned, moving away from Cleo immediately, trying to come for me because he knew, in one look, in one moment, I was hurting.

I pressed a hand to my chest where my insides were rearranging themselves to fit around this love. This grief.

"Mei Zhen," Lin said, reaching for my hand to give it a squeeze. Her dry, smooth skin grounded me. "Breathe, Mei Zhenette Raisinet."

I grinned a little at the nickname. In Cantonese, you could add "ette" to the end of a given name as a nickname, and Lin had come up with the silly endearment years ago. Every birthday she even bought me a massive box of Raisinet candies. I breathed then, and it felt like the first breath after nearly drowning. Painful and sweet.

"Rocky," Henning said, suddenly in front of me, so much taller than me I had to crane my neck back to meet his gaze. "You okay?"

No, I wanted to shout, *I'm in love with you, and it feels like a prison sentence confined to solitary because you'll never love me, too.*

Instead, I smiled weakly. "I think the makeup's making me nauseated."

The concern in his expression fell away with a sharp bark of laughter. He slung an arm like a lasso around my shoulders to tug me into his front, holding me while that bright laughter rolled through his barrel chest. I let myself press my cheek to his sternum for a moment to clock the vibration and the knock of his heartbeat against my skin.

"You don't need it," he assured me, peering down at me with crinkled eyes and smile lines. "But you look damn beautiful."

It was said so flippantly, so off-the-cuff I couldn't doubt his sincerity.

"Thank you," I said, embarrassed by the warmth I felt in my cheeks.

"Wow, I don't think I've ever seen you blush," Cleo teased as she joined our little huddle.

I scowled. "Don't get used to it."

She grinned, holding her hands up in surrender. "God forbid Mei Zhen be soft and adorable."

"Damn right," I agreed, but some of Cleo's sweetness seeped beneath my skin like anti-venom to battle the toxicity of my love and heartbreak. "No one ever called a dragon cute."

"I think Cleo just did," Henning quipped, his eyes shining with contentment as he stood huddled with his women.

I tried to ignore the resurgence of heat in my cheeks. "Whatever."

Cleo and Henning shared a look at my expense, but it was filled with fondness.

"All right, then," Lin declared, clapping her hands briskly as she bustled us back in front of the white hydrangea bush. "Let's get a photo of the three of you."

Henning gathered Cleo and me in each long arm, securing us to his side with a hand curved around our waists. I felt the heaviness of that strong hand burn through the thin satin of my dress, beneath my flesh and into my very bones. Tears pricked at the backs of my eyes, but I forced myself to blink them away and enjoy this moment.

Kate should have been there enjoying this moment with her family, and if she couldn't be here, I'd enjoy it enough for the both of us.

Lin raised her camera, and the flash went off.

"Smile," Henning said, leaning slightly into me and speaking out the corner of his mouth. "You look beautiful, Mei."

I closed my eyes briefly, swallowing the sweet poison, and then forced myself to smile brighter.

His hand squeezed the curve of my waist. "I'm sorry Daiyu can't be here for you, and Old Dragon has to stay with her." He didn't add that he was staying with her because we didn't want her to be alone when she passed, and that could happen any day––no, moment––now. "I know it's a poor as hell substitute, but it wouldn't be the same for Cleo and me if we couldn't share this with you, too."

He was trying to kill me. Clearly.

Guilt crashed over me. Here I was lusting after Henning when I'd committed myself to taking care of him and Cleo in Kate's stead. What kind of selfish creature was I?

"I'm sorry Kate can't be here," I echoed his sentiment, the words brittle and cracking to pieces on my tongue. "I know it's a poor as hell substitute, but I wouldn't be able to do this without you guys."

Henning made a little noise of sympathy and understanding in the back of his throat before turning to press a kiss into my hair. Cleo poked her head around his side and grinned at me. When I stuck out my tongue at her, she giggled, and there was yet another *flash* as Lin captured the moment.

Lin peered down at the photo on the screen of the camera and grinned. "Henning and his girls."

Henning and his girls.

And there I was, aching with the desire to be his *woman*.

Damn, I was so going to hell one day.

And maybe, if I'd been a better person, one who didn't lust after impossible men, I'd have noticed the tinted windowed black sedan that crawled down the street a little too slowly, the glimmer of a camera lens flashing out the back window.

But I didn't, and I wasn't.

And that was the night everything went to hell, not just my soul.

CHAPTER ELEVEN

Mei

BRIAN STOOD ME UP.

Cleo couldn't believe it, and I got a little satisfaction from seeing my sweet friend so outraged. She even stomped her heeled foot in indignation and shook her fist in the air like an angry Italian.

Honestly, I didn't give a fuck.

Brian always smelled like bong water and cigarettes. The idea of dancing with him was enough to make me gag, so I hadn't been looking forward to it.

But the asshole was supposed to help me out with the after-party at Turner Farm. I didn't know the first thing about dealing drugs, and truthfully, I'd just figured I'd stand by while Brian did the dirty deed. I wasn't in it to make money. I was in it to buy enough street cred to figure out what happened to Kate.

And now, I was on my own with a backpack waiting in my locker filled with cocaine and marijuana.

I was also alone, sitting on a white-clothed table, sipping from a plastic cup of overly sweet punch while I watched Cleo and her date swirl around the dance floor. The gym was decked out in glittering streamers, blue and silver balloons, and a large banner that said Congratulations Class of 2015. It was all so cheesy and juvenile to me. I wanted to be by Daiyu's bedside with Old Dragon. At the Axelsen house watching TV with Cleo or chatting at the kitchen table with Henning and Lin. Anywhere felt better than here. I felt like a fraud for even trying to fit in.

But Ma had encouraged me to go. She wanted me to have as many normal high school experiences as I could even though she knew, unlike Dad, that I wasn't a typical high school girl.

You only live once, she said, and the sentiment coming from my mother lying in hospice was enough to bring me to my knees.

I felt the weight of both Daiyu and Kate with me as I sat there, like they were ghosts pressing reassuring hands to each shoulder. I wanted to live for both of them, soak up as many experiences as I could because they were both robbed of their fill too young.

A couple of brave souls had come over to ask me to dance, but they didn't even seem surprised when I turned them down. I didn't like to be touched, and the idea of being held close by a sweaty-palmed teenage boy wearing too much body spray was repugnant. Besides, I knew they were only attracted to the makeup and the red satin halter neck dress Ma had helped me order online.

Red, she'd insisted, *for luck*.

The only thing I'd need luck for tonight was drug dealing at the after-party, and I didn't think that was what Ma had in mind, but it still made me feel good to wear it. I'd facetimed her and Old Dragon from the Axelsen house for a few minutes, and she'd cried seeing me in her favourite colour. I'd almost cried, too, because it was a rare feeling to see my parents so proud of me, and because I knew this was one of the last times she'd have the opportunity to.

I was interrupted from my boredom and morose contemplation by the buzz of my phone in my black clutch.

Henning: Cleo told me about that asshole. You doin' okay?

My smile was instantaneous, so wide it ached in my cheeks.

Mei: No "I told you so"?

Henning: I figured it went without sayin'.

I laughed then caught eyes with a guy I recognized from the soccer team and transformed my features into a glare lest he think I was beckoning him over.

Henning: Seriously, though, you good?

Fuck, he was such a good guy. It always amused me, the sidelong looks people gave him when he was wearing his club leathers, the patches boldly declaring him a 1%er, an outlaw. Henning didn't give a shit, though, and neither did Cleo or me. He was the best man we knew, bar none. A white knight didn't just come in shining armor. My knight came in leather.

Mei: Fine. Just a little annoyed because I don't put on a dress for just anyone, and this dance is criminally boring.

Henning: Thought you'd say that. Go outside.

Mei: ??

Henning: For once, do as you're told without askin' questions, Rocky.

A little tremor of desire slid down my spine. I was a rebel at heart, but that didn't mean I objected to Henning's occasionally bossy ways.

I slid off the table and landed on my high heels easily. Cleo caught my eye from the dance floor, concerned that I needed her. I waved her off with a little smile before turning to make my way out of the gymnasium through the exit in the girl's locker room.

A couple made out against the lockers, but I ignored them, heels clicking against the floor as I walked through and pushed into the warm, humid summer air. The sun had set long ago, but the parking lot was lit with yellow streetlamps, and the dance committee had strung lights through the trellis leading down the main walkway.

It was more than enough light to see Henning leaning against his gleaming white and black Harley-Davidson Road King. He'd changed out of the suit he'd worn to drop us off into his usual dark wash jeans, heavy leather boots, cut, and long-sleeved white tee. With his wavy, overlong hair shifting like gold wheat in the summer breeze, he looked like a rebel loitering outside a bar, just waiting to cause trouble.

Every inch of me throbbed as I took him in, every molecule attuned to the wild beat of my heart yearning for him. How strange and powerful it was, the way *knowing* changed my every atom from yesterday to today. I knew I could never go back to before when he was just my best friend's dad. Just my sort-of friend. Just Hen.

Now, I'd never think of him or see him without a wish attached to his name.

"Hi," I said, lame and soft because I wasn't used to this.

To the shyness that came from loving a man so far out of my league.

He grinned at me, white teeth flashing against his dark gold stubble as he pushed off the bike and strolled over to me.

"Hey, Rocky," he murmured, low and slow in that way that made my blood heat.

"What're you doing here?"

He shrugged, but amusement crinkled the sides of those too-bright blue-green eyes. "I figured I'd better check in, make sure you weren't huntin' down Brian to give him a piece of your mind...or fists." He paused when I laughed a little. "And I figured, if you were still here, you'd spend the whole time watchin' over Cleo and not havin' any fun for yourself."

I bit my lip because of course, he was right. Zander was a good guy as far as I could tell, but Cleo seemed to draw some serious jerks into her orbit because they wanted to leech out some of her sweetness. It didn't hurt to be careful.

"You know, we're both gonna have to learn to let her have more independence," he mused, a wry twist of his mouth. "She's eighteen, and it's a good age to make mistakes. She hasn't done much of that yet."

"She can make mistakes," I argued. "I'll just be there to help her with the aftermath."

He stared down at me, expression gone soft. "Yeah. Yeah, I figure you will be."

Understanding passed between us, a gentle current of loyalty that spoke of our shared love for Cleo and, maybe a little, for each other.

"Still," he said finally, straightening a little and then raising his hand between us. It was huge; long, thick fingers and a broad palm. There were scars across the back of it from land mine shrapnel and a tattoo of the Norse god, Thor, on the inside of his forearm. It was a mean-looking hand, a threat wrapped in skin, but it was all softness as I automatically slid my hand into his. “It would be a fuckin’ crime not to have at least one dance with you in that red dress.”

He tugged me then, a fast jerk that had me falling off-balance in my heels to land hard against his chest. His chuckle rumbled through him and into me as he wrapped his other arm around my hips and started seamlessly to lead me into a dance.

“Can’t sing for shit,” he confessed. “So, you’ll just have to imagine music playin’.”

I didn’t have to try very hard.

The thump of my heart was a deep bass, the rush of blood in my ears a symphony of strings, and the sharpness of my breath the twang of an acoustic guitar. The low rumble of cars on the street beyond the parking lot and the faint spill of noise from beneath the gym doors were quiet enough to make us seem completely isolated. Only Henning and me alone in the world.

It was a dangerous sensation, one that made me feel braver and more hopeful than I should have dared.

“Do you think you could ever fall in love again?” I found myself asking him.

He paused mid-step, then smoothly continued, his gaze fixed over my head. “That’s a complicated question.”

Bile surged to the back of my tongue, an unpalatable mix of guilt and hope.

“You’re a complicated man, so I didn’t expect anything less.”

A twitch of his full, pale mouth. “You might be the only woman to think so. I’ve been called a simple man my whole life.”

“By who?”

He shrugged a little, but there was remembered pain in his expression, an echo of hurt from the past. “You’re not the only one with a disappointed father.”

That surprised me. I’d never thought Henning could disappoint anyone.

He'd been to war for our country, studied medicine to help the ill, and he was one of the smartest, kindest men I'd ever met. Anger curdled my stomach because I understood all too well what it was like to have parents who were never satisfied with your accomplishments even though you always did so well.

"Obviously, he was a dumbass," I concluded.

To my delight, he chuckled and spun me under his arm before pulling me close again. "That he was. Thank God for Lin."

I looked up at him, seeking answers with my gaze.

He sighed heavily. "Curiosity killed the cat, Rocky."

"Good thing I'm not a cat, then."

Another flicker of a smile. "My father, Soren, wasn't a good man. He fled some scandal in Denmark and immigrated here. Knocked up a girl within the first month, and a month after I was born, she took off. He always used to say I should've felt lucky he kept me at all, but I think it would've been easier if he hadn't."

"Did he hurt you?" I whispered because the idea was too abhorrent to speak with conviction.

Another stiff shrug. He pulled me closer, chest to chest, but I knew it was because he didn't want me to see his face. The scent of his leather cut and pine-rich cologne settled the queasiness in my stomach.

"Sometimes. He liked his belt more than his fists. It stopped for a bit after he met Lin, and she moved in. She didn't like his violence, and you know Lin, she wasn't shy about tellin' him to cut it out. He was a drinker, though, and before long, he was hurtin' her, too. Mostly, though, he stayed away for days then weeks, drinkin' and carousin'. Wouldn't be surprised if there were other Axelsen bastards out there. By the time I enlisted, he was only poppin' up every couple of months. I think he got sent down for somethin' at one point, probably assault. Lin took care of me until I graduated and enlisted. We were happier without that motherfucker. The only good thing he ever did was take out a life insurance policy. The payout went to Lin and me when he died. I was nineteen. The army paid for most of college, and I used the insurance money to pay for incidentals and livin'. After that, it left enough to pay for the house and Kate's real estate licensin'."

"There's something karmic about that," I decided. "Flowers blooming from the shit he'd heaped on you for years."

A huff of laughter. "You're the only woman I know who can be poetic and curse at the same time."

I grinned up at him. "I'm multitalented like that."

"You are," he agreed, finally tilting his gaze down to mine. It was startlingly sombre. "*Rén zhōng zhī long.*"

A dragon among men.

I blinked dumbly up at him. "Hen…I'm not so good as that. Trust me."

"I do," he said easily. "I trust you with Cleo, and she's my whole heart."

I swallowed thickly. "You know I'd do anything for her. For both of you."

Something in my voice must have alerted him to the gravity of my meaning because he stopped our gentle rhythm and let go of my hand to grasp my chin. When he tipped my face up, his was so close I could count the striations in his bright eyes even in the dim light. He was so beautiful, I almost couldn't breathe.

"Bein' loyal doesn't mean takin' on the world to right your loved one's wrongs, Mei. You understand that, right?"

I understood it, sure, but I didn't believe that.

Nightmares of the carnival plagued me every single night. I woke with Kate's name in my mouth and the phantom taste of blood on my tongue. My heart pounded out a tattoo on the inside of my rib cage that said *fix this, fix this*.

I couldn't go back in time, but I could help Henning and Cleo find closure. I could help Kate's ghost find peace.

Henning shook me a little by the shoulders, then lifted me against him until only my tiptoes rested on the ground. His face twisted into a snarl, but I wasn't afraid because I knew in my bones he would never hurt me.

"Don't be a noble idiot, you hear me?"

"I could say the same of you," I retorted.

We stared at each other then, too similar to stand down to the other. There was a saying in Chinese, *a fight between a dragon and a tiger*, a conflict that was too evenly matched to result in victory for either.

It wasn't the first time I'd thought of Henning in those terms. As a tiger, also his zodiac sign, and my equal match. And it wouldn't be the last.

He was still so close, curled over my body like a shield. Maybe that was why I did it. Or the fact that his arm around my lower back had constricted, so I was flush against him, only a narrow ribbon of heat between our bodies.

Probably, it was the fact that I was just seventeen years old, and I'd figured out I was in love for the first time in my life.

Whatever the reason, I found the courage to throw caution to the wind, rise up on my toes again, and kiss him.

His facial hair was coarse, a sting against my skin in direct contrast to the plushness of his mouth on mine. I didn't have the courage to part his lips with my tongue, but the gentle contact was more than enough to light fire to soul and burn new pathways down to my sex.

I understood then why there were so many poems and songs written about the significance of a single kiss and also that none of them could do justice to the simple yet utterly profound meeting of two mouths.

It only lasted for three heart-pounding, bone-quaking moments, but they were the purest moments of my entire life.

Followed swiftly by the most mortifying.

Henning shoved me away roughly, staggering back as if I'd stabbed him. His expression was broken open with horror and something too like disgust for my trembling heart to suffer.

"What the fuck, Mei Zhen?" he demanded, using my full first name as he only did when he was furious with me.

I licked my lips, unconsciously chasing the taste of him. It only made his scowl deepen.

"I'm sorry—" I cut myself off because I wasn't sorry. In fact, I'd never been less ashamed of anything in my life. "No, no, I'm not. I wanted to do that."

"Since when?" he snapped, rubbing at his mouth with the back of his hand as if I'd left poison there.

"Does it matter?"

"Yeah, it fuckin' well does matter. You've been sleepin' under my roof, basically livin' in my house part-time for years, and if this isn't a new development, I'll feel sick as fuck that I didn't notice your...your crush before and cut it off at the pass."

My hands were shaking slightly, so I clutched them behind my back. "Fine. It's a...new development."

"Thank fuck." He closed his eyes, tipping his head to the sky as if praying for deliverance. "Then you won't have any trouble stoppin' it."

"Stopping what? My feelings for you?"

"Fuck." The curse was so vicious I flinched, and he winced in return, reaching for me automatically because he'd been a source of comfort for so long it was instinctive. "Dammit, Mei. Why?"

I laughed, a bitter little thing that clogged my throat. "Why? I think the question should be *why not*? You're the best man I've ever known, Henning. You saved Kate and Cleo first, but there's no doubt you saved me, too. I wouldn't have survived what happened at the carnival without you. I wouldn't be surviving Mum's illness now without you either."

"I don't deserve the hero worship, but I can live with that if it's what you need to believe. I cannot and will not live with this...whatever that just was," he said, struggling to find the words and growing more frustrated because of it. "I'm old enough to be your fuckin' dad!"

"Hardly," I scoffed. "Sixteen years isn't that much."

"Mei," he said in a muted roar, finally touching me again but only to shake me by the shoulders once more. "There are more than just years between us. I've lived an entire lifetime compared to you. Been to fuckin' war, killed men, and watched them die. Came home, married a woman, and adopted a daughter. You're just a teenager graduatin' high school, and you're my daughter's best friend. This will not happen."

"Don't reduce me to the years I've lived. I've watched a woman I love be murdered and die. I'm watching my own mother suffer and fucking wither away every single day," I said, chin tilted, eyes burning in my skull. "You don't have to return or even like my feelings for you, but I will not be ashamed of the way I feel. You're my white knight, and it doesn't matter if you're too old or too outlaw or too whatever else you want to throw at me. I know in my bones that I'll always feel this way about you. You see me, Henning, even when I feel invisible, even when I want desperately to remain unseen. That might not mean anything to you, but it means everything to me."

He stared at me, vibrating faintly, eyes almost panicked with anger and confusion as they scoured over my face. "Don't romanticize me. I'm a fuckin' outlaw biker, for fuck's sake, Mei."

"An off-white knight, then," I agreed, but my chin canted even higher in the air so I could look down my nose at him as I reiterated. "But still *my* off-white knight."

I stepped away from him, his hands falling off my shoulders to hang limp at his sides. I backed away to the gym, searching for the knob blindly behind me and then clinging to it like a life raft.

"My love for you isn't conditional on you loving me back," I told him even though my heart hurt, my head hurt, my very soul hurt. "So this won't ruin anything between us unless you want it to. I hope you don't. I know I'll never be yours that way, but having you in my life is better than nothing. I...I don't have many people I love, and I've already lost too many."

He blinked at me, breathing hard, staring like I'd grown snakes from my head and transfixed him with my gaze.

I left him like that, opening the door and sliding into the locker room without another word. And when I went back to the dance I felt more alone than I ever had before.

CHAPTER TWELVE

Henning

USUALLY, A RIDE THROUGH THE NIGHT STREETS OF CALGARY ON my bike calmed me. In the days followin' Kate's murder, I'd ride through the empty city for ages in the small hours of the night while Lin stayed at home with Cleo after she fell asleep. There'd always been somethin' restless and yearnin' in my soul that was only soothed by the vibration of the powerful metal beast beneath me and the growl of Harley pipes in my ears.

It did nothin' to still the calamity of emotions wreakin' havoc inside me that night.

The stoplights reminded me of Mei's vibrant red dress and painted mouth, such a strikin' difference to her usual black. The starless sky an acute reminder of the inkiness of her silken hair spillin' around her shoulders, brushin' my cheek as she'd kissed me.

Fuckin' kissed me.

What the hell had she been thinkin'?

We were family, in a way, and I was sixteen years older than her. The idea of a romantic relationship with my best friend's daughter was wrong and utterly fuckin' impossible.

Only...

Only...

Alone on the back of my bike with my thoughts, I could reluctantly admit to myself that I understood why she might have developed feelings for me.

She was right.

We got each other.

Mei wasn't just a touchstone and guardian to Cleo but also to me. The late nights when we both hadn't been able to sleep, sketchin' silently together in the kitchen or shootin' the shit while we drank Longjing tea on the back porch lookin' up at the stars. The iron bond we'd forged in the trauma of Kate's death had been re-enforced over the last five years of shared memories and a growin' understandin' of each other as individuals separate from the parameters of our socially accepted roles.

Mei was more than my daughter's best friend, and she had been for a long time.

That didn't mean it was okay for her to kiss me or that I wanted her to do it again. Whatever she thought about her experiences and maturity, she was a kid to me, the same age as my daughter. She was so off-limits, my brain couldn't even fuckin' compute an alternate reality where she and I would be *together*.

But I couldn't deny the tangible connection between us. The fact that this girl had become as important to me as Lin, Kate, and Cleo, yet she had no definable role in my life.

If it was confusin' for me, it had to be complicated as hell for her.

So, I could forgive her the kiss even though I knew it would haunt me. I could forgive her for thinkin' she was *in* love with me 'cause the love we shared was so difficult to put in a properly labelled box.

Still, nothin' would come from it.

Mei and Cleo would go off to college together and experience all the newness and wonder of a new settin' with new boys to fall for and break hearts over. Mei would forget her feelings for me 'cause, let's be fuckin' honest, I was the least acceptable object for her affection, and she'd realize it as soon as other men came into the picture.

It was strange, though, how even comin' to that reasonable conclusion ached somewhere inside me like a bruised rib. It had to be that I didn't want to cause Mei pain, even unwittingly. I hoped my rejection didn't have to change our relationship completely 'cause the idea of my life without her in it felt deeply and maybe a little perturbingly wrong.

I didn't have long to dwell on the situation, thank fuck, 'cause Old Dragon had pulled through for me and got me a meetin' with someone from Seven Song triad.

Not the Dragon Head himself, but close.

The Golden Door Inn was a narrow two-story building in Chinatown sandwiched between a restaurant and a tailor's shop. The Chinese sign above the door proclaimed it had no vacancy, and I doubted it ever read otherwise. This was not an establishment for those outside of the "know," and the know were those in the Seven Song triad.

I parked my bike under the sodium light of a streetlamp directly outside and walked into the building without issue, even though the space between my shoulder blades itched with the sensation of multiple eyes on me.

A huge blond man walked into a bar in Chinatown...it sounded like the beginnings of a terrible joke, but there was nothin' funny about enterin' the main foyer to find three Chinese gangsters with guns levelled at your chest.

"Hello, Mr. Axelsen." The man in the centre of the inverted triangle, a step behind the other two but clearly in the position of power, was dressed in a perfectly tailored suit and tie, diamond cuff links winking at his wrists, matching ones in his ears.

I'd never understood the gaudiness of gangsters. Bikers kept it real with silver rings and wallet chains, practical accessories that made our punches sharper and the possibility of theft extremely fuckin' unlikely. Rollin' around in gold and flashy designer brands was askin' for attention from all the wrong kinds a people––thieves and police.

"Hello, Mr. Kuan," I returned blandly in Cantonese. "Good of you to meet with me."

A little smile that was cocky despite its size. "I had to see what kind of man would walk into my place of business when he has so clearly done me wrong. If you have big balls or a small brain."

"Maybe it's both," I suggested with a flicker of a raised brow to show how uninterested I was in playin' games.

His smile curled tighter. "Maybe. Come, take a seat."

The left side of the room opened up to a small bar and seatin' area with little tables and worn wooden chairs that looked like they'd crumple under my weight. I pulled one out and flipped it backward to straddle the back as we took seats around one of the tables. It was a little thing, but the wood was a better shield than nothin', and I didn't trust these motherfuckers at all.

"Is this visit at the behest of your president?" Jiang asked as an older lady appeared at our side with a bottle of rice wine and two glasses.

She filled them efficiently and placed one in front of me.

I recognized the offerin' of food or drink, and took a small sip of the pleasantly dry wine even though I didn't want to.

Jiang mimicked my action with raised brows, clearly pleased.

Five minutes in his presence and I was already exhausted by the ritual of détente.

"No," I finally answered. "But I don't think you'd've taken my request for a sit-down if it was sanctioned by Rooster."

"No," Jiang agreed easily before straightenin' slightly, a sly expression elongatin' his features 'til he looked fox-like and too-clever by half. "Is it, perhaps, about your wife?"

Rage hit me between the eyes, rockin' me back, obliteratin' my sense of reality. For a long moment, I could only focus on the need to throttle the man for even mentionin' Kate, for thinkin' he could bring up her murder like it was gossip at a fuckin' tea party.

My fists clenched and unclenched beneath the table.

"No," I ground out, so guttural it hurt my throat. "Though, you got information about any of your people puttin' a hit out on my wife, it'd be good you come clean about it. I'll find out eventually."

"Will you?" His mildness made everythin' offensive, as if nothin' about the situation was interestin' or worthy. It took serious effort to keep red from cloudin' my vision, my judgment.

Jiang's long, thin fingers stroked the little clay urn of rice wine as he contemplated me. "I meant no offence. Only, I've heard you believe the wrongdoing lies at our doorstep and you are quite mistaken. I did some digging of my own when word spread after her death that it was Seven Song responsible, and at the risk of insulting you further, I might note that your wife was a prostitute with many clients and a pimp who was notorious for having enemies."

Fury burned through me, deep inside my marrow, so I felt like I might combust from the inside out. I focused on breathin', in for four, hold for seven, and out for eight, then lifted my gaze to Jiang and ruthlessly cut myself off from all feelin'. A trick I'd learned as a boy when my father took his fists to me that was compounded by my years of trainin' in tactical breath work in the military.

"Not here for that, like I said. I'm here to focus on the problems of *now*. Those bein' this feud between you and The Fallen that's cropped up like a weed in an otherwise prosperous playin' field."

"A playing field *you* changed by delving into heroin and meth."

"A playin' field you fuckin' lit on fire by stealin' some of our dealers first."

He blinked at me, and there was surprise there. He wasn't expectin' someone so unruffled by his taunts, so calm in the face of his pomp and threatenin' circumstance.

He'd've done research on me. Doctor, dropout, tattoo artist, single dad, and widower. But you couldn't read a person's soul in a report. You couldn't test the strength of their character from a collection of facts found on the internet.

I wasn't just a thug and he'd expected that.

Under other circumstances, I might've sighed at the common judgment.

Then again, how could any man who went by the name of Axe expect to be seen as anythin' other than a weapon?

"What are you proposing exactly, Mr. Axelsen? Sitting here without the weight of your president at your back, you're hardly in a position to negotiate a truce."

"Actually, I am."

Jiang cocked an eyebrow.

I sucked in a discrete deep breath, ready to gamble everythin' on this one conversation. "Rooster's a sack of shit and most of the brothers are unhappy with him. Might not have his support, but I got the support of the mother chapter of The Fallen, and there's no authority higher than Zeus mother-fuckin' Garro."

Jiang flinched just slightly, a coilin' of tension in his spine drawin' his posture even straighter. It caused a hank of styled hair to fall over his forehead into his right eye, and for a moment before he fixed it, surprise in his eyes and youth in his features, he looked like a young man. Just a boy really sittin' in a slightly dilapidated inn in Chinatown.

"And, with the sanction of Zeus Garro at your back, you propose what exactly?"

"A division of assets. You keep the heroin and meth trade; we stick to weed and weapons. We don't step into each other's territory, and we got any disputes outside of that, we have a sit-down like fuckin' gentlemen."

"Outlaw gentlemen?"

I shot him an appraisin' look. "Says the man in head-to-toe designer shit."

His eyes sparkled as he nodded, and I could tell he was havin' fun. That, no matter what circumstances had driven him into crime, he enjoyed its seedy underbelly.

I recognized the look, maybe, 'cause despite my conflicted feelings of shame around it, I did too. There was no way to mimic the high stakes of war, the metallic bite of adrenaline on the back of your tongue, in real life like a life of crime.

"It's not rocket science, but it'll keep bodies from pilin' up," I allowed. "Neat and fuckin' tidy so long as you agree to it."

"You'd go behind Rooster's back on this?" he murmured, leanin' forward slightly for privacy even though we were alone outside the thugs waitin' at the door.

I knocked my knuckles against the table lightly. "If you're ready to go behind your brother's."

More shock, fairly well guarded by the shutterin' of his lids as he took a sip of rice wine. He hadn't expected me to know about the tension between them.

Truthfully, I hadn't, not for sure.

But Old Dragon had briefed me a little about the infamous Chinese brothers from Hong Kong. Kasper was older by ten years, more established but also more set in his ways. He'd come to Canada a grown man whereas Jiang had only been a teen. It made a difference, and even if it was just a small one in ideologies, it was enough of a crack for me to wedge open with a fuckin' crowbar.

"You say this because you know my brother does not work with white men. He will not go quietly away from the idea of vengeance. You killed one of our own and stole from us. I'm a more forgiving man than he."

"We'll return what was stolen. We got no use for those drugs anyway. And I'm not talkin' to Kasper for a reason, Jiang. I came to *you* 'cause your brother might be Dragon Head of Seven Song, but this isn't Hong Kong, and I think you get that more than he does. You want to survive in Canada with the bikers, the Quebecois mafia, the Indigenous gangs, and all the rest, you got to learn to play nice when it counts."

"You speak Cantonese. Your wife had dealings with Chinese foreign nationals and Chinese-Canadians through her real estate business. So, I imagine you think you know something about our culture? This can't be true if you sit there straight-faced asking me to betray the trust of my brother. Family, Henning Axelsen, comes before all else. And honour is a very close second."

"It does," I agreed, openin' my palms to reveal my trump card. "Which is why I'm sittin' here askin' you to make a decision independent of your brother, not against him. If this conflict escalates, if we got a gang war on our hands in the streets of Calgary, no one is safe. Fuck you or me, we signed up for this shit. But what about my daughter?" A pause, a little pocket of silence that exploded between us when I whispered, "What about your boyfriend, Eero?"

Jiang was across the table with a gun to my temple in an instant.

Happily, I'd known that was comin' so I had the rice wine cup smashed, a shard of ceramic in my hand and raised to his jugular in about the same amount of time.

He breathed heavily, a bow strung taut across the table ready to release all his fear and fury at the threat of me.

I didn't flinch.

I didn't even bat a fuckin' eye.

That's somethin' they teach you in the sandbox. You get in front of an insurgent, you never show fear. Not even in the instant before certain death.

And I knew, somewhere in my gut, that I wasn't dyin' at the Golden Door Inn at the hands of Jiang Kuan.

"Which would your brother have a harder time with, do ya think? That fact that you're fuckin' a *white* man or the fact that you're fuckin' a white *man*?" I murmured, cognizant of the thugs at the door who'd drawn their guns but remained where they stood across the room, waitin' for a sign from their boss. "Smart of you to hide from him."

"How the fuck do you know that?" he snarled, the pressure of the gun against my temple a cold, painful bite. "How the *fuck* would you even find that out?"

"Give a thug an education, and there's no tellin' what he'll do," I snarked softly. "When it comes to protectin' his family, he'll do damn near everythin'."

Jiang stared into my eyes for a long moment, every muscle in his face tensed. Whatever he found there seemed to settle somethin', and he slowly sat back into his chair, though the gold-plated pistol stayed on the table in easy reach.

"You want to keep livin', I'm sure you'll find a way to make sure that knowledge never leaves your mouth again," he stated demurely, as if he wasn't threatenin' me.

"You want all of us to keep on livin', I'm sure you'll find a way to see what I'm offerin' and work with me to find an amicable kinda solution," I replied with an easy smile.

Even though, beneath my breastbone my heart was poundin' like machine fire.

Jiang leaned back in his chair as if I'd given him a choice he could live with, as if he'd been the one to bring it to me myself, and he said, "Talk to me."

So I did.

It was a gamble, an enormous one.

Jiang could've killed me on the spot for revealin' I knew his secret. It didn't matter the colour of your skin or your criminal outfit, homosexuality was still viewed cruelly by any kinda thug. I had Jiang's life in my hands, and he had to trust I was just as vulnerable if he was gonna let me live.

Unfortunately, or fortunately, my plan involved goin' above Rooster's head to Zeus, the leader of the entire fuckin' Fallen MC, which put me and mine in just as bad a position as Jiang.

The way I saw it, it was the only way to untangle this fuck fest without rivers of blood runnin' through Calgary's streets. Seven Song would get their product back and uncontested rule over the hard drug trade, and The Fallen would keep to our gun runnin' and weed production.

I just needed Jiang to convince his brother it was a wise idea.

When I finished talkin', Jiang looked at me with somethin' like respect in his eyes and said, "*Zuk nei hou wan*, Axe. You'll need it. I don't take kindly to men who threaten me...or mine," he acknowledged with a glower, cedin' the point that I was right about his boyfriend.

I made a silent oath to buy Old Dragon somethin' expensive for Lunar New Year. I didn't have a clue how he knew about

Jiang's sexuality, but the old man still had connections in the underground, and he didn't hesitate to use them for me.

"I will speak with him tonight, but I make no promises. He does not take kindly to opinions that are not his own. The problem is," Jiang continued, almost conversationally, pourin' more rice wine into his cup, "I am not in charge of the triad. Kasper is."

"You can bend his ear."

"Not as much as you may think," he admitted wryly. "He is much older than me, and he has been doing this his own way for a long time. I am the muscle, not the mind. I think you understand very well the position I am in. A Vanguard is only a different kind of enforcer."

I tipped my head in acknowledgment. "I've often wondered if it wouldn't be better, the mind and the muscle in one body takin' control."

Jiang's smile was sharp as the edge of the *dao* sword secured to his hip. He tipped his rice wine cup to me and waited for me to match the gesture before he said, "You and me, both."

CHAPTER THIRTEEN

Henning

The Fallen clubhouse was a shitty building on the outskirts of the city in the industrial district. Once, it had been some kinda warehouse, but the club had turned it into a clubhouse with a main room complete with a shoddily built bar and a collection of bunk rooms in the back. A row of motorbikes was parked in a sloppy line along one side of the building, their chrome backs glintin' harshly in the light from the huge industrial lights loomin' over the parkin' lot.

It was a Friday night, so the place should've been packed with brothers and biker groupies, but the air was still, thick with heat and eerie silence. When I pushed through the door, the main room with the makeshift bar, comfortable and well-used furniture, and stained wood floors was completely empty.

A chill skittered down my spine.

"Prez?" I called out, my boots thunkin' against the floorboards, overly loud in the ringin' quiet.

"Back here, Axe."

I moved through the room to the back hall and to the left to our chapel, the room we held meetings and formal shit in. The door creaked ominously as I entered.

Rooster sat at the head of the long metal table smokin' a cigar with Hazard at his side. He was a thick man, built like a minotaur with colossal shoulders and no neck. His face had that sandblasted, cracked quality of a biker who'd spent many years on the road, so he looked even older than his fifty years. I knew he struggled with arthritis in his knees, and they popped like bubble wrap every time he swung on and off his bike. He rubbed at the left one now, a nervous tell.

Somethin' was wrong.

Then again, in this life, somethin' was always goin' wrong.

And there was the very likely notion that I was projectin' my restless worry onto my president. If he so much as suspected I'd done anythin' like negotiate a truce with the Seven Song without him, he'd have my neck in a noose swingin' from the rafters in the back of the warehouse.

Not an exaggeration.

We'd seen it done before.

"Took you long enough," he grumbled without lookin' at me, a tactic he took up to show how beneath him we were. "Sit your ass down. We got news."

I took the free seat on his right side, ignorin' the way the cigar smoke stung my eyes.

Only then did Rooster look at me as if he was waitin' for me to start a conversation I had zero context for. He waited a long fuckin' time 'cause I didn't speak unless I had somethin' important to say.

"Seems those motherfuckers are targetin' us for a reason,"

Rooster began. "You know your wife was fuckin' a member of the Seven Song 'fore she died?"

The words hit me like a bullet between the eyes. I rocked back in my seat, mind blanked with white noise and pain.

Of course, I'd always known there was a possibility one of Kate's old johns had been a 49er, one of the triad foot soldiers, maybe someone even higher up in the ranks. She'd had a passable workin' knowledge of Cantonese before I'd even started teachin' her, and she was always drawn to Mei and Lin's culture, integratin' little culture nods and traditions into our family dynamic. I figured it was 'cause Lin was important to me, those traditions a part of my life 'cause of the woman who wasn't my mother in blood only, but a little part of me had always wondered.

Not much else made sense about her murder.

It was just so fuckin' personal. So gruesome and deliberate.

You didn't kill someone like that without a motive like... love.

Only there'd been nothin' in her personal effects after her death to link her to anyone specific and the Seven Song triad was notorious for hatin' white people.

Not for the first time, I cursed the fact I'd let sleepin' dogs lie after I pulled Kate outta that life. Yeah, it made it easier for her to move on, but it made it impossible for her daughter and me to move on without her or any of the answers to the fuckin' question her death left behind.

"No," I said finally. "She had a life before me. We didn't discuss it much."

Rooster's fist was the size of a small boiled ham, pink and fleshy as it contracted on the table. "Well, she fucked one of 'em, and then she fucked one of 'em right over. That's why these motherfuckers are comin' after *my* club now. 'Cause'a *you* and your whore ex-wife."

Rage exploded behind my eyes, ringin' between my ears. I

braced every muscle against the urge to slam his smug mug to the table, feelin' the satisfaction of his nose crackin' like an egg against the metal. Hazard would get involved, his fuckin' brown-nosin' lackey, but I could handle him. I didn't even have my gun on me 'cause I didn't want to get caught carryin' at Mei and Cleo's school, but I didn't need it to take Rooster and Hazard out.

The military had made me into enough of a weapon on my own.

But no.

I wasn't gonna take on an entire motorcycle club and a Chinese gang at the same time. I had a daughter at home who needed me. And I had no goddamn doubt that Rooster was speakin' shit to incite me to violence.

I just didn't know why.

"I highly fuckin' doubt my dead wife's ex-lover from over a decade ago would be targetin' the club––the most notorious, deadly outlaw motorcycle club in the fuckin' country––'cause he's still nursin' a broken heart," I drawled, but my mind was racin'.

Why was Rooster tryin' to pin this on me? I'd been tellin' him for weeks to lay off Seven Song's turf and focus on what we did best. We raked in a ton of cake and only fucked with people who tried to fuck with us. Startin' a goddamn gang war was suicidal.

Rooster glowered at me, but Hazard shifted uneasily in his chair like he was nervous.

"I'm thinkin' the triad doesn't take kindly to the fact we raided their warehouse and decided to jump ashes and deal heroin," I continued. "If you're worried, Prez, I say we start there and dial that shit back *hard* before they retaliate for the warehouse attack."

To be fuckin' honest, I was shocked they hadn't come at us

already. They weren't the type of organization to fuck around with revenge.

"Goes to show you don't know shit, as per usual, Axe," Rooster crowed. "My son and Hazard caught wind of a man at a bar near Chinatown who was talkin' about this 'White Snake' fella who fell in love with a hooker and almost destroyed the whole fuckin' triad."

"And naturally any mention of a hooker would refer to Kate?" I asked woodenly, even though I knew Rooster. He'd got his club name for a reason. The man liked to drag out his stories 'til everyone was hangin' on to every word and dole out information sparingly so you had to rely on him. He was a cocky piece of shit who always wanted the attention on him.

Not a great trait for a criminal if you asked me, but no one ever did.

"Well that's just it, seems the White Snake was connected to your wife. The guy mentioned that he cut this bitch to pieces with *dao* swords at a fuckin' summer festival."

Bile rose so quickly to the back of my throat, I almost couldn't stop myself from hurlin' on the table. Who the hell was this White Snake associated with Kate? I knew she'd done work with Kasper Kuan, but he was as Chinese as they came, and the name implied the soldier was a white man.

Had Kate been having...an affair?

I couldn't believe it. Not 'cause we had a passionate physical relationship, but 'cause *we didn't*. After the sexual abuse and mutilation she'd experienced at the hands of her pimp, Jimmie Page, and her clients, Kate was not only terrified of sexual acts, she still had lingerin' pain that made it basically impossible for her to become aroused even if she'd wanted to. We'd had an arrangement where I could take care of my needs discreetly, but I never spent the night with another woman or saw one more than once.

Despite that, Kate and I had loved each other in a way that

had saved each of our lives. I'd been depressed and alone after bein' discharged from the army, workin' myself into some kinda early grave at the hospital like fucked-up penance for the lives I'd taken 'til she and Cleo gave me focus and a reason to live. And Kate had been so deep in the pits of hell, she'd forgotten to hope for anythin' else. The bond between us was unusual, hell yeah, but it was deeper than blood.

So, an affair? It was unfathomable.

"You don't look convinced," Rooster noted. "Well, let me tell you this. When Hazard got his hands on him in the back alley, the bastard admitted there'd even been a kid there. He thought she'd probably died that night too."

Mei.

Fuck.

Immediately, my mind's eye conjured the image of Mei barely fuckin' standin', clutchin' a Chinese *dao* sword in both hands while a shard of bone protruded from one arm and blood poured from her head and nose. Even bloody, even broken, she'd found the will to stand in front of Kate and try to defend her.

My heart turned over in my chest like an engine tryin' to restart.

"It was him." The words dropped from me like a stone, heavy and sure.

Rooster's grin was a slow, mean curve of his thin mouth. "It was him, brother. And tonight, you get your chance to confront the motherfucker."

The heavy silver rings on my right hand *click-clicked* against the tabletop as I drummed my fingers to release some of the energy coilin' inside me.

"Where?"

"There's a party tonight at Turner Farm. I was gonna send Dunkirk and Whitey to distribute, but I figure you ought'a go, too."

You'd think a former army man would have a problem with drug dealin', law-breakin', and general outlaw culture, but the truth was, motorcycle clubs drew a lot of disenchanted army vets into their ranks. We knew how to follow orders and enjoyed a sense of structure, but we'd lost sight a long fuckin' time ago of what we were fightin' for, and our own financial or, in my case, personal, gain was as good a reason as any to get our hands dirty. Lord knew they'd never be clean again after what we'd been told to do overseas.

And then there was the simple fact that once you've been to war, you never really come back. A part of you was always lookin' for the next fight, itchin' for some kinda violence to let some of the steam outta the pot.

So I didn't have a problem with the illegal nature of what The Fallen did. I just didn't like how goddamn stupid they were about it.

"I've told you, we need outside dealers," I reminded him. "It's too fuckin' hairy gettin' caught with our own product on the streets. Especially at a damn party with frat boys and girls with parents waitin' for them to come home for curfew."

"We got product to move, don't give a fuck how it's moved, but it's gotta go," he grunted.

"It's too hot to sell triad shit in Calgary. I thought we were outsourcin' it to other chapters?" There was a pause, and the truth dawned on me. "Fuck, no one else wants to take on the heat."

My prez glared at me, but I ignored it and pressed, "We own our lane. We're good there. Why merge into a different lane and risk everythin' with a collision?"

"Fancy fuckin' degree makes you think you're smarter than me, huh, Axe?" he hissed, blowin' smoke out through his teeth like an angry bull.

I didn't say anythin', but that was answer enough for him.

Rooster scowled at me and then slowly, eyes fixed to mine,

lowered his cherry-ended cigar onto my hand where it lay on the table. I didn't move away, and I didn't flinch when the burnin' end pressed into the knuckle of my pinkie. The sizzle and pop of dissolvin' flesh was followed by the stink of burnt hair and skin.

He was a man of creativity only when it came to belittlin' the men in the club. I'd once seen him shove a prospect's face into a pile of dog shit on the sidewalk outside the clubhouse and piss on a brother's sleepin' face in a bunk room after he slept with a groupie Rooster'd wanted for himself.

"You keep talkin' back to me, Axe, I won't see fit to help you with this little vendetta you got against the Asian pricks, you hear me?" he threatened before finally liftin' the cigar off my hand.

I didn't let so much as a twitch give away the pain in my fuckin' hand and the anger riotin' beneath my skin.

The part of me that had never made a great soldier wouldn't let it lie without another little push. "You think it's safe? We haven't heard word from Seven Song since we looted their warehouse. Thought we'd lie low 'til the other shoe dropped. Heard it straight from your mouth just the other fuckin' day."

Hazard shifted in his chair. Just a little creak of wood and rustle of cloth against stiff leather, but it was enough to draw my eye. He avoided mine, starin' at the table like it was playin' porn.

Somethin' was goin' on here. I knew it in the way the hairs on the back of your neck stood on end in the electric air before a storm. A warnin' written in the response of my body to a threat I couldn't see yet.

It could have been that Rooster'd had me followed, but I didn't think. If he knew about my meeting with Jiang, I'd be dead already.

No, this reeked of somethin' like guilt.

Rooster puffed on his cigar and blew the smoke straight

into my face. "I did. And today I'm sayin' I want you, Whitey, Dunkirk, and Cedar to go to this fuckin' party and deal shit. I'm givin' you a pound'a grass, thirty-five grams of coke, and whatever heroin you can carry."

That was a fuck ton of product for some college party. Enough, if we were caught by the cops, that we'd go away for more than simple possession. At least the fucker was sendin' me with Cedar, the only member of the club I actually considered a brother and would trust to have my back.

"Why so much?"

Rooster scowled at me. "'Cause I fuckin' said so."

I lifted a brow, but didn't say anythin' else 'cause I didn't want another fuckin' burn, and I'd pushed enough for now even though the plan didn't sit well in my gut.

"What does tonight have to do with Kate?" I dared to ask 'cause fuck Rooster. He knew damn well the only reason I'd patched into this club was to get information on her killers, and he'd been none too forth fuckin' comin' about the info, yet now he finally had some.

He kept me waitin' while he discarded his ruined cigar, opened and cut off the tip of a new one and then lit it. After takin' a nice puff, he blew the smoke directly into my face.

Anger rolled through me, bangin' hard against the walls I'd built around it over the years. My father had been an angry motherfucker, and mostly, I refused to let myself be the same. It had been too long, I realized then, drummin' my fingers fast and hard to calm myself, since I'd had a really good fight. Since I'd felt skin split under my fists and blood hot against my skin.

Tonight, I thought, would change that.

"We got reason to believe the Song, including the man you've been lookin' for, will be at this party tonight. You see 'em, you tag at least one and bring him back to the clubhouse for Shrap to interrogate. You get me? After we get what we need about their operation, you're free to do whatever the fuck to the motherfucker who had a part in killin' your wife."

I sucked in a sharp breath through my teeth, battlin' for control. How long had Rooster been sittin' on this information about Kate? I knew in my fuckin' bones it wasn't a coincidence that they'd found out the name of someone involved with her murder at the same time he and Seven Song triad were movin' in on Rooster's territory and threatenin' his own dream of eclipsin' the Entrance chapter's income and power.

What was that sayin' about lookin' a gift horse in the mouth?

"What's his name?" I asked, already standin' up to leave.

Rooster was annoyed, with Hazard, probably, for sharin' too much with me, and with me for bein' too independent of his authority. I'd never make a lieutenant in his club 'cause he was too damn threatened by me to put me to any good use.

I was his weapon, and tonight, it was obvious he wanted to put me to good use.

"Kang," he said. "Kang Li."

CHAPTER FOURTEEN

Mei

Turner Farm was creepy as hell.

Even lit up by the string lights and bonfire raging in the empty field beside the barn and log house, the entire setting was eerie, an obvious choice for a horror flick where the pretty girls die first. Bodies writhed to the thumping music in the blown-out windows of the dilapidated farmhouse, shadowed outlines against the red lights someone had plugged into a generator thrumming loudly away outside. Huge sections of wood planks were missing in the walls of the barn where some kind of drinking game tournament was taking place, and even though I couldn't see them, I could hear people fucking in the long grass behind the house.

I'd never been out this way before, but I'd heard of the place. It was a popular choice for underage parties because it was outside of Calgary in the middle of nowhere. The closest town was Fort Normandeau, an abandoned fort that got the odd tourist or two but had next to no permanent residents.

It was the perfect place for my first errand for Seven Song triad.

"The key is not to look nervous," Kang told me dryly as we divvied up the drugs between us.

He was the one to pick me up after prom in a sleek black BMW, the window rolled down, a cigarette hanging between his lips and a Rolex flashing on his wrist. I had to give it to Chinese gangsters. They had flash and style in spades.

He'd also told me that he went by the name Broken Tooth. When I'd asked him why the hell he'd want to be called that, he'd only shrugged and explained most of the men in the triad had monikers like it.

For privacy, he'd said, but also for a sense of brotherhood.

Like Henning calling me Rocky.

I couldn't deny there was a magical kind of bond in giving and receiving a nickname.

I was beginning to understand, in a way I never had before, why people turned to gangs. If you felt alone and misunderstood by society, there was no better feeling than not only being accepted by a group but also feared by that same society that had rejected you in the first place.

"I'll be fine," I lied, trying to be convincing as I accepted little plastic bags filled with powdered drugs.

"You need to do a line to relax?" he asked, zipping up the pockets on his travel wallet before lifting his shirt to secure it around his torso. It was a clever way to keep the drugs on him while keeping them concealed.

"No, I don't do drugs."

Kang fixed me with his cold stare. I fought the urge to fidget and let him look his fill. I'd changed out of the red dress into my usual black jeans, a black tank beneath my leather jacket, and my heeled leather boots. The drugs were in a little black purse I wore across my body.

"Why do you want to be a part of Centre Street?"

It was a good question, one I was ready for. "I've been trapped by the expectations of my parents my entire life. I want to live my life for me. I never fit in with their lot, and I want to find my own way and my own people."

"And you think a criminal outfit is your lot?" he asked, tone dry enough to peel like paint.

I rolled my eyes. "You saw me fight, Kuan. You ever seen a girl do that before?"

His hesitation was answer enough.

"Trust me, this is where I'm meant to be," I said, and there was enough truth to my words that they rang clear and true.

Kang didn't have to know I was meant to be here to find whoever killed Kate.

But it begged the question now that I was so close to finding answers, what would I do if I found them?

The men who'd killed her and the person who'd ordered the hit.

Did I want them imprisoned and on what evidence? She'd been murdered years ago, and the trail had long ago gone cold.

Did I want them dead?

My heart shivered a little in my chest. Not with fear, but with dark delight.

Yes. I wanted them dead. They didn't deserve to live when Kate did not.

More than that, I wanted them to *suffer*.

And maybe that did make me the kind of person who fit in better with outlaws than respectable society folk. The barbarism of criminality made sense to me.

"Okay, I'll be close by, but you take the barn, and I'll do the house. We'll meet out back by the field in two hours and check in. If you haven't managed to sell shit, this is the end for you."

This time, a shiver of fear, a cold zipper closing up my spine.

"Whatever," I said with a flippant shrug I didn't feel.

I moved past him, biting down a shudder when our shoulders brushed. Something about Kang unnerved me. He didn't blink enough, his predatory gaze unflinching. It alerted something primal in me, an urge to flee.

Don't trust this man, my gut cried.

I didn't, not really, but who else was there to trust at this party?

I wondered with dread why Brian hadn't shown up at prom. He was a drug dealer, sure, but he'd been excited for the dance. He'd even bragged nonstop about a white suit he'd bought that he thought made him look as dapper as Charlie Chan.

As soon as I left the bathroom, the party swallowed me whole. There were people everywhere, clogging the arteries of the rickety house, barely moving even when I shoved past them. Everyone from our grad class seemed to be there, hundreds of kids because we went to a big public school. At least Cleo was home with Lin. There was no way I'd be able to do this with her around.

The first slap of cool air against my face when I pushed outside was a welcome relief. The shadows clung to everything, so deep in patches of the lawn it looked as if the universe had devoured whole sections of the yard. I kept to them, slinking around boisterous groups and a few couples doing very depraved things in the darkness. I wasn't sure if it was the eerie setting or the strange light cast by the bonfire, but everyone seemed more animal than human, their teeth gleaming red, their features elongated by shadow.

I shivered in my leather jacket and ducked into the barn.

I instantly recognized Michael Hannigan, one of those jock-types who always seemed to thrive in high school and fade after graduation. He moved with a kind of frenetic energy, as if he himself knew the end of his glory days was nigh. There was something about his agitation that called to me. He was holding court in the middle of a large group, which made approaching him risky, but I figured if I could get the King of Cal Oaks High to buy some of my shit, everyone else would soon follow.

I sucked in a deep breath, righted my shoulders, and moved toward the popular crowd I had never, not once, spoken to before tonight.

Michael caught my eye almost immediately, head and shoulders taller than most of the people surrounding him. His eyes gleamed, red-black like a demon's, and for just a second, his mouth curled, a cruel promise.

Okay, he seemed to say, *come here and play*.

He didn't know I'd faced worse adversaries than him. If I could fight Jiang Kuan and stand up to Henning Axelsen, I could face Mr. Popular without fear.

"Hey, Hannigan," I greeted with a chin lift, stopping just beside his little group to lean casually against a wooden pole. It creaked under my slight weight ominously.

He stared at me a moment more before jerking his own chin. "Marchand, what's up?"

A few of the girls, all of them wearing next to nothing, shot me warning glances. I almost snorted at the idea that I was after Michael. He was as far from Henning as I could imagine and, therefore, not of any interest to me romantically.

"Nothing much, unfortunately," I started with a little sigh. "Just bored out of my skull. This party is lame."

"Yeah," he agreed slowly, turning a little more to face me properly. "You got any ideas how to fix that?"

I let a smile move across my face, slow and warm as melted wax. My hair shifted over my shoulder, a sleek sheet of inky silk, and I watched as Michael took it all in, as he blinked and licked his lips.

"Maybe," I suggested, biting the edge of my lip. "Depends on how bored you are...and how much you want to pay?"

He laughed, a quick bark. "You prostituting yourself now, Marchand? Isn't your daddy rich as hell?"

Michael knew he was. Years ago, before they'd learned better, the rich and popular crowd had tried to recruit me to their ranks. The daughter of Florent Marchand would have been a perfect fit for them, in theory. In reality, I didn't give a shit about them or anything they gave a shit about themselves.

I rolled my eyes and spoke over the twittering girls who thought his comment was a little too funny. "I wasn't offering myself. Just a little party favour..."

I unzipped my little bag and pinched a little baggie of white powder between my fingers. It was easy to flash it his way, just a quick peek to entice his interest.

His eyes bulged, almost grotesque in the darkness. "How much?"

"How much do you want?"

He looked at his crew, a collection of twenty odd girls and boys who all seemed to hang in suspended animation around him, just waiting for his cue. One of his buddies clapped him on the back and grinned.

"What the hell," he decided. "I'll take whatever you got. It's our last night as high schoolers, better make the most of it."

I didn't have to manufacture the smile that claimed my mouth, but I wondered if anyone could look at me and think I wasn't feral, intent on wickedness that far surpassed drug dealing to teens in an abandoned barn.

They didn't empty my collection, but they put a large dent in it. I'd never really gone to high school parties, so I was shocked by the ease of their expertise as they took three bags of coke and started to divvy one up into clean little lines on a small mirror a girl produced from her purse. Another guy took a baggie of weed and set to rolling a joint with the well-oiled movements of a habitual smoker.

It shouldn't have shocked me. I knew The Fallen probably dealt to teens all the time, but it seemed absurd to me that my peers would want to risk their health, security, and potentially their future on a bit of chemical fun.

Michael neatly snorted a line of coke, then eyed me where I stood impassively in the corner watching them. A mean expression flashed across his face, there and gone.

"Have a line," he suggested, offering me a rolled-up twenty-dollar bill.

"I'm good."

"It wasn't a question." He stepped closer, caging me into the wall with his towering physique. It annoyed me that men always seemed to do that, using their bodies to intimidate in a way most women never could. "Daddy's good little girl too prudish to do a line of coke with me? How do I know you aren't some kind of narc?"

Anger shivered over my skin. Rationally, I understood he was manipulating me, but I was triggered all the same, my emotional response too immediate to balance out with logic. I had the rolled-up twenty in my hand before I could even think about it.

"'Cause she's with me."

The answer didn't come from me or from Michael.

But I knew without turning exactly who that voice belonged to. The low, quiet weight of Henning's voice would be familiar to me underwater or whispered down a faulty telephone line. I knew it better than I knew my own.

But why the hell was he *here*?

Before I could turn around, a large hand was reaching over my shoulder, gripping Michael by his button-up and then slamming him against the wall on the right side of me.

Henning's body brushed mine as he stepped forward into his caged prey, his profile a snarling menace.

"You like to force women to get high so you can take advantage of them?" he growled into Michael's face.

I'd never seen Henning like this. So much an outlaw. In his leather cut, the blazing skull motorcycle patch of The Fallen on his back, his hair a mess of waves around his jaw, lips peeled back over strong, sharp teeth, he looked like a wolf trapped in a man's body. An animal about to snap.

A little shiver worked down my spine, but this time, it was a dark current of arousal.

"She sold this shit to *me*, man," Michael argued, struggling against Henning's grip.

In response, Henning wrapped his other hand around his neck. How strange I'd thought Michael so large when in comparison to Henning, he was only a child.

"Call off your attack dog," one of the girls, I thought her name was Felicity, hissed to me, gripping my arm too tight.

It was the cold water plunge I needed to shake off my shock.

I stepped forward to place a hand on Henning's tensed back, the muscles dense as stone. "Hey, hey, it's okay."

His head swivelled slowly to face mine, and his feral expression didn't change. "I'll deal with you in a second, Mei Zhen. Step off."

I backed up immediately.

Henning's was the only authority I'd ever acknowledged, and it was impossible to disobey him when he looked like that.

Capable of murder.

He turned back to Michael, and I watched the way his hands flexed and popped with tightening tendons, squeezing around the teen's neck.

"You listen to me," Henning hissed. "You ever heard of The Fallen MC?"

Michael nodded hard. The Fallen was an international

organization, but it was Canadian originally, and every citizen knew the motorcycle club. It was a part of the cultural underbelly. Something parents told children about as cautionary, scary stories before bed.

"Good. So you get if you touch one hair on Mei Zhen's head, I'll take every one of yours along with your fuckin' scalp. You get me?"

Tears raced down Michael's cheeks, but he nodded again, and Henning released him. Done with his threats, Hen turned to me, tagged my hand, and dragged me out of the barn without hesitation. I looked over my shoulder to make sure Michael was okay, but a crowd of girls had swarmed him, and I knew he'd be fine.

"Henning," I snapped, trying to dig my feet into the hay-strewn ground to wrench my arm out of his hold. "Stop it, you're acting like a heathen."

He didn't acknowledge my words. I focused on keeping up as he took us around the far end of the barn where the shadows were inky thick and quiet. A little gasp fell from my mouth when he whipped me around by my hand and then thrust me back against the wet, warped wood of the building. His teeth snapped next to my throat, a physical threat he couldn't find the words to embody.

"Hey," I tried to soothe, smoothing my hands down the bulging arms that held me pinned. "Hey, Henning, I'm okay."

"You think this is *okay*?" he mocked, his glower carved like granite into his face. "You think bein' a seventeen-year-old drug dealer is *okay*?"

Indignation sparked in my belly. I canted my chin up to peer down my nose at him. "I think doing what's necessary to find out who killed Kate is *more* than okay. You manhandling me and bullying me is not."

Henning swore savagely and pushed off me to pace in a tight circle, hands tearing through his hair. I stood frozen in place 'cause even though I knew he would never hurt me, seeing him like this, so...unglued, scared me in a different kind of way. There was a flutter in my heart but also lower, between my thighs.

"You have no fuckin' clue what you're involved with," he finally growled, turning sharply on his boot to crowd me again. "For a smart kid, you're bein' a goddamn idiot about this. Why can't you just leave all this alone? Be a kid while you can. You're ruinin' your life with this vendetta bullshit."

"It's not a vendetta," I spat, insulted by the idea. "It's justice. Kate never got any for her murder, and the idea of her stuck in purgatory somewhere fucking haunts me. I promised her I'd take care of you and Cleo, but I also made a promise to myself that I'd find answers to what happened to her."

"You are a seventeen-year-old kid," he roared in my face, slamming a fist into the wall beside my head. "Operatin' in the underworld with the likes of me and the fuckin triad is *not* an acceptable option for you."

"You're not my dad!"

"No," he shouted, anguished now. "No, I'm not. I don't wanna be. But whatever I am to you, I thought you respected me more than this. I thought you loved Cleo, your parents, and Old Dragon--*me*--more than this. Did you even stop to think what we would go through if you were incarcerated for dealin' drugs? Or, worse, if these motherfuckers found out you were just dealin' for them so you could spy on them?"

I blinked up at him, shocked by the agony waterlogging his tone and the sight of it in his turquoise eyes.

"God, Mei," he muttered, the steam suddenly going out of him so his big shoulders sagged and his head dipped low, close enough I could feel his warm breath on my face. "You want somethin' from me I got no power to give you, but that doesn't mean I don't got a magnitude of love for you in my heart. You told me you couldn't stand losin' another person you love? Well, don't make me go through the same."

A quivering, bruise-tender silence bloomed between us. I didn't know what to say. His words made my chest ache, but I'd spent years forming my future and my identity around the idea of seeking justice at all costs. I didn't want to give it up and I didn't know if I could, not when I'd come this far.

"This is my test, and then I'm *in*," I tried to explain to him, clutching at the lapels of his cut. "I fought Jiang Kuan and impressed him, Hen. I can do this."

He screwed his eyes closed so tight it looked like it hurt, and when they opened again, they blazed like the blue on the inside of a flame.

"You hear me, Mei Zhen, you will not get involved with these fuckers."

"It's too late for that," I whispered.

"Have you done their initiation ritual?"

"No..."

"Then it's not too late. I'm gettin' you outta here, and when I get home, you better be waitin' for a serious talkin'-to, kid. This goes way beyond the fuckin' pale. You are neck deep in so much shit you can't even look down to see how fucked you are."

An uncharacteristic wobble gripped my lower lip before I bit it still. It hurt to feel like a helpless, foolish idiot in Hen's eyes, but it hurt even worse to get why he felt that way.

I was being reckless, sure, but I didn't know how to sit on my hands and let the world spin on in its fucked-up ways without having some kind of *say*.

Henning shook me gently and my attention snapped back to his aquamarine eyes, bright even in the shadow of his brows. "For once, will you do what I say and get outta here? Please, Rocky."

It was what he did next that undid me.

His broad forehead tipped down to press to mine, and he

closed his eyes, a pained expression on his rough-hewn features.

And I knew he'd never love me the way I loved him.

Like I was the oxygen he needed to breathe.

But at least he loved me like this.

Like losing me would be living with half a lung.

"Okay," I said, succumbing to authority for one of the first times in my life, but doing it freely because this was Hen, and I knew if I pushed, I'd lose him and maybe even Cleo and Lin. "I didn't drive here, but I'll order a ride home."

A spasm wrenched his expression before it smoothed out in relief. When his eyes opened again, they were dark and fathomless.

"Thank you," he whispered in Cantonese before pressing a kiss to my forehead where his own had just rested.

Before I could say anything, a shadow shifted away from the opaque darkness, swallowing up the cornfield behind Henning's head. I opened my mouth to warn him, but I was too late.

Kang appeared out of the blackness on a smooth leap, his body fluid as an arrow. He brought the handle of his chopper blade down on the side of Henning's temple, and the man I'd always thought of as indestructible crumpled to the ground.

Before I could say anything, frozen with shock and horror, Kang grinned wickedly at me, his teeth glinting like the blade in his hand.

"I knew having a pretty face would work in our favour." He chuckled hoarsely, nudging Henning's big body with the toe of his expensive-looking black cowboy boot. "These heathens would have shot you first and asked questions later if it was a man dealing on their territory."

I swallowed roughly as Kang bent to press Henning's hands together, producing a zip tie that barely fit around his big wrists to lock them together.

"What're you doing?" I asked, my voice weak.

He peered up at me as if questioning my sanity. "He's a *gweilo* with The Fallen." His lips puckered before he spat on Henning's chest. "They're racist pieces of shit who raided one of our warehouses and killed three of our men two weeks ago."

"He's probably not alone," I hastened to mention as Kang braced himself on his knees and grunted, rolling Henning's massive body onto his shoulders before he staggered to a stand. "Those biker guys always travel in packs."

"Luckily, so do we," he said with a grin that was mostly a grimace, sweat beading on his hairline from the effort of remaining standing under Henning's weight. Honestly, it was shocking that he could carry the larger man.

I tried to think fast. How the hell could I get Henning out of this situation without putting myself in danger too and condemning us both to a beating, torture, or worse...death. My palms were sweating, a bead of moisture trickling down the deep crease of my destiny line, then down off my middle finger.

It reminded me of the Chinese fortune teller all those years ago at the fair.

You must not be too hard and unyielding, too focused on death and the dark.

If you don't learn this, the tragedies of your life will overtake you.

Fuck.

I'd entered into this deal with the devil to get justice for Kate, Cleo, and Henning, not to condemn the rest of the Axelsen family that remained standing.

"What about selling the rest of the product?" I asked, trying to keep the panic from my words as I followed Kang into the shadows of the cornfield.

Kang's laugh was hollow, a cough instead of something from the belly. "Oh, the Vanguard will forgive you that. You caught the white whale, Mei Zhen. Don't worry, you will be rewarded generously. Not punished."

A hideously horrified giggle burbled up in my throat, but I forced it down with a painful swallow. If Kang thought abducting Henning was anything but the worst kind of punishment for my thirst for vengeance, he was fatally wrong.

I thought *fatally* because I'd killed Kang before I let him do anything to Hen.

I just didn't know how I'd manage it without putting myself in danger, but then, I didn't care about the night's outcome for me.

All that mattered was saving the only hero I'd ever known.

CHAPTER FIFTEEN

Mei

THEY WERE WAITING FOR US AT THE HEART OF THE CORNFIELD IN a small clearing cut around three rotten and tattered scarecrows fixed to wooden poles.

One of the men, dressed impeccably in a dark grey suit, was in the midst of cutting down the remains of the scarecrow from the middle cross when Kang and I pushed through the cornstalks into the clearing. Four unknown gangsters in a half moon with legs spread and arms crossed in front of their torsos, ramrod straight posture, were at attention.

Waiting, no doubt, for orders from the two most notorious triad members in the province.

Kasper and Jiang Kuan.

I'd never met Kasper before, and I'd never hoped to. As the Dragon Head of the entire operation in Calgary, I'd have to be committed to Seven Song for *years* before I was worthy of being called into his presence. Seeing him now, in a dark cornfield lit only by the bright moon and stars overhead and the headlights from a sleek black SUV they'd driven into the cornfield, I was struck by how utterly unimpressive he seemed. Mid-height, carrying extra weight beneath his chin and in his cheeks, discernable even under the well-cut suit, with thinning black hair, he seemed like any other Chinese businessman. The only reason I knew he was the Dragon Head was the deference his position allowed him, and the way he carried himself, as if he expected one of his men to lay across a puddle for him so that he wouldn't sully his designer shoes.

Next to him, Jiang, tall, strong, and beautiful enough to walk down a runway, seemed God-like.

Something was chilling about Kasper's normalcy, though. It reminded me of a quote I'd read once about the banality of evil. And there was no doubt, looking at the crime boss in the still dark, that he was a special kind of evil.

Kang took Henning to the now-vacant cross, and together with the other man there, they propped Henning against the wood and fixed him there with grunts and heavily knotted rope. I kept to the shadows at the edge of the circle, unwilling to draw attention to myself until I knew how the hell I was going to help Henning.

"I don't like this," Jiang murmured quietly in Cantonese. "I told you there was another way to handle this."

I had the sense they were waiting for something. Everyone seemed fixed on the path that led out the opposite side of the circle, no doubt leading to a road on the other side of the Turner Farm acreage.

I shivered, hugging myself as I slipped deeper into the cornstalks.

"It was always going to come to this," Kasper said, his voice oddly rough like he'd smoked a pack a day from his youth. "You must learn, *Dai tai*, that the only way to deal with someone who opposes you is to put them in the ground."

Jiang gestured to Henning, who hung like a macabre ornament from the wood cross. "And he is our enemy? Why not kill the president and be done with it? We both know who ordered the club to steal from us."

"This is the man they say killed Stray Dog at the silo."

"No doubt at the orders of Rooster Cavendish."

Kasper shrugged elegantly. "No doubt."

"Then why?"

He sighed, an older brother beleaguered by the stupidity of the younger. "Because fear is a powerful motivator. We took their women as if it was nothing. After they hand over the product, we kill this man in front of them. They leave cowed, *Dai tai*, and malleable. We can always use mules to cart our product."

"I told you I brokered a deal with one of the brothers. We don't need to do this shit out in the back field at a high school party, Kasper. For once, listen to me."

"We do what I say, when I say it," Kasper contradicted coldly, without even looking at his brother. "This is a lesson that will be taught with blood, not peace, as all lasting lessons should be."

When Jiang opened his mouth to say something, Kasper held his hand up to stop him. "No, *Dai tai*, I will not hear another word. You may speak when you are spoken to, and that is it until I decide you are worthy of respect again."

I watched Jiang's hand clench and fist at his side, but he didn't say another word.

Seconds later, I heard what they'd been waiting for.

The distinct rumble of Harley pipes.

As if summoned by the noise, the stalks to our left rustled before revealing three men in their Fallen cuts, one of whom I recognized. Henning was kind of a lone wolf outside of his family, but if I had to say he had a best friend in Calgary, it would've been Cedar, the man stalking through the trampled grass behind two mean-faced bikers. His gaze darted up to Henning, and he grimaced but made no move to rescue him.

Ice water slithered through my veins.

What the fuck was going on?

Behind us, only a hundred and fifty yards away, my graduating class continued to party without a clue about the criminal standoff taking place in this field. I wondered if I screamed loudly enough if it would do any good and decided against it. It would probably only succeed in getting both Henning and me killed faster.

The ground was rumbling now with the vibration of the powerful Harley engines. One appeared at the head of the spear, a huge bike with ape handlebars. I knew who the man was before he even swung off his bike and unclipped his helmet.

Rooster Cavendish swaggered a few feet forward and crossed his arms over his barrel chest as he stared down the Kuan brothers. Behind him, five more men parked their bikes, and one of them yanked a hooded man off the passenger seat and dragged him forward, throwing him at Rooster's feet. When the man tried to squirm to his knees, Rooster delivered a brutal kick to his face, steel boot connecting with a wet crunch I could hear across the small clearing.

The man stilled instantly.

Another man, I thought in the dim light he might have been Hazard, one of the brothers Henning had also been to war with, stepped forward with an arm full of saddlebags and tossed them beside the prone man.

"Your fuckin' China White and the piece of shit you wanted picked up," Rooster grunted, feet braced, face fixed into a fierce scowl.

He should have looked terrifying, but there was sweat pouring down his face and a nervous tic in one fist, opening and closing like a gaping fish out of water. He was the president of The Fallen MC in Calgary, and he looked...terrified.

I shivered, my gaze cutting up to Henning tied to that fucking post. He was starting to come to, face spasming with pain, the blood on his face drying to a flaky, deep red-black.

Wake up, wake up, I thought desperately as if that would help.

For the first time, I understood what Henning had been trying to tell me about being in over my head.

"Where are the women?" Cedar demanded, crossing the perimeter of the clearing to get to Rooster and the rest of his brothers. His head was on a swivel, trying to see into the surrounding darkness.

To the left of me, Jiang went noticeably still while Kasper let out a wooden laugh.

"I'm thinking about keeping them." He didn't move, barely even blinked as he studied the bikers very visibly carrying guns and knife sheaths on their person. He could have been talking about the weather. "You can get a good price for women these days, especially young ones like your daughter."

Hazard made a sound like a muted roar in his throat and took a step forward, but Rooster clapped him on the shoulder and shoved a foot into his leg, taking the younger man to his knees.

"Stay," he ordered gruffly.

And Hazard, a grown man, an outlaw biker, stayed, head bowed, knees getting wet in the muck of mud and straw on the ground.

"You didn't tell me you took their women," Jiang murmured so quietly in Cantonese, I could only hear him because I was only a metre and a half behind him.

Kasper didn't even spare him a glance. "It's good, then, I don't report to you."

"Why would you keep that from me?" Jiang insisted. "You

know the blond biker came to me with a deal. It would have been helpful to know we already had the situation under control."

"Are you accusing me of keeping secrets, *Dai tai?*" Kasper said so low, it was barely a sound, yet the vibration of violence could be felt in the air.

Across the clearing, Rooster shouted, "Are we fuckin' doin' this or what? I gave you what you asked for."

"Technically, my Red Pole was the one to find the biker who killed our man at the silo," Kasper said in that flat, metallic monotone that set my teeth on edge.

I sucked in a sharp breath at his words.

"I was the one who got him here, ain't I?" Rooster demanded. "Now hand over the women, or I won't be responsible for some'a my trigger-happy brethren."

Holy *fuck*. Rooster was *giving* them Henning as some kind of payment. I stared at the man I loved slumped on the wooden pole and prayed to God, my ancestors, anyone I could think of to save him.

Kasper raised his brows. "That threat is empty. If you open fire, we will return it, and none of us will leave this farm." The air itself seemed to still as he hummed over his decision and then flicked his fingers. "Fine, bring them forward," he ordered in Cantonese.

A man unpeeled himself from the group of thugs to his right and disappeared into the stalks.

"While we wait..." Kasper tipped his chin at a man with the number 438 tattooed on his neck, denoting his role as Deputy Mountain Master, Kasper's vice-president essentially, moved forward to collect the hooded man.

Two more followed, gathering the saddlebags filled with heroin.

But my gaze was fixed on the hooded body as it was thrown

at Kasper's feet. Jiang, beside him, stared at the figure with something like mounting shock, his face blanching.

"Who is it?" he whispered.

"Trash I asked The Fallen to pick up so I wouldn't have to sully my hands," Kasper said mildly, and with a nod, the Deputy Mountain Master reached down to rip the hood from the man's head.

Jiang made a sound I'd only heard once before, the same one Henning had made when he'd seen Kate strung up and bleeding to death in the basement of the House of Horrors. A sound like something had died in his chest.

The man at Kasper's feet was shifting in and out of consciousness, his breath rattlingly wetly in his throat from damaged lungs. His face was a mottled mess of swollen flesh, bruises, and dried blood. Once, maybe, he had been attractive, and maybe, if he survived the night, he could recover enough to be so again.

But I had the distinct and gut-wrenching feeling he would *not* survive the night.

Jiang trembled as he seemed to gather the pieces of himself together. When he spoke, his tone was as stripped bare as his brother's. "How?"

"How?" Kasper asked disdainfully, finally showing emotion, and it was *anger* curdled by a bone-deep disgust. "I know *everything, Dai tai*. When will you get that through your rabbit head? You have never been able to hide anything from me, and you never will."

"Why, then?" Jiang asked, desperation just skirting into his tone. "You don't need to... I won't see him again."

"You won't," Kasper agreed, almost pleasantly, and then, before I could blink, the Deputy Mountain Master had a pearl enamelled gun in his hand, and he was pulling the trigger.

The *bang* was blast, the radius kicking Jiang back a few steps, and I went along with it, sliding deeper into the stalks away from the horror. They had forgotten me, for the moment, but I was uninitiated. They wouldn't let me survive the night unless I took a vow to join Seven Song, and now, finally, I couldn't think of a worse fate.

Because the poor man, clearly Jiang's beloved, was dead on the ground, blood and grey matter splattered around him like rotten tomatoes.

And Jiang?

He didn't move a muscle, not even to blink, not even it seemed to breathe. Yet I could feel his despair in every inch of my body. It echoed through the clearing and back in a feedback loop.

Kasper stepped over the body between them as if it was nothing and lightly slapped his younger brother's cheek. "Do not keep secrets from me again, *Dai tai*. If you do, you'll meet your lover much sooner than you should."

The commotion of the triad soldiers bringing The Fallen women into the clearing drew my attention away from the horrifying scene in front of me. A handful of women ranging in age from elderly to teen ran across the clearing, but not one of them was Cleo. I let out a heavy exhale at the same moment Henning, finally, woke up.

"What the fuck," he bellowed, struggling against his bindings so hard that the rotted wood post swayed dangerously.

When he caught eyes with Rooster, he stilled, eyes blown wide with shock as he took in the situation.

"You betrayin' one've your own?" he questioned, a soft burr of a growl.

Rooster scoffed. "Like you weren't workin' to take my place as prez. I see you, Axe, always tryin' to undermine my fuckin' authority."

"'Cause I didn't want shit to lead to this," he shouted, twisting his arms until blood started to coat the ropes.

"Oh," Rooster drawled as the women ran to the men behind

him. He paused to pat a teenage girl on the shoulder as she went by and then grinned a manic grin at Henning. "This was inevitable. The fuckin' triad pricks think they can take our shit? They'll find they're mistakin'."

"Rooster," Henning tried to cajole, but it was too late.

Rooster had come with his own agenda. A stupid, violent, and bloody one, but an agenda all the same.

He pulled a gun smoothly from his shoulder holster and shot Kasper Kuan in the gut.

Instantly, everything dissolved into chaos.

This was gang warfare, and I was a seventeen-year-old girl hiding in the cornstalks. Henning's voice rebounded in my head, telling me I was a stupid girl throwing my safety to the wind just for a chance at retribution. For a moment, as gunfire peppered throughout the clearing, I squeezed my eyes shut and wished for it all to be over.

And then I remembered that Henning was still tied to a fucking pole in the middle of the two factions and that *neither* would protect him now.

I was on my feet before I realized I'd moved, my hand curling around the short tactical blade I had stowed in my boot.

Two soldiers were helping Kasper Kuan out of the field back toward Turner Farm and their vehicles. In the distance, where the grad party still droned on, I could hear the beginning of female screams as the sound of bullets echoed through the lot. Jiang was engaged with Hazard, fighting hand to hand, while a few more skirmishes took place. Rooster was shielded by the propped-up body of one of his dead brothers, shooting at Kasper's retreating body and yelling promises of retribution.

And amidst it all, Henning, strapped to that wet wood, the pole frayed from the strain of holding him.

I sucked in a deep breath, trying to find bravery and then, failing that, trying to remember Kate's voice in my head and the promise I'd made to protect her family.

I darted forward, ducked around Jiang as he took Hazard to the ground, and then sprinted toward Henning. He was bleeding from a bullet wound to his left thigh, but otherwise, he seemed unharmed. When he saw me running toward him, something in his face gave, collapsing into grief and horror.

Rocky, he mouthed.

I slammed into the pole, unable to curb my speed thanks to the adrenaline electrifying my blood. The chopper blade shook in my hand as I raised and lowered it against the ropes binding Henning's feet. They gave way after another hit, and I went to work on his hand, on my tiptoes, sawing at the plastic because I didn't have a good angle or enough leverage to cut through them without hurting Hen.

"What the fuck?" he whispered. "Get out of here, Mei Zhen. *Now*."

"Not without you." I didn't even recognize my voice, it was so shrill and weak with terror. My heart beat louder than the increasingly infrequent gunshots in my eyes.

The ropes finally gave way, releasing one of Henning's hands. I rocked back to my heels and watched as he flexed and twisted his wrist to resume the blood flow. I was about to work on his other hand when he shouted my name and pushed me *hard* to the dirt.

I twisted onto my back instantly, in time to watch Kang flying at Henning with his *dao* sword raised. Only, he wouldn't have been flying at Henning, but at *me* if I still stood where I'd been two seconds ago.

Kang had been going for me, no doubt after seeing me let Henning loose.

I swallowed the surge of bile in my throat as Kang missed his swipe, just a foot too far away to connect with the biker. Henning kicked the blade with the thick sole of his boot, but Kang had a good grip on it. Changing tactics, Hen stepped closer, too close for a proper strike with the chopper blade by

Kang, but close enough for him to land a heavy fist against the Asian man's jaw. Kang's head snapped back audibly.

Behind Henning, Rooster had given up shooting after Kasper, who'd fled, and turned his attention to Kang and Henning, the only remaining fight other than Jiang and Hazard who were locked together rolling on the ground.

"I told you I'd get you a face-to-face with Kate's killer," Rooster crowed as he dropped the body of his Fallen brother and started his own retreat, flanked by two brothers with guns raised. "I always follow through with my promises, Axe."

Henning didn't respond, but I could see the coiling of tension in his core as he digested this information.

Kang had been one of the triad soldiers to kill Kate.

The revelation hit me between the eyes. I'd known he'd given me the creeps, but it was more than that. I'd heard that hissing whisper of his before, at the top of the stairs in the House of Horrors. He'd been the one to push me down the treads.

I jumped to my feet, curled my sweaty palm around the blade of my knife, and waited for a gap in the fight between Kang and Henning. A moment later, after Kang hit Henning in the ribs with the butt of his sword, and Henning returned a roundhouse punch to Kang's throat, causing him to choke for breath, I moved.

I'd been training for years to see fights in slow motion, to read my opponents and exploit their weaknesses. My adrenaline and decade of practice drowned out the pain, the fear, the worry, and all that was left was the cold blade of retribution.

I lunged deeply, extending my arm to chop the blade the way it was built to, a strong sideways slash like I was halving a watermelon. Only it cut deeply into the soft side of Kang's belly, smoothly until I hit the bottom protrusion of his ribbon. The knife lodged there, and as he spun away from the pain, the handle was wrenched from my fingers, leaving me weaponless.

I stood there dumbly for a second, expecting Kang to go down. To drop to the ground and *die*.

That was always how it happened in the movies.

But Kang was a triad Red Pole, the enforcer of Seven Song. He'd been fighting for longer than I'd been alive, and he had his own wealth of adrenaline to carry him through the hurt.

He didn't go down. Instead, he turned that recoil into leverage to swing his torso back around, *dao* sword angled and raised to come down on my throat.

People say their life flashes before their eyes before they die, but mine didn't do that. All I could think about at that moment was Henning. I was afraid for his life. That he'd make it out of this godforsaken field alive and that my death wouldn't scar him forever.

The blade stopped a foot from my neck, stuck in the side of a huge, strong hand tattooed with "love" across the knuckles and shrapnel scars like pockmarks on the fingers.

Henning grunted painfully as he stopped the blade with his hand, leaning his weight across my body to catch it in his non-dominant left hand. Kang pushed harder, severing Henning's pinky finger completely.

The sight of the bubbling, bloody stump was enough to spur me into action again. I took advantage of Kang's preoccupation to pull my knife from his side with a wet, sucking sound. Blood flew as I cocked it back for one last strike.

This time, when the chopper blade sank into Kang's flesh, it severed his carotid artery, and he immediately fell to his knees, garbling on the blood flooding his throat.

My numb fingers dropped the blade.

"Rocky." Henning's voice was stripped bare, raw wires cackling with electricity.

I turned to face him only to see Rooster over his shoulder. Something like a squawk emerged from my throat, but not before Rooster laughed and wrenched Henning back by his bloody hand. He dropped to the base of the wooden cross and with a little, innocuous *snick,* he handcuffed Henning there.

"I hope you bleed out before the pigs arrive," he sneered into Henning's blanched face. "But if not, you're a better fall guy for this mess than I ever coulda hoped for."

I launched myself at Rooster, kicking out the side of his leg so it gave with a loud *pop* and *crack*. It gave out, and he went careening to one knee. Leveraging every ounce of my slight weight, I brought my fist down hard on Rooster's cheek.

I would've kept going, blind with fury and rage, but someone pulled me off him before I could beat his fucking face in.

"Mei, stop." It was Cedar, hauling me away from Rooster as another Fallen brother bent to help his president to his feet. "You stupid girl, fuckin' *stop*."

"Kill her," Rooster ordered, florid with pain.

"No." This time was Jiang Kuan, of all people, who stepped forward over the prone body of Hazard with his gold gun trained on Rooster. "You are not murdering another innocent tonight."

In the quiet of the new standoff, I heard the distant sound of wailing sirens. I dropped out of Cedar's hold to tend to Henning, who was drained of colour, but still trying to curl around me like a human shield. I let him but focused on tearing a strip off his shirt to wrap around his hand, trying to stop the flow of blood.

"I could shoot you where you stand," Jiang offered. "Or I could let you get away, say goodbye to your loved ones, and go to bed one last night knowing I'm coming for you."

"Fucking coward," Rooster spat. "You wouldn't dare."

Jiang studied him for a moment, canted one shoulder, and then a bullet was fired.

It took me a moment to realize it wasn't Jiang who fired the gun, but Henning. An unfamiliar Glock was steady in his right hand, the barrel still trained at his ex-president. Rooster slumped in his brother's hold, blood weeping from a hole in the right of his chest.

Jiang looked down at us as the brother supporting Rooster dropped the man and ran for cover himself, jumping on his Harley and tearing out of there.

"The cops'll be here in minutes," he told us after a moment, and then before we could answer, he spun on his heel, bending to pick up the dead body of his lover carefully in his arms, and then disappearing into the dark.

"Take Mei."

I didn't realize what Henning was saying or to whom until Cedar's hands were lifting me again.

"What?" I asked dazedly.

Henning was looking over my shoulder at Cedar, his gaze solemn. "You did what you had to do for your mum, man, but fuck, do this for me. Get Mei the fuck outta here."

Cedar hesitated for only a moment before his fingers curled tighter around my shoulder bones, and I was tugged into his front.

"I'm so sorry, brother. This...this wasn't how I wanted it to go down. But they had Mum, and you know, I owe her everything."

"Don't got time for that shit, Cedar. Please, you're forgiven if you take Mei."

"No!" I shouted, finally seeing through the haze of adrenaline and shock to the heart of what was happening. "NO! I am not leaving you here, Hen! Cleo needs you. Lin needs you. What will they do if you don't come home? Please, please, get up. We can figure out how to get you out of those cuffs--"

"Rocky," he said, so softly the sound was like a tender caress after all the evening's violence.

I shivered and fell to my knees, dislodging Cedar's hold so I could walk on my knees to Henning. "Don't make me leave you."

"I'd pay any price for you," he whispered fiercely, his blood-soaked hands clutching at my face so hard it almost hurt. "Is that enough love for you, Rocky?"

It was *too* much. So much I was drowning in it, sinking beneath the turquoise of his eyes into the deep, dark awareness hidden in the folds of my heart.

This was why I loved him, because there was nothing he wouldn't do for those he loved.

It was crazy, almost, the lengths he would go to. But if anyone understood, it was me. I'd cut my heart right out of my chest if it meant he'd be safe and happy.

He smoothed those bloody hands over my cheeks up into the hair over my ears so he was palming my entire head. Only then did he tip forward and press his forehead to mine to whisper, "I won't be gone long. Five years tops for manslaughter or some shit like that. I'll ask Zeus over in Entrance to use his club's lawyer. It'll be fine, Rocky girl."

"It won't," I sobbed. "We need you. You don't deserve this."

"Neither do you," he reminded me, so fucking calm it made me want to rage at him. "You've got your mum to think about and your future. Do this for the both of us, yeah? You got in over your head, but I'm here, and I won't ever fuckin' let you down."

"No," I begged, clinging to his thick wrists. "Please, don't do this. We can both get away."

"No, we can't. But you can. Just...take care of Cleo, please. And Lin. She's a tough old bird, but she needs people to fuss over, yeah?"

"Henning," his name broke on a sob as it exploded from my throat. I ducked my head into the curve of his neck and pressed my lips to his pulse point just to feel it throb.

"You gotta get goin'. *Now*, Mei."

"I love you." The words burned through my belly and throat like dragon fire.

Henning shuddered at the heat of them and pulled me away just to press his own kiss to my forehead. It felt like a benediction from a priest, a holy anointing.

"I love you," he promised, and it was an oath.

Sirens shrieked through the air now, right in front of the farmhouse at the front of the property. Red, white, and blue lights cast apparitions in the black sky overhead.

"We gotta go," Cedar demanded, tagging my arm to wrench me away from Henning.

"No!" I screamed, scrambling to plant my feet in the muck.

Henning only watched mutely as his friend and betrayer dragged me away. His hand was still cuffed to the post, a stub where his pinky finger used to be still spilling blood through the makeshift bandage.

I bit Cedar's arm, blood flooding my mouth as he cursed. Before I could get away, he yanked me off my feet and slung me over his shoulder like a sack of potatoes, stalking through the grass with Faith and his mother, Denise, following in his wake.

I craned my head to look back at Henning, refusing to lose eye contact until the cornstalks closed around us, and he was gone from sight.

Tears ripped from my eyes and scorched into my hair line, and snot clogged my nose as I struggled to breathe. The agony of sacrifice, guilt, and heartbreak sundered through me like a thousand hot blades. I didn't even know then that it would be the last time I saw Henning Axelsen for eight long years, and the next time I did see him, he'd hate me just as much as he'd once loved me.

PART II

"A crisis is an opportunity riding the dangerous wind."
— *Chinese proverb*

CHAPTER SIXTEEN

Mei

Eight years later

2023

I hadn't been to a hospital in eight years, and three people could have compelled me to change that.

One of them had called me weeping that very day.

"Mei," Cleo had said, sobbing my name the way a disciple sobs for the mercy of their God. "I'm in the hospital, a-and I need you."

I hadn't seen Cleo in just over six months. We still met up every few months now that I lived in Vancouver, but they were clandestine meetings in tucked-away restaurants with low ratings on Tripadvisor because she didn't want Henning to know that we still spoke.

It hurt to be kept like a secret by my best friend, a forbidden thing hidden from a man who hated me and whom I still loved so fucking much.

But to be kept at all, given the circumstances, was far more than I deserved, so I met Cleo whenever she was down in Vancouver, no matter the time or day. Even if I had work, I found a way to be there for her.

I owed her that and so much more after what I'd taken from her.

She never made me feel bad for it. If anything, she seemed embarrassed and upset by her own desire to keep our continued friendship secret.

"I can't live without you," she'd say sometimes, holding my hand too-tightly in a mildew-scented café. "But he can't live with knowing I still see you."

He being Henning Axelsen.

The man who'd taken the fall for my actions and spent two years in prison.

I understood Cleo's conundrum, and I assured her all the time that I didn't care about being her little dark secret. She meant more to me than anyone else left in my life, save Old Dragon.

I'd do anything for her.

Even if that meant visiting a hospital again for the first time since Daiyu died in hospice back in Calgary.

Even if it meant potentially facing the biggest mistake I'd ever made and seeing Henning again for the first time since I'd gotten him arrested.

My hands shook as I took off my helmet and clipped it to the handlebar of my bike. They kept shaking as I entered the hospital through the automatic doors, the scent of antiseptic and sickness a toxic mix in my lungs. I hit the button to the sixth floor, where Cleo had told me they were keeping her another week to make sure she recovered well from the seven separate surgeries she'd had to undergo to stay alive. They'd taken what remained of her womb from her body, stitched up her brutalized sex, fixed the internal damage from eleven stab wounds, and sewn each one closed.

I squeezed my eyes shut so tightly that white spots bloomed in the darkness of my lids. I had to be strong for her now. I wouldn't cry when I saw the state she was in. I'd be strong and sure and gentle as a summer's breeze. I'd be her best friend and her caretaker and her mother and her sister. I'd be whatever Cleo needed me to be.

By the time I reached her room, I was breathing slow and steady, wrangling my erratic heartbeat into something fairly normal.

It all went to shit the moment I stepped into the doorway and laid eyes on her, though.

Cleo lay in the hospital bed, pale as the white sheets, her face mottled and swollen with fading bruises like the skin of a rotten fruit. Her left leg was outside the blanket, casted from hip to ankle, and there were bandages on both hands, peeking out from beneath the collar of her hospital gown.

She looked next to death.

I knew this because I'd watched my mother die in a hospital bed just like this.

Fresh horror and desolation overlaid the echo of both still reverberating through my heart so many years after Daiyu's passing, and for a long moment, I forgot how to breathe.

My entire body focused so intently on Cleo that I didn't notice the hulking presence of a man until it was too late.

"Who are you?" a low, smooth male voice demanded seconds before I was shoved into the wall beside the door, punching the air from my lungs.

After years of training, my response was automatic.

I jerked my knee into his groin and drove my knuckles into his throat simultaneously.

He wasn't expecting it.

Then again, most people didn't look at my five-foot-three height and slim build and assume I knew how to defend myself.

The man buckled in on himself, gasping in pain. I stepped out from between his body and the wall, tugging my jacket back down over my hips.

"I'm Mei," I told him coldly. "I'm here for Cleo."

Before I could step forward, he grabbed me, lightning-quick. His grasp on my forearm burned with pain, but I didn't give him the satisfaction of cringing when I looked up into his face.

Oh.

He was gorgeous.

I forgot myself for a moment and stared at him, shocked to find not only such a beautiful Indigenous man in Cleo's room but also one in the colours of The Fallen motorcycle club. It wasn't usual to see people of colour in predominately white motorcycle gangs.

He scowled at me fiercely, but it didn't impact the nature of his good looks at all. If anything, that strong-featured face and long dark hair suited his brooding expression.

"Who are you?" I asked, not as harshly as I would have a moment ago.

Because I liked this man standing guard for Cleo. I liked that he didn't let anyone, even a seemingly unassuming woman, saunter into her hospital room.

"That's Kodiak," a whisper responded from over my shoulder. "Ignore him. I try to."

I spun on my heel, wrenching my arm painfully from his hold.

Because Cleo was awake.

Her grey-green eyes were almost translucent in her brutalized face, devoid of all colour, like they'd been drained of water.

But they filled with tears the moment our gazes locked, and I was hit with a flood of memories: Cleo laughing when I tried vodka for the first time and spat it out all over both of us, Cleo crying with me when I told her my mum's diagnosis, Cleo sleeping beside me, face sweet with dreams, lashes casting long shadows on her cheeks.

Love filled me overfull until I had no choice but to burst.

Tears fell fast and silently down my cheeks, a mirror image of hers.

"Glory," I whispered, forcing the words through my too-tight throat.

My hand shook as I reached for her, walking closer until my thighs hit the bed, and I could press that hand to her head. She tilted her weight into my touch and closed her eyes, lips forming a tremulous smile glossed by her tears.

"You came," she croaked.

"Always," I promised.

"I'm sorry," she whispered through her panting breaths, her lids flashing open to reveal panicked eyes. "I need you. I-I can't do this without you. I tried for days, and I-I just can't..." She dissolved into inconsolable sobs, hissing at the pain of them wracking her recovering body.

I sat on the edge of the bed and bent awkwardly at the waist to press her face into the curve of my neck, cupping the back of her head as she cried and cried. My shirt grew soaked, my neck tight with the salt of her drying tears, but I barely noticed. All that mattered was that Cleo was *alive,* and I was with her.

After a long time, her sobs turned to whimpers and hiccoughs. She clutched at my jacket with one hand, the knuckles bruised and split in a way I recognized meant she'd fought back against her attacker. My heart throbbed like an open wound in my chest, but I held back my own meltdown until later when I was alone.

"I'm so sorry," I whispered to her, stroking her greasy, dull hair. "I'm so sorry I wasn't there to save you."

She sucked in a shaky deep breath. "I had a whole motorcycle club at my back, and they couldn't save me. I know you think you're a superhero, but don't take this on, too. Okay?"

I nodded even though I wasn't sure I could do as she asked.

"I was so dumb," she whispered, eyes closed, body growing limp with exhaustion. "I was so stupid, Mei. It makes me want to die how stupid I was to believe him."

"Not stupid," I snapped, too harsh. Kodiak half stood where he'd taken a seat in a chair near the window, ready to intervene if I upset her.

I sighed and kissed Cleo's hair. There was still a faint trace of the same Vera Wang perfume she'd worn as a girl. "You're not stupid. You're the sweetest, kindest, loveliest person I've ever known. And that psychopath took advantage of you."

"I just wanted someone of my own," she admitted, words slurring as she fell rapidly into sleep. "I'm so stupid. I deserved to die."

"Don't ever say that," I snapped again, a little too loudly, but Kodiak didn't move this time. "Don't ever say that about yourself. You did nothing to deserve this, okay?"

She didn't respond because she was asleep.

Carefully, so I didn't disturb her, I twisted to look at the huge biker folded into the small chair in the corner. He was bent over, forearms to thighs, hands hanging between his legs, head heavy on his shoulders, hair a dramatic curtain framing his shadowed face. When he sensed my gaze, he looked up at me with haunted eyes.

"Has she been talking like this a lot?" I asked him quietly.

He hesitated a moment, then nodded.

"Like she deserved what happened to her?"

Another nod. A hard swallow that he forced down with his entire body.

"Oh Glory," I whispered, bending to kiss her brow. "My sweet girl."

"How much do you know?" he whispered roughly after a long moment.

"Just what I read in the papers," I admitted with a little shiver.

"It was worse than that." Dead voice, dead eyes like black volcanic rock in his face. "So much worse than what they wrote."

I recognized the haunted pitch of his voice because I'd carried it in my own since Kate died, and it had only worsened after that night at Turner Farm.

He'd been there, maybe, or done something or not enough of something to land Cleo in that place where she'd been found brutalized by a madman.

I pressed another kiss on Cleo's head to the shorn hair beside her temple. She wiggled closer in her sleep, murmuring lowly before I stroked her cheek, and she settled once more.

"I don't know who you are," Kodiak surprised me by saying in that same low, cold voice. "But I haven't seen her so animated since it happened. You're gonna stay with her, right? She...fuck, she needs all the help she can get."

I sucked in a deep breath so I didn't sob, and then I nodded. "Yeah, I'm going to stay with her."

Cleo startled with a harsh gasp, clasping at my hand so tightly I hissed. When I met her gaze, it was panicked, pupils blown wide.

"Don't leave me," she begged with the urgency of someone who had woken from a nightmare believing it was reality. Unfortunately, for Cleo, it was. "Please, Rocky, stay with me, okay?"

I was thrown back to that night so many years ago in the basement of the House of Horrors when Cleo's mum looked at me with that same desperate urgency.

Take care of them, she'd begged.

I'd made an oath there that I'd failed to keep throughout the years, but I renewed it then as I looked into Cleo's beloved and brutalized face.

"I'm not going anywhere," I told her earnestly, carefully lying down on the edge of the bed so I could gather her gently into my arms. "I won't leave you ever again so long as you want me."

I didn't care what it meant. I'd do anything to keep my word to my best friend, even if it meant facing Henning again for the first time in almost a decade. Even if it meant I compromised all the work I'd done over the past eight years to keep my first oath to Kate.

I held Cleo close to me, the scent of hospital in my nose, the memory of our dead mothers in my mind's eye, and I knew I'd rather die than lose Cleo along with them.

CHAPTER SEVENTEEN

Axe-Man

Once, a psychologist came sniffin' around the clubhouse, wantin' to interview some brothers for a paper she was writin' about the outlaw complex. She was tryin' to sort out how men became criminals. Why they were drawn to gangs and outfits like moths to flame.

I'd asked her, *what's the worst thing that's ever happened to you?*

And do you know what she fuckin' said?

When I was nine, our family dog, Daisy, died. I was devastated.

Behind me, Wrath had laughed a cruel, gratin' cackle that made the psychologist back up three steps.

I hadn't laughed or scoffed. I'd just told the bitch to get lost. There was no way she could understand any of the men in this brotherhood with so little of her own tragedy as context.

'Cause that was it.

The glue or the catalyst or the flamin' thing that drew us all together as one unit against all else.

Tragedy.

Every single man in The Fallen MC had been through hell and come back, willingly or not. We didn't have just one hardship, one tiny tale of woe. We had a string of them like black beads in a macabre rosary.

Most of these men were broken beyond repair. Even the ones who found the love of a good woman weren't miraculously *repaired* by their connection. That love just made breathin' a little sweeter 'cause it gave them somethin' to live for.

We were all broken, and we didn't try to fix shit about each other.

We just stood together against all the tragedies of the world that inevitably came for us, and we tried to ease the burden as much as we could, even when it seemed impossible, even when it meant riskin' our lives for each other.

I could still remember the day Zeus Garro showed up at Fort Hudson Prison with my old friend Bat at his side. He was a hulkin' man, bigger than anyone else I knew. It would have been funny, watchin' him cram himself into the tiny phone cubicle if I'd been in a place to find anythin' funny.

"Brother," he'd said into the plastic phone, the thing tiny in his huge paw. "It's been too long since I set eyes on ya, and I gotta say, I'd rather it was happenin' under better circumstances."

I'd stared at him.

"Let me get straight to it, then. I know the Calgarian fucks turned against ya, one of their fuckin' own." He paused to swallow back the roar of anger buildin' in his voice, shakin' off the yoke of rage like water on a wet dog. "Want you to know that's been dealt with."

"Dealt how?" I'd already put Whitey, Dunkirk, and Rooster into early graves. What else was there to take care of?

"Sent some brothers from my crew with Bat to clean up there. We're startin' from scratch. Onc'a my men stayed back to help recruit and set up a new crew. It's somethin'a his speciality, so Calgary'll be in better hands now than it ever was with motherfuckin' Rooster in the chair."

I didn't say anythin', mostly 'cause if I'd been a quiet man before the clink, I was near on silent now.

Zeus appraised me with shrewd eyes, brows lowered over them in a glower I knew masked a sharp mind. "What they did to you wasn't right, brother. Rooster wasn't dead, I'd do the deed myself. Fallen don't turn against Fallen."

One of my brows ticked up in a small show of incredulity. It was club lore that Zeus killed his own damn uncle to gain the presidency of the mother chapter.

He grinned wolfishly in response, leanin' close to the glass. Some basic human instinct in my nervous system screamed at me to lean away from the predator, even separated as we were by the partition.

"Some things are thicker than blood, and this brotherhood is one'a 'em. Someone does one'a mine wrong, they pay for it with their life, and that payment is takin' the hard way, you get me? Any other chapter'a the club, you'd'a seen that, but 'specially in *my* club. People think biker moral codes are a little shaky, but I see things fuckin' clear. There are no bad deeds done to those who fuck with the good people'a The Fallen. *My* people. Other clubs, gangs, civilians, they all know that 'cause my reputation precedes me." Another feral grin. "So the men who ride with me and their families are safe. Or safe as they can be livin' the kinda life we gotta lead."

My gaze found Bat, who opened his hands to me in silent offerin'. I just didn't get what it was on offer 'til later.

Zeus echoed the movement, leanin' back to open his hands and shrug pseudo-casually. "Listen, we haven't talked much about my past, but I was in the joint for a spell, too, and I got kids. I get what it is to be parted from 'em." He hit his fist against his chest brutally. "Kills ya every fuckin' day."

I swallowed thickly but didn't say a word. Barely a minute went by when I wasn't thinkin' and worryin' about Cleo.

"Wanted to come here and offer to look after your girl for you while you're inside. I get we've only spent two weeks years ago gettin' a feel for one another, but you know Bat and you know Smoke. They're good men, and our club's full'a'em. Bat told me your girl and your stepmum are lookin' to move. The club's got a house in a good area in Entrance. You want it, it's theirs. Couple'a the guys, they got kids too, good ones. They'd be happy to meet your Cleo. Not to mention, I got a daughter 'round about her age, and fuck knows, my girl could use some more goodness in her life."

"Why?" I demanded through my gritted teeth, my fist clenchin' and unclenchin' on the table.

I'd learned the hard way, many times, not to trust anyone. Even though I'd fought with Bat, had his back as much as he had mine, it went against everythin' I'd hoped I'd learned to trust this man and even my friend to look out for the only two loved ones I had left in the world. The impression he'd made on me as a good man beneath the violence and edge of aggression, a man with a keen mind to back up his brutal fists, didn't matter much to me at the moment.

Zeus stared at me then, his eyes glintin' like silver blades. For all his height and weight, the scars visible on his knuckles, and the tatts peekin' out of his shirt, there was a kind of gentleness in his expression. An openness like he was exposin' somethin' to me he didn't often offer to people.

"I'll tell ya the full story one day, but let's just say I was fucked by my club once too. Went to prison for what they made me do one day. I don't like to see it happen to a man I'm told is a good brother. A brother I *know* to be a solid man."

"So what, you take care of my girls, and when I get out, I

transfer to your chapter and do your dirty work? I was an axe for Rooster. I won't be one ever again."

Zeus shrugged. "You can do whatever the fuck you want, man. You get out, and it suits ya to hang around the club, get a feel for the kinda brotherhood we got on offer, then yeah, that'd be cool. I'm thinkin' we'd be fuckin' lucky to have a man like you in the fold. Every brother in the club's gotta choose what kinda role he wants to play and how it plays to his strengths. You don't wanna be the axe, fuck, we already got a blade for an enforcer. You could do whatever the fuck. But you get out and want shit all to do with the club, then yeah, sure. I get it. One chapter fucked you, maybe you're too burned. There are no strings here, honest to fuck. I'm here 'cause the kinda man I am, I couldn't know there was a good man who'd been fucked over wastin' away in a cell worryin' about his daughter without protection."

We locked eyes, takin' each other's measure. After six months in prison, I'd learned more than I ever fuckin' wanted to about readin' people, and I saw nothin' but sincerity in that man's face.

"I'll leave ya to think on it," he said, knockin' his knuckles against the glass like a goodbye.

He got up, clapped Bat on the shoulder, and then went to the door to get the guard to let him out.

Bat took his place, pickin' up the receiver to say, "You remember those nights lyin' on top'a buildings in the cold lookin' up at the stars while we waited for daybreak? We wondered what the fuck we were fightin' for? Just eighteen-year-old kids without a fuckin' clue."

He leaned closer, nose almost to the plexiglass. His face was one I'd seen at so many dangerous moments of my life, a touchstone amid the chaos. I trusted him the way only military men can trust each other, a bond forged in dirt and violence, in blood and tears and sweat and fear so blindin' it threatened to blot out all the rest. He'd aged and changed over the years, but those black eyes in that face were the same ones I'd trusted to have my back since I was eighteen.

"I got more than one thing to fight for now," he continued. "My boys, Steele and Shaw, just like you got Cleo. But I also got a brotherhood, the kind we lost after we were discharged; the kind that seems so foreign to you sittin' there behind bars 'cause a brotherhood of bastards put you there. The Fallen gave me a home when I was homeless, lost somewhere back in the Afghani forests, my spirit thin as a fuckin' ghost. You saw him give that snot-nosed teenager, Jonathon Booth, a chance at a different kinda life, and that man's a brother now, good as they fuckin' come and thrivin' wearin' our cut. They can give that to you, too, brother. To you and Lin and Cleo. You just gotta take that first fuckin' terrifyin' step and trust someone again after bein' betrayed."

He'd left me then without gettin' an answer.

But three weeks later, Lin and Cleo moved to Entrance, BC.

And two and a half years after that, I followed them when I got out early for good behaviour.

It was the best decision I ever fuckin' made, second only to marryin' Kate and adoptin' my Cleo.

That was only reinforced now after my worst fuckin' nightmare had come true and my daughter, my fuckin' Glory, was raped and left for dead by a fuckin' serial-killing psychopath.

Seth Linley, "The Prophet," was dead. Killed by our club enforcer, Priest McKenna. It shoulda made me feel somethin' good, relieved, or vindicated, but instead, I felt my anger calcify like somethin' undernourished. My fury wanted to fuckin' *feed,* and what the fuck could I feed it if not the blood of the man responsible for almost murderin' my kid?

It was two weeks after the assault. After Kodiak and Priest found her in a fuckin' field beside Bat's dead wife, Amelia. Over a week since Priest saved Bea from that lunatic and took him down.

But I could not get a handle on this fuckin' anger.

Without my brothers, I would've been out on a violent tear through Entrance, lookin' up old enemies just for a chance to get some blood on my hands to feed the beast ravenin' at my soul.

As it was, Wrath's blood would have to do.

My fist connected with the hard edge of his chin, slammin' his head back with a *snap*. Wrath Marsden was a big man, nearly as big as Zeus, who was a fuckin' giant, and he was a mean sonovabitch who'd been workin' as a thug on the streets since he was a teen. Landin' a hit on him was a fuckin' miracle, one he'd probably allowed me 'cause I needed it so bad.

Curtains and Boner hooted and hollered from outside the ring, urgin' us on.

Box n' Burn was Wrath's gym, backed by the club. King had suggested it when Wrath was fully patched in, sayin' it was a good business idea but also a great idea for the club. A place for us hotheads to let off steam when needed.

Mostly, it was to give Wrath, whose own woman had been murdered years ago, somethin' to do with his life now that she was gone.

Wrath swiped his forearm over his bloody mouth and grinned at me with red-painted teeth. "Not bad for an old man."

I bared my teeth at him and launched a combination at his head--jab, jab, right cross, upper cut. He dodged or blocked them all, then immediately countered with his own flurry of powerful strikes. One hit me in the side just over my kidneys, pushin' the air from my body in an explosive exhale.

"Feelin' good now?" Wrath taunted.

I wiped his blood from my knuckles across my cheek like war paint and grinned ferally at him. There was too much anger and horror in my chest to purge in a mock fight, even against a tough opponent like Wrath, but it was better than nothin'.

"Hey, Axe-Man," Heckler called from the office doorway. "You got a call."

"Next hit wins," I told Wrath a second before I lunged for him.

He took an instinctive step back, which I'd counted on because my lungin' foot was placed just behind his heel. He tripped backward, fallin' into the rope and bouncin' lightly back up with perfect timin' to meet the hammer of my fist against his cheek.

I loomed over him, pantin' viciously, sweat pourin' from me like salted rain. When he stood back up, workin' his jaw, I tore off the gloves with my teeth and offered him my hand.

"Dirty play," Wrath praised, takin' off his own gloves to clasp hands with me. "You've come a long fuckin' way from the rule abider you were when you first stepped into this ring."

I rolled my eyes. "Most gyms praise etiquette. Not playin' dirty."

Wrath grinned, that mean curl of lips that didn't quite reach his eyes. "Yeah, well. Those gyms aren't owned by The Fallen."

"Axe-Man," Heckler hollered again, wavin' my cell in the air. "You got a call, man."

"Who is it?"

"Kodiak."

A chill instantly swept through my body. I was leapin' up and over the boxin' ring and stalkin' toward him with a scowl the next moment.

"You didn't think I'd wanna know it was Kodiak on the fuckin' line?" I growled. "He's lookin' out at Cleo's bedside."

Heckler shrugged, but there was an edge to his expression, a childish kinda petulance that coiled that anger in my belly a little tighter. I shoved him into the wall and wrenched my cell outta his hand.

"'Lo," I said into the speaker. "What's wrong?"

There was a brief pause. "Nothin' wrong, exactly. There's some girl here to visit Cleo, though."

I sighed, suddenly fuckin' exhausted. "My girl's got a lotta friends. As long as they don't upset her or some shit, it's good for her to have the company."

"Yeah, man, I know. Just...I don't recognize this one. There've been the usual girls in and out the past couple of weeks, but this one's new."

"You sure?"

"Woman's got a face you don't forget. Not to mention, I'm sittin' vigilant at the bedside of a woman who means somethin' to me who was attacked. I'm thinkin' if there's a time I ever forget a face connected with Cleo, it won't be for a good few decades at least."

I grunted my own agreement, then trapped my cell between my shoulder and ear so I could grab my gym bag and wrestle my tee out from inside. The cotton stuck to my skin as I pulled it over my head, but I was in a rush. If there was some strange girl in with Cleo, there was no way I wasn't headin' over there to check it out.

"I'll be there in twenty-five," I told him. "Cleo's okay?"

"She fell asleep the second this girl put her hands on her," Kodiak said in that muted voice of his, a little awe creepin' into the deadpan.

We both knew Cleo hadn't been sleepin' for shit since the accident. Only the drugs the nurses gave her for the pain helped, and I dreaded what we'd do when she was discharged soon.

Who the hell was this girl with her?

Cleo was a reporter at the local newspaper in Entrance, and she had a ton of friends, though none as close to her as Bea and the rest of the Old Ladies in The Fallen. If it wasn't one of them with her, I assumed it was some woman from the paper I'd never met before. The girls who worked with my daughter there tended to make themselves scarce when I was around. It could've been my cut, the club, but they seemed fine to visit when it was King or Nova standin' vigil with Cleo, so I suspected it had more to do with my temperament than anythin' else.

"Call me if anythin' changes," I told my brother, who grunted in affirmation before hangin' up.

"All good?" Curtains asked from behind me.

I turned to face our red-headed hacker, scrubbin' a hand over my face and back into the hair I'd tied back for the fight. The band came loose, and the heavy mass of gold swept down across my shoulders.

"Some new visitor for Cleo."

Curtains had huge green eyes on his pale face, his gaze sharp as fresh sea glass. "You want me to do some diggin'?"

A flood of warmth in my icy chest. Curtains was practically a kid next to me, but there was no denyin' he was one of my closest brothers in the club. We were both geeks in our own way. I was the only man in our chapter other than King who'd been to university, and Curtains was born some kinda genius. We got each other, and we worked together on club financials and business specs.

But none of that meant anythin' without this right here.

The casual, easy offer to look into someone for my peace of mind.

I clapped the kid on the shoulder and squeezed. "Yeah, let me head down there and figure out who she is. Could just be some sweet girl from Cleo's office."

"Could be," he agreed, but we both knew with the world we lived in that the odds of easy answers were slim.

Zeus was in the waitin' room when I arrived at the hospital, sippin' on a thin Styrofoam cup of coffee that looked miniature in his hand. A group of female nurses nearby whispered to each other as they checked out the huge dude in the recognizable leather cut. They were frightened, yeah, but more they were curious, lustfully intrigued. It never failed to amaze me how well trepidation coupled with desire. The moment they noticed me, their titterin' increased.

When I cocked an eyebrow at Zeus in question, he shrugged and fell into step with me down the hall to Cleo's room.

"Kodiak called. Said he had a bad feelin'."

A ripple of apprehension rolled down my spine. I picked up my pace.

"He say why?"

Zeus shrugged, rubbin' a hand over his beard. "You know The Bear, just said he gotta feelin'."

Yeah, I knew Kodiak and his feelings. They never signalled anythin' good.

We reached the open door of Cleo's room, and the knot of tension in my gut loosened when my gaze locked on Cleo fast asleep in her bed. I had to force breath into my lungs at the sight of her like that even though she was actually lookin' better every day. No parent seein' their kid broken up in a hospital bed breathes easy, though. I seriously doubted I ever would again.

I'd let down the two most important women in my life, and it was nearly impossible to live with that.

"Didn't mean to make you worry," Kodiak said quietly from his sentry position. "Wasn't thinkin' straight. 'Course, I triggered you."

I shrugged, sweepin' a hand back over my hair as I sucked in a steadyin' breath. "No harm. It pays to be cautious."

My gaze was pulled back to the bed, lookin' over at the girl who'd ticked Kodiak's fuckin' spidey senses. She was thin, pale skin inked in black designs peekin' out the sleeves of an oversized leather jacket, dark hair like black silk on the rough pillowcase.

Stirred by my gaze, she shifted her head outta Cleo's neck, uncoverin' a pretty face I knew all too well even after all this time.

I took an instinctive step back, slammin' into the door so it banged hard into the wall. The loud noise woke both girls up, twin sets of blinkin' eyes trained on me, one pale greenish-grey and the other black.

Blood roared in my ears, drownin' out every other sound. My muscles twitched, clenched so tight they fought the urge to release. Emotions stormed my insides, tearin' at the seams of old wounds, pullin' out stitches that should've dissolved long ago.

The dark-haired girl recovered first, slowly easin' out of bed so she didn't jostle Cleo, and then gainin' her feet. She was older, eight years older than the last time I saw her, but *fuck*, she looked the same.

Slippery black hair movin' around her shoulders like black rain, wide eyes under delicate winged brows. A mouth that looked as pink as pomegranate juice. The only differences were the tattoos visible on her low forearms, another coilin' from her back over the side of her neck, and the last of a childish plumpness dissolvin' from her face, leavin' the ridge of her cheekbones sharp above the faint hollows in her cheeks. A distant part of my brain noticed she'd grown into a real beauty. The knock-you-down-drag-your-heart-straight-outta-your-chest kinda beautiful no red-blooded man could resist.

Mei Zhen Marchand in the fuckin' flesh.

"Henning," she said in that smooth, feminine voice, and the tension inside me *snapped*.

I was movin' without thought, eatin' up the space between us and then haulin' her into the air by the lapels of her leather jacket, the same one she'd found at a thrift shop in Calgary one day with Cleo and me. I pushed her none-too-gently against the wall and leaned close to snarl into her face, but the scent of her fragrance hit me in the face like a slap.

Cherry blossoms, fresh and sweet.

It threw me back to all the hugs we'd shared, to the memories of sittin' across from each other at the kitchen table, the scrape of pencil on paper as we sketched, the sound of her laughter mixed with Cleo's, the vision of the two of them curled together like yin and yang in another hospital bed the day after Kate was killed.

Grief and fury tangled in my gut like fire and gasoline, racin' up my throat, so when I spoke, the heat of my words made her flinch.

"What the fuck are you doin' here?" I growled into her face. "I told you to stay the fuck away from us."

"Cleo needed me," she said, totally calm and cool.

Her eyes always looked black from afar, but up close, they were warm and rich as something alive—tilled soil, pine bark, mink.

I snapped my teeth at her, furious with us both. "She needed us both eight years ago, but you fucked off. What she needs now is *peace,* and you've never known what the hell that is."

She opened her mouth to say somethin', but I couldn't stand one more word from that mouth, so I pressed one hand over it and leaned even closer, my nose brushin' hers.

"You stay the fuck away from my family, Mei Zhen. If I see you around here again, you'll learn just how much prison changed me, you understand? I am not your friend, and you sure as fuck don't want me for an enemy."

"Dad," Cleo tried to interject, but I couldn't take my eyes off the ghost trapped in my hold.

"I promised Kate I'd take care of her," Mei whispered, eyes beseechin' and wide. "Of both of you."

"Yeah, well, you're eight years too late to keep that oath," I snarled. Done with her, done with the way my heart pounded like a fist against my ribs, I tossed Mei's slight frame up and over my shoulder in a fireman's carry.

Cleo's protests followed me as I stalked out the door and down the hall to the staircase because I wasn't waitin' for the elevator. I took the stairs down two by two, nearly jumpin' from step to step. The feel of Mei against me burned through my clothes to my skin and down into my bones.

Later, I'd realized she hadn't struggled at all. The girl I knew could've put up a decent fight, even against my bulk, but she just lay over my shoulder like a sack of potatoes.

A few nurses protested when I reached the main floor and prowled through the admission area, but the second they caught sight of my Fallen MC cut, they fell silent and wary.

The moment I passed the automatic glass doors onto the sidewalk, I dropped her unceremoniously to the ground.

My chest was heavin', heart racin' so madly in my chest I had no hope of catchin' it and wranglin' it into a steadier pace. It hurt to watch Mei straighten, to see the way she bit at the end of a faintly tremblin' lip to keep it still. It hurt to watch the familiar old defiance flare in her expression as she set her shoulders straight and looked up to meet my gaze.

It hurt to see my own pain reflected back at me, years of confusion and loss and anger as tangled and deep as the roots of an old growth tree.

"She needs me," she said, voice strong and sure. "What she just went through...please, Henning, don't make her recover alone."

"She won't be alone." I felt like hollerin', like some mournful wolf callin' for a home that no longer existed. "She's *never* been alone. I got her back, *always*, and now we got a family who'd never abandon us. Not for anythin'. You're not a part of that, and you never fuckin' will be again. So leave now before I do somethin' I regret, and don't you ever fuckin' think about comin' back."

She stared at me, chin canted at the haughty angle she'd perfected when she was twelve. Only, she wasn't the same twelve-year-old girl who'd stood broken and bloodied before my dyin' wife with a *dao* sword in her hand, ready to defend them both.

I had no fuckin' clue who she was now, and I didn't want to know. If I never saw her again, it still wouldn't be enough. I wanted her scrubbed from my brain, her name erased, her presence purged.

I wanted to be rid of the agony of lovin' and hatin' her and the confusion that arose in the thin line between the two.

"I'm sorry," she said, so soft I almost didn't hear. "I'm sorry for everything that happened. That I was the reason you went to prison and that I couldn't see you until it was too late, and you'd already started to hate me. I'm sorry for so many things, but most of all, I'm sorry I hurt you. You're still the best man I've ever known, and you deserve a lot more than what I did to you. There hasn't been one day since I last saw you that I haven't loved you both from afar. So fine, I'll go, and I'll stay away from you, but I can't promise I won't be here for Cleo. Not when she needs me."

"Leave her alone," I demanded, steppin' forward, fists curled. "I mean it, Mei."

Her smile was thin and self-mockin' as she started to back away, hands in the pockets of that ridiculously oversized leather jacket. "Don't you remember, Hen? I've never been much good at following orders."

She turned on her heel and jogged lightly around the building toward the side parkin' lot, a flash of black hair caught in the wind my last sight of her. Still, I stood there for a long time, breathin' like a stuck bull, tryin' to exist around the wound she'd reopened at the heart of me. Maybe another time, when my daughter hadn't been raped and left for dead, I could've remained unaffected by the sight of my old friend, my old downfall.

But my armour was in shambles around my feet, broken to bits by my sense of failure and horror havin' been unable to protect Cleo. So the blade of Mei's reappearance had pierced me right through my already failing heart, and now, all I could do was stand there in the entrance to St. Katherine's hospital bleedin' out with no hope of bein' saved by the doctors or nurses inside it.

"So that was Mei."

I wasn't surprised to hear Z's rough growl behind me, but I still tensed, an animal response to another predator approachin' when I was weak.

My only answer was a grunt.

He was silent for a long spell, just standin' next to me in solidarity. It never failed to amaze me that a man built like a weapon could so often know the perfect way to soothe his band of unmerry men.

"It's funny," he said at length, clampin' a hand on my shoulder. "How our demons can have such pretty fuckin' faces and cause us so much damn pain."

"She broke Cleo's heart." My voice was weak, stripped bare by the emotion tearin' me up from the inside out.

"She broke yours, too," he said, heavy and firm, so there was no room for me to argue with him.

"Not much left to break by the time she got around to it," I half denied.

Z's pause was long enough to make me want to squirm like a kid caught in a lie. No one in the club knew anythin' about my history before I arrived in Entrance fresh from the joint, save Zeus and Bat. I'd never had reason to regret them knowin' 'til now.

"You got one'a the biggest hearts I know, Axe-Man, so I can't say I agree with that shit. But sometimes we gotta tell ourselves lies to get through the hard times, so I'll leave you be."

"Appreciated," I muttered sarcastically, even though some of the tension in my shoulders dissipated in relief.

When Zeus wanted to, the man was like a dog with a bone about these things, and I was in no frame of mind to handle probin' questions about Mei.

"Just to say," he added, and I tensed again, knowin' he was about to land a final blow. "Cleo obviously kept in touch with the kid. She obviously loves her the way Cleo loves everyone in her heart. Balls to the wall, ride or die. Your girl is a *giver*, just like her dad. Seems to me, if she called Mei, it was 'cause she needed her right now. And she needs her right now 'cause the road she's on to healin' from this horror? She's gonna need to *take,* and there are only a handful'a people Cleo feels comfortable doin' that shit with. You get me?"

I swallowed the stone that was lodged in my throat and actively worked to unclench my fists.

Yeah, I knew.

I knew firsthand just how ironclad the bond was between

souls bound together by trauma. I'd watched a normal childhood friendship between girls blossom into a relationship the likes of which I'd never seen 'til I moved to Entrance and watched King with Mute, Boner with Curtains, Harleigh Rose and Lila, Cress and Lou, Zeus and Bat, and Bat and Dane. Some friendships would never die, even when you buried them alive, and I knew in my gut Cleo and Mei's was one of them.

The thing that pissed me off as much as it scared the hell outta me was that after my reaction seein' Mei today, I was worried our relationship was one of them as well.

And I didn't know if I had the strength I needed to put the final nail in that coffin, just as I didn't know if I'd be able to survive another betrayal from that girl I used to love.

CHAPTER EIGHTEEN

Mei

The drive from Vancouver to Entrance wasn't long, especially without traffic clogging the winding artery wrapped around the mountains along the coast of British Columbia, and the scenery was gorgeous enough to make the time slip by pleasantly enough.

Unfortunately, neither the mountains nor the silvery blue-grey of the ocean under a wintery cloud-covered sky or the dulcet tunes of Labrinth through the Bluetooth in my helmet could take my mind off impending doom.

And doom they would be because eight years after being scorned by Henning Axelsen, I was on my way to his very doorstep.

I had no doubt if he was home, he'd slam the door in my face.

Maybe he'd even call the cops.

But I told myself I didn't care.

Eight years might have passed, but what bearing did time have on the storage capacity of the human heart? Ma had died almost a decade ago, and I missed her every single day. It was nearly the same for Kate. Cleo and I hadn't seen each other for ages, and she'd still called me from her hospital bed days after a psycho fucking serial killer cut her up from the inside out and left her to die in a fallow field.

Eight seconds, eight years, eight decades, I didn't give a damn.

My Cleo needed me, I'd do whatever it took to be there for her.

Even if it meant I had to face the biggest mistake I'd made in my life.

My palms were slick with nervous sweat in my leather gloves, and the hum of the bike beneath my body didn't soothe me the way it usually did. I drove a Kawasaki Ninja motorcycle, a far cry from the growling rumble of a Harley, but today it reminded me too much of being on the back of Henning's bike, the sensation of his strong body manipulating the heavy machinery with ease, the feel of his warmth soaking into me through the leather on his back.

Even though Cleo and I had kept in regular contact with emails, Skype calls, texts, and the occasional letter, and then, after I moved to Vancouver, with infrequent coffee dates, I still felt the loss of her presence in my life like a phantom limb every single day so the idea of seeing her again, of holding her, and caring for her after this new nightmare she'd endured was a gift I would cherish no matter what.

No matter that it meant facing Henning after his violent reaction to seeing me at the hospital six weeks ago. I'd only seen such fury on his face twice before. The day he found Kate strung from the ceiling of the House of Horrors and the day Rooster's Fallen Men had betrayed him.

To think he might hate me as much as he did Rooster Cavendish or the people who killed Kate made acid eat through the lining of my gut.

But I'd never been the kind of woman to shy away from confrontation, not when I was fighting for something that mattered.

And Cleo mattered to me more than almost anyone.

When she called me two weeks ago for our weekly check-in, she'd been sobbing. These great, tearing sobs seemed to crack open her entire chest. She hadn't begged me to be there for her, but she'd come close, and I'd never heard Cleo beg for anything before. Her body was healing, but she was living in a state of perpetual fear since the assault. I'd read once that fear and trauma made people regress to an earlier state. Hospital patients frequently asked for their favourite childhood stuffed toy or their mothers.

Cleo couldn't have her mother, but I was happy to be stand-in for her stuffed rabbit. If she wanted me by her side through her journey of healing, I'd be there. Even if it meant fighting her own father to do so.

I shivered in my leather jacket and opened the throttle a little more.

Years ago, after what went down, I'd written to Henning.

Letters and emails, so many of them I had a drawer stuffed with "return to sender" envelopes and a folder in my inbox labelled Henning filled with emails he'd probably never even opened.

After my first visit to the prison, he refused to add me to his visitor list, and when he got out of prison two years later, I was too much of a chickenshit to try to visit him again.

He'd made his decision clear.

He'd fallen on a sword for me, but the consequence was eternal banishment from his life.

Sometimes, I wished he'd let me bear the consequences of

my mistakes back then, not only for his sake but selfishly, for my own. Maybe then I'd still be someone to him.

As it stood, he was still everything to me.

I was twenty-five years old, and I'd only ever been in love once, and maybe even to say that was misleading. I'd only ever loved once because I was *still* in love with him.

The best man I'd ever known.

When Florent sent me away after that night at Turner Farm, I'd been forced into daily therapy sessions. My therapist there, Mr. Cox, had proclaimed that I only thought I was in love with Henning because he was the first man outside my family to show me kindness. I'd told him he should get a refund from the university that issued his psychology degree because he was a shit therapist.

You didn't fall in love with someone simply because they were *nice*. Nice should be a given, a social prerogative. You fell in love with someone because they felt like the only person who could see through your skin and bones straight down to the soul, and even knowing all of you––the good, the bad, the motherfucking ugly––they still accepted you.

As terrified as I was to face Henning and, therefore, the biggest mistake I'd ever made, I was also unaccountably *giddy* at the idea of seeing him in the flesh again. He was forty now, aged in ways I hadn't had the chance to digest at the hospital, living a life full of question marks I'd finally be able to answer.

I only knew the basics of Henning's life after he got out, because Cleo was deliberately vague about him. After he'd left prison, he'd transferred to the notorious mother chapter of The Fallen MC, run by a man by the name of Zeus Garro, who was as infamous as his club. They owned the Sea to Sky Highway, the strip of asphalt that linked the entire province of British Columbia together like a vital artery, and ran drugs and guns up and down the coast. There might have been other gangs in Vancouver, a few small ones on Vancouver Island, but there was nothing to rival the stronghold The Fallen had on the whole province.

Though many tried.

I'd been surprised to learn Henning would go back to the club after the disaster that befell him with Rooster's Calgary chapter. He'd never been naturally criminal or rebellious in my estimation, not like me. Yet last I'd heard, and not from Cleo, Henning was an officer for the club, the Treasurer and Secretary, who ran their finances and laundered their money.

From doctor to money launderer.

A shift that had occurred largely, I knew, because of me.

I'd made him into a criminal, so could I really judge him for staying the path so many years later? What hospital would let him practice with a criminal record?

I turned a long curving corner up a steep incline and then levelled out, a carved wooden sign with wolves and bears appearing to my left.

Welcome to Entrance, BC.

The town presented itself like a postcard as I hit residential streets and then, Main Street. It was quaint, the buildings old and carefully maintained, the streetlamps antique, and the main square prettily landscaped even in the cold winter months. The cold air was scented with the brine of the ocean wafting up from the bay where I could just make out the tops of sailboats bobbing on the waves. I could see why Cleo would love it. It was as pretty as a picture.

The only incongruous detail came from the line of shiny-backed motorcycles parked outside of a place called Stella's Diner. Within the huge front windows, I could see two booths packed with men in leather cuts, the back of one clearly depicting a skull with fiery wings and the top rocker reading *The Fallen*. The sound of my own motorbike must have alerted those closest to the door to my presence because a dark-haired man packed with muscle walked to the window to study me through the glass where I waited at a red light. He was handsome even from afar, something about him tickling the back of my mind.

The light turned green before I could think more about it, and I gunned forward, letting the GPS on my phone give me directions through the Bluetooth in my helmet to the place Cleo now called home.

It took a further twenty minutes to reach the secluded address, but as soon as there was a break in the thick forest, I understood why Henning had chosen the spot to make their home. The large lake was bright in the grey light, a polished pool of melted-down aquamarine the same shade as Henning's eyes. At its edge sat one house, a rustic log cabin built of dark wood with a painted green front door. As I pulled up the gravel driveway to park before the separate garage, that front door swung open, and a familiar figure filled the space.

Cleopatra Joan Axelsen.

I swung off the bike in one fluid motion, taking off my gloves as I went. My hair caught in the helmet as I pulled it off, but I ignored the pain and dumped the bucket to the ground, already running toward the stairs.

I took them two at a time, heart thumping so madly I thought I might faint before I reached her.

Happily, I didn't.

It had only been six weeks since I visited in the hospital, and we'd gone much longer stints without seeing each other, but under the circumstances, it was six weeks too many. Even the two weeks it had taken me that long to figure out how to take time away from Vancouver to temporarily move up here to be closer to her had dragged on painfully slow.

My sight was blurry, warped by tears, as I reached out for her mid-step, but I caught the motion of her reaching right back, gripping me by the forearm to tug me into her body.

Vaguely, I was aware of a clatter as something fell to the deck, but it was only later that I realized it was a pair of crutches.

We pressed together gently because Cleo was still so weak, but our molecules fused back together so tightly it seemed organic, two magnets meeting after years apart. Once again united the way we were always meant to be.

I wasn't sure who it was who sobbed first, an explosion of tears pressed out of the eyes and gasping mouth, but the other soon followed.

We stood on the front porch in the cold, wrapped so tightly there was no space between our bodies, her face in my neck and mine in hers. There were so many reasons to cry that we cried for a very, very long time. I cried for our separation and the ways her body was different against mine, brittle and frail like she hadn't eaten in weeks. I cried for what was done to her and taken from her. I cried for the shame of not being there to protect her and for the way she still smelled the same, like Vera Wang perfume, after all these years apart.

Mostly, I cried because holding her felt like coming home.

"My Mei," she murmured into my hair, clutching me tight enough to hurt, her nails curling into my leather jacket. "My Mei."

I pressed a kiss on to her temple and then peppered more all over the side of her head when it was obvious one wasn't going to be enough. The bruising that had mottled her face in the hospital was gone now, at least, and only a faint scar at her right temple was still visible. I kissed it three times as if my lips could erase the history of the mark.

"Hi, Glory," I whispered, forcing the words through my too-tight throat. "I'm so fucking sorry it took me so long to get here. That...that I wasn't here in the first place."

She made an animal kind of whine in her throat, pressing impossibly closer. "You're here, now. Just...just promise you won't leave again like you did before. I need you."

My heart ached like a fresh wound. I pulled back to cup Cleo's beautiful, gaunt face in my hands and promised in the same voice I'd once promised her mother, "I'm not going anywhere, okay?"

She placed her hands over mine on her face, one arm bent at a sharp angle by the cast that stretched from below her armpit all the way to her wrist. "Thank you."

Someone cleared their throat from behind Cleo in the doorway. Without thinking, I turned us so I was in front of Cleo before swirling to face the stranger.

My protective instincts were a little laughable, considering the woman had been inside Cleo's home with her, and it was even more ridiculous when I saw the fine-boned, almost waifish blonde who stood there. She was unbelievably pretty, almost doll-like, with wide blue eyes and thick pale hair that curled over the breast of her pink sweater dress. The wickedly sharp knife she had clutched easily in one hand seemed completely out of place on her person as did the swell of an unmistakable pregnant belly beneath her dress. Not only did she seem too young to be a mother, she seemed too...ridiculously pure to be a teen mum. I wondered snidely if it had been an immaculate conception.

"Oh," Cleo exhaled on a little laugh, stepping up beside me to take my hand. "Mei, this is my best friend, Beatrice Lafayette. Bea, this is my Mei Zhen Marchand."

Bea and I stared at each other for a long moment, both of us warring, I thought, with our respective importance to Cleo. She was her *best friend* now, but she still called me hers like I'd been born to her. A feeling I reciprocated.

I wondered how much Cleo had changed that her new best friend wore pink unironically and looked like some kind of Barbie doll when her old best friend was in shit kickers and the same vintage leather jacket I'd worn when we were teens.

"It's nice to finally meet you, Mei," Bea said, her voice sweet as sugar pie, perfectly in keeping with her image. She lifted the hem of her loose sweater dress to slide the knife back into its sheaf strapped around her thigh and bent to pick up Cleo's discarded crutches. After handing them off to her, she offered me a slim hand, one I shook after a moment's hesitation. "I wish it was under better circumstances."

I nodded, because I didn't have anything else to say.

Luckily, we were distracted from awkwardness by the need to get Cleo inside. I realized immediately that she shouldn't have been out of bed, let alone out in the cold. She was rail thin, her bones harsh shards like glass threatening to poke through her skin. It was difficult for her to even manoeuvre the weight of the two huge casts. The main room of the cabin was fairly huge, the kitchen along the back wall with a big island and hanging copper pots above it, the living room to the right, and the dining room with a massive raw edge wood table set to the left. Above the kitchen was the exposed hallway of a second story, a wooden railing separating the floor from the drop below. Big rough-hewn wooden beams arched overhead, and massive windows along both sides of the house exposed a view of the lake to one side and the forest to the other. The furniture was oversized to fit the scale of the space, dark wood, deep chocolate leather, and homey touches like a handknit blanket thrown over the couch and books here and there over different surfaces.

It was completely unlike Henning and Cleo's small bungalow in Calgary yet it suited them--Henning--perfectly.

I lost my breath to its perfection, literally sucking in short, sharp breaths as I took everything in while Cleo led me to the L-shaped leather couch. My fingers traced the ink over the cushions, swirling patterns I knew had been made by Henning's expert hand in coloured ink pens.

It was only when we were sitting beside each other, knees

pressed together, our tangled hands between us, that I finally took in the changes in Cleo herself.

And I lost my breath even more to that.

She clearly wasn't well.

I knew from her texts that she was recovering from the assault by the serial killer the media coined "The Prophet," but it looked as if she was held together with barely a hope and a prayer. Her once gorgeous, thick golden-brown hair was cut in a ragged, awful style, short as a boy's, and her bones pressed too-hard against her skin, deep hollows beneath her cheekbones and around her wide, dulled sage-green eyes.

I pressed a fist to my mouth to keep in the sob, taking Cleo's thin hand with me when I did.

Her expression collapsed in on itself, lips trembling, brows bowed under the strain of her frown. "I know...I don't look so pretty anymore."

"You'll always be beautiful," I told her honestly. The other girl, Bea, was totally forgotten even though she sat three feet away in a chair. "But this...God, my heart breaks just looking at you. What did he do to you...?" I let the question trail away because it was rhetorical, but Cleo seemed to take it seriously.

"Everything," she whispered. "Everyone says I should talk to someone about it. I-I had some meetings with a trauma psychologist at the hospital, but...how can I find the words?"

She swayed toward me, planting her face in my neck so she could whisper her heartbreaking words against my ear. "He took my womb from me, Mei. I'll never have kids."

My eyes squeezed shut so tightly I saw exploding stars. Idly, I wondered if I was watching my heart fragment into pieces.

Cleo had always wanted children. She was the kind of girl who grew up thinking about her wedding to a good, kind man with a stable job and living in a house with a white picket fence and two-point-five children. She was wholesome, not because she'd been raised in a wholesome environment by wholesome people, but because she *had not*.

All my sweet Cleo had ever dreamt of was *peace*.

And peace to her meant a big family she could shower her love and goodness on.

I'd never even thought about having children. How could I when the man I loved in a way I knew I'd never stop had been taken from me when I was just seventeen?

"I wish I could switch places with you," I murmured helplessly, curling my arms around her. "I wish I could take away every bad thing that's ever happened to you. I should have been here to protect you."

"You and Dad are so similar," she said on a shaky exhale. "You can't protect someone from their own free will. It was my decision to go down this path, and now, I have to deal with the consequences."

"Not alone," I declared.

"No," she agreed, snuggling closer, pressing her face so tightly to my neck I wondered how she could breathe. "I was so stupid, Mei. Everyone around me was falling in love, and I wanted that so badly I forgot that I might not have a great romantic love, but that doesn't mean I'm unloved."

"Never," I agreed, trying to speak through the stranglehold of emotion around my throat. "You have so many people who love you. And even though I haven't been around enough the past eight years, there wasn't a single day that passed where I didn't think about you or miss you so much it hurt to breathe."

"I missed you," she said, an expulsion of breath like a desperate confession to a priest. "I know Dad won't like it, but I need you. I don't care if it isn't fair to ask you to be here. I don't care if it hurts you or him. I don't have anything left..." She sucked in a harsh breath. "I don't have anything left but *need*. Do you know how wrong that feels?"

"Yes, because you're the most giving, loving person I've ever known." Tied with Henning whom she'd no doubt learned it from. "But it's time for you to take as much as you need."

"I don't know how," she whispered brokenly. "I'm just so empty. I don't know how to fill myself up."

I forced myself to breathe slowly through the pain crushing my chest. My hand found a soothing rhythm stroking her hair, and I settled back into the pillows, taking her with me so she was lengthwise along the big couch.

"Do you know the concept of *gwaan hai*?" I asked her.

"Doesn't it have something to do with business?"

"It can. But the elemental meaning of Chinese *gwaan hai* is building personal relationships where both parties are willing to do whatever it takes to help each other. It implies a sense of moral obligation between the two. It's used in business a lot, and people talk about how it can lead to corruption, this idea of scratching each other's backs. But I believe any relationship worth having should be based on *gwaan hai*. If I love someone, I'm more than willing to do what needs to be done to bring them happiness, success, and joy. And the way I love you? That isn't an obligation, it's an *honour*. So please, honour me by trusting that I want to give you everything and anything you need. Not just because of what's happened to you. Not just because I promised Kate I'd look after you. But because I love you in a way that I *need* you to take what I have to offer, so really, you'd still be the one giving to me in the end."

Cleo's breath was a soft, warm puff against my jugular as she digested my words. I loved that she still took her time to understand something important and that her words, when spoken, were still so weighty.

"Okay, Rocky," she whispered. "I'll give you what you need."

"Thank you, Glory." I kissed the crown of her hair. "Now, what I need after that long drive is a nap. Do you think you could handle that?"

Her laugh was just a long exhalation, but it felt like a gift. "Yeah, I can handle that."

"Then hush."

It took Cleo about three minutes to fall into a deep sleep, her body weight sinking fully into my side. Only then did Bea, the forgotten friend in the chair beside us, shift forward and brace her arms on her thighs to stare me down. She was too pretty, too sweet in pink even with a knife I knew was strapped to her thigh to take very seriously, but I appreciated her gravitas.

"One of the first things she said when she came to was your name," Bea said quietly. "She's talked about you before, but this was different. It was like the only thing that could stave off the panic burning through her was you."

"We've been through a lot."

Her gaze narrowed. "Yes, I know. But that was eight years ago. She's different now, and I'm worried she called you here because trauma makes people want to move backward instead of forward. She hasn't needed you in the eight years you've been gone, and I don't think she really needs you now."

"I won't leave unless she tells me to go," I said through bared teeth.

But the idea made my chest throb like an echo in an empty cavern. The idea of leaving Cleo like this when she so desperately needed help was anathema to me. If she wanted me to leave at any point, I would, but until then, I could put up with cold blondes in the shape of Henning and Bea and anyone else who wanted to make life difficult for me in Entrance. It wasn't about *my* comfort. It was about Cleo's.

"I hope she does," Bea admitted without remorse. "I hope she realizes tomorrow, today, when she wakes up from her nap that everything she needs is already in Entrance, and you're just a ghost that should be banished back to where you came from."

"Harsh words for someone with a bow in her hair."

"Don't judge a book by its cover." She sniffed and sat back, crossing her legs so her short dress rode up to reveal the bottom edge of her sheathed knife. "The monster that did this to Cleo was after *me*. If you think I don't feel one hundred times more guilt than the glimmer I saw on your face, you're wrong. I'll protect her now better than I did before, even if it means protecting her against someone she thinks she can trust."

"I'd die for her, so don't talk to me about trust," I snarled softly.

"Maybe," she agreed slowly. "But I've heard enough about you to know what you're like, Mei Zhen. And sometimes, to heal, you have to lay down the sword and expose your underbelly. You might die for her, but that's not what she needs right now, and I don't think you're strong enough to be soft for her."

"If you've heard about me, then you know what it took for me to drive into this town with the intention to stay when a man I used to care for more than almost anything told me I wouldn't like what happened if he ever saw my face again."

She raised a pale brow, and I remembered that Cleo had mentioned her best friend in Entrance was hooked up with The Fallen's enforcer, a man so infamous in the underworld for his unflinching, exacting violence that people called him the Priest of Death. She looked a little something like that now, a blonde with a pink bow in her hair and violence shimmering in her wide blue eyes.

"Speaking of, how do you plan to deal with this? Axe-Man doesn't want you here. The rest of us don't want you here because we know all you'll bring is drama and painful memories to two *good* people who have already been through too much. Tell me I'm wrong."

It was strange to hear him called *Axe-Man*. I knew his club name was Axe back in Calgary, but I wondered at the new moniker and the distinction between the two. I also wondered if the Henning I knew existed within this Axe-Man everyone here seemed to know.

"I can't promise there won't be drama." I knew Henning's stubbornness because it so exactly matched my own. He wouldn't let me waltz back into their lives without throwing up obstacles every two feet. "But I can promise I know when something is worth fighting for. I learned that the hard way, but I'm not stupid, and I've learned it now. Cleo is worth fighting for."

"And Axe-Man?" she asked, flinging the words at me like daggers.

They slipped between my ribs and inflicted so much pain I almost lost my breath to them.

Anger surged in the wake of the pain, an instinctive, defensive response I'd honed since I was young. If I was threatened, I threatened back. But Bea knew that about me, it seemed. Knew enough to cast shade on my ability to be a soft place for the Axelsens to land in the rough wake of Cleo's trauma.

I refused to prove her right even though a small, niggly thing at the back of my mind worried she was.

I tipped my chin and levelled her with a cool glare. "I'll try to stay out of Henning's way when I can. If he works or something, I'll be here with Cleo when he's gone and leave well before he gets home. I'm not here to hurt him anymore. I'm here to heal where––who––I can."

Bea stared at me for a long moment, face perfectly implacable, before she looked away out the window to the gleaming blue-green lake the same colour as Henning's eyes.

"I didn't know his real name," she murmured, almost to herself, a little grimace catching at the corner of her mouth.

I didn't say anything. It didn't surprise me Henning hadn't shared. He'd never been much for conversation, and he was a loner by choice. Another reason I was surprised he'd joined up with the club again, let alone this chapter so infamous for its tight bonds.

"He's always been the strong, silent type," Bea continued softly, looking down at her hands as they smoothed over her swollen midriff. "I've been in this house hundreds of hours over the years, and I only know a handful of things about my best friend's dad." Her mouth twisted. "Now this has happened, and all we want to do is help them. Cleo and Axe-Man. Cleo, I can do." She turned to face me again, eyes flashing with conviction. "I love her, and it doesn't matter that you loved her first. I'm going to be here for her, too, so we'll have to make our peace. Maybe together, we can bring her back to life.

"But Axe-Man? I don't have a clue how to help him. A man like him whose daughter has been attacked and maimed right under his nose?" She shook her head and hissed in sympathetic pain. "I don't have the first clue how to get him out from under that pain. All I do know is that word of his outburst at the hospital spread like rapid fire through our ranks, and based on that, it's clear to me he hates you. And Axe-Man isn't a man who emotes much, let alone like that. So you promise me you'll stay clear of him as much as you can, or, Mei, friend of Cleo or not, I'll have my man escort you out of town."

Her smile was sinister. "And trust me, he's a whole lot scarier and more convincing than me."

"Are you done?" I asked mildly even though my hand trembled a little as I stroked Cleo's hair.

Bea's laughter was broken off at the ends, discordant notes struck on an out-of-tune piano. "Oh no, definitely not. We all know now that you're the reason behind Axe-Man going to prison, so don't expect a friendly welcome party. We'll put up with you around Cleo, for her sake, but otherwise, you're on your own."

This time, it was me who laughed roughly, a cough that tasted of blood. Bea's threat was no threat at all. I'd been on my own for so long I never hoped for anything else.

At least, not anymore.

CHAPTER NINETEEN

Axe-Man

I was bent over Bat's torso with a buzzin' tattoo gun in my hand, finishin' off the weepin' angel in tribute to his recently deceased wife. I'd just shaded into the skin beneath the left side of his ribs when the chime over the doors sounded, followed by the click of expensive shoes across the wood floors.

Street Ink Tattoo Parlour was famous across the globe.

Mostly, this was 'cause Nova Booth, fellow brother in The Fallen MC, had a fuckin' gift. The man could make even the lamest idea from a customer into pure art. It didn't hurt he was easy on the eyes. The shop's social media was filled with photos of him tattooin' or in various states of undress to show off his own heavily inked, gym-toned body.

It was also because of his woman, Lila Meadows. I'd been around her the past five years, and none of that time had dulled the impact of her beauty. She just had that kinda strikin', sensual, inherently womanly beauty that made your heart beat fast and your dick go hard. She'd become the face of Street Ink years ago when Nova first started tattooin' all that deeply tanned gold flesh with dozens of flower-themed tattoos. Fans called her Flower Child, but Nova'd been the one to do it first. Now that Nova'd got his head outta his ass and they were finally together, blissfully, obviously so, their coupledom had brought Street Ink even more notice. Lila ran one of those couple's accounts on social media that had over a million followers.

Third and final, though, was me.

Yeah, former military man, once doctor, Henning Axelsen was now a revered tattoo artist.

Who'da thought it?

The reputation I'd started to hone in Calgary meant nothin' in prison because most of your life before the cage meant shit all inside. But Harper Correction Facility, where I'd spent two years of my five-year sentence before gettin' paroled, was one of the five sites Corrections Canada chose for a pilot program that established roughshod tattoo parlours within the prison. As a doctor, I thought it was a clever way to reduce the aggressive spread of HIV and other infections. As a prisoner, I was fuckin' thrilled.

Tattoos in prison were like patches for motorcycle clubs. Most inmates got them, even if they didn't want them, so they could be associated on sight with their group. It was a form of protection, identification, and, in a place where self-expression was stifled practically to death, it was a way to remind yourself about who you were and what you stood for.

Of course, I signed up for work detail my first week in the joint, and thanks to Zeus's connections greasin' the wheels, I got one of those coveted spots.

We had old gear and few supplies, but the program was a fuckin' hit, and we were busy every damn day. The skills I had as an artist and the time I'd spent at Battle Scars Ink meant I was the most in-demand artist in the place. Even though I'd been associated with a white motorcycle club, every inmate of every race came by to be inked by me.

It was a helluva way to make friends and keep myself protected.

And more than that, it kept me sane in the monotony of prison life and the isolation from my kid.

When I moved to Entrance after I was released, I'd met Nova--the same kid I'd witnessed Zeus take under his wing so many years before--and the rest was history.

The good kind.

So yeah, there I was, a tattoo artist for one of the most famous establishments in North America with a waitlist longer than my arm and appointments booked six months in advance.

All this to say, an expensively dressed customer walkin' into the shop wasn't weird. We had movie stars and rock stars within these walls a fuck ton. This customer shouldn't'a made the hair on the back of my neck stand on end.

But it did.

Without turnin' around to see the intruder, I knew somethin' was *wrong*.

Bat felt me tense and went alert himself, body like a weapon coilin' in the chair.

I turned on my wheelie stool to face the door, and the moment I did, I knew.

Mei's reappearance had somehow heralded the reappearance of all my fuckin' demons.

Jiang Kuan stood at the reception desk as if he was waitin' to talk to the receptionist who was currently on the phone.

But his eyes were on me.

And he was smilin'.

Motherfucker.

I turned off the tattoo gun and tossed it with a clatter to the metal worktable pulled up to my station before I was on my feet prowlin' toward him.

Jiang didn't even blink before turnin' on his heel and calmly walkin' outta the parlour.

I followed him, aware that Bat, Nova, and one of our artists, Jae Pil, were all at my back.

Jiang stopped around the corner in the small alley between Street Ink and the clothin' store next door. Even surrounded by four bigger men, the Seven Song triad member just stood casually with legs braced apart and his hands in the pockets of his thousand-dollar suit.

"Henning, it has been a long time," he murmured in Cantonese. "I wish I could say you look well, but..." A one-shouldered shrug. "Honesty, it is a virtue."

"What the fuck are you doin' here, Jiang?" I barked in English for the benefit of my brothers. "A little far outside your territory, no?"

He looked up at the mural on the side of the tattoo shop, the huge-ass image of Lila amid a chaos of flowers with the words *marry me* beneath it, and he smirked a little before returnin' my gaze.

"If you mean Alberta, we've...relocated in the past few years. Maybe you didn't notice, being in prison."

"I've been out for five years," I said flatly, crossin' my arms over my chest.

I'd always been a big guy, even as a kid.

Big, slow, and dumb, my dad had liked to say.

Years in the military had honed that size, but it was the two years inside that had turned me into what Cleo called a mammoth. Crossin' my arms like that just accentuated the idle threat my body always posed.

Jiang's gaze flicked down the length of me, and the line of his shoulders tensed visibly.

I grinned a grin that was also a threat and watched him

blink.

"Yes," he said, clearin' his throat. "I've kept an eye on you over the years, of course. Which brings me to here and now. I want a meeting with your president."

I arched a brow as Nova let out a bark of incredulous laughter behind me.

"And why in the fuck would I set that up?" I asked dryly.

Jiang opened his palms to the sky, gold watch strap flashin' in the dim light caught between buildings. "There is no call for animosity, Henning. I told you once, and I will tell you again, I had nothing to do with your wife's death."

My snort burned my nostrils. "So you said. But you had a fuckuva lot to do with me goin' down for manslaughter."

"And for leading your lovely Mei into the dark embrace of the triad?" he continued, a little too sweet, eyes glitterin' as he set the bait for me.

One, two, three, four.

I counted as I dragged a deep, steadyin' breath in through my nose, but it did little to tamp down the flames burnin' in my gut.

"What do you want the meet for?" I was proud of the way my voice sounded: cold, devoid of a single emotion or inflection.

Jiang grinned then, a sharp pull of thin lips over perfectly capped white teeth. With a flourish like somethin' from one of the k-dramas Cleo liked to watch, he pulled a folded collection of papers from the inside of his jacket and snapped them open before danglin' them between us.

When I didn't take them, he sighed. "Really, Henning, the worst they could do is give you a paper cut."

"Don't call me that," I demanded, snappin' the papers from his grip. "Name's Axe-Man."

He snickered. "You bikers and your nicknames, always so on the nose."

"And Broken Tooth wasn't?" I asked cruelly, referrin' to Kang Li.

He made a soft noise of agreement, but I wasn't listenin' because my eyes were scannin' the documents, and what they found was not fuckin' good.

"No way this goes through," I growled, shovin' the papers into Bat's chest beside me.

He grabbed them, but my focus was on the Chinese gangster.

Jiang didn't smile, but his eyes were dark with pleasure. He liked the production of this intimidation, liked havin' violent men on his hook.

Done with his flash, done with this fuckin' conversation and the Seven Song's reappearance in my life, I flicked open the holster of the hatchet I always had danglin' from my belt, and within the span of a blink, the weapon was up in my grip and spinnin' through the air at Jiang.

He stumbled back, too slow to react as the small axe embedded itself in the wood of the heritage house boutique three inches to the right of his face. Before he could recover, I was on him, hand on the smooth, worn handle of the weapon, body curved over Jiang's smaller form, teeth snappin' inches from his blanched face.

"Listen here," I grumbled low, my free hand comin' up to fist in his designer shirt. "We aren't in Calgary anymore, and I'm not the man you once knew with bastards for brothers and the remnants of a moral conscience. I'm a brother of the mother chapter of The motherfuckin' Fallen MC, and if you come at me, at us, I got no qualms about carvin' you up like a Christmas ham. You get me?"

Jiang swallowed thickly, but his eyes narrowed into a glare. "I came here to speak as businessmen, not heathens on the edge of battle."

"Do. You. Get. Me?" I grunted, pullin' the axe from outta the wood so I could press the sharp edge to the hinge of his jaw.

His sigh feathered over my neck. "I should have known better than to do business with a brute. Yes, I understand. Now, move off and take my words to the president. I want to speak to the man who actually makes the decisions. Not the brawn who protects him."

I could feel my brothers at my back, vibratin' with tension, wantin' to get in on the action, but they held back to let me run the show.

I chuckled into Jiang's face. "Like I said, Vanguard, I'm not the man you used to know. They called me Axe because I was only a weapon. Now, I'm the Treasurer for The Fallen and 'the man who actually makes' the business decisions for the club. So you want a meet, I'll think about it. And 'til then, you got eight minutes to leave city limits, or I'm comin' after you with more than a hatchet."

When I shoved off him, Jiang was slow to peel himself off the wall, doin' it in a casual way like he'd decided to be pressed there. He adjusted his cuffs, smilin' slightly as the gold links winked in the light.

"How is your daughter doing after her unfortunate meeting with that murderer?" he asked, smooth as a hiss.

I lunged forward, but he was ready for me this time. A silver revolver like somethin' from an old Western was suddenly thrust up into my bearded chin.

"Uh, uh, uh," Jiang cooed. "My words weren't a threat but an olive branch. I know you haven't forgotten what happened to your wife all those years ago. You aren't the kind of man, I think, to let sleeping dogs lie."

"You want, I'll blow his damn brains out, Axe-Man," Bat offered coolly, and I didn't have to look over my shoulder to know his always present Colt M45A1 was levelled at Jiang's head.

"You so much as mention my daughter again, I'll cut out your tongue," I told Jiang.

A sly smile spread across his face, but he lowered his eyes in deference to my threat. "Of course, *Axe-Man*. I was merely offering an incentive. You set up this meet with Zeus Garro, I'll give you the name of the reason your wife was murdered."

Aware of his gun pressin' into my gullet, I didn't make a move for him, and he slipped away from me and the wall, backin' away down the alley with his hands casually stuffed into his pockets, eyes trained on me.

"As always, it was a pleasure doing business with you," he called before turnin' on his heels and disappearin' around the corner.

"Escort him outta town," I said without lookin' back at my brothers.

Without a word, I heard the sound of Nova's slightly uneven stride headin' around the side of the buildin' to get his bike. I knew he'd call in whichever of our brothers was closest to help him tail the Chinese crime boss outta city limits.

Bat didn't move an inch, but he waited for Jae Pil to head inside before he sauntered up beside me and crossed his arms.

"How is it nightmares never seem to die?"

I snorted, scrubbin' a hand down my face. "You find the answer to that, let me know. I've been tryin' to kill them for years."

Bat clamped a hand down on my shoulder, shakin' it lightly. "Yeah, brother, me too."

"We don't need more shit to deal with," I muttered, feelin' the weight of my past bearin' down on not just me, not even just Cleo and Lin, but the club. This group of brothers and their women and children who'd become my home. "We've had enough shit to deal with."

"The shit'll never stop comin', man. The life we signed up for? It's filled with the lowest of lows," he noted, as always, wiser than any man had a right to be. "But we got the highest of fuckin' highs along with it, and it's those we gotta cling to. Go home and hug your daughter. Take tonight to be grateful we came out the other side of a fuckin' serial killer in our midst with your daughter *alive*. Tomorrow, we'll deal with what comes. We always do, and brother, just in case you were thinkin' of pullin' your same old martyr shit, we deal with it as a club, you hear me?"

"You're a pain in the ass, you know that?" I asked to deflect from the fact that his words had found purchase in my chest, puncturin' somethin', an abscess, a never-healed wound that made me breathe a little easier.

"Yeah." He grinned, then sobered, lookin' over my shoulder at one of his many ghosts. "Now, get gone. Give Cleo a kiss for me."

I would, not just 'cause I needed to hold my girl every time we'd spent time apart to remind me of what I'd nearly lost, but 'cause Bat *had* lost someone to The Prophet, his own wife. And every time I looked at my brother, I knew we could have easily been in each other's place. And every time I felt that guilt of knowin' my loved one had survived, it helped to know Bat was happy I had that.

"You'll tell Z?"

Bat laughed. "You think he wasn't Nova's first call outta here, you're wrong." He laughed again when he pulled his vibratin' phone from his pocket and showed me Z's contact info on the screen. "Go, I'll deal with this for tonight, and tomorrow, we'll meet at the clubhouse."

I pulled him into me, pressin' my forehead to his in a quick gesture of profound thanks, and then turned on my heel to head for my bike.

Even with an escort outta town, I wouldn't feel easy 'til I saw Cleo home safe with my own eyes.

CHAPTER TWENTY

Mei

"We really have to do something about your hair, Glory."

Cleo and I were in the steamy bathroom adjacent to her bedroom on the main floor of the cabin. I'd insisted she take a shower even though she had refused in a way that made it clear she'd been refusing to shower for days. Bea's low-lidded glance confirmed it. The sweet and sour blonde had to leave to go to a doctor's appointment––The Fallen's death dealer had shown up in his terrifying red-headed glory to retrieve her––and I was glad to be alone with my best friend. She was softer with me, that bristling energy she had since the attack lowering to an easier frequency. It made it simpler to manipulate her into the bathroom and sit her on the lip of a glorious free-standing tub before a massive picture window while I adjusted the temperature of the handheld showerhead.

She didn't even fuss when I stripped her down to her underwear, but then, I didn't try to relieve her of those before helping her to sit in the tub. I imagined she wouldn't like to be naked following the assault, and the slight tremble in her lower lip when I forwent their removal spoke volumes.

Her eyes were closed now, her body lax in the cradle of the big tub as I gently worked warm water and a sudsy washcloth over her skin. Sometimes she made a little humming noise, and sometimes she flinched when I passed over the fresh pink of barely healed wounds. There were so many knife marks––eleven––all over her body, in the softest places in a woman's flesh, like The Prophet was trying to punish her for her womanliness.

When I spoke, she peeked through one lid.

"My hair?" Her hand went up to grab the ends where they should be laying over her shoulder and encountered nothing but air. There was a splash as her hand dropped abruptly back into the water.

My heart clutched at itself, hungry for retribution against a dead man.

"Yeah," I said casually, reaching over to grab the shampoo and lathering it between my hands before I shifted to straddle the tub behind her back. My bare feet slid against the bottom of the tub, but Cleo grabbed my ankles to steady me and then held on. "What do you think about a cute blue pixie cut? You're pretty enough to pull it off, and I bet Lin would love to get her hands on you."

Her nose wrinkled as I started to work my fingers into her scalp. "I don't think I could pull off crazy-coloured hair."

"Why not?"

Her shrug slapped water against the rim of the tub.

I tipped her head back in my hands, massaging the base of her skull so her lids fluttered with pleasure as she looked up at me.

"Did I ever tell you why I got my first tattoo?"

Her green-grey eyes flashed wide open, alert and interested suddenly. "No. We weren't speaking much at the time. I always wondered."

"You could have asked," I told her gently, only ever gentle for her. "I got this one right here."

I used one soapy hand to lift the hem of my black shirt. Two koi fish swam in a kind of yin and yang around my belly button, one red and the other black.

Cleo twisted slightly to better see it, a wet finger reaching out to almost touch the design. "Dad drew this on your cast in the hospital after...after Mum died."

I nodded. "It wasn't a good time in my life, then after losing Kate, and when I got this, having lost you and Henning. I was... struggling, and the only thing that brought me peace was the idea that things could only get better from there. That *I* could only get better from there. Rock bottom feels like a hellish place, but there's some peace in knowing you can only go up from there, you know? It's a fresh start. The perfect time to reinvent yourself. The koi evolves into a dragon only after reaching the end of a long, often dangerous and painful journey."

"Do you have a dragon tattoo somewhere, too?"

I tried to hide my flinch, biting into my lip so the physical pain could ground me from the emotional slap.

"No," I murmured. "I haven't gotten there yet."

She took a long, silent look at the koi fish, at the spiderweb caught beneath the base of my breasts, at the chain links arched beneath those and the flowers growing between their gaps. When her eyes met mine, they were fathomless, an enigma of unimagined pain.

"Did it hurt?"

"Sometimes. The skin is thin on the inside of the arms, the upper thighs, the ribs."

"No," she said softly, mouthing the words instead of truly

speaking. "Did it hurt to get your life story written into your skin for everyone to see? Does it hurt when people look at them and know?"

A little shiver bit into the base of my spine that had nothing to do with the cooling bath water.

"A little," I admitted, gently pulling her back against the tub so I could rinse the suds out of her choppy hair. "But it feels good, too. It's hard enough to live with baggage without being ashamed of it. It feels fulfilling to be unafraid of someone knowing what's happened to me."

Cleo was quiet for so long, I wondered if I'd pushed too hard on tender buttons. Her gaze was fixed out the large window on the right side of the tub into the dark trees lining the back of their lakefront property.

"It's hard," she admitted finally when I'd finished rinsing her down and pulled the plug. "When anyone looks at me now. I feel like they c-can..." She sucked in such a deep breath she winced as her lungs filled to bursting. "...like they can tell what I let happen to me."

I stopped, the towel in my hand unfolding to the floor with a whisper. Tears fought merciless with the backs of my eyes, trying to fall. A sob was lodged like a knife in my throat.

My knees gave out, dropping hard to the slate floors, but I didn't feel the pain. I abandoned the towel and reached out to cup her beautiful, tragically pale, gaunt face.

"You didn't *let* anything happen to you," I whispered, and even though the volume was lost to my agonized fury, the words were filled with conviction. "I don't care if you flirted with him. If he made you feel special and seen and you fell in love with him. I don't care if you agreed to meet him in secret when you shouldn't have. None of that matters to me or *anyone* that would ever hear about the absolute tragedy of what happened to you, Cleopatra. Goodness, love, and kindness are *never* meant to be rewarded with violence and hatred. Sometimes the worst kind of people are attracted to the best kind of people, like moths to a flame, because they want to suck out your light and corrupt it. The blame for that has everything to do with Seth Linley and his broken mind and absolutely nothing to do with you deserving it. Do you understand me?"

Huge tears like dewdrops collected on her lower lids, trembling there for long seconds before falling down her pale cheeks into my fingers and palms. She trembled, her hands shaking as she reached up to clutch at my wrists.

"Do you promise?" she gasped between quiet sobs.

"Oh Glory," I breathed, ripped apart by her anguish. "I swear it. If you believe anything I've ever said or done for you, please believe this. Sometimes bad things happen to good people for no better reason than that they shine so bright they're incredibly alluring to someone swallowed up by the dark."

"I-I don't know how to live through this," she confessed, shaking harder now, clutching at me so tightly that I lost feeling in my hands. "I wake up and feel like I should have died like Amelia. It would have been so much easier than living in this body and this mind. I feel like...like they betrayed me."

"They didn't. You didn't. *He* did."

Her eyes searched my face, scalpel sharp, searching beyond skin and blood and bone as if the truth lurked somewhere deep under my flesh.

"They tell me that," she said woodenly. "But it's hard to believe them. It's hard not to think after what happened to Mum...maybe the Kay women are cursed, or maybe we do something––"

"No." My word cracked like a gunshot through the space, making Cleo jerk with surprise. "Absolutely not. Neither of you deserve what happened to you, Glory. If I have to tell you every day for the rest of our lives, I'll do it. I can be very relentless, you know."

A little smile flickered and died along her mouth. "I know."

"And besides, you aren't a Kay anymore, and you haven't been for a long time. You're an Axelsen, and we both know Axelsens are like bamboo. You might bend under harsh winds, but you never *ever* break."

Cleo's grip pulsed tighter around my wrists before she tipped her head to lean her forehead against mine. We stayed like that for a long moment even though my knees ached. I would have stayed there for days if she needed that.

But a little creak in the wood floors startled us both into jerking away and turning toward the door.

Henning stood there, his big body taking up the entire doorframe. Arms crossed, muscles coiled like heavy ropes beneath his brightly tattooed skin and tight tee. He looked absolutely terrifying in that leather cut. His thick, carefully groomed beard made him seem even more heathen than I'd remembered, his hair longer, spilling in messy waves all around his shoulders. It should have softened him, maybe. Instead, he looked like a wild man with wild eyes staring at us. A predator stuck indoors.

"Henning," I said, an exclamation of shock.

Whatever softness had lingered in his expression was obliterated by the sound of his true name from my mouth.

"I warned you, Mei Zhen," he growled softly, almost a purr. "I told you to stay the fuck away."

"I asked her to come," Cleo said, pulling herself awkwardly to a stand using her one good arm and leg. She was in a soaked-through sports bra and boy shorts, with short, wet hair slicked back, pale limbs trembling with cold, but she looked so resolute standing there, and it took my breath away.

"Cleo--" Henning started to argue, but she didn't give him a chance.

"No," she insisted even though her teeth were chattering faintly. "No. I asked Mei to come to the hospital, and then I made her promise she wouldn't leave me again. I never told you because I thought it would hurt you, but I've seen Mei every few months for years now. She's...she's my family. *Our family*. I don't care what happened before." Tears came, great big ones that rolled down her face like waves even though her voice remained strong and sure. "Her heart has always been in the right place, and she should be, too. That right place is here, Dad. With me."

With *us* lingered in the air unspoken.

I was still on my knees, frozen in place by Cleo's show of strength, by Henning's awful, vibrating hatred of me. I wanted to flee as much as I wanted to stay there forever.

It was the perfect vantage point to see the way he looked at her, then. To see the awful weight of emotions play over his face: anger, frustration, helplessness, fear, and finally, grief so deep it cut new lines into his face beside the mouth and eyes.

He opened his big hands, ineloquent, struggling with it. He stared at them as if the lines in his palms might hold answers, and then, when they didn't, he looked at me. It was an old glance, a beseeching one. The way he might have looked at me eight years ago when Cleo asked for something he didn't want to give, when he knew I'd act as a translator between the two of them.

Realizing his slip, he wrenched his gaze away and ran a rough hand through his hair, the ends tangling around his fingers. It was so much longer now, brushing over his shoulders past his collarbones in a rich golden mass of waves. Looking at him, it was impossible, even though it was deeply inappropriate, not to imagine tangling my fingers in that hair. They twitched at my sides, and I curled them into tight fists so my nails cut half-moons into my flesh. The pain grounded me.

"Please, Dad. I need her here," she said, no less sure but softer. She swayed on her feet a little, unbalanced without her crutches. I stood, knees popping, and wrapped the towel around her before offering my arm to help her out of the bathtub.

Henning watched the two of us, gaze remote now, mask firmly in place. This was Axe-Man, not Henning. A new beast, one I had no experience with. One who hated me with palpable vitriol.

"She's here only when I'm not," he finally ground out, hands fisted at his sides. "And not alone. One of the brothers'll or their women'll be here, too."

"Dad," Cleo tried to protest, but this time, Henning was done.

"I don't trust her with you," he said, gaze snapping to mine to deliver the vicious blow. To watch how it landed like a flurry of fists against my breastbone, vibrating through my heart until I thought I heard it *crack*. "So you want her here, fine. But not without supervision and not when I have to be here to breathe the same air as her. Let that be good enough, Glory. It's more than I'm comfortable givin', you hear?"

"I hear you," Cleo muttered, wrapping an arm around my waist as she stepped out of the tub beside me. It could have been because she needed the extra support, but I thought it had more to do with offering it to me.

"Harleigh Rose is here to see ya," he grunted. "I'll send her in to help you get dressed, and then we'll have dinner. Lin's bringin' homemade barbecue duck and *cong you bing* for dinner."

Another punch to the gut. Sharing food was everything in Chinese culture. By deliberately leaving me out of dinner—with Lin's fucking delicious scallion pancakes, no less—he was making a point.

Cleo might think I was her family, but to Henning, I was decidedly *not*.

"A word outside before you leave," he ordered me, already turning around to depart on stiff steps.

Cleo and I stood still and silent for a full minute after, waiting for his lingering anger to dissipate.

"I'm sorry," we both started to say at the same time.

We didn't laugh at the synchronicity the way we might have in the past. We'd both been through too much to find such a little thing very funny, but it still felt good.

"I am sorry, though. He has a right to be angry with me, and it can't be easy to see me again after all this time. After...everything that happened."

Cleo sighed, an unwinding ribbon of weariness. "You know, he wasn't so mad in the beginning. Even those first few weeks in prison. I think he kept waiting for you to show up. It was only when you didn't, when he realized you'd left us, that he started to hate you like that."

Hearing that did something dangerous to my chest. A lightening, a sensation that floated through me that felt terrifyingly like hope.

Because if he hadn't hated me that night at Turner Farm for putting him in that position, if he hadn't hated me when the police showed up after I'd been spirited away and hauled me to the station in cuffs, if he hadn't hated me when he'd been charged with manslaughter after Florent Marchand promised to send him away for good, and he'd only started to feel that righteous fury when I'd disappeared for good, what did that mean?

It was impossible not to love a man who was willing to go to prison for you, but I'd never thought about the heart of a man who was willing to go to prison for a girl.

Because a man like Henning wouldn't go to prison for just anyone.

A family member, certainly. Maybe a friend who'd done or would do the same for him like Bat.

But the only reason a man like that went to prison for a girl like me was because, maybe, some part of him considered her *his* girl. Not romantically, no, but still, something strong like family, family we'd chosen for each other.

My heart thundered, and suddenly, I couldn't breathe.

The thought of Henning sitting there in a dark cell during those first few months, waiting for me to visit, willing me to be there because he loved me and he believed I loved him, only to slowly realize that he was wrong.

And I hadn't.

It broke my heart all over again.

The last time I'd spoken to my father, I'd threatened to hit him if he ever showed his face to me again. Now, I wished I could see him, just to take out this poisonous anger on his stupid, arrogant face.

"Rocky?" Cleo murmured. "I know Dad was mean, but don't trust it. He's all bark and no bite."

My laugh was a one-syllable cough. The Henning I'd known was exactly the opposite—no bark and serious bite. I doubted he'd lost those cruel teeth after a stint in prison and almost a decade with the most notorious outlaw MC in North America, but it was sweet of her to say so.

"Mei Zhen," Henning barked from somewhere in the house.

Cleo bit her lip. "You'd better go. But...you'll come back tomorrow, right? Dad works at Street Ink Tattoo Parlour. He's taken lots of time off to be with me, but I think it's good for him to have his routine. It's good for me, too. He takes off around ten every morning to go to the gym before work, so I'll see you after that?"

"You will," I promised, carefully wrapping my arms around her still-towel-clad body to give her a hug. "I won't break a promise to you again, okay?"

When I pulled away, I offered her my curled index finger and outstretched thumb. A glimmer of a smile pulled her lips before she met my fingers with the mirror of my own, forming a heart the way we had so often when we were young.

"Think about what I said," I urged her as I started to back away. "I'm Old Dragon's granddaughter, after all, so I'm very wise, you know?"

This time, a full smile. "Sure, you are."

"And the hair, think about that, too."

"Pink," she blurted, a little surprised by herself, eyes round, before she tried to shrug it off, awkward with one arm casted and wrapped in crinkly plastic to keep it from getting wet. "If I did it, I'd want it to be pink."

I beamed at her. "Pink dye and coffee at ten-oh-five tomorrow morning, Glory. See you then."

And even as I walked toward the kitchen, feeling like I was approaching a gangplank and my talk with a hateful Henning Axelsen, I felt lighter than I had in years. Because I'd made Cleo smile three times, and it was only my first day with her.

CHAPTER TWENTY-ONE

Axe-Man

The sight of Mei holdin' Cleo reverently in the bathroom, sunk to her knees on the unforgivin' slate tile to be eye level with my girl while she promised her that Cleo'd done no wrong in fallin' for the psychopath who'd assaulted her would be seared into my brain for the rest of my livin' days.

It wasn't only that Cleo hadn't let anyone but Bea, Harleigh Rose, Cressida, and me touch her since the assault. Not even Lin, her grandmother. Not even Loulou or Lila or Buck's wife, Maja. Only Bea, 'cause they were best friends, and they'd bonded over their association with the sick fuck Seth Linley. Only Harleigh Rose, 'cause she'd been assaulted by her ex-shit-for-brains-boyfriend Cricket before she'd put a knife in him and ended his life. Only Cressida, 'cause she knew the weight of staggerin' grief after thinkin' she'd lost King for months last year and 'cause she was Cressida, everyone in the club's touchstone––sister, mother, friend––even to the ones who didn't bond in the usual ways.

It wasn't even that Cleo'd refused to take a bath since she got home from the hospital, and I suspected it had a lot to do with bein' vulnerable for any period of time in a half-naked state.

It was that I hadn't seen the beauty of that connection between Cleo and Mei in eight years. I'd forgotten, somehow, buried under the layers of history and shit shovelled over top of it, how they made each other shine brighter.

Somethin' about Mei's strong-willed spirit relaxed Cleo as if she trusted her friend to deal with the harshness of the world so that she herself wouldn't have to bear the weight of it as much. And somethin' about Cleo's trust and gentleness eased the restless, vaguely antagonistic aura Mei often used as a shield.

They were fuckin' beautiful together. Always had been.

It shouldn't'a rocked me the way it did, maybe, given I didn't give a fuck about Mei anymore. I told myself as I stalked back down the hall into the kitchen and livin' room that it was just the shock of seein' her again at all.

But my heart was beatin' a tattoo on the inside of my ribcage, and I didn't know what shape it would take, fearin' it'd have somethin' to do with *her*.

The girl I'd gone to prison protectin'.

The girl who'd fuckin' abandoned us.

"Whoa there." Harleigh Rose's voice broke into my thoughts, pullin' my gaze to where she was sittin' on the butcher block island chewin' a piece of Hubba Bubba gum that snapped between her teeth. "You look ready to bludgeon someone to death with your bare hands."

I grunted, too frustrated to find the words for everythin' rollin' around inside me.

But I felt her eyes track me as I braced my hands on the

counter before the sink so I could stare out at the calm turquoise of Lake Mead. It was the reason I'd bought the plot of land and encouraged the club to invest in the surroundin' acreage. This kinda beauty deserved to remain unspoilt by developers and the slow spread of Entrance spillin' bigger and bigger over the valley between mountaintops.

It was the kinda beauty Cleo and I deserved after all the ugly we'd left behind in Calgary.

"Axe-Man?" Harleigh Rose was closer now, not touchin', 'cause she wasn't like that, but close to comfort, voice pitched low and soft instead of its usual brassy, confident drawl. "I don't think I've ever seen you so mad, not counting when we couldn't find Cleo. What's wrong? Should I call Dad?"

"No," I said, 'cause Zeus would just laugh, probably thinkin' this was some kinda fucked-up fate, and I couldn't escape it. For an outlaw with a record and blood on his hands, Zeus Garro was bizarrely romantic.

Then again, his romance with Loulou would turn anyone into a fuckin' sap.

H.R. hesitated, then perched her hips beside mine, body facin' the opposite way into the kitchen. "Does this mood have anything to do with the pretty Asian girl who visited Cleo in the hospital a few weeks ago?"

"Damn brothers," I muttered. "They gossip worse than high school kids."

She laughed, head tipped back just like her father. "Ain't that the truth? Boner was so mad he didn't get a glimpse of her. He offered fifty bucks to anyone who'd tip him off to where she was at if she showed up again."

My scowl deepened, gaze cuttin' to H.R. to see she was watchin' me with an arched brow, one of those knowin', feminine smiles on her mouth.

"She meant somethin' to you once?" she asked, 'cause even if news of Mei's visit had made the rounds, I knew Bat, Smoke, and Z wouldn't share my history without permission, and even curious, none of the brothers or their women wanted to bother me with gossip when I was still dealin' with everythin' that had happened to Cleo.

"Once," I acknowledged tersely.

She hummed, blowin' a pink bubble, then poppin' it with a snap. "Unresolved history's got a way of comin' back to haunt us."

"Bit young to be dolin' out wisdom, H.R."

"Hey, age has got shit all to do with it. I'm marrying the love of my life in six weeks, I've got a great job, a kick-ass hound and house, and I'm generally amazing. You should be *begging* me for life advice."

I snorted 'cause it was impossible not to be charmed by Harleigh Rose. She'd been raised around bikers her whole life, so she knew the language and religion of a biker and his club. Talkin' to her was like shootin' the shit with one of the brothers, only she was smart in that way of women who seemed to inherently understand emotions and shit I'd always struggled to put words to as if she'd been born with them on her tongue.

It was a dangerous combination 'cause it made you want to open up to her, and I liked bein' closed off just fine.

"I know you like doing things yourself," she said, readin' my mind in that eerie way. "I know you think at the end of the day the only one you can rely on is yourself, and I know it because I used to be like that, too. Some people would call you a martyr, maybe, but I think you've just been alone so long you can't see what's right in front of you." She shifted, those bright blue eyes as sharp as broken glass cutting to the heart of me. "A brotherhood and a family who've all got your back."

"You think I don't know that when you're here after a long shift at the hospital to be with my girl 'cause she needs community? I must look dumber than I thought."

"Not dumb," she mused with a quirk of her mouth. "Just stubborn."

"Year of the tiger."

H.R. had a knife from the butcher's block in her hand and levelled in Mei's direction before I could move.

"Who the fuck are you?" she demanded and then seemed to draw the conclusion herself because there was a little bit of wonder in her voice when she said, "Mei?"

Mei's smile was flat and flimsy as pressed tin. "Pleasure to meet you. I meant no offense"—she gestured to the knife—"when I said year of the tiger. It's just in his nature to be stubborn and solitary."

Somethin' caught fire in my chest, scorchin' up my throat. Somethin' that tasted bitter on the back of my tongue.

"You don't know shit anymore," I told her coldly before takin' the knife carefully from H.R.'s grip, slidin' it back in the block, and addressin' her. "Cleo's waitin' for you in the bathroom. Can you help her get dressed while I talk to this one?"

Her gaze narrowed as she looked between Mei and me, and for a second, I wondered if she'd refuse. Born and raised a biker girl, she wasn't exactly obedient or easy-goin' for anyone other than her future husband, Lion Danner.

But then her mouth softened, and she nudged me with her shoulder in a little show of camaraderie that spoke volumes. If I needed her, if Cleo needed her, she'd do anythin' to meet those needs.

"Sure, Axe-Man," she muttered with a little grin before the expression collapsed into a suspicious glare she aimed at Mei that she maintained the entire time she walked through the kitchen and down the hall to Cleo.

"Is there some mandate in the mother chapter of The Fallen that everyone has to be pretty and mean as a snake?" Mei quipped, slouchin' against a wooden pillar like she didn't have a care in the world.

Years ago, her comment would have made me smile. Such a little thing, a pretty thing herself with such a sharp-edged tongue. Unbidden, I had the thought that she'd fit in here in Entrance 'cause she was right in a way. Everyone here was like a cactus in bloom, lurin' people close but not close enough to touch.

Just like her.

"You won't be spendin' enough time around them for it to matter much either way," I said as I stalked toward the front door and opened it, gesturin' her to precede me outside.

She stared at me for a long moment before pushin' off the post and glidin' out the door, just to maintain some pretense that the move was her choice and not my order.

The smell of her cherry blossom scent lingered in the air behind her. I held my breath as I walked through it, slammin' the door behind me.

It was one of those late March nights that was shockingly cold, the sky clear of clouds and velvety dark against the shine of the stars. The lake was hammered metal, gleamin' and corrugated with little ripples from the mild breeze.

Beautiful.

An awful fuckin' settin' for this talk with a ghost who never should've resurrected herself. Her presence deconsecrated somethin' about this peaceful haven I'd carved out for Cleo and me. It made it unsafe, somehow, even though I knew logically, even after all this time, even after what she'd done, Mei'd never do anythin' to put Cleo and me directly in harm's way.

It was more that I didn't want memories of her here. I knew I'd walk up the steps tomorrow after work and see her mirage outta the corner of my eye, a girl in a too-big leather jacket swallowed up by shadows but still shinin' like somethin' that'd hurt your eyes if you looked at it too long.

"It's so beautiful here," she said, the prompt I needed to

shake off this stupid nostalgia-tinged romanticism and get down to why I'd put myself out here with her in the first place.

"Don't get used to it," I grunted and had the bittersweet pleasure of seein' her jerk a bit, slapped by my harsh words.

Her jaw clenched, the angle sharp and slightly square. She didn't look at me, and I wondered if it was for my sake or hers.

"You've got to know, the only reason I'm lettin' you step foot in my house is 'cause I'd make a deal with the devil to help Cleo feel better. I'd sacrifice anythin' to take it all away from her. Lettin' you in..." I meant the house, but we were both aware it was more than that. *In* to the house, *in* to Cleo's life, *in* to my space again. "Is conditional on you stayin' the hell away from me and Cleo reportin' that every day with you is golden, you hear me?"

"I hear you," she whispered.

Her hand wrapped around the post next to the railin', and she leaned into it like she needed the help stayin' upright. Moonlight spilled across the side of her face, and I couldn't remember if she'd always been this exquisite. So damn pretty cast in moonlight, she seemed ethereal, like she'd dissolve if I tried to touch her.

I clenched my fists tight and refocused.

"I got a visit at the shop today. You wanna guess who it was?"

Her eyes skittered my way, then slipped away just as quickly. "Who?"

"An old friend of yours, Jiang Kuan."

I was watchin' for it, and even though it'd been eight years, I'd once known her face well enough to read all her tells, so I caught the way her lids flickered as if tryin' to tamp down a secret that might show in her eyes.

"Oh," she said, and that was it.

"You still hangin' out with that crowd?" I demanded.

The lingerin' softness she'd maintained from bein' with

Cleo or the submissiveness of guilt she'd assumed vanished in a blink. Her chin jutted forward at that fuckin' obstinate angle I used to be so familiar with, and she glared at me sidelong, mouth petulant.

"You don't get to tell me to essentially fuck off and then demand to know about my life, Henning."

"You call me Henning one more time, I'll keep you from Cleo. I don't give a damn that she wants you. She's survived for near on a decade without you. She can do it again," I threatened darkly.

She didn't know I wasn't certain I had the heart to see the threat through, and I was grateful.

A long sigh, just louder than the cold breeze rushin' through the long grass. "Old Dragon and I settled in Vancouver's Chinatown a while back. I see Jiang around sometimes. It's unavoidable."

My gut said she was lyin' somehow, but I was already done with bein' out in the moonlit dark with her alone, so I didn't push it.

"I find out you got more to do with him than that, you won't like it," I warned.

Another weary sigh. "You know, *Axe-Man*, I never thought I'd see you again, but when I did think about our reunion, it didn't involve you threatening me so much."

"You must have a poor imagination."

A little mockin' grin curved her lips before she nodded, pushin' away from the railin' to finally face me. She looked at my right ear instead of up into my eyes, and for some reason, it irritated me. I wanted to wrench her little chin up and force her gaze on mine.

My short nails dug into my palms and broke the skin, but I didn't loosen them.

"We've got eight years of secrets between us and zero trust. I get you want a brother here when I'm with Cleo. I can even pretend it doesn't kill me to think you might wonder if I'll hurt her or put her in danger. But if you remember anything about me, remember this..."

Her eyes flashed up to me then, slicing through me like an obsidian blade. "I'd die for her just as happily as I'd die for you. No amount of time will ever change that. And no amount of hate."

Without another word, she bowed to me a little in mock servitude and then ambled down the stairs to the Kawasaki Ninja parked nearly out of sight under a flat bit of land between trees. I watched as she plunked on the black helmet, swung a nimble leg high over the seat of the bike, and settled onto it with the ease of a long-time rider.

The engine revved. Nothin' like the sweet growl of a Harley, but somethin' else that still resonated in my biker-lovin' heart. When she peeled around in the gravel lot, she did it with flair, stones sprayin' out behind her in a wide arch, rainin' down on the edge of the porch stairs with little *clinks*. I watched the glow of her tail lights 'til they disappeared down the tree-lined drive.

When the door opened behind me, I wasn't surprised, but I still braced. Harleigh Rose was only gettin' more and more like her dad the older she got, and I knew her comment would cut near to the quick as Mei's last, darin' glare.

"A present from Lion," she murmured as she stepped up beside me, knockin' the side of a half-full glass tumbler into my arm. "Looked like you might need a glass."

I snorted but accepted the glass and knocked back a long swig of the smooth whiskey. "Try the entire bottle."

"You say the word, we'll kick that girl outta town," she offered easily.

A little of the burn in my chest eased off 'cause I knew they would. The whole fuckin' club would ride out en masse to drag Mei kickin' and screamin' out of Entrance. The fantasy made me grin.

"But you won't say it," she noted, cuppin' her elbow in one hand and her own glass of whiskey in the other. "You'll let her invade your space and your peace just because Cleo needs her."

"Hey," she said, half laugh, shrugging a little when I glared at her. "I get you, Axe-Man. I don't even disagree with your decision. I'll just say...be careful. Eight years is a long time for someone to change a whole lot in good ways and bad."

"I don't give a fuck how she's changed. I'll avoid her, and she'll avoid me."

"Mmm," she hummed. "In my experience, ghosts haunt us even when we leave the place they died. Sometimes there's no exorcising them."

"I'm not payin' for your dime store wisdom," I grunted.

She laughed but got the hint, leanin' into my side just a little before goin' quiet. Sippin' good whiskey with a girl I considered somethin' like a niece to me was just the peace I needed after the chaos of Mei whipped through my ordered life. I hadn't been alone a single night since Seth had taken Cleo, a brother or their old lady or their kids always rotatin' through our house with food, with drink, and with a fuck ton've comfort. For the thousandth fuckin' time in the past five years since I'd transferred to the Entrance chapter of The Fallen, I felt grateful for the gift of them I wasn't sure I'd ever find a way to deserve.

CHAPTER TWENTY-TWO

Axe-Man

ENTRANCE WAS NOTHIN' LIKE CALGARY. IT WAS A SMALL BUT growin' town that had the kinda charm you'd see in a fuckin' Hallmark movie or a children's book. Main Street was a seven-block stretch of heritage buildings in brick or various revival styles painted in pastels or earth tones intermingled with stretches of green spaces and parks. It was late March, the snow recedin' from everywhere but the mountaintops, and the blossoms were already peekin' out on the cherry trees, pink buds frosted by the cold mornin' air.

It was fuckin' idyllic, and I didn't take it for granted even for a second.

For a kid who'd grown up with nothin' in a trailer park outside of Fort McMurray, I'd always appreciate the beauty of British Columbia and this town we'd made our home.

It was the people, too.

The brother, Wrath, who owned Box n' Burn and worked out with me every mornin' for ninety minutes before headin' across the street to Stella's Diner or down the road to Honeybear Café & Bakery for a coffee and a sandwich, both places filled with patrons who greeted me with a grin or an up nod.

Me. An ex-con proudly flyin' the colours of his notorious outlaw motorcycle club.

Sure, some citizens gave me the stink eye, but for the most part, the townsfolk liked the club. We held charity events, helped mediate disputes 'cause no one much trusted the police after the corrupt Staff Sergeant Danner was arrested for tryin' to kill King Kyle Garro and for murderin' a fellow cop, Riley Gibson, two years ago, and we kept other criminals from doin' damage inside town borders.

It felt good to be accepted, admired even, for bein' exactly who I was. It was somethin' I'd struggled with my whole fuckin' life, and findin' it here gave me a kinda peace I'd yearned for a long time.

So walkin' into Honeybear Café after my workout, still damp from my shower, revved with the adrenaline of a good workout, I didn't expect to see anyone I knew outside of the regulars.

The bell over the door chimed as it swung shut beside me, but I stood frozen in the doorway, starin' at Mei Zhen Marchand as she smiled at Lauren Hatfield behind the counter. She was wearin' that fuckin' leather jacket again, unzipped over a semi-translucent black top even though it was goddamn freezin' out and she had next to no body fat to keep her lean form warm. It exposed the black, line-etched tattoos on her neck and the ribbon of flesh between the shirt and her low-slung black jeans. I noticed a small axe on the side of her throat that made my pulse pound. With her ink-dark hair shimmerin' over her shoulders, the alabaster of her skin, and the only spot of colour in her pouty mouth, she looked like some kinda badass Asian version of Snow White.

The sight of her kicked me in the teeth and again in the

fuckin' gut.

'Cause, fuck, she'd been a pretty kid, but she was a gorgeous woman.

My teeth ground together as I fought through the inappropriate punch of desire and the swift right jab of anger.

"What the fuck are you doin' in here?" I grunted as I stalked forward.

Mei's pretty smile faltered, then fell off her face as she turned to look at me. There was devastation in her features for just a second before she rearranged them into a mockin' smirk. She tilted her paper cup of coffee at me.

"Morning sustenance. Cleo told me this place was the best in town. I've never tried a dirty chai latte before, but I have to say..." She took a sip, her mouth leavin' a red imprint on the white lid. Unbidden, the image of that same stain on my skin flashed behind my eyes. "It's fucking delicious."

"This is my place. It's off-limits," I told her, crossin' my arms to underscore the point.

Laughter danced in her warm, dark gaze as it moved over my obstinate pose. "Oh-kay... Harsh of you to take my new favourite drink from me, but I guess I could duck into Stella's Diner next time."

"No, that's mine, too."

She cocked a brow. "You want me to starve while I'm in town, Axe-Man?"

I'd wanted her to call me that, so why the fuck did it feel wrong? Why the fuck did the sight of her in my town feel so invasive, like somethin' crawlin' painfully deep beneath my skin?

"Just stick to places I don't like," I suggested blandly. "Wouldn't do for local business for me to stop patronizin' them just 'cause the sight of you there ruined my appetite. We both know you won't stick around long enough for them to recoup their losses with you."

Her flinch was small, but then, I'd never seen her flinch before. It wasn't like me to be such an asshole, but Mei'd always managed to bring out the more aggressive side of my nature, even back in the day when we'd been close.

"Right," she whispered, lookin' down at the little honey bear stencilled onto her cup, rubbin' her thumb over it like she could erase its smile. "Well, I'll get out of here before I spoil your post-workout meal."

Lauren cleared her throat from behind the counter, shootin' me a frown before she passed Mei a paper bag already damp with fresh grease stains. "Your breakfast sandwiches. Tell Cleo I slipped in some extra avocado for hers, yeah? And if she'll accept it, give her my love, okay?"

Mei bit her lip as she accepted the bag and nodded, duckin' behind a curtain of silky hair as she started for the door.

Before she could get by me, my hand was snaggin' her arm. I stared at the sight of my big, tatted palm wrapped around her slim wrist for a moment 'cause I hadn't meant to touch her. Hadn't meant to stop her.

"Listen, you stay away from me, I won't cause you problems here," I said, a little gruff 'cause it was as close to an apology as she was gonna get.

She didn't look at me, just nodded and carefully wrenched away from my grip. "Sure, Axe-Man. Whatever."

I opened my mouth to say somethin' else, anythin' else that might drag that sloe-eyed gaze back to mine, that might light the same fire in her I felt in my gut, but I didn't get the chance.

A scream from the back of the shop ripped through the room.

Instantly, everyone moved.

The other coffee seekers ducked and started runnin' for the door.

Mei and I moved simultaneously toward the source of the scream. I had my axe unclipped from its holster, the smooth wood handle gripped in one palm and my gun in the other. Mei had dipped down to pull a wicked-lookin' knife from her boot, the blade shinin' new mornin' sunlight into my eyes.

"Put that away and get outta here," I demanded, already movin' around the register to the door leadin' to the back kitchen.

Mei didn't answer, but I could feel her like the heat of a fire at my back.

In the kitchen, two bakers and a front-of-house clerk were huddled around the entrance to an office on the right.

"Everyone good?" I called, careful to aim the gun at the ground.

No one flinched at the sight of me, but they were all fuckin' green like they'd seen somethin' to twist their stomachs.

"Yeah," Lauren's voice drifted out from inside the office, weak and warbled. "But you'd better see this, Axe-Man."

The little crowd parted for me so I could move into the office, where Lauren stood in front of her desk. I followed her line of sight to the bloody carcass of a headless raccoon that was pinned to a picture frame by a cleaver-like blade.

"Note?" I guessed, steppin' forward.

I could feel Mei behind me, hoverin' in the door and takin' stock.

"I-I didn't have time to open the office earlier this morning because Judy couldn't make it in. I hopped on the line to help Kerry and got caught up in the lunch rush… I don't know how long this *thing* has been here for." Lauren's hand trembled like a newborn bird as she handed me the blood-soaked paper.

The Chinese characters were familiar to me.

Follow and obey.

I looked up at Mei, whose face had lost all colour.

"You know anythin' about this?" I demanded.

Her glare was sudden and ferocious. "The fuck? You assume because the threat is written in Chinese that I'm involved?"

"Well?"

"Fuck you, *Axe-Man*."

"What the fuck am I supposed to think when you show up and suddenly I got triad threats comin' out the fuckin' wazoo, huh?" I demanded, steppin' forward to shake the paper at her.

A fleck of raccoon blood landed on her cheek and when she angrily dashed at it with her thumb, the red streaked beneath her eye like the mark of a warrior.

"I'm here to help, not cause you any problems," she snapped, steppin' toe to toe with me so she could poke her sharp taloned finger into my chest as if I wasn't a head taller and a hundred pounds heavier than her.

"I seem to remember you sayin' that once before, and it ended up with me behind bars for two years."

Her hand flexed hard on the handle of the tactical knife she held like an extension of herself. "I see old age has made you *stupid*, because anyone with half a brain would know I arrived this fucking week, and I've never stepped inside these doors before today."

"You've always been good at lyin'."

Her flinch that time was only the twitch of an eyelid before she recovered. "Lauren, we met for the first time this morning, right?"

"Yeah," she replied shakily, no doubt wonderin' why we were fightin' in her office like two cats in a hen house.

"Check the security footage if you don't believe me," Mei seethed. "Or, instead of wasting both our time, you can let me help."

"Oh, so you do know somethin' about this." I gestured to the fresh kill on Lauren's desk.

"I know if the body is here, the head is somewhere else."

As if on cue, my phone started vibratin'. I pulled it out of my pocket and re-holstered my gun in the same move without takin' my eyes off Mei.

"Yeah?" I answered.

"Axe-Man," Bat replied, soundin' even more grim than his usual grimness. "Stella just called. Seems she found the head of a fuckin' raccoon nailed to her bathroom mirror at the diner this mornin'."

Across from me, Mei's smile cut like a bloody line across her face.

The Fallen Compound took up an industrial-sized block on the outskirts of the "polite" side of town, between the tidy upper-class neighbourhoods with their big houses and manicured lawns and the tiny cracker-box houses with chain-link fences and Beware of Dog signs on the other. It was nothin' like Rooster's clubhouse had been back in Calgary.

For one, it was a hub of business.

Edge Truckin' operated out of the far-left side of the property with its own gate in the ten-foot fence, closin' the property from the public after hours. Beside it, Hephaestus Auto & Garage with its four huge bays open to the forecourt, brothers millin' about workin' on repairs and custom bikes. It was famous in the biker community, not just 'cause a notorious MC owned it, but 'cause the brothers who worked there under Zeus and Bat did fuckin' beautiful work.

Then tucked up against the river cuttin' through the back of the property, the clubhouse. A one-level sprawl of brick and mortar with a massive depiction of The Fallen's emblem, a skull with burnin', tattered wings spray-painted on the front by Nova himself. It was tidy, with window boxes tended to by Lila and a little garden with picnic tables off to one side of the asphalt lot.

None of it looked criminal, but then, that was the point.

It was only the club and the cops who could spot the little ways it protected its members from intruders or pryin' eyes. The high fences backed by slightly transparent black screens impeded visibility, and the two entry points operated on remote mechanisms that locked with strong bolts and passcodes. The doors on the buildings, heavy and metal, only opened outward to prevent forced entry, and the clubhouse was so closely backed by the river to prevent a sneaky approach from behind and also offered an alternate mode of escape if we were boxed in.

It was, more than anythin', a second home. A sacred, safe place for men who'd been mocked or punished by "normal" society for the choices they'd made or been forced to make in their lives.

I fuckin' loved it, and the knot of tension between my shoulders uncoiled slightly when I rode into the forecourt and backed my white Harley into the line of bikes beside the clubhouse.

"Axe-Man," King said from his perch on one of the picnic tables where he was writin' in one of his ever-present notebooks. Our resident biker poet. "Everyone's waitin' inside."

"But you," I noted, clippin' my bucket to the handlebars before makin' my way over to Zeus's eldest kid, a man now, one I respected better than most.

The wind pushed his yellow hair into his face as he grinned at me, leanin' back on his hands in a faux gesture of innocence. "I like the fresh air."

"It's cold as hell, and you know it."

The grin dropped, replaced by that searchin' gaze that so adeptly picked apart grown men and divided them into their pieces. It was instinct to look away, but I forced myself not to.

I had a lot to atone for, but I refused to be ashamed of my past, especially when it was threatenin' to haunt my club.

"Heard you had two visitors yesterday," he drawled. "Unusual for you."

I grunted but leaned a hip into the side of the table and crossed my arms. King had somethin' to say, and it'd do no good to rush him.

"H.R. said she's gorgeous," King noted.

Ah, so that was the priority. Not Jiang and the business with the club. Not the dead 'coon at Honey Bear Café. For the romantic, the girl would always come first.

"She's a kid," I rebuked with a one-shoulder shrug.

And she was. Twenty-five. Sixteen years younger than me.

Cleo's best friend.

And that was the least of our fuckin' problems.

"Cress said the same thing 'bout me at first." His eyes sparkled in the pale winter sunlight, so light a blue they seemed nearly transparent. "'Til I convinced her otherwise."

I snorted. "Yeah, well, she tried that once before, and it didn't work."

"Uh-huh," King murmured, but there was triumph rich in his tone, and I cursed myself for givin' anythin' away, especially to him. "So she loved you, once."

"She didn't know the meanin'," I ground out, irritated with us both and with Mei for even bein' the source of this conversation. "She was seventeen and confused."

"Loulou married Dad at seventeen," he noted, implacable, starin' me down like we were ten paces out and ready to draw pistols. "You think she was confused?"

My teeth clenched so tight, my jaw *popped* ominously. No

one knowin' Loulou Garro could ever say she'd been a lost and confused seventeen-year-old. A two-time cancer survivor, cut off and physically assaulted by her father, neglected her entire upbringin' by her parents to the extent she took on a criminal nineteen years her senior as a fuckin' pen pal, Loulou'd been mature beyond her years.

"Mei isn't Loulou."

"Nah, I figure not," King mused, but it was a trap, and I knew it. His pretty face and casual, easy-goin' demeanour belayed a mind as sharp as the edge of a blade. "But if Cleo called her to her side, I figure she's special enough in her own way."

I glared at the boy, the muscles in my arms jumpin' ominously as I clenched my fists. "Your sister offered to have the club run her outta town, and here you are, makin' like you wanna roll out a red carpet for her."

King peered at me, thumb worryin' at the pages of his notebook, somethin' workin' behind his eyes I couldn't read. Finally, he jumped off the table in an explosion of graceful movement only a young twenty somethin' could manage and clapped me on the shoulder before headin' to the clubhouse.

"There's not a man in this club without demons, Axe-Man. When a man's got a rare opportunity to exorcise them, he's gotta take it if he ever wants a chance in hell of findin' some long-lastin' happiness."

"Why do you think I told her to fuck off?" I muttered as I followed him up the stairs.

A flicker of a smile, but he didn't say anythin' else, and his silence was smug. For a twenty-three-year-old kid, he shouldn't'a been able to see so much, know so much, but from the time I'd first met him ago, he'd always been like that. Those pale eyes were scalpels, cuttin' up human flesh and scrapin' past bone to the heart of people.

It was fuckin' eerie.

I turned King, and Mei, from my mind as I moved through the clubhouse to the long side room exposed by carved wooden doors pushed open and manned by our prospect, Carson.

He held out the small cardboard box for my phone without a word.

King and I dropped them in, and I clapped the kid on the shoulder before I moved into the smoke-filled room and the long wood table wreathed by my brothers.

Zeus, as Prez, sat at the head of the table. On his right, our VP, Buck, the only old-timer remainin' from the club before Z ousted his uncle as President. He was in his early sixties but still big and fit as a bear, his hair gone to silver as bright as the rings on each of his thick fingers. Across from him on Z's left sat my old friend, Bat, our Sergeant at Arms, and the seat beside him was left vacant for the Treasurer.

Me.

When Zeus had offered me a place in his club if I wanted it, whichever place I chose, I'd been fuckin' relieved not to have to take up the mantle of enforcer the way Rooster'd once forced me to do. That role was taken by Priest McKenna, arguably the scariest motherfucker ever born, a man whom I knew based on my medical trainin' was an honest to God psychopath who enjoyed dismantlin' our enemies the way most men enjoyed dismantlin' a good burger. Since we'd welcomed Wrath Marsden into the fold some years back, we'd even added a second enforcer. His immensity, rage, and history of violence made for a good contrast against Priest's wraith-like, cold, and mechanical brutality. They sat side by side toward the other end of the table, as different as night and day but still somehow compatible.

Left to my own devices, I'd fallen naturally, even a little gratefully, into the role as Treasurer and Secretary of the club. I'd done my major in mathematics, and I'd always been drawn to numbers just as I was to art. So I enjoyed my role keepin' the club's books, figurin' out how to clean our money, where to invest in legal businesses, and where to tap into illegal interests. I even did the books for Nova at Street Ink.

And I was fuckin' good at it too.

Since I'd taken over, with the help of Zeus and then King as he'd gotten older and when his dad did a stint in prison, we'd made the club into a multimillion-dollar organization.

It got to the point where Zeus offered my services to other chapters to help them set up their own business ventures.

But today wasn't about club assets and allocations.

It was about new threats.

More specifically, threats *I*'d brought to my club's doorstep.

"Mornin'," I murmured to my brothers as I took my chair and pulled my glasses from the inside of my cut.

"Hey, bro," Boner said, louder than the chorus of "heys" from the rest of the group. He leaned over the tabletop closer to me, his young face eager and bright with curiosity. "Heard you got a new lady lover."

"She's not my goddamn lover," I snapped.

Across from me, King coughed to hide his snort of amusement, and Buck raised his brows at my uncharacteristic show of temper.

"Oh sweet," Boner crowed, pivotin'. "So you don't mind if I get a look at her, decide she's worth pursuin', and make a go at her?"

Curtains slapped his best friend on the back of his head. "Get a brain, would ya? We got more important things to talk about than who you can dip your wick in."

Boner pouted. "I was just doin' my due diligence. Bein' a good brother. I don't wanna chase some skirt Axe-Man's got a stake in."

"Not only do I not have a 'stake,'" I growled, tryin' and failin' to stay calm. The past twenty-four hours had worn my patience clean away. "I don't want that 'skirt' mentioned again in my goddamn presence. Got me?"

Boner blinked at me, shocked by my aggression.

"Got. Me?" I repeated through clenched teeth.

"Yeah, man."

I swept my gaze through the rest of the brothers at the table, searchin' for confirmation and findin' it in a series of confused or amused nods and chin lifts.

"Now the pleasantries are over with," Zeus mused from his reclined position in his chair, fingers steepled over his mouth, though I thought I could see the edge of a grin in his beard. "Maybe we can get down to business."

"My guest yesterday," I concluded. "And that fuckin' threat at Honey Bear Café today."

"Yeah, but somethin' else I think might tie in," he added, gesturin' to Bat to pick up the thread.

"Stella's here in the garage's office with Loulou," Bat started. "She came in this mornin' in a rage with a bloody takeaway bag she tossed onto the seat'a the Harley I was workin' on. There was a decapitated raccoon head inside. Stabbed through with one of her own kitchen knives."

Priest produced the said bloody bag, droppin' it on the table with an unceremonious wet thunk.

"Nasty," Boner muttered.

"You don't blink an eye at dismembered humans, but a raccoon is gross?" King asked.

"Dude, raccoons have like a whack ton of diseases," he countered, nose wrinkled.

Zeus, as he often did, ignored them.

"There was a note." He picked up from where Bat had left off, jerkin' his chin at Wrath, who pushed the crinkled white-lined paper into the middle of the table.

I snatched it up.

The script was cramped and spiky. I adjusted my glasses

and read, "Follow and obey. The same damn thing was written on the one at Lauren's bakery."

"Apparently, some fucker has been pressurin' Stella to sell the business for a few weeks now. Comes in every Wednesday mornin' like clockwork to buy a goddamn coffee. It started friendly enough, but he's been escalatin'. Last week, she said he squeezed the coffee cup so hard it burst all over the counter when she refused to sell again."

"Why the fuck would someone want to buy Stella's so badly?" King asked. "It's a damn good diner but nothin' outta the ordinary."

"Same with Honey Bear Café," Curtains added.

"Cress might fight you on that, but you're right," King agreed, starin' off into the distance the way he was prone to do when he was puzzlin' shit out.

"They both do good business," Buck allowed. "But not at the level that warrants a fuckin' takeover like this."

"Not alone, maybe," Curtains mused, pullin' up somethin' on his laptop before spinnin' it to show our end of the table. "But Stella said he was an Asian guy, right? Well, a corporation has bought six houses on Crest Street, Bones's Barber Shop, and a strip mall between us and Stoneridge just off the Sea to Sky Highway."

A shiver of premonition trickled like ice down my spine as I leaned across the table to pull Curtains' computer closer. I squinted at the screen for a second before reachin' for my reading glasses.

"Fuck. I think if you do a search, you'll find that same corp's got a bid in on two square blocks of warehouse district directly beside land we own and an agricultural acreage that butts up to Angelwood Farm." I rubbed at my temples. "This does not say good things."

The industrial land housed our weapons depot, but only Priest, Zeus, Bat, and I knew the exact location to keep shit on lockdown. Angelwood Farm was one of our favourite settings for interrogations, beatings, and puttin' enemies' bodies to rest. Havin' a rival criminal organization as our neighbours at either location was untenable.

"What're you thinkin', brother?" Zeus asked, lookin' unruffled as fuck 'cause the man'd been to prison twice, had his wife abducted, his daughter assaulted, and his son believed to be dead for more than half a year. This shit was nothin' to him. Which didn't mean he couldn't care less. What made Z not only the best leader of this chapter but the whole damn Fallen empire was his ability to give a shit about everythin' without losin' his goddamn mind.

In this business, too much crazy and horrible shit happened. You'd patch in on a Monday and go crazy by Thursday.

"I'm thinkin' an old acquaintance from Seven Song visited me yesterday, and we got threats against local businesses today… They're obviously linked."

"You got history with the triad?" Wrath spoke up for the first time, leanin' forward on thick forearms.

"Some."

He arched a brow. "Worked with the Red Dragons youth gang when I was a teen. The Chinese triads don't fuck around. If they're comin' up to Entrance, it means they got their eye on some prize here."

"Maybe they've already maxed out their potential in Vancouver," Curtains suggested. "They use the casinos and real estate to wash their money, only the Gambling Board's cottoned on to them recently, and housing prices are through the fuckin' roof in the city. Makes sense for them to move up the Sea to Sky in search of new opportunities."

"Only we own this fuckin' corridor," Zeus growled. "And the T-Squad owns the local casino. There's no way they're lettin' the triad in on that cash cow."

"No," Curtains agreed. "But they don't really need to work *with* the Thunderbird Squad," he said, referrin' to the local Indigenous gang. "They just need to funnel enough money through straw men they send through the casino. As long as they don't use their own gangsters, which they aren't stupid enough to do, they'll be able to get away with launderin' a decent amount of cash."

"Fuck," Bat murmured.

"That's about the size of it," Zeus agreed. "Right. Curtains, do some work on findin' out which triad this corp buyin' up land in town is tied to. Red Dragon and Seven Song are two different beasts, and we need to know who we're dealin' with. Last I heard, they fuckin' hated each other, some bad blood that goes way back. Look into that, too. Get every motherfuckin' thing we can use against 'em. We don't want outsiders buyin' up Entrance wholesale, and we sure as fuck can't afford for another syndicate to buy land near our fuckin' burial grounds. Let's get Pigeon, Carson, and Ransom doin' the rounds in town, seein' if they've approached any other businesses. And Axe-Man? What's your bead on this Jiang Kuan?"

"He said he wants a meet with you. The last time I saw the man was eight years ago when we tried to save our own asses when Seven Song and the Calgary chapter were warrin'. It didn't go down the way we hoped, obviously. He and his brother work together, but they didn't exactly see eye to eye back in the day." I hesitated, knowin' Carson was standin' behind me. "Jiang had a white male lover back then. Kasper didn't approve on either count. The night shit went down––*I* went down––Kasper murdered his brother's man right in front of him. We could use that if we gotta."

I heard the shuffle of Carson's feet behind me and turned to address him. "Use it against *Kasper*, brother. Not use Jiang's sexual preferences against Jiang. You get me?"

Carson didn't meet my gaze for a moment, starin' at his

boots. He was still young, and even though he was wickedly in love with his high school sweetheart, Benny, it was hard to be a gay man in an MC, even one as progressive as Zeus Garro's. Finally, he looked up with a familiar obdurate expression and gave me a nod.

"Jiang's a wily one, but he's more westernized than his older brother. It might be worth it to feel out what he wants and if it's the same thing Kasper Kuan wants," I suggested.

Zeus stared at me for a long moment, and I could read his expression after years of practice.

This is bringin' up ghosts for you. I'm sorry, but I'm gonna need ya on this anyway.

I jerked my chin up at him and nodded back.

"Set the meet. Tomorrow, dawn, somewhere on our turf. 'Til then, keep an eye out in town for triad blood."

"They're easy enough to spot, the flashy fuckers," Wrath muttered, and despite myself, I grinned, 'cause it was the damned truth.

"On another note," King said. "H.R. and Danny are gettin' married in six weeks, and we still haven't thrown the guy a bachelor party."

"Says he doesn't want one," Zeus muttered. "And I'm on board for that."

Boner rolled his eyes. "You're such a dad. The dude needs a bachelor party. It's basically a crime against nature not to say goodbye to the good ole single life without a proper send-off."

"Meanin' strippers," Buck confirmed.

"Well, yeah," Boner agreed. "Leave it to me, I got this."

"I'm his best man, so you can help *me*. If I left it up to you, you'd turn the whole thing into some kinda bacchanalia," King corrected.

"No fuckin' clue what that is, but it does sound sexy."

"Talk about this shit on our own time. Church adjourned," Zeus declared, thumpin' his fist on the table.

Everyone echoed his movement before gettin' up and filterin' outta the chapel.

Bat and I stayed at the table as everyone else left.

"No Kodiak again today," Bat noted.

"He's up at the house."

My friend slanted me a look. "He's appointed himself Cleo's fuckin' watchdog since everythin' went down."

He had, and I wasn't gonna complain about it. Kodiak was a quiet sonovabitch, but he was smart and fierce as hell. He wouldn't let anythin' happen to my girl when I couldn't be there, and it took the edge off my panic whenever I was away from her to know he had her back.

"Just be careful, yeah?" Z said. "The kinda men we are, someone who inspires that kinda loyalty in us often inspires other kinds'a feelings."

I bared my teeth at him. "He's not gonna hit on my daughter after she's been fuckin' attacked. Kodiak doesn't deserve you even sayin' that."

Zeus blinked calmly at me, openin' his hands on the table. "Not sayin' he would. I'm sayin' loyalty and love are two sides of the same coin. Just don't be surprised if the situation develops into somethin' more."

I shook my head. "I know H.R. was attacked once, but what happened to Cleo...it's different. It's like what happened to her mum. I don't think..." I sucked in a deep breath through my teeth, warrin' with the impotent rage and agony in my chest. "I don't think a person ever comes back from that in a way that makes them feel safe to fall in love like that again. I hope to fuck I'm wrong, but she's already sayin' the Kay women got some kinda curse."

The silence that blanketed the table was punctuated only by the sounds of the brothers in the main room.

"Maybe," Zeus agreed, mouth pressed tight in an unhappy line. "But let's hope not, for Cleo's sake. She's got a whole family'a badasses at her back, and she always will. Hopefully, that gives her the shield she needs to feel safe again."

"Eventually," Bat agreed with his own wry grin.

"How're you doin'? How're the boys?" Z asked.

The Prophet had murdered Bat's wife, Amelia, leavin' their twin boys without a mother.

Bat scrubbed a hand over through his black hair and loosed a long, windin' sigh. "Let's just say, thank fuckin' Christ for Tempest and Dane."

"Who would'a thought one of the biker groupies would make such a good nanny?" Z chuckled.

Bat did not.

With a glower, he said, "Tempest was never a fuckin' groupie. She was just a girl in a tough spot. Trust me, she's saved us more than we ever saved her."

Z held up a hand in surrender. "No offense meant, brother. She's a good woman."

When Bat levelled that glare at me, I only smirked. "Got nothin' but good to say about her, man. I'm guessin' Dane is with her and the boys, now?"

A grimace contracted his face for a second before he could smooth it out. "Yeah, they get along well, and the boys love 'em."

Z and I locked eyes for a second, both wonderin' how Bat would take it if his best friend ended up with his nanny.

I didn't have all day to shoot the shit like the rest of the brothers out in the clubhouse, though. Pushin' outta my chair, I leaned on the table and knocked my knuckles against it in farewell.

"Where're ya goin' now?" Z asked. "Thought we'd go over some numbers this mornin'."

"Later. We want the low-down on Jiang Kuan before the meet tomorrow, I got someone I need to talk to."

CHAPTER TWENTY-THREE

Mei

Purgatory Motel was a hellhole painted all in pink.

The neon sign teetered on its metal pole over the cracked asphalt parking lot, pink light flickering on a dingy once-white background. It announced there was no vacancy, but it was obvious just looking at the place that it had never been fully booked in its entire existence. The long, low building was shaped like an L and tucked into the back of the lot on the side of the Sea to Sky Highway. The doors were painted the same obnoxious pink as the trim, the walls a paler shade like the inside of an unclean mouth. There was a rust-sided Harley-Davidson in one parking spot and an ancient Caravan with yellowed curtains in the windows in another.

A total dump.

I loved it.

I'd grown up staying with my parents in Fairmonts, Four Seasons, and Dogwoods. Hotels with sleekly appointed bellhops and impeccably turned-out reception staff.

The pot-bellied man sitting behind the desk at Purgatory Motel wore a thin white tank top through which I could see his profusion of thick, grey chest hair and a heavy chain that dug into the thick rolls of his neck. When I checked in, he didn't greet me by name or expand on the wonders of the local culture or activities.

He grunted at me and handed over an old-fashioned key without even asking my name, only extending his opened fist for the cash I offered.

Room 7 was on the second and highest floor at the end of the L. It was hard to get to, for anyone who might want to get to me, but it was also hard to escape. I tested the security of the iron railing and judged the distance to the ground floor. If I eased myself over the railing slowly, I'd be able to make the leap with no problem.

I had to shove my shoulder into the door to get it to budge open, scraping back over pink shag carpet that carried the smell of cigarette and musk. There were two double beds, a single nightstand and set of drawers, and a small boxy television with actual bunny ear antennae I'd only seen in old movies.

I laughed as I dumped my duffel bag on one bed and did my walk through the space, checking for hidden cameras and anything particularly disgusting. Other than the pink bathtub and the stained towels in the bathroom, it was clean in the sense there were no bugs.

When I sat on the bed and a little dust cloud exploded, I laughed again and bounced a little on the creaky box spring.

"Yeah, this seems right," I muttered, falling back to stare at the popcorn ceiling.

I was in Entrance to pay penance for the ways I'd done the Axelsens wrong eight years ago. Staying in this ridiculously awful place was only appropriate.

Besides, it offered a quick getaway on the highway and an

easy trip down to Vancouver if I was called home for some reason.

After Axe-Man practically banned me from frequenting any reputable place in town and the whole headless raccoon debacle, I'd popped in to give Cleo her sandwich and a kiss, leaving that huge, silent bear of a brother, Kodiak, to take her to her rehab appointments at the hospital so I could see to some shit back in Vancouver, including a visit with Old Dragon.

It was late when I finally dragged myself back to the motel, the wind drawing cold claw marks across my face and through my hair as I slumped up the steps to the second story. I was exhausted in a way I hadn't been able to shake since Cleo called me from the hospital. It was the weight of guilt, I knew. That I hadn't been with her, not only to save her that day from the psychopathic killer but that I hadn't been there before that to lead her down a different, less desperate path. Maybe it was egotistical to think I could have made that difference...she had the best dad in the world, Lin, a new best friend who wore pink unironically, and an entire motorcycle club taking her back. What difference would I have made, really?

What difference did I ever make, other than to ruin nearly everything I touched despite my best intentions?

Daiyu used to say I didn't know how to do anything gently. My love was violent. I threw my heart against unsuspecting acquaintances, trampled on it myself before they could pick it up off the ground, and when I stuck it back in my chest, torn, dirty, beating a little less madly than before, I didn't even bother to wipe it off. It was a reckless, dangerous kind of love that hurt those I tried to care for as much as it hurt me.

It seemed like so many Chinese folklore tales Old Dragon had grown up telling me, the tragedy of the Butterfly Lovers and the Legend of the White Snake, like even Madame Cheung had told me in the red tent that night at the carnival, I was doomed to love and live alone. It didn't seem to matter if the love I had to give was platonic or romantic. I clearly wasn't a good influence.

I was brooding on this when I opened the door to my room, so I wasn't paying attention like I normally would have.

Which was why, when a large figure moved in my periphery, I reacted the way I'd been trained to my whole life.

With violence.

It was dark in the room. The intruder hadn't bothered to turn on any lights to better surprise me, but I could tell at a glance that he was huge, at least double my size. When he reached for me, I grabbed his arm and spun into his body, curling my spine slightly as I tucked up against him. Position secured, I leveraged his momentum to toss his weight up and over my back. He went crashing onto the closest bed, his legs thwacking into the wall, a booted foot going straight through the plaster wall.

But he had hold of my arm still, a fierce grasp I couldn't disengage from. When I tried to wrench away, he took advantage of my lack of balance to tug me closer, rolling onto his shoulders to wrap strong thighs around my torso and throw me over his prone form on to the bed between his legs. I landed badly, my shoulder cracking against the pink-painted wood headboard.

Instantly, I tried to get to my feet, but he moved fast for such a big man, twisting onto his front to pin me to the bed with his thighs, two rough palms shackling my wrists.

I was about to headbutt him when he finally spoke. "Is this the way you greet everyone that comes knockin' nowadays?"

"Henning?" I gasped, because the man above me was big enough, but his hair was dark and short.

He made a chuffing noise like an irritated bear, transferring one of my wrists into his other hand so they were both pinned in one palm before he reached to flick on the horrible frilly pink lamp beside us.

The rosy light illuminated his craggy face, and a black toque embroidered with The Fallen MC patch pulled down low over his forehead.

"Ah," I said. "If you want an apology, you'll be waiting a while. I'm not sure what kind of girls you hang out with these days, but the *usual* kind of girl will do exactly what I just did when she finds an enormous slab of strange man meat in her room uninvited."

"Nothin' about you is or ever has been usual," he countered.

He was so close, his body pressed all along mine. Thick thighs as unforgiving as steel bracketing my hips, a huge hand easily clasping my wrists, the other braced in the pillow beside my head. It was meant to be a threatening position, but now that I knew it was *him*, it was dangerously sexy. A few inches south and he could rock his cock against my groin, zipper to zipper, the friction delicious. A few inches north and he'd be sitting on my chest in perfect position to feed his cock into my greedy––now drooling––mouth.

When I wrenched my gaze from his groin back up to his face, his bright eyes were locked on my mouth. I held my breath as he slowly raised his hand from the flat pillow and unhooked my lower lip from my teeth. The pad of his thumb came away with a streak of blood, and we both watched, transfixed, as he started to bring it to his mouth as if to lick it away.

Unbidden, a little breathy groan escaped my lips, and just like that, the moment was punctured.

Axe-Man practically leapt off me, moving to the other side of the room to lean mock-casually against the dresser holding the TV. He crossed his arms and stared at me as if I'd invited him over myself, and he hadn't just shown up like a total creeper in my room.

"You're being very creepy," I informed him, in case he was unaware.

For a second, his frown faded into blank shock, and then his lips twitched.

Just for a second.

But it was basically a smile.

Or as close to one as I'd gotten in eight years, and I'd probably ever get again.

It was almost absurd how victorious I felt seeing that like I'd won gold at the Olympics or a Nobel Peace Prize.

And honestly, given the hostility between us, I thought I might've deserved one.

"You're one to talk. How the fuck did you know about the raccoon today?" he demanded.

"Oooh." I decided if he could pretend to be casual, I could too. I adjusted on the bed, sprawling across the pink sheets, hair a wild black aura around my head, arms propped beneath the pillow. "Well, obviously, my real motive in moving all the way to Small Town, Canada, was to terrify the local shopkeepers, so I woke up early, trapped a 'coon, sliced and diced it, and put the pieces around town like a macabre scavenger hunt."

"Cut the shit," he snapped, stepping forward as if he wanted to stop me physically.

I wished he would.

Though, the Henning I'd known had never been so quick to anger, even with me. He'd always been steady, with a gravitas that made him even keel even in the wildest circumstances.

"I don't know what to tell you. I didn't have anything to do with it."

His eyes narrowed. Maybe to someone else, he would have seemed terrifying looming in the shadows with that dark hat pulled low, his leather cut proclaiming him a 1%er, the hatchet sheathed at his hip. But I hadn't seen him in nearly a decade, and was I thirsty for the sight of him, to catalogue all the ways he'd changed and the ways he hadn't. I wished hopelessly that he'd just rest there for a while and let me sketch him.

"Mei." He clapped his hands together to get my attention. "I said, you know who did."

I shrugged. "No, I don't. But given the threat was in Chinese, it seems viable it was one of the triads."

"Which one?"

I rolled my eyes. "Again, I *do not know*. What I do know is that the Red Dragons and Seven Song have basically declared war. It wouldn't surprise me if one or both of them were trying to extend their reach outside of Vancouver for more security and influence."

"How do you know that? And don't even think about lyin' to me, Mei."

"Oh." I mock shivered. "Is the big bad biker going to hurt me?"

His grin was a wedge of white, wicked teeth in the pink-tinged shadows. "You'd like that too much, I think. No, I'll just forbid you to see Cleo."

"You wouldn't." But I wasn't sure. He really did seem to despise me almost as much as he loved his daughter. I'd never seen him deny her anything she truly wanted, but it was reasonable to assume I might be the first.

"I would," he snarled softly, unfolding his arms to stalk forward and plant a knee on the foot of the bed so he could lean over me. "When it comes to protectin' my family against you, I'd do anythin'."

"I would *never* hurt Cleo."

"Not intentionally, maybe. But you did eight years ago, and I got a feelin' you'd do it again."

"You don't know me anymore," I argued, rearing up to plant a hand on his chest and shove him back. "If you want my help, you can fucking ask *nicely* for it."

"I don't want your fuckin' help. I want you to be honest for once in your selfish fuckin' life and tell me what you know about the situation so I can protect my family," he roared, shoving off the bed to pace the small strip of pinkish-brown carpet in front of the beds.

Whatever fun I'd been having dried up and died in my chest. I sat up, scooting toward the headboard, and wrapped my arms around my knees.

"I don't know much, Axe-Man. Whether you choose to believe me or not. I know about the turf war because I lived in Vancouver, and the police are trying to keep the media out of it, but gang violence has been escalating. Almost eight years ago, the Kuan brothers extended their operation to Vancouver and instantly clashed with the Red Dragons, who'd been in town for decades. The Dragon Heads hate each other, but I don't know the story there." I swallowed thickly past that lie as it lodged in my throat. "I don't know why or if it was them scaring Lauren and that other woman. It's just a guess that they might be looking for ways to secure their hold as they get ready for a full-scale war."

"You know a lot about it," he accused, but he sounded weary, deflated.

He had never been an angry man, or even a sad one despite all the things he'd suffered through in his life, but he seemed so tired now, almost hollow like he had nothing left to give. It made me ache to fill him up, to give and give all I had just to ease his pain for a second.

The hardest thing was living with the truth even an eight-year separation couldn't kill. I still loved him. That man was more than a man to me and always would be because he was also my hero, and no matter what ending they got, the mythological Jason and Hercules, the superheroes Batman and Spider-Man, they lived on eternally for the impact of their good deeds. And Henning's goodness lived on inside me. I'd grown around it.

And I could see it now, watching him bear the weight of worry for his club in the face of this new threat, for his town, for his daughter. It was so much for one man to carry, too much.

The yearning I had to help him carry that load was a physical, sharp ache in my chest.

"You know Old Dragon still has friends in the triad," I reminded him. "I keep an ear to the ground."

It was more than that, but I couldn't tell him.

I knew he'd never forgive me, already, but if he knew the truth, he'd never speak to me again, and he'd forbid me to see Cleo. Even though part of me wanted to be honest with him, I couldn't risk not seeing my best friend. I might've been unsure whether I was a good influence in her life, but for better or worse, *she* wasn't, and I wouldn't abandon her––again––when she needed me so badly.

"What I want is for you to stay outta this," he demanded, cracking his knuckles. It drew my attention to his left hand, where his pinky used to be, before Kang severed it with his *dao* sword.

Noticing the direction of my gaze, Axe-Man snapped his fingers to get my attention. "Yeah, Mei. I lost a finger and two years of my life last time you got involved in shit that was beyond your pay grade. Maybe this time I can trust you've learned enough to fuckin' *listen* to me for once and keep your nose outta this."

I canted my chin up but didn't resist the urge to tug a pillow into my lap, hugging it reflexively. "I could help. I'm not the same seventeen-year-old girl I was back then."

"No? Then prove it by doin' what you're told."

"I've never been much good at that," I admitted, biting into my torn bottom lip again. "Especially not when people I care about are at risk."

"No one is at risk," he snarled, his knuckles white as he clenched his fists. "You think I'm gonna let a damn thing hurt Cleo ever again? You think I'm gonna let some fuckin' triad close in on my town after we were just ravaged by a fuckin' religious lunatic who carved up women for fun? I'm the one who's got a stake in this, not you. You might've moved here for Cleo, but don't think for one second this place will ever be your home."

His words were embedded in my skin like needles in a pin cushion until pain radiated from every pore. I ducked my head because I deserved his anger and malice. But I couldn't bear for him to see the tears surging to the backs of my eyes.

"Right," I murmured, fiddling with the edge of the pillow. "Okay. I'll stay out of it."

"Is that a promise?" he demanded, and when I didn't meet his gaze, he surged forward again to grasp my chin between his knuckles and tip my face up. The movement dislodged a tear, and he tracked its movement down my cheek, fingers spasming slightly on my face, before he fixed his angry eyes on mine. "And, Mei, you don't want to fuckin' lie to me ever again. I'm not the soft man you once knew."

And I'm not the helpless girl you once knew, either, I wanted to say but didn't.

Instead, I sucked in a little breath, twisted my fingers together in my lap under the pillow so he couldn't see them, and once again, I lied to Henning Axelsen. "Sure, I promise I won't get involved."

He searched my face for a long moment, and even though he hated me and that hate was evident in every inch of his expression, I drank in the sight of his gorgeous face. My throat was clogged with such a tangled mess of sorrow and desire, I could barely breathe.

"I'll hold you to that," he swore, and there was a cracking in those lake water eyes like ice before the thaw. "It's for your own good, too, ya know."

"Sure." I nodded, but this time, he was wrong.

Being here with him and Cleo in Entrance was for my own

good. Taking care of them was the *only* good I'd ever done or attempted to do in my life. It gave purpose to my existence.

Axe-Man nodded curtly, dropping his grip on my chin like I'd burned him. He subtly shook out his hand at his side as he moved toward the door and opened it.

Before he left, because I'd never been a cautious girl, I added, "Oh, Axe-Man?"

He paused, so big in the doorway he made it look like a hobbit's house.

"Have you considered why they wrote the note in Chinese when both Stella and Lauren are white?" I watched thoughts cross his face like storm clouds. "It's not because I'm in town. I think it's because *you* are. It's been a long time since shit went down in Calgary, but the Kuan brothers are the kind of men who never forget. They're powerful enough, so they rarely have to."

"You think the note was for me."

"I think there are questions we never answered back then that are still relevant."

"It's not a bad point," he conceded reluctantly, knocking his silver rings against the doorframe. "But I'll be the one to answer them, not you."

"Aye aye, captain," I said with a mock salute so that when he closed the door, he did it with a glower.

I flopped to the bed the second he left and blew hair out of my face with a loud raspberry.

"Well," I said to the popcorn ceiling. "How long will it be before he finds out I'm dating Jiang Kuan?"

CHAPTER TWENTY-FOUR

Axe-Man

ENTRANCE BAY MARINA OCCUPIED THE ENTIRE RIGHT SIDE OF THE bay and was filled year-round with an assortment of fishin' boats, small and large sailin' vessels, and big to enormous yachts. It was a hodgepodge like Entrance was a hodgepodge, different social-economic groups co-existin' but rarely minglin'. It made the marina quaint, and the shingled, faded red and navy-blue buildings clustered at its mouth added to the aesthetic. Eugene, Z's cousin, had a huge fishin' boat docked in the shadowy pier near the sheer cliffside overlookin' the ocean.

It was the perfect place to meet Jiang and his lot. Public enough to discourage violence, but private enough to discourage noisy passersby from stickin' their noses in.

Zeus, Bat, King, and Wrath were with me on the boat while Priest and Nova waited at the top of the rampway to pat down our guests when they arrived.

Curtains was hidden in the captain's hold on the ship with

his computer, ready to start trackin' the bastards as soon as one of us could slip a trackin' device on them.

"You look rough, brother," King pointed out without lookin' up from his leather-bound notebook. Kid was always writin' in it, cover folded back, book propped on his knee as he scribbled with a stubby pencil he often wore behind one ear. "Somethin' stop you from gettin' a good sleep? 'Cause I'm the one with a baby, and I look a helluva lot better than you."

"You're just better lookin'," I deadpanned.

King flashed me his movie-star smile. "Ain't that the truth. Still, you gotta take care'a yourself, man. For Cleo's sake at least."

"You don't think I'm tryin'?" I demanded. "Triad comes to town on the heels of that fuckin' psychopath, and you think I can get a wink of sleep?"

It was that and more. Not that I'd reveal anythin' to King, but my altercation with Mei the night before had left me feelin' outta step.

I tried not to let myself think about Mei. If I did, my thoughts splintered along the divide of our past—the girl I'd known before prison and the girl who put me there.

The girl from before had been a fixture in my daily life for years. We'd been bonded by the trauma of losin' Kate and by the loneliness we both felt bein' different than the people we tried so hard to fit in with. There'd always been this fundamental, elemental understandin' between us. Like we had the same language written in our blood and bones.

I loved Cleo more than anythin' in this world, and I'd loved Kate and Lin, felt that I owed them everythin'. But I'd never felt so understood as I had in those late-night hours sketchin' and shootin' the shit with Mei in my little kitchen.

But that was gone.

Now, eight years and a shit ton of wrongdoin' separated us irrevocably. Mentally, I knew she couldn't be trusted. I'd gone to fuckin' *prison* for her, done it, if not happily, then righteously, proudly, 'cause I'd valued her and her future more than my own. And she'd just...abandoned us. *Me*. Without a word.

Then eighteen months later, she'd turned up at the prison as if nothin' had happened when everythin' had changed.

I didn't know this girl. She wasn't––couldn't be––my Rocky anymore. She was just some dangerous allusion to a past when I'd been soft and stupid. I couldn't afford to be those things anymore, especially not for her.

Fool me once, and all that shit.

The problem was the...muscle memory. I couldn't seem to keep my hands off her. I didn't have to tussle with her like that, straddlin' her small but subtly curved and muscled form, pinnin' her hands and thighs with my body in a way that reminded me I was a man and she was no longer a girl.

She'd always been gorgeous, but now...

I had to remind myself that her loveliness was all deception. Beneath the beauty, she was one of the most dangerous people I'd ever known. She'd even proven it last night by findin' a way to flip me over her damn back.

It was just my goddam luck that I found that sexy as fuck.

And last night, after lyin' in bed tossin' and fuckin' turnin' for hours worryin' about the triad, about Cleo's mental health, about the club, I'd finally fallen into visceral, carnal dreams about Mei Zhen fuckin' Marchand.

Even now, in the weak light of a late winter sun, I couldn't shake the phantom feel of her small breasts in my hands, the texture of her cunt against my tongue, and the noises my subconscious had manufactured for her when she came around my cock.

A full-body shudder of disgust rolled through me and shook me free of the memory.

King was studyin' me and winced when he saw my shudder,

mistakin' it for somethin' else. "Yeah, I got you. Still, we can handle these fuckers."

I raised my brows. "You dealt with the triads before?"

He shook his head. "They can't be worse than the fuckin' cartel."

I snorted. "Not worse, maybe, but just as lethal. Different. The raccoon at Stella's and Honey Bear Café? They're playin' with us, King. Playin' like a motherfuckin' tiger with a mouse. We're just cluin' in, but they're already three steps ahead. Guarantee that."

"Fuck," he muttered, and then his eyes darted over my shoulder, and he slipped his notebook into his back pocket. "They're here."

Jiang was immediately recognizable at the forefront of a group of four. He was taller, leaner, and dressed like one of the K-drama movie stars Cleo loved so much. I shook my head as the gold of his flashy gun sparkled beneath the flap of his trench coat.

"Is he wearin' a fuckin' sword?" King muttered.

Wrath, steppin' up beside me, crossed his arms. "A lotta 'em do. They got a shorter, straight-edged blade called a watermelon chopper, but Jiang's got a proper *dao* sword."

"I always forget you worked for them," I murmured, crossin' my own arms and bracin' my legs military-style as the gangsters passed Priest's and Nova's scrutiny and were escorted down the ramp toward us.

"The Red Dragon's youth gang," he amended. "They were just startin' out and desperate for muscle, so they made me a bouncer at one of their clubs and had me jumpin' ashes at the door even though I was a white kid."

Jumpin' ashes was the Chinese slang term for dealin' heroin.

I side-eyed my brother, realizin' for the millionth time how little we knew about him. Really, how little the club knew about the histories of any of its brothers. Zeus knew the most, bein' Prez, but sometimes, I fuckin' marvelled at the trust he had in us. This ragtag group of criminals who each had hearts of gold under all the tatts and records and bad attitudes. How did he sense it?

I'd stopped trustin' my gut instinct for that kinda thing around the time Mei left me to rot in jail.

"They gonna recognize you?" Zeus asked as he stepped up beside us, Bat and King takin' up his other side so we flanked him.

Wrath grinned the way a wolf might've grinned, all teeth and peeled-back lips. The guy was so good lookin' it was a town joke that any of the single women would make a deal with the devil for one night with the biker even though he never took notice of any of them. But I could not fuckin' see it.

Dude was the scariest motherfucker I knew.

Priest used to take the cake on that, but he had Bea and a little one on the way now. It made him more dangerous 'cause he had somethin' to lose now, but it also made him *human* in a way he'd never been before.

Wrath'd lost his humanity along with his heart when his woman was killed a few years back.

"I wouldn't worry about it," he assured us, then wiped the smile from his face when the group hit our row of boats, and Priest and Nova led them across the planks to our boat.

"Not very hospitable, taking our weapons when you retain yours," Jiang called in an almost friendly tone as he stepped up the ladder and onto the boat.

Zeus shrugged a shoulder. "You wanted a meet when I'd rather never'a set eyes on your ugly mug. Beggars can't be choosers."

Jiang's smile was thin as he struck a pose—hand on hip, pushing back the trench coat to show his empty holsters, the other drumming his fingers against his thigh. "Well, we make concessions when we deal with infamy and you are infamous, President Zeus Garro. What a delight it is to meet you in the flesh."

Zeus's response was to cross his arms over his chest and cock an eyebrow.

Jiang laughed in delight. "You certainly do live up to your reputation."

"Then it won't surprise you when I say I don't give a fuck 'bout your expectations. The only reason we're meetin' is 'cause you rolled into *my* motherfuckin' town and threatened *my* motherfuckin' townsfolk and *my goddamn motherfuckin' brother*. So quit the act and settle up. What has you so desperate to meet?"

Jiang's persona fell away from one second to the next. Now, he stood straight as a rod, facin' us head-on, chin tipped down so he could stare at us through narrowed eyes. When he spoke, it was a hiss. "I'd think again about your attitude, Garro. I'm here because once, a very long time ago, your associate Axe-Man tried to help me, but mostly, I'm doing this as a favour for a friend. In fact, I could get my own ass in a sling just by extending this little courtesy. I always told them trying to help you lot would be like pulling a cow up a tree."

It was a Chinese expression that didn't translate properly to English, but we all understood his meaning.

Zeus shifted position just slightly, rollin' to the balls of his feet, hands curlin' into loose fists. He'd have his beloved brass knuckles in his pocket, and I could see his desire to use them.

I felt it, too. My hand curlin' around the handle of the hatchet at my side.

"A favour to who?" I demanded, 'cause somethin' about that didn't sit right.

Jiang only raised both brows at me in haughty disdain before addressin' Zeus again. "I'm here to *warn* you. My brother has set his sights on Entrance. He believes it's a good foothold to dominate the Sea to Sky passage, and he wants it for Seven Song."

"Yeah, we figured as much based on the dead animals he's left our shopkeepers," Zeus drawled. "Too bad this foothold's been owned and operated by The Fallen MC for decades, and we won't ever give it up."

"Without a fight," Jiang amended with a click of his tongue. "Because my brother isn't well versed in the word *no*."

I wondered if he realized how he touched the scar on his right cheek, the same scar I'd watched Kasper slice into his face the night I went to jail. It didn't surprise me that Jiang still worked with his brother even after all that. Chinese cultural emphasis on family before all else was so deeply embedded, Jiang probably thought he still owed everythin' to his older brother even though Kasper'd killed his lover and publicly scarred and humiliated Jiang himself.

I'd been willin' to stand by Rooster for too long, and he wasn't even blood, so I couldn't pretend I didn't understand where he was comin' from. Loyalty as a fundamental characteristic was a double-edged sword I'd cut myself on one too many times.

"You sure you wanna take us on?" Zeus was sayin', flippin' open a blade to clean under his nails. "We're not the Calgary chapter ten years ago. We're the fuckin' mother chapter of The Fallen MC, and we got allies up and down this province. You wanna go to war with us and the Red Dragons, be my guest. You'll be torn apart an hour after you fire the startin' gun."

"I don't want to go to war with anyone." Jiang opened his palms to the sky as if beseechin' God for peace. "That's why I'm *here*. To warn you. He wants access to the marina, a financial hold on the town, and power. But he isn't the only one. The White Snake, the leader of the Red Dragons, has his eye on Entrance too. The car dealership owned by a Reece Ross? They're in negotiations right now to take over the lot. They've also got their eye on Purgatory Motel and Main Street B&B. It's the devil you know," he said with a dramatic flourish to himself. "Or the devil you don't. You can go to war with him––and with us––or we can reach an agreement. We'll let you run your guns and weed, but you mule our heroin and cocaine from the Washington border up through Whistler."

A growl worked low in my throat because that was the same deal Kasper'd blackmailed Rooster into acceptin' after takin' some of the club's women hostage.

He lifted his open palm, and one of the silent men behind him placed a stack of papers in it. Jiang accepted the package without looking at it and offered it to us. "It's all very above board. We've laid out fair terms and percentages, and all you need to do is agree."

When no one stepped forward to take the contract, Jiang tossed it at our feet. Without hesitation, Wrath unclipped his flask from his belt and poured booze on the papers. Before he was done, I was lightin' a match from the Eugene's Bar matchbook in my pocket and droppin' it to the papers.

They went up instantly, flames cracklin' in the air at our feet. The boat deck was fibreglass, so we didn't have to worry about the fire spreadin'.

Only after that did Z give me the nod.

I stepped forward, boots almost in the flames, and stared down Jiang Kuan. "The Fallen MC isn't for sale, now or ever. You want what isn't yours, you better be prepared to die for it."

"This didn't go well for you last time, trying to stop our progress," Jiang reminded me.

"No, but I got a whole different brotherhood at my back, and they're the kinda men who are happy to live free and die hard for what matters. Now get the fuck outta our town."

CHAPTER TWENTY-FIVE

Mei

I DIDN'T KNOW WHY I THOUGHT VISITING LIN'S BEAUTY Emporium would be a good idea, except that Cleo desperately needed some pampering, and I hadn't seen Lin in years. I wasn't as apprehensive about seeing Lin as I had been about seeing Axe-Man because she'd actually responded to my letters and emails over the years. We weren't close like we used to be, and she'd only come with Cleo to visit me in Vancouver once before declaring she felt wrong keeping it from Axe-Man. Still, she seemed to understand without me having to cut myself open and bleed myself dry that some fairly...awful things had kept me from the Axelsen's side in those eighteen months after Axe-Man went to prison. She still sent a massive box of Raisinets along with Cleo for my birthday every year, too, which had to mean something good.

So maybe I thought it would be, I don't know, *fun*. Going to the salon with my bestie and getting our nails done while we caught up with Lin. We used to do it in high school, Cleo choosing something pastel and pretty while I waffled between red and black. Lin's old salon had these huge faux leather massage chairs we could lean back in while we got our toes done, and we'd sit facing each other for our manicures afterward. It was so innocent and fun, a little ritual we'd done every month to pamper ourselves, but mostly, to bond.

I wanted that again even though I should've known recapturing such a thing was like trying to bottle smoke.

Cleo wasn't in a good place that day, either. She'd never been a grumpy girl, always sweet, a little shy even though she was social and personable, and eager to laugh and enjoy. Now, she was sullen, lower lip curled under, hands caught up in the overlong sleeves of one of Axe-Man's old Street Ink Tattoo Parlour hoodies. The cast fit beneath it, but I thought she'd chosen it as a way to hide her body. She'd always loved pretty things, but since the attack, I hadn't even seen her in colour-coordinated pajamas. It was like she felt beauty had betrayed her.

"Do you want to go home, Glory?" I asked as I helped her out of the car and passed over her crutches. "We don't have to do this. It's supposed to be fun."

That lower lip wobbled before she curled it between her teeth. "No. No, I need to get out of the house. It's starting to feel li-like a prison. A mental institution." I winced because both settings hit a little too close to home. "I need to *breathe*, you know?"

"Even if it's stale beauty salon air?" I teased.

A little grin. "Even then." She sighed so heavily it stirred the uneven locks of hair over her forehead. "It's just that...I feel so tired all the time. Not just from lack of sleep but like I was fundamentally exhausted of being myself. Of being in my body and but also just of being *me*."

I swallowed the whimper in my throat at the idea of that kind of pain and self-loathing. Stepping closer to crowd her against the car, I gently cupped her face and pressed a kiss to each cheek. I'd never been a physically affectionate person with anyone but the Axelsens, and even though it'd been eight years since we'd spent any kind of real time together, the impulse surged through me like rain over a drought-dry field.

"Why don't we pretend for an hour or two, then? You can be whoever you want to be. We both can."

"Who would you want to be?" she asked, that inquisitive personality that made her such a good journalist peeking through her misery. "Why would you want to be anyone else when you could be you?"

I laughed so loudly that a mother putting her child into a car seat in the minivan a few parking spots away from us startled.

"Oh Glory, you've always had such a skewed vision of me."

Her face spasmed with horror, and she ducked her head. "I guess I'm not a great judge of character."

"No, no." I tipped her chin up and smiled with a healthy dose of self-mockery. "I'm the problem here. I guess it's hard to see yourself the way other people do when all you can fixate on are your mistakes."

Her eyes widened, head reeling back as if I'd hit her. A little gasp escaped her mouth before she swallowed thickly and nodded. "Yeah. Yeah, that feels true."

"Okay, so for this next hour, why don't you pretend to be *my* Glory. The kindest, sweetest, brightest, and most curious woman I know."

"And you'll be *my* Rocky?" she asked suspiciously like she didn't believe I'd go for it.

Which, I mean, was fair. I hadn't felt like Cleo's Rocky in such a long time. It seemed like a beloved shirt I'd outgrown and forgotten.

"Yes," I agreed, holding out my hand in the shape of half a

heart, waiting for Cleo to mirror and join it with her own. "I will."

"*My* Rocky is a smart-mouthed badass," she reminded me with arched dark brows. "But she also has the most loyal and loving heart."

It was my turn to swallow thickly, forcing the self-disgust I'd felt for the past eight years down my gullet where it burned in my belly.

"Okay, let's do this."

"You know," she said as she manoeuvred on her crutches up the sidewalk and over to the glass front entrance in the middle of the shopping centre. "I used to come here with Bea."

I didn't say anything as I opened the door for her because I was afraid the words would come out jealous and bitter.

But Cleo proved she knew me well when she hobbled into the shop and turned to flash sparkling eyes at me. "But it was never really the same, so we didn't do it very often. We made our own rituals. It felt wrong to step on ours."

We exchanged little grins that felt almost shy, like we were both almost embarrassed by how much we'd missed each other.

"Mei Zhenette Raisinet!"

I wheeled toward the sound of that familiar voice a second before I was hit by someone even tinier than I was. My laughter exploded out of my chest at the impact as Lin squeezed me in a hard, tight hug.

"Lin," I whispered, curling around her, pressing my nose into her hair to find it still smelled faintly of rice water.

"It is good to see you," she whispered back in Cantonese, still holding me a little too tight.

I'd often wondered if Old Dragon had broken his promise and told Lin exactly what happened when I went home that night after the events at Turner Farm. It just didn't make sense that she could still be so...kind without knowing I hadn't had a choice in my disappearance back then.

But then, Cleo didn't know, not really. She only had a vague sense that Florent had done something inexcusable, and we no longer had any kind of relationship.

And she still loved me.

In fact, over the years, it was *me* who had kept a greater distance between us, thinking she deserved better.

I shook off my introspection as Lin stepped away enough to clasp me firmly by the cheeks to inspect my face.

"Too pale," she declared, dropping her hands. "Too thin. It's good I brought in mooncakes for you. Salted egg yolk and red bean."

On cue, my stomach rumbled, and the three of us laughed right there in the centre of the busy room like we were back in Axe-Man's Calgarian bungalow.

"You know I'll never say no to your mooncakes, Lin."

"You'll never say no to me at all," she declared with an arched brow and narrowed eyes.

I laughed again as she led us to a long row of black massage chairs almost like the ones she used to have. I helped Cleo get settled in the chair, forgoing the massage so it didn't press against any of her still-sore muscles or contusions. The salon was still relatively empty so early in the morning, which was why I'd decided we should come in. Cleo didn't need to feel like people were whispering about her or that she had to field a bunch of questions from well-meaning townsfolk. Taylor Swift was playing from the speakers, and the salon was bright and cheery, with one red-painted wall and a few huge acrylic landscape paintings on the others.

"Those are gorgeous," I murmured, almost without realizing it.

The woman painting my toes, Agatha, grinned at me.

"Don't let Lin hear you, she'll take any excuse to brag about her boy."

"Lin!" I gasped. "You're dating someone?"

Agatha, Cleo, and Lin all laughed at me.

"I'm afraid I closed up shop a long time ago," Lin said happily, expertly painting the toes peeking out of Cleo's cast a sparkly, pretty purple. "Agatha is talking about Axe-Man. He did all the paintings in here."

"Close your mouth," Cleo teased me the way she used to. "You could catch fish in there."

I shut my jaw with an audible clank as I sought out the paintings again. Axe-Man had only just taken to painting with acrylics back in Calgary, and he'd been super secretive about his studio in the garage, so I'd never seen what he was working on. From the looks of it, he had massive amounts of talent. The canvases were vibrant and detailed, but there was something almost abstract about them that evoked feeling. The sunset over Entrance Bay was all peaches, the pinks and oranges and warm yellow tones of the fruit as if the sun was bursting over-ripe across the sky. The view of the lake I now recognized as the same one beside his house was gloomy, the trees on the far shore jagged and overcrowded like soldiers waiting solemnly to die. It should have been a sad painting, but it was oddly peaceful.

"He could make a fortune off these."

"He doesn't sell them," Cleo told me, staring at that one of the lake as if it called to her. "They're meant to be gifts. Sometimes he sets out to paint one for someone. A birthday or Christmas or Lunar New Year. But sometimes he paints one and realizes he did it for someone without realizing it."

I tugged the sleeve of my tee over my wrist, suddenly acutely aware of the art I'd stolen from him already. As an artist myself, I'd always known it was highly unethical to steal his work the way I had, but I couldn't bring myself to stop. Once I had the koi fish inked around my belly, I was addicted. Now, I had twenty-two tattoos all over my body, each of which had originally been drawn by Henning's hand.

Axe-Man, I had to remind myself, not Henning.

A different man now than he had been.

It was funny that I felt so unchanged when he obviously was not. It was like I had fossilized around this need inside me. My wants and needs had calcified at the time and place I'd discovered my love for Henning Axelsen and then abruptly been torn from him. Anyone seeking to excavate me, *know* me, ultimately failed because they couldn't know my core motivation. Why I got up in the morning and went to bed at night. They couldn't know I was stuck in time trying to right irreversible wrongs.

They couldn't know what a tragic mess I was inside, that the only clear, bright thing I curled around protectively was my love for the Axelsens and my need to take care of them. Even from afar. Even in strange, morally grey and slightly macabre ways. Ways that would make *Axe-Man* hate me even more than he already did.

It wasn't that it was too late to change my path. It was that I didn't want to.

It wasn't that I couldn't change who and why I was. It was that I refused to.

"Does he have a girlfriend?"

The words were out before I could stop them. I wanted to cut out my own tongue for being so obvious. Seventeen and dumb all over again, only this time it was worse because Axe-Man was still my best friend's dad, and now, he couldn't even stand the sight of me.

It was Lin who answered, and she did it softly. In a way that was meant to be kind, I thought, but instead, it just embarrassed me even more. "He dates. But not seriously. Not for long."

"He's always said he only needs us," Cleo added, but she didn't do it with that girlish pride she'd had when she was younger, happy to have a dad who loved her after a childhood without.

She said it like it made her sad, but she'd only just realized that.

"I wouldn't get your hopes up."

I hadn't been paying my normal attention to my surroundings, but the salon had filled up, and a small group of women had approached our row of chairs. The woman in front was absolutely beautiful. Like someone from a magazine or a movie, so nearly perfect I almost didn't believe she was real. She wasn't the one who had spoken, but she stared at me with brilliant blue eyes that held a wealth of reservation. Even though she was young, maybe even younger than me, there was a seriousness to her aura and her positioning, like she'd been elected the leader.

The woman beside her was holding a baby with a curly mess of golden hair and a plump little fist wrapped around the rich brown strands of his mother's locks. They looked like a modern-day version of Madonna with baby, both beautiful, both serene. In a cream knit dress with suede booties with her big hair in loose waves, she was just as pretty as the blue-eyed blonde, but she didn't seem to demand the same attention. And she was the only one who didn't look like she wanted me to leave town on the next bus.

It was only because of the last two women that I knew they were affiliated with The Fallen. They were wearing leather, the eldest woman in skintight black leather pants with a matching lace-up corset and the other in a cool, vintage brown jacket and motorcycle boots. They both looked weathered in the ways bikers tended to, wind-blown and sun-cracked and worn in by life and exposure to the elements.

If I'd been a complete stranger, I would have loved to

approach them. They seemed like my kind of people, at a glance, cool and composed and secure in their own unique style and personalities.

But my life was never like that.

So they'd obviously heard of me, and what they'd heard they did not like.

"Yeah, bitch, I'm talkin' to you." The woman in head-to-toe leather stepped forward pugnaciously, jerking her chin up at me.

"We haven't met, so I'll forgive you for getting my name wrong," I replied blandly. "My name is Mei, not bitch. Don't forget it."

"Oh, we know who you are. Everyone in this town will know who you are by lunch, so don't go expectin' Lauren to sell you shit from Honey Bear after that. No one wants you here, you get me?"

"Winona," the brunette with the baby scolded, stepping forward and rocking her fussy baby at the same time. "That's enough."

"Not nearly," the older blonde added with a glare for good measure.

"I want her here, Hannah." Cleo's voice stilled the group of women like smoke in a beehive, the vibration falling almost completely flat. "Does that not matter to any of you?"

"Sweetie." Hannah frowned and moved to step toward her, but Cleo held up a slightly quivering hand.

"No. I guess you heard Mei was messed up in some stuff a long time ago. But it was just that, a long time ago."

"Around the time your dad was sent to the clink," the original aggressor, Winona, snapped.

"Yeah," Cleo agreed, and I could tell she was going for calm nonchalance, but she was starting to shake, and there was a faint tremor in her voice that broke my damn heart. She hated conflict, always had, so this had to be hard for her. "But you don't know how or why she was messed up in that or about all the years before when Mei was family to me, my dad, Lin, and my mum. You don't have a clue, so don't stand there and pretend you have enough information to pass judgment."

"Cleo," the young blonde, the pretty one with some kind of imbued authority, stepped forward, and the more aggressive two shrank back even though Winona sneered a little. "They're coming on strong, but they mean well. We're all just worried about you. We want the best for you."

Her eyes cut to me, and I could practically hear the words *and she's clearly* not *it* echo in the room.

"I want the best for me too," Cleo admitted on a shaky exhale. Unable to resist, I reached over and took her hand, glaring at the women myself for upsetting her like this. "And Mei's part of that."

"You did just fine the past eight years without her," Hannah pointed out, but it wasn't with the same cruel joy as Winona.

"Did I? I wonder," Cleo said softly, staring down at her casted leg and maybe, her ruined womb.

The brunette with the baby made a wounded noise before shaking her shoulders as if flinging water off her back. "That's enough, all of you. The last thing Cleo needs is a public freaking showdown. We came here to get our nails done, same as the girls. Let's leave them to it. I've got a limited window before Prince starts wailing, and Benny's alone at the shop."

Winona shot me another vicious glare, but Hannah only gave me a defiant look like she was displeased, and the other blonde sent me a long, assessing stare before smiling warmly at Cleo.

"We'll see you tonight?"

Cleo's own smile was tremulous, but she nodded. "We haven't had a proper girls' night in forever, Loulou. Of course it's still on. It's been too long since I've seen Angel and Monster, too, so bring them? I also promised Ares I'd read his English project over."

"They miss you," Loulou replied and didn't hesitate to walk around my chair to get to Cleo. Once there, she leaned forward to hug her. "I miss you, too. We're always here if you need us, yeah?"

"Yeah," Cleo whispered back, blushing with happiness.

Loulou nodded and moved away, taking the baby from the brunette as she went. I watched her coo to him, smiling and laughing at his baby sounds. I wasn't sure if it made me feel better or worse to know she was a good person and her prickliness was only reserved for me.

"We're a protective bunch," the brunette said, pulling my attention back to her. She'd also made her way over to Cleo and stroked her hair absently while she addressed me, like affection was second nature to her. "We have to be."

I didn't know what to say because I got it, I did, but it still sucked.

"I know I made a really stupid mistake with...with *him*," Cleo muttered, referencing Seth Linley, The Prophet. "But I wish people would stop treating me like I'm four years old. I made a mistake, and *I'm* the one paying the consequences. You guys have to just...let me. It's demoralizing that you think I'm suddenly incapable because I'm a victim of something."

The other woman pursed her lips as she considered that. "That's fair, honey. It's different, but when we thought King was..." She sucked in a painful gulp of air like even the thought made her feel like drowning. "...dead, everyone treated me like I was less than because of my grief. Like I couldn't even tie my shoes without help. I realize now that it was because my loved ones were suffering too. Not just because they'd also lost King but because seeing me suffer was agony for them. Their way of coping was helping me, even if it was too much. I'll talk to them, but also, remember, if you can, that it's because we love you so much. We'd all give a kidney to take even an ounce of your pain away from you."

Cleo closed her eyes, breathing deeply to control her emotions for a moment before she opened her glittering eyes and squeezed her friend's hand. "Thanks, Cress. You know I love you, too, right?"

"Always," Cress agreed, kissing her brow before pulling away to smile at us both. "Now, honestly, I have to do something about my nails. You wouldn't believe how much damage running a bookstore does to your hands, but it's not pretty." She paused for our weak chuckles and then softened again. "We haven't been introduced, Mei, but I'm Cressida Garro. I run Paradise Found Bookstore on Main Street. You should pop in some time for a cup of tea and a natter. I have a feeling we could find a lot to talk about."

It was the first olive branch I'd been extended since I came to town, and I was shocked by its impact. For a moment, I forgot how to breathe. Just that simple act of kindness felt astounding in the face of so much hate.

"Thank you, I will."

Cressida smiled at me, blew a kiss at Cleo, and then turned to join her group on the other side of the shop.

Cleo let out a gusty sigh and slumped deeper into her chair. "God, that was rough. I'm sorry, Rocky."

I shrugged one shoulder. "I wasn't exactly expecting a red-carpet welcome, Glory. In a way, it makes me happy to know that you and Axe-Man have friends who are so protective of you."

"Yeah," Cleo agreed, her eyes shifting over the group of women. "You know, when I first moved here, they really did roll out a red-carpet welcome. They helped Lin and me move into a little house off Main Street because Dad was still in prison. Even though he wasn't here, wasn't even a member of the chapter, they all folded us into their community. Dad's been struggling with you back in our lives, but he'll get over it, and when he does, everyone will see how much they're missing out on not having you for a friend."

"I admire your faith," I said dryly because I could so *not* see that happening.

Cleo narrowed her eyes at me the way Lin was prone to do. "You're pretending to be *my* Rocky, remember? And my Rocky is confident."

"Right, I'm the best. Anyone would be lucky to know me. I enrich the lives of those around me just by breathing."

"You know, I remember Old Dragon used to say sarcasm was the lowest form of wit."

I laughed because she was right, even though my belly clenched at the mention of my grandfather. He'd started developing signs of dementia five years ago, and three years after that, I'd had to move him into an assisted care home because I wasn't capable of working and taking care of his needs full-time. It had almost killed me to move him even though it was a really nice, *really* expensive home, and it had almost killed me again the first time he forgot who I was and called me Daiyu. I still visited him every week, and I'd continue to do so even while temporarily living in Entrance.

"The brunette seemed nice," I said, just to change the subject.

"Oh, Cress is the loveliest. She brings me graphic novels to read every weekend because I still don't feel up to going into town much."

"She doesn't look much like a biker's wife. That Winona person, though, fits the cliché pretty well..."

Cleo laughed at my expression. "They don't usually spend much time with her because she's kind of...yeah, a little mean and negative all the time. She must have caught them at the clubhouse on their way here or something. Despite what you say today, The Fallen babes are actually really kind. They wouldn't leave Winona out even though they don't vibe with her much."

"Well, I believe it of Cressida."

"Yeah, she was actually King's teacher when they first met. She used to be kinda judgy back in the day, but she's been through a lot since then, and now, I don't think she has a cruel bone in her body."

"Teacher in college?" I clarified.

"High school," she admitted, then laughed again at my expression. It was rusty, still, a little broken like the clang of a cracked bell, but God, it was precious. "I know, it was quite the scandal. Cress was fired, or maybe she quit, but they've been together ever since. You should see them together, it's like..." She sighed, eyes dreamy. "It's like the most epic love story in real life."

"And I take it Loulou is Loulou *Garro*, Zeus Garro's wife?"

"Yep. Another scandal, another epic love story." At my look, she expanded. "Zeus is like nineteen years older than her, and they got married when she was seventeen."

Nineteen years.

Married at seventeen.

I ached to talk to Loulou suddenly. What had it been like loving Zeus at seventeen? Had it felt like being awoken from a lifetime of slumber? Like realizing suddenly who you were and why you'd been put on the earth?

And what had it felt like to be loved like that in return?

Zeus Garro had been brave enough, kind enough to her and himself to pursue love when society had told them not to. And look at the results? They were married, a living love story according to Cleo, and she'd mentioned kids as if they were her own.

She was living a dream I'd had since I was seventeen, too. Only my dream had gone from highly improbable to never fucking happening.

"You okay?" Cleo asked me.

I cleared my throat and fixed a smile between my cheeks. "Wow. Is there something in the water here?" I joked, but really, my heart was beating too hard against my breastbone.

Cleo's gaunt face pinched tighter. "Yeah, I wondered that, too. Like I said before, it was hard feeling so alone when everyone I loved seemed to be finding their perfect match. It's not their fault. I was just weak and stupid enough to fall for an awful allusion instead of the real thing."

"Hey, *my* Glory doesn't talk about herself like that, remember?" When she rolled her lips under her teeth as if to zip the bad words inside, I sighed and reached for her hand, tangling our fingers. "I don't think that kind of love can be forced, no matter how much we long for it."

"Have you ever been in love?" she asked, cocking her head with a frown as if the thought had never occurred to her.

A rabid, wild laugh rose in my throat, but I swallowed it, and my voice choked when I said, "I guess I'm still waiting for my white knight to come and sweep me off my feet."

She didn't have to know that I'd already met him, already loved him, and had no hope remaining that he'd ever want to sweep me away unless it was straight into the dustbin.

"Hey, what about the big bear of a man, Kodiak? He's hot," I suggested with a waggle of my eyebrows.

Cleo made a face like she'd swallowed a lemon. "No way, he's way too *bossy* and *rude*."

"I don't think I've heard him speak more than ten words, and he's always around you."

"Yeah, well, I guess he saves them all up to boss me around," she grumbled so mulishly I had to laugh.

"I think it's cool he's so ready to take care of you," I confessed. "It makes me feel better, if a little bit jealous, to know you've got all these people to love and that love you."

Lin's gaze was heavy on me, as it had been the whole interaction, watching me as if to relearn me. Something about what I said seemed to resonate with her because while Cleo's toes were drying, she got up and returned shortly after with a Tupperware filled with paper towel-wrapped mooncakes.

My mouth watered when she offered me the container. I lifted a golden brown, scalloped-edge round pastry and bit into it with relish, moaning as the flavour of salted egg yolk dissolved on my tongue. She usually only made them for the mid-autumn festival, and it warmed me straight through to my bones to know she'd gone out of her way to bring them today because she knew I loved them.

"You're in public," Lin reminded me, which made Cleo cough out a laugh.

I rolled my eyes in bliss and moaned even louder.

This time, when Cleo laughed, it was full enough for The Fallen women on the other side of the salon to hear. It was a little win, but it warmed the icy recess of my heart enough to make the rest of our trip bearable.

CHAPTER TWENTY-SIX

Mei

THE NIGHTS IN ENTRANCE WERE LONG. BACK AT HOME IN Vancouver, I worked a lot at night because that was when my creativity seemed to surge, but the dingy pink walls of the motel were not conducive to making art, and the only thing I could manage to draw or write about was Axe-Man. Which was kinda the point normally, given that I'd made my living creating a fictionalized version of him. But these weren't the kind of drawings I could submit to my editor. Pages filled with his big hands, the blunt-tipped fingers and that stub for a pinky he'd sacrificed to save me, the wide palm topped with rough calluses, and the pocked scars from shrapnel he'd got overseas. The tattoos over the back of his fingers on each hand in a cool, gothic script--*love* and *loss*. They looked like working man's hands, not an artist's tools. Not dexterous, fluid fingers, but weapons. Those hands had killed people. I'd known because

I'd seen it that night at Turner Farm, and I had no doubt they'd done damage since.

So why was I so obsessed with them?

Maybe because they seemed like such a perfect symbol of Axe-Man's dichotomy, the artist and the savage. I wondered, briefly, if that's why they called him Axe-*Man* now. It suited him, and even though I hated the idea of never calling him Henning again, I liked that he'd chosen that as his new moniker.

Mostly, though, I was obsessed with his hands because they were so fucking sexy.

The rest of the pages were sketches of those hands on my body. Wrapped around my throat in a slight chokehold. Pressed too hard into my hips so they left faint bruises. Filling up the space between my thighs that ached for him just thinking about it.

I tossed my pencil to the bedspread and face-planted in my sketchbook. Happily, I didn't have a deadline looming, but my editor still liked to see progress on my next project every few weeks, and so far, I had nothing (appropriate) to show her.

A knock on the door stirred me out of my fevered restlessness.

I rolled off the hard mattress, landing on the balls of my feet and grabbing my tactical blade from the bedside table simultaneously. I wasn't expecting any visitors, and I'd learned the hard way not to open the door to strangers over the years without a weapon at the ready.

When I pulled the door open with the chain still attached, I saw Jiang Kuan smoking a cigarette and leaning against the balustrade. The sodium lights cast his steeply angled cheekbones in vivid yellow, the hollow beneath in black. He looked like a *jiangshi*, the Chinese equivalent of a zombie-vampire hybrid. Something monstrous and dead inside wrapped in a dangerously pretty package.

I should have known better than to let him in, but that option had been taken from me long ago.

"*Mui mui*, aren't you going to let me in?" he asked after a moment, stepping forward to blow smoke through the crack in the door directly into my face.

I scowled at both his rudeness and persistence in calling me *Mui mui*, a term of endearment that meant both little sister and girlfriend. Still, I closed the door in his face to unlock the chain before opening it again, dragging him into the room by the collar of his shirt. If one of The Fallen MC saw him at my door, I thought they might shoot me first and ask questions later, given my reputation.

Jiang allowed himself to be pulled into the room and then pushed down onto the first bed, the one I used as a desk and couch. When I plucked the cigarette from his mouth, he didn't even protest as I stomped to the bathroom to put it out in the sink and then throw the butt away.

When I returned, he was lounged back on one elbow, looking through my sketches. He had long, elegant fingers meant to play the piano or stitch silk, yet they were used predominately for torture and the odd murder.

"Your next book should be erotic," he suggested, pushing the image of Axe-Man's huge hands palming my backside toward me over the duvet.

I perched my butt on the dresser, crossed my arms, and cocked a brow at him. "Can you forgive a girl for being a little horny? My boyfriend is gay, so I don't even reap the benefits of being in a committed relationship."

Jiang didn't smile at me, but mirth was hidden in those dark eyes as he blinked at me with faux boredom. He didn't particularly like to be reminded of his homosexuality even though it was his natural state. Years of bigoted talk amongst the triad members and Kasper killing his boyfriend eight years ago had left him in a strange limbo state. He was only attracted to men and refused to date a woman in any real sense, but he was forced to appease Kasper or else face the consequences, which were, quite honestly, dire.

So he used me.

I'd been playing at being Jiang's girlfriend for the past five years.

Not out of the goodness of my heart but because we had a deal.

Gwaan hai.

I scratched his back, and he scratched mine. It had started out as a business deal, but over the years, I'd come to reluctantly care for Jiang. The truth was, other than Old Dragon, he was my only constant. Years of public dates in fancy Vancouver restaurants and showing up on his arm at charity events had led to real conversations about who we were and what we wanted out of life. Even though we both knew we weren't the kind of people to ever get what we actually wanted.

I felt for him and related to him in a lot of ways. He couldn't be who he wanted to be, couldn't be with someone he truly wanted to be with, and that was a kind of hopelessness I felt echoed in my own heart.

More than that, I owed him a lot. He'd helped me get out of the hellhole Florent had banished me to, sent my work into the right hands to secure my first publishing deal, and saved me from feeling desperately alone. We relied on each other and even loved each other in our own ways.

"Why are you here?" I asked him. "I told you I couldn't have you showing up."

He gave me a long look and then shrugged one shoulder as he went back to looking at my art. "Kasper asked about you last night. He mentioned we hadn't seen you around in a while and that it was high time I put a ring on your finger."

"You know that's never going to happen," I reminded him. "I

draw the line at marriage. Especially when you haven't exactly been holding up your end of the deal lately."

His end of the deal.

Finding out who killed Kate and getting me access to them.

I knew who'd done it. Jiang had discovered the truth from Kasper one night three years ago.

The White Snake, the Dragon Head of the Red Dragons triad.

A man who had emerged in Vancouver some sixteen years ago as an unknown and quickly united the various tongs in Chinatown under the united front of the Red Dragons. He'd reigned uncontested in the city until Kasper and Jiang had moved in from the east.

At first, I thought it was too tidy. That Kasper was just giving up the White Snake to justify his desire to crush the Red Dragons. But then I'd found out the White Snake's real identity thanks to the Seven Song's old asset, the infamous hacker Obsidian Swan.

His given name was Maxwell Dutton.

Armed with that knowledge, I'd found a connection between him and Kate by scouring through old Calgary PD records. Maxwell Dutton had done a stint in the clink for aggravated assault against a man who'd been charged with sexual assaulting Kate Kay. According to the report, he'd found Kate being cut up by the assaulter and beaten him nearly to death.

So why the hell would Maxwell Dutton have killed Kate if he'd beaten up a man who assaulted her?

Jealousy was one reason, and murders had been committed for less.

But why the ceremony of it? Why the distinctly Chinese bent of the murder? Death by Lingchi was an old-school punishment, and death by metal was one of the five ways to kill a triad oath-breaker, according to the "five thunderbolts."

It was clear Maxwell Dutton had some in with the triads

even back then. Otherwise, he would never have risen to the rank of Dragon Head as a white man, but I was missing some key piece of the puzzle. How did he get from point A to point B with a little layover to murder Kate on the journey?

Jiang had a theory that the White Snake had been trying to pin it on Seven Song, knowing about Kasper and Jiang's connection to Kate through their real estate dealings.

I wasn't so sure.

What I wanted was an opportunity to confront the White Snake, but that had proved nearly impossible.

I'd tried to break into their office building downtown, but the security was so tight, even Obsidian Swan hadn't been able to get past the system without triggering an alarm.

Jiang had heard he was supposed to be dining at Mott 32, so we'd made reservations the same night, but he'd never shown up.

There were countless other attempts over the years to pinpoint the elusive leader of the Red Dragons, but I'd never come close. Kasper hadn't even seen the man in over a decade, and he refused to meet with him even when the Kuan brothers reached out to negotiate new territories.

We'd reached a stalemate.

"That's the other reason I'm here," Jiang admitted. "Obsidian Swan was able to hack into the calendar of Red Dragon's Incense Master. He is supposed to be travelling with the White Snake up to Whistler in two weeks. They leave from Vancouver Thursday at midnight."

"If they're on the move, it's going to be hard to approach them, let alone identify them," I argued, but a frisson of excitement sparked like a fuse trailing down my spine.

"You'll figure it out," he noted blandly, and despite myself, I felt warmth knowing he found me so competent.

There was, by the sheer nature of our agreement, a stone bridge of trust between us. I could get Jiang killed and vice versa. It felt good to be trusted by someone after so long, even if it was because we had no other option.

"You just want me to take out the White Snake so you and Kasper can swoop in and take over their territory," I pointed out, turning to put the electric kettle on because Jiang and I liked to share a cup of green tea when we met.

"Well, two birds, one stone and all that," he said with a sharp smile, pulling himself up to the headboard so he could lean there and cross his legs. He looked faintly ridiculous in his three-piece designer suit and Ferragamo loafers in such an ugly, pink motel room, but he seemed entirely unaffected by his surroundings. "If you wanted to take out Zeus Garro while you're at it, you'd solve all my problems."

"You know I'll never touch The Fallen MC," I said, trying to keep the sudden rage from my voice even though I couldn't keep my lip from curling back over my teeth.

He raised both hands in surrender. "You've told me a few times, yes. You know, I met him today. Your Axe-Man could be a caricature of a biker."

"And you could be a caricature of a Chinese gangster," I noted, pouring the hot water through the strainer filled with puffed rice and green tea leaves. "It doesn't make you any less dangerous. Did you try to make a deal with them like we discussed?"

"Did you really think they'd take it?"

"No, but it makes me feel better that you tried." I carried the steaming mug over to Jiang and placed it on the table beside him before sitting cross-legged on the bed in front of him with my own cup. "I still think it's suicide for the triad to go after the Red Dragons and The Fallen simultaneously."

"It makes sense to Kasper, and you know he doesn't listen to my advice."

Since he'd discovered Jiang's relationship with Eero eight years ago, Jiang was Vanguard in name only. Oh, he was invited to meetings with the inner sanctum––the Incense Master, Deputy Mountain Master, White Paper Fan, and Straw Sandal––but his input was not appreciated. He was given his directives and expected to follow them.

"I don't know why you put up with it," I said softly because it hurt me to see the way Jiang had diminished over the years, his spirit shrinking behind the dark lens of his gaze. "You could be so much more than what he allows you."

"I don't know why you pine for the blond Viking, but you persist in trying to pay penance for things that were not your doing. Do you see me judging you for it?"

"I put him in jail, Jiang," I said tiredly, rubbing a hand over my face because we'd had this conversation so many times before.

"No, *I* put him in jail. *Rooster Cavendish* put him in jail. *Henning Axelsen* put himself in jail. He made that choice to take the heat so you could go on and live your life, *Mui mui*, not so you could waste it by living in the past trying to banish old ghosts."

"If you had the chance to make Kasper pay for killing Eero, would you?" I whispered.

Jiang went so still that it was as if he was in suspended animation. He didn't blink or breathe for one long minute.

"I don't think about that kind of thing," he finally said stiffly.

"You do," I bet, my voice a glistening blade sliding between his ribs, performing an autopsy without his consent. "You think about it in bed at night when the space beside you is too cold and empty. You think about it on the anniversary of his death every year and the anniversary of when you two met. You think about it when you look at Kasper out of the corner of your eye when you believe he isn't looking. You can't fool me, Jiang, because I know what it is to love in a way that never dies. And if that love is taken from you unjustly, I know what it is to live with revenge as your life's purpose. You can pretend as long as you'd like that you don't want to take Kasper down one day for what he did to Eero and what he continues to do to you, but I'll always know the truth. And if, no, *when* that day comes, I'll be here to help you take your vengeance. Not because of our deal, but because I know you want that peace for yourself just as much as I do, and I think you deserve it."

The air between was thick, humming with tension. There was a chance he'd hurt me for saying that, that he'd hit me or choke me out for daring to speak so candidly. But Jiang had never hurt me, and I didn't think he was capable of it even now when violence simmered in his eyes.

I'd just tapped into a rage that was already there, like sap beneath the bark of a tree.

"I'm going to pretend you didn't say that," he finally responded, the words slow as that same sap, dripping sluggishly in the cold room. "And I'm going to leave now before I do something I regret."

"Like hurt me?" I asked mildly.

He levelled me with a cool glance. "Like hug you."

My mouth fell open a little as he took a long slung of his hot tea and then placed it back on the nightstand before getting up to go to the door.

"Lock this behind me," he ordered, making me roll my eyes. "I'm almost certain I wasn't followed, but Kasper is paranoid these days. I told him you were on vacation, but if he finds out that vacation is in the home of The Fallen, even I can't protect you, *Mui mui*."

"I know."

"Call me on the burner when you know what you want to do about the White Snake. Stay safe," he demanded. "And stay smart. Don't embarrass yourself with apologies to that great oaf if he won't listen to the reasons you were forced to hurt him."

"Yes, Cupid," I snarked, but Jiang, used to my sarcasm, only gave a beleaguered sigh and then slipped out the door.

A moment later, he knocked on the door, and it was my turn to sigh as I got up to lock it behind him.

Ten minutes later, I'd tidied up my sketches and was lying on my belly in the bed as I looked up the Sea to Sky Highway on Maps to try to figure out where I might be able to ambush White Snake with Jiang's help, when there was another knock on the door.

I stared at the pink wood for a moment, wondering if I'd heard it correctly over the swell of WILDES on my portable speaker.

Another knock, this one heavier, the side of a fist instead of the knuckles.

I shot up to my knees and lunged for my knife on the nightstand just before the door creaked and banged open two inches, the chain straining to hold against the intruder.

My heart galloped in my chest as I jumped to my feet and assumed a ready position with my knife in my right hand, raised in front of my chest at an angle. I had no idea who could be after me because there were *too* many options.

Kasper Kuan and the Seven Song, the Red Dragons, even The Fallen MC.

A flash of metal appeared between the door and the frame and the chain gave with an anticlimactic *clink*. The door burst open in the next second, revealing a huge man with deadly intent in his gaze.

"You wanna tell me why Jiang fuckin' Kuan was cozyin' up in your room just now?" Axe-Man demanded, his hatchet in hand, chest heaving, brows knitted heavily over enraged eyes.

For the first time in my life, I was actually frightened of Henning Axelsen.

CHAPTER TWENTY-SEVEN

Mei

My heart banged so loudly in my chest, I was certain Axe-Man could hear it even over the low swell of music. Maybe he could because my momentary silence seemed answer enough to his question. He stalked into the room a few steps before slamming the door shut behind him with a rattle that shook the walls. In his leather Fallen MC jacket, a white tee with Street Ink Tattoo's skull and tattoo gun emblem on it stretched tight across his prominent pecs, dark denim, and heavy, silver accented motorcycle boots, big hand wrapped around the wooden handle of the axe he'd used to cut through the lock on my door, he looked every inch the biker. Nothing like the off-white knight of my youth and everything like a night-time predator.

A shiver rocked through me so hard it felt as if the hand of fear had ripped my spine out my back.

The smile that curled his mouth in his blond beard was meaner than any glare I'd ever seen. He advanced, and I matched him, moving backward, step for step. When he noticed the tea still steaming slightly on the bedside table, his nostrils flared. He stepped over to pick up the mug, the ceramic so small in his ungainly hand. After sniffing it, he threw it against the wall with a muted roar.

"What the actual *fuck*, Mei Zhen?" he demanded. "You sleeping with this fucker now?"

"You know he's gay," I managed to choke out, trying to maintain my dignity but unable to because fuck, he was terrifying.

But even more than that, he was arousing.

It was wrong to be so seduced by the sight of a large man, shaking with the restraint of holding his anger inside, but there was something about it. The contrast, maybe, between the awesome nature of that rage and his ironclad control of it.

I wondered what that viciousness and restraint might do in other contexts, and my nipples pebbled obviously beneath my thin black tank top.

"I don't know shit. He could be bi, he could be pan, he could be whatever the fuck, Mei. The question is, are you sleeping with this motherfucker who almost ruined your goddamn life? Why the hell did I go away if you were just going to join up with the fuckin' Seven Song, huh?"

"No one asked you to martyr yourself for me," I snapped. "I told you it was my mess, and I was happy to take the heat. I was a minor. I would've gotten two years tops for killing Kang Li, and I could've claimed self-defence."

"You were eighteen in six months. If you think they wouldn't've pushed for you to get the max after bein' involved in triad and biker gang warfare, you're even stupider than you were at seventeen. And if you'd gone down in that mess, you would've missed your last days with your mum. You think I was down with that happenin'?"

He couldn't have known that I'd missed those last days

anyway, but his comment broke the last of my restraint. I'd been living with this anger toward the world, but mostly myself, for so long that only a thin barrier separated me from its chaos.

"Oh, fuck you!" I shouted, storming forward to poke a hand in his hard chest. "You have no clue who I am now, and don't pretend you give a shit. Is your hero complex wounded that I didn't turn into the fancy medical doctor I wanted to be when I was young so I could live out your dreams of medicine too? Are you pissed I'm not married or some shit already with two-point-five kids and a fucking white picket fence? Because if you are, then you're even stupider than you were at thirty-three. I was *never* going to end up as society's ideal. Florent's ideal. And you more than anyone should know that because that was one of the things we had in common."

"I don't give a single fuck you aren't a doctor," he bit out, shoving his axe back into the sheath on his belt so he could take me by the shoulders and shake me gently. "I give a fuck you're still fuckin' suicidal hangin' out with the wrong goddamn crowds. And why? Why the ever-lovin' fuck would you be invitin' Jiang Kuan into your room for a cozy midnight chat, huh? If Rooster was still alive, I'd be checkin' for him hidin' in your fuckin' closet."

I glared up at him pugnaciously, chin jutted forward like a dare. "It's none of your business."

It was. In fact, it couldn't have been *more* his business because it was for him. Always for him and for Cleo.

Axe-Man's bearded jaw worked hard as he chewed his anger into smaller pieces. "If you've stayed friends with him over some mis-fuckin'-guided attempt to get justice for Kate, I swear to fuckin' God, Mei, I'll turn you over my knee and tan your ass so hard you won't be able to sit for a goddamn *year*."

"I'm not a child anymore, *Axe-Man*," I sneered, shoving at him with two hands.

He didn't even budge.

"You think I'd threaten to spank you if you were?" he asked, his voice so dark, so rich, it felt like black velvet tied around my throat just a little too tight.

The palpable vibration of fury between us seemed to fluctuate into something different, a little heavier, a lot more electric. It felt as if there was a current of power strung between his chest and mine, and if we weren't very, very careful, one or both of us might combust.

"You think you can scare me into doing what you want?" I hissed. "Because I hate to break it to you, Mr. Big and Bad, but you don't scare me at all."

"Oh yeah?" His voice was stuck somewhere in his throat, guttural in a way that made my belly swoop. "That's 'cause you were used to dealin' with a softer man. There ain't nothin' soft about me now, and you'd do well to remember it."

"Or what?" Giddiness and desire so fierce they were *violent* surged through me. I was shaking slightly, filled with an excess of energy that needed some place to go. "You wouldn't hurt a fly if it wasn't threatening you or yours."

"Yeah," he agreed easily, eyes so bright a turquoise they seemed to shine with unholy light. I was so lost in them, it took a moment for the cruelty of his words to sink in. "But you *are* a threat. The biggest threat I've faced in eight years."

My face spasmed with pain before I could curb it, and I reverted to that seventeen-year-old Mei I'd sworn was dead and buried. It was just that anger was so much easier to feel than hurt. "Fuck you, Henning."

My hand lashed out for his cheek without conscious direction from my brain. I was fast; I'd trained my whole life to be so, but Axe-Man still caught me neatly at the wrist and, in a flash, had my hand twisted behind my back, his body pressed up against mine and his mouth at my ear.

"I told you not to call me that. Don't fuck with me, Mei," he growled, his breath hot against my neck, making me shiver and then shiver again so hard I bit my lip. "You don't want to push me."

I threw my head back, hoping to catch him in the teeth, but he dodged me enough that I only connected with the edge of his jaw, the blow softened by his thick beard.

"I think I do," I taunted, grinding my ass back into his groin until he hissed and pulled his hips back. But not before I felt the telltale bulge of an aroused cock. "Why? You think I can't handle you?"

I wasn't sure what we were really talking about anymore. It had devolved from trash talk into something filthier, something that made my womb clench and my thighs tremble. That big, powerful body curled over mine, holding me still, was enough to make me shamefully, ridiculously wet. I could feel the dampness seep through my underwear into my spandex workout shorts.

When you've wanted someone for half your life, the single touch of his hand on your skin could light a bonfire in your soul.

"You fuck around with me long enough, you'll find out."

"Is that a dare?" I practically purred, but there was that edge of violence still curled in my belly. A kind of anger and desperation that made me want to fuck him as well as fight. I wanted to rail against him for shunning me and eat him alive after years of hungering for him. "Because you know I've never been able to resist a good dare."

Throwing caution to the wind, I turned my head sharply to sink my teeth into the meaty part of his pectoral. He let out a sharp bark of shock, using his hand on my twisted arm to push me away, but it only succeeded in dragging my teeth diagonally across his chest. Over the place above his pounding heart.

"Fuck!"

He shoved me away lightly, only to spin me by the shoulders so I was facing him. I had time to notice that my teeth had broken through parts of the thin tee and even his skin, little pinpricks of blood staining the cotton before he hooked a foot around my leg and tripped me. Instead of falling forward onto the bed where he could trap me, I rolled my momentum to the side, slamming against the wall. When I saw his hands come for me, I ducked under his arms and slid between his body and the wall to dart across the room.

His footsteps thundered behind me, too close. Before I could open the door to flee or force him out of my room, he was on me, pressing me into the door.

"Just tell me the fuckin' truth for once in your life. Why the fuck are you still dealin' with the triad, Mei?" he growled.

"I don't have to tell you anything," I countered, stepping hard on his inseam so he released me with a grunt of pain. "You won't trust anything I do tell you anyway."

"True," he growled as I spun to face him, pushing his hand into my sternum and flattening it so I was forced back up against the door.

My heart knocked loudly at my breastbone as if it were calling for Axe-Man to answer.

"You worry about your shit, and I'll worry about mine," I snarled, pushing both hands against his chest to get space.

Only, he was an immovable force.

Thinking quickly, almost panicked by his proximity after so long without his touch, I braced against his chest to bring my feet up to his thighs, climbing up his body so I could wrap my thighs around his neck and squeeze. He didn't realize what I was doing fast enough. Grunting against my groin, he wrapped his hands around my thighs to pull me off him, but I locked my feet together and refused to let go.

He cursed and panted hotly into my fabric-covered pussy, and suddenly, I lost focus, my grip weakening at the effect on my libido. Taking advantage, he pried me off his shoulders and slammed me into the door again, pinning me to the wood like a splayed butterfly.

His eyes were narrow, blown black by his pupils. We were both panting so hard that our chests brushed, my nipples abrading against his chest hair through the thinness of our shirts.

"Get the fuck off me, Henning," I demanded, wriggling against him only to feel the ridge of a distinctly hard cock against my stomach.

My eyes flashed up to his in surprise, mouth falling open.

Axe-Man glowered at me as if it was my fault. His hand moved from my shoulder to my throat, palming the entire thing. My pulse hammered against the hard press of his thumb at my carotid artery and the press of his iron-hard thigh as he adjusted, placing it just so between my thighs.

I gasped, head thudding against the door as I fought to regain my equilibrium.

I wasn't a virgin, and I wasn't a stranger to rough play in the bedroom. In fact, I loved the physicality of sex the same way I loved the physicality of martial arts. I wanted to fight and fuck, bite and suck, groan and whimper.

But this...this was almost too much, like the energy under my skin would split me apart at the seams.

And I wasn't sure anymore what we were doing.

We'd been fighting, but now...

Would Axe-Man really fuck me?

His eyes were fixated on my mouth, so intense I could feel the heat of that stare like a burn. To soothe it, I poked my tongue out to wet the tender skin.

"Fuck you," he whispered thickly.

"You don't have the balls," I dared, quiet because I didn't have enough breath in my body, but still firm.

"You're the biggest mistake I ever made," he told me, so cruel and cold, hand flexing around my throat just tight enough to restrict my breath for a beat before he released the squeeze.

I reared up, biting into his lower lip so hard it broke the skin, and his blood burst on my tongue. The iron tang made me moan. I'd been so hungry for him for so long that it seemed nothing short of cannibalism would satisfy me.

But maybe taking him into my body in other ways would curb the urge.

I held his bleeding lower lip between my teeth and flicked my tongue over it with a humming moan.

The next instant, he was on me.

Using the hand on my throat, he tipped my neck to expose the skin at the curve of my neck and shoulder, fixing his teeth there with a rough grunt. I shivered, pinned by his body and his teeth to the door. Wet flooded between my legs, and I grounded down on his thigh shamelessly, aching for the friction. The years-long hunger for this man roared to life inside me like a well-constructed bonfire gone dry in the heat just waiting for a lit match to set it aflame. It was powerful, so profound, for a moment, I was almost afraid of my own desire.

Axe-Man moved back, his thick thigh the only thing keeping me upright for a moment as he hooked his fingers in the neck of my tank top and wrenched, ripping the fabric down the middle. It fluttered listlessly to my sides, exposing my small breasts and pebbled brown nipples to the cool air and Axe-Man's lusty, hateful gaze.

He bared his teeth at me as he took in the sight, hands finding my hips to hold me still as he dipped his head to take a nipple into his mouth. When his teeth closed around it, I *keened*, an animal, vulpine sound that echoed through the room and back to me. Squirming against his leg, head thudding against the door, I weathered his attack on my breasts without an ounce of grace. I was reduced to mindless pleasure, clutching at his hair and wrenching hard to keep his attention there.

Within minutes, I was ready to come, writhing like a creature in its death throes. Axe-Man seemed to sense my tension and pulled away with a wet smacking sound, his lips damp and red, my nipples tight and bruised by his attention, the swells of my breasts peppered in bite marks that looked so fucking hot I almost climaxed at the sight of them.

"Not so fuckin' fast," he growled between clenched teeth.

He pressed a palm into the wet, bruised skin of my chest to hold me there while the other made quick work of thumbing open the button on his jeans and unzipping his fly. He was too close for me to see his cock, but I could feel the heavy weight of it slap against my trembling inner thigh as he pulled it out. The crinkle of foil told me he was fishing in his pocket, and a second later, a condom wrapper was between his strong, white teeth, and he was tearing it open. He spat the used foil to the ground and gritted his teeth as he sheathed himself in latex and immediately pressed himself to the wet seat of my shorts.

I gasped at the contact, clutching him, but he swore and stepped back, prying my hands off his body.

"Don't touch me," he ordered even as he dropped me to my feet on the floor to shuck off my shorts and panties in one fell swoop. Still bent slightly, he knuckled my soaking wet pussy as if testing my readiness, and then, apparently unsatisfied even though I was leaking down my thighs, he spat on my clit.

I shuddered, rocked by how sexy that was, but he was already standing up again and pressing close. I watched in a haze as he sucked his wet knuckle into his mouth with a low growl and then palmed my ass to heft me up against the door again. The second I was pinned, he notched his cock at my slippery entrance and thrust forward to the hilt.

My head cracked against the door as I threw it back on a soundless scream. I convulsed around his girth, my pussy struggling and failing to relax. One of his hands shifted to secure my weight so the other could cup the back of my head, an instinctively protective move I knew he was unconscious of making.

He grounded deeper, the hair at the base of him grinding against my clit in a way that started a friction fire.

"Fuck," I gasped, clawing at his shoulders until I drew blood and made him hiss.

"Take it," he ground out, collecting my clawing hands in his then holding them above my head so my entire centre of gravity was focused on where we were connected.

I hung there like an ornament as he fucked into me, his thrusts so deep they kissed my cervix with a twinge of pain that almost instantly blossomed into pleasure. The door rattled loudly in its frame as he pounded against me, the wet slap of his balls against my sopping cunt a sharp underscore to the bass beat.

When I came, it happened so suddenly it was like being hit by a train. One moment, I was clinging to sanity, and the next, I was broken open by the impact of that runaway cock. Vaguely, I was aware of Axe-Man releasing my hands, using one to muffle the screams pouring from my mouth and the other to squeeze between our bodies to brutally pinch my clit. On the heels of the first orgasm sparked another, this one sharper, almost painful.

I screamed until I couldn't breathe, slumped against Axe-Man and the door, water-logged with an excess of pleasure.

My mind was gloriously, blissfully empty, so when Axe-Man made an animal noise of dissatisfaction, I canted my hips to accept him deeper automatically. When he took both my ass cheeks in his hands and clenched tight, dragging my entire body forcibly up and down his thick cock, I dug my fingers into his hair and held on desperately.

And when he fixed his teeth over my throat, biting deep

enough to bruise, I tipped my neck lower to expose myself to the pain and ground down into his every thrust, working myself to yet another impossible climax.

"Fuck, you're the most dangerous thing I've ever known," he grunted a moment before growling as he slammed himself to the root inside me, his cock kicking against my swollen walls so hard I knew he was coming.

For an absolutely insane moment, I wished he was coming inside me, flooding me with his seed so that when he pulled out of my used cunt, it would leak down my thighs. The image tipped me over the edge into another bone-quaking orgasm that made my teeth ache.

I lost consciousness for a moment, and when I found reality again, I was being moved. I opened my eyes just as Henning pulled me off his cock like a used condom and tossed me on the bed closest to the door. My body bounced once, twice, before settling limply, dislodging the pencils and the loosely stacked pile of sketches I'd organized earlier so they fell to the ground.

I watched in a kind of fugue state as Henning stalked to the bathroom to dispose of the condom and then prowled back into the room while doing up his fly. He didn't look at me at all. My heart had moved into my throat as he moved to the door, pulling it open and stepping a foot outside without a word to me.

Only at the last second did he look back, his eyes so narrow with vitriol I couldn't see any of that oxidized copper blue. He looked... I sucked in a breath as our eyes met and locked... He looked like he hated me.

No, that wasn't strong enough.

He looked like I'd killed every dream he'd ever had. Like I'd betrayed him irrevocably. Like he couldn't stand the sight of me.

Me.

I was lying there, limbs akimbo on the bed, bruised from

his teeth, wet and swollen from his cock, red thong still attached to my left ankle like the last hanger in an empty closet.

And the truth came back to me in a rush, a cold wave as fierce as an avalanche landing on my chest. I lost my breath to it.

Because the truth was he might have been the hero in my story, but I'd always be the girl who'd made his a tragedy. Nothing would change that. Not finding Kate's killers, not loving and caring for Cleo. Not even fucking him the way I'd fantasized about for years.

He wrenched his eyes from me, jaw working, and then shook his head even as he stalked back toward me.

For one heart-stopping, breath-halting moment, I felt hope.

And then he plucked my used panties off the end of my foot, wiped his hands off on them like he couldn't stand the stain of me on his skin, and stalked right back out the door. It closed with a resounding clamour, loose in the frame from his break-in and our vigorous bout of sex.

I lay there, cooling, breaking apart as the last of my hope dissolved in the vinegar of his malice. One single tear trickled out my eye and into my hairline, but it was all I allowed myself.

After all, a part of me deserved that.

A part of me longed for it. The sex and the punishment for what I'd done and how I'd failed him.

But enough was still enough.

I wasn't going to make myself into Axe-Man's punching bag as some kind of act of forgiveness. I was going to do exactly as he'd ask and avoid him like the plague.

That didn't mean I'd abandon Cleo.

Or my journey of vengeance for Kate, especially when my motives had become so much more complicated than that.

But I was officially done pining after Henning Axelsen.

He was dead and buried inside a man I didn't know and didn't love named Axe-Man.

CHAPTER TWENTY-EIGHT

Mei

I WAS ASLEEP WHEN MY NEXT GUESTS CAME TO VISIT. THE ferocity of my orgasms and the emotional roller coaster of my interaction with Jiang, compounded by the euphoria and heartbreak of finally having sex with Axe-Man, only to be deserted by him, led me into a deep and troubled sleep. I was dreaming of a Chinese dragon undulating through the sky in a graceful dance until suddenly, a parliament of owls appeared on the horizon and started chasing the dragon through a dark forest. Owls were bad omens, harbingers of death, and I knew the moment they caught up with the gorgeous serpent in the sky, it would die. In the end, I was the dragon, and the sharp beaks and claws of the night-hunting owls had descended on me, chipping off scales to sink deep into flesh.

I woke up with a painful cry, snapping into a seated position only to be shoved back down on the bed. Panic, already awoken by the dream, surged through me like lava flowing through the mouth of a volcano. A horrifying scream tore from my throat before a fleshy hand clamped over my lips, pressing me hard into the pillow.

The face above me was familiar. The Red Pole for the Seven Song in Vancouver grinned and yipped at me the way a fox did, manic, giddy in the way of a predator with trapped prey. Behind him, I counted three other shadowy figures, and I knew I stood no chance of getting out of this situation without harm.

"Hello, Mei Zhen," Ashes Li said in Cantonese, showing me the Chinese *gun* staff in his free hand before lifting it for a strike. "Kasper sends his regards to you and your friends at The Fallen MC."

I reared up, sharp nails aimed for his face, connecting with soft flesh as I raked them down his cheeks. Before I could attack further, one of the other men was collecting my hands and pining them to the pillow.

Ashes grinned at me, leaning down to whisper hotly in my ear, "Hold still. This should only hurt a little."

Like most triad gangsters, Ashes Li was a liar.

It hurt so fucking much that before long, I passed out into cool, black oblivion.

CHAPTER TWENTY-NINE

Axe-Man

I DROVE THROUGH THE NIGHT-DARK STREETS OF ENTRANCE AND up into the mountains for hours. Cleo was safe at the house with Loulou, Lila, and Harleigh Rose and probably all snuggled up in the California king-sized bed I'd spoiled my girl with. Nova and Lion were shootin' the shit waitin' for me to get home.

But I couldn't make myself turn the bike toward Lake Mead.

My demons were chasin' me through the dark, and the only way I knew to outrun them was on the back of my Harley-Davidson Softail Deluxe FLDE. It was a custom beauty Bat and the boys had spent weeks on in at Hephaestus Auto to turn it into my dream stone-washed pearl and chrome steed. The thrum of the purrin' engine was the only thing loud enough to mute the thoughts roarin' between my ears.

How had the night turned to such shit?

It'd been easy enough for Priest and Nova to slip the

trackin' devices into the weapons' sheaths they'd confiscated when the Seven Song triad members had met up with us on the boat, and even easier to track them once they left us. Jiang's lackeys had travelled back down the mountain to Vancouver, where they belonged, but Jiang'd stayed north, goin' up to Whistler for the afternoon to meet with dealers in the area before headin' back down to Entrance.

I knew 'cause I'd been the one to tail him.

It was a prospect's job, really, and Carson, Ransom, or Pigeon could've used the practice stalkin' outta sight, but I felt responsible for the triad's interest in Entrance and our club, so I took it on. Our receptionist, Sara, at Street Ink rescheduled my appointments, and the girls headed over to the house to keep Cleo company.

What had started off as a borin' kinda self-imposed punishment took a fierce turn when I followed Jiang down the twistin' Sea to Sky Highway all the way to the turn-off for Purgatory Motel.

The same pink monstrosity housin' one Mei Zhen Marchand.

I sat on the idlin' bike in the deep shadows outside the pitifully low lights in the Purgatory parkin' lot and watched as Jiang got out of his Mercedes and walked up the stairs to the second level. He lit a cigarette before he knocked at number 7, and when the door was opened, he was yanked inside urgently.

The way one might haul a lover into one's arms after a long separation.

Acid had boiled in my stomach and surged up my throat, threatenin' to choke me. Jiang had once had a male lover, but what the fuck did that matter? I knew brothers in my own club that'd fucked around with men a time or two but still considered themselves straight. Maybe Jiang was somewhere in the middle of the sexual spectrum, and why the hell wouldn't he want Mei if he was into women?

She was...

Fuck. The truth was she was fuckin' immaculate. So beautifully constructed that even after years of distance, my fingers still itched to pick up a pencil, a pen, or a piece of charcoal and work out the fine details of her face on paper or canvas.

The idea of Jiang stainin' it with his criminal, blood-stained fingers enraged me even more than the idea that Mei might've eschewed my sacrifice to remain in contact with the triad.

But why?

I didn't give a fuck who Mei slept with. She was a grown-ass woman with no relationship to me other than bein' friends with my daughter.

And it wasn't like *I* wanted to touch her. Even if I had, it would have been hypocritical to write off Jiang as too blood-drenched and criminal when I'd been killin' insurgents and then other criminals for decades now.

Still, the rage burned bright and brighter still as I sat in the dark and stared at the closed door to her room for forty minutes while she entertained the Vanguard of the Seven Song triad. I tried not to let my imagination get away from me, but it was a losin' battle, given I made my livin' as an artist.

By the time Jiang appeared in the door, lingerin' for a moment as if he was reluctant to leave, I was thrummin' with fury.

How dare she? I thought on repeat. *How dare she do this?*

As if I had a right to judge. As if I was the same man lookin' out for her back in the day or, worse, a new man with a strange and horrifyin' interest in who she might take as a lover.

I convinced myself I was just angry at another betrayal as Jiang pulled out of the parkin' lot, so minutes later, I stalked on foot over the asphalt and up those peelin' pink stairs. Took them two at a time, my blood pumpin' from more than just exertion. By the time I was knockin' at her door, I was mad with emotion.

So mad, it was like I was possessed by another man.

One so filled with hate and confusion that he couldn't think straight or see clearly.

That same man, more monster really, tussled with Mei when she refused to be fuckin' honest or straightforward with her answer. Pinned her against the door when she was bein' too squirrely. Fixed his teeth in her neck 'cause the long, pale column was too temptin'. Sucked marks into her flesh 'cause it was too clean. Ravaged her breasts 'cause suddenly reason was a foreign concept, and all that was left was body urges and violent, repressed desires.

I fucked her like I hated her. Usin' her. Tryin' to forget exactly who it was I was drivin' my dick into, only she kept remindin' me in a myriad of inescapable ways. That goddamn cherry blossom scent. The absurdly silky texture of that raven-wing hair. The strong muscles in the small, lean body offset by the new discovery of curves, the plumpness of her ass totally palmed in each hand, and the slight but pretty swell of her white, red-tipped tits.

I was lost in a toxic cloud of rage and lust, everythin' tinged pink like the motel around us. If someone'd asked for my name and address, I would've blanked, only capable of gruntin'.

It would've been possible, maybe, to blame my ferocious animal response on the fact that I hadn't fucked since before The Prophet's assault on my daughter.

It would've been possible to blame the rage on the fact that Mei had used and abandoned me eight years ago, and the wound had never healed, festerin' and oozin' for near on a decade without closure to stitch it closed.

But none of those excuses mattered.

The truth that only served to fuel my fury even as I let myself loose on her body was that I wanted her.

Plain. Simple.

I wanted to bury myself inside her. Wanted to tame all that

wild, reckless energy with my cock and a strong hand on her throat, her tits, her sweet little ass. Wanted to stamp my possession on every inch of that black-inked, white-washed skin 'til she glowed with colour from my lips and teeth and brutal hands.

It wasn't about anger, not really, unless it was anger with myself for capitulatin' to this dangerous degree of lust. It seemed, when I was balls deep in that snug, delicious cunt, that I'd found nirvana, and I'd never get enough.

It scared me through to my fuckin' bones, so after I'd lost half my soul to my climax, I'd flung her away like a discarded bit of trash, washed my hands on her panties like she disgusted me, and left her wet, swollen, beautiful as all the best kinds of sin on that horrible pink bed.

She hadn't noticed that I'd pocketed that red scrap of lace.

Her eyes were squeezed shut when I noticed a piece of loose art paper at the base of the bed and crumpled it up along with the underwear to be secreted away in my jeans for later.

Eventually, it was the urge to see what was penned on that paper that stopped me from ridin' aimlessly through the night.

I pulled over on one of the back roads leadin' down the mountain to Lake Mead, the entire stretch of water shimmerin' like hammered metal below me, ringed by the dark triangles of evergreens. My hand was tremblin' when I dug into my pocket and retrieved my stolen goods.

The lace was still wet, fragrant with the salt-sweet musk of her pussy. I was a dirty old man, but I lifted them to my face and took a deep drag of the scent, scenes from our fuck flashin' behind my eyes 'til suddenly I was hard as steel again.

"Fuck." I sighed, shovin' the underwear deep into my pocket again, resolvin' to toss them when I got home. Even though a part of me knew I wouldn't.

The crumpled piece of paper was hard to discern at first even though the sky was clear, the moon a round silver coin catchin' the light of the sun and beamin' it down brightly on the Earth. I sucked in a breath when I realized it was a picture of me stylized almost like a Dark Age comic book, heavily shadowed with deep dimensions. My hair and beard were both shorter than I wore them now, but otherwise, it was a clear representation of me. In the illustration, I was shirtless, muscles bulgin', jaw clenched, and eyes closed with my head thrown back like I was in ecstasy. Which made sense, given a figure who was distinctly Mei-shaped even from the back, was ridin' my cock.

"Jesus fuckin' Christ," I muttered, adjustin' myself in my jeans. Straddlin' a bike with a hard-on was damn uncomfortable.

Some of the guilt eatin' at me subsided seein' evidence of Mei's desire for me. She'd reacted with genuine carnality back at the motel, but I'd still been rough with her, like I'd never been with a girlfriend and only a little with biker groupies. It was a part of me, that dominatin', rough, and somewhat cruel side of my sexuality, that made me feel wrong. I'd tried so hard most of my life to be a good man, even if I'd never been a lawful one, and those dark needs always threatened to eradicate that.

But with Mei, she'd seemed almost...turned on by my savagery. More, she'd matched it. I could still feel the throb of her teeth marks over my left pec and the sting of her scratch marks over my shoulders. It was unbelievably fuckin' hot to let myself go like that.

Even though it shouldn't have happened with *her*.

And it wouldn't. Not again.

Even if my dick was tellin' me somethin' different.

The problem with it was that she was just different enough from before to be intriguin' to me. I found myself wonderin' if she still loved longan fruit, if she ate standin' up like she couldn't bear to sit still unless she was drawin' somethin'. If she still smelled like cherry blossoms, a question I'd answered hours ago in the affirmative. If she laughed more and fought less. What she did for work now? If she wasn't a doctor liked she'd always imagined, was it somethin' more physical, which I'd always thought would suit her—a physio, a park ranger, even an MMA fighter?

The questions plagued me like an overly catchy tune. I woke up to the same music every day and went to sleep with it still stuck in my goddamn brain.

What I'd whispered to Mei before I came was true. She was a danger to me and mine. 'Cause even though she'd hurt me, abandoned me, I hadn't managed to weed out the last of those roots dug deep in my soul that told me to care about her. As a result, I couldn't stop thinkin' about her. I couldn't stop hatin' her, but I was intrigued more than was healthy.

"Fuck," I muttered again, shovin' my hand through my tangled hair 'cause I hadn't bothered to put on my bucket when I'd taken off like a bat outta hell from Purgatory.

The cold wind slappin' at my face helped to calm me some. Enough that I realized I left her with a busted open door in a sketchy as fuck motel.

I warred with myself for long minutes. The part of me that didn't want to see her ever again, who tried to convince himself he didn't care about her well-bein', with the part of me that'd never stopped wonderin' about her, worryin' about her. After what'd happened to Cleo, I couldn't rest without at least checkin' on Mei again.

A drive-by would be good enough.

If I didn't feel good about it, Lion and Nova were with Cleo, so I could spend the next few hours 'til dawn freakin' out over my lack of self-control in the shadows beside Purgatory Motel as well as I could anywhere else.

I had no fuckin' clue what Mei was doin' hangin' around with Jiang, but it couldn't be good. Fuck, she'd always been stubborn and one-track-minded, but could she really still be pursuin' the cause of Kate's death? Even after she'd killed Kang Li, who'd admitted to bein' one of her murderers?

The parkin' lot was quiet when I pulled up on the side street, but that wasn't exactly surprisin' at three in the mornin'. Still, somethin' like a sixth sense told me to get off my bike and check out Mei's door, make sure it was secure enough to last the night before I could send one of the prospects over to fix the latch for her.

When I walked past the reception, the thin pink blinds twitched, a face disappearin' behind the fabric. A little shiver of forebodin' scuttled down my back.

I picked up my pace as I climbed the steps quietly, stalkin' down the open-air hallway to the last unit, #7. The door was mostly closed, but it wasn't sittin' well in the frame. To test it, I pushed on the painted wood lightly.

It swung open with a soft gasp.

I stepped away from the doorframe instantly to avoid anyone waitin' inside. My gun was in one hand, the hatchet in my other before I could even process the situation.

"Mei?" I called out.

Only the whistle of wind flowin' into the room answered me.

Fuck.

I crouched and leaned forward slightly to look around the frame. No one was in sight inside, but someone could've been hidin' in the bathroom. Even though I had a feelin' it was empty, I stepped into the room on careful feet, clearin' it before headin' to the bathroom. I slammed the door open with one extended arm while I waited around the corner, but no one emerged.

Satisfied I was alone, I went back to the beds, noticin' the rumbled sheets on the one closest to the bathroom. There was blood splatter on the pillow. Enough of it to mean someone had hurt Mei considerably.

My heart was beatin' in my stomach, tossin' up my long-ago dinner 'til I thought I'd be fuckin' sick.

I'd left her in an unsafe place without thinkin' 'cause I was throwin' a fuckin' tantrum over an eight-year-old betrayal. What kinda man was I to leave her undefended behind a broken door?

Granted, Mei was probably the most dangerous woman I knew discountin' Tempest, who could hit a movin' target from twenty yards away with any kinda firearm. But it wasn't good enough.

Someone had taken Mei, and it felt palpably, woefully like my fuckin' fault.

What if they found her days later in a field, half dead, split open by a knife, broken in more than just bones...

I sucked in such a deep breath it ached in my lungs, forcin' myself to do the 4-7-8 technique they'd taught me in the military to calm the fuck down before I had a damn panic attack.

This was not the same situation as Cleo.

Even logically knowin' that, my heart was a sick, rottin' thing in my chest as I searched the room and found a dirty boot print on one of Mei's sketches strewn on the carpet. It was big enough to be a man's foot.

I called Bat, instead of Zeus, on autopilot. Bat'd been there through me through war, through Kate dyin'. He was always the first brother I'd call.

"Brother," he answered, voice rough with sleep but instantly alert.

"Someone got to Mei."

Readin' the panic buried in too shallow a grave in my chest, Bat cursed softly. "You at Purgatory?"

"Yeah. Gonna have a look around, but she could be anywhere."

"Right." There was a voice in the background I didn't listen to very closely. "I'll be there in twenty."

"The roads are empty. Make it fifteen."

"Fifteen," he agreed, before ringin' off.

I knew he'd make some calls himself and turned my mind to searchin' the rest of the motel. Startin' with the person behind the flickerin' curtain at reception.

This time, I let my boots pound against the metal stair treads so they knew I was comin'. When I pushed open the door to reception, and it smacked into the opposite wall, the man behind the desk was already cowerin' behind it.

"Get up," I demanded, stalkin' forward with my gun held loosely in one hand.

I used the other to wrap around his shirt collar and drag him half up over the desk. He made a noise of distress, arms flailin' as he thought about tryin' to pry my hands off and then decided compliance was best.

Maybe he was smarter than I'd given him credit for.

"Who was here tonight?"

"I don't know. I don't fuckin' watch the comings and goings. Got better things to do."

Then again, maybe he was a fuckin' idiot.

I looked at the small TV playin' old *Degrassi* reruns and arched my brows. "Sure, ya do. Now, tell me who rolled up in the last two hours."

"It's a free world!"

"This shithole is on the Sea to Sky Highway, so no, it's not a fuckin' free world," I hissed at him, draggin' him up by the shirt to sneer down into his face. "It's The Fallen MC's world, and you know who makes the rules in it? Motherfuckin' *me*. So start talkin', or I'll show you why they call me Axe-Man."

"Fuck," he spat. "Knew I shoulda taken the job at Evergreen Gas instead."

My laughter was a bark. Cressida had been abducted from that same place years ago, and it was a popular spot of conflict on the sex, drug, and human trafficking routes up and down the province.

"Too late. Now, talk."

"Some Asian guy came before you in a fancy Merc, then I heard your Harley before I saw you. Wasn't until an hour or so after you left that they came."

"Who?"

"How much is it worth to you?" he tried, glarin' up at me.

Stupid, fuckin' asshole.

"How much is it worth to you?" I growled, pressin' my gun to his temple. "Every second you drag this conversation on is another second someone I care about could be dyin'. You won't help me, I'll take out some of this rage on you. How'd you like that?"

The sharp ammonia scent of urine permeated the space as the middle-aged scumbag peed himself.

"A couple of Asian guys again. All dressed in suits like they were goin' to a fuckin' red carpet or some shit."

"Did they visit the girl in room 7?"

He glared at me, but when I moved the gun from his temple to his slightly parted mouth and thrust it inside, he shivered and tried to speak around the barrel. When I pulled it out, he spat, "Yes. Okay."

"Did they take her anywhere?"

"They disappeared around back with her about half an hour ago," he muttered.

I threw him back over the desk. He landed half in his chair and fell to the ground on his elbow, lettin' out a squawk of pain.

"You didn't think to call the fuckin' cops?" I asked even though the cops were bigger fuckin' idiots than this guy. "You see a girl taken in the middle of the night, and you think she's down to party?"

"Fuck you!"

"No," I murmured, knockin' my fist against the desk. "You're the one who'll be fucked if I find out this girl died 'cause you're a fuckwit. If you believe in God, I'd start fuckin' prayin'."

Without another word, I turned on my heel and walked out. The side of the motel was cloaked in pitch black with absolutely no lights to make the grounds safe beyond the dingy light of the parkin' lot. Cursin' under my breath, I turned on my phone flashlight and prowled around the buildin' with my gun raised.

There was nothin' but dirt and stray rocks that had tumbled down the steeply inclined mountainside behind the structure.

'Til I reached the far side and found two huge blue dumpsters overfull with trash.

And in one, a pale, fine-fingered hand inked with the Chinese symbols for *faith, hope,* and *honour*.

"Fuck," I shouted, sprintin' toward the dumpster and launchin' myself up over the rim into the muck, mindless of the filth. "Mei, Mei!"

I threw garbage off her body, searchin' for the extent of the damage, terrified to move her if the wounds were deep or cripplin'.

Bruisin' was already bloomin' on her naked body, and when I removed the burlap sack from her head, one eye was swollen shut, and both her cheekbones split open along with her lower lip. There were no compact fractures, but there could've been internal bleedin' 'cause it was obvious they'd beaten her into unconsciousness. I vehemently hoped that her nakedness didn't mean they'd sexually assaulted her, but it was hard to tell because we'd had sex only hours before.

"Rocky," I called, tryin' to rouse her.

"Axe-Man?" Bat's voice echoed across the parkin' lot.

"Back here!" I hollered as I carefully collected Mei into my arms.

She seemed so small like this, naked and limp and covered

in contusions and lacerations. Her heartbeat was steady but low.

A moment later, Bat and Dane both appeared around the far corner, joggin' toward me with their guns out. When they stopped at the dumpster, they both cursed in tandem. Any other time, I would've laughed. Since the moment Dane got back from bein' MIA overseas for years, he and Bat had practically been joined at the fuckin' hip. I wasn't even mildly surprised they'd shown up together at one thirty in the mornin' 'cause Dane'd been helpin' out with Bat's twins, Steele and Shaw, now that their mum was dead.

Instead, I ordered, "Bat, take her while I get the fuck outta here."

Bat stepped forward so I could gently lift Mei's cold body over the metal lip of the dumpster and into his arms. He curled her instantly, protectively to his chest. Dane offered a hand to me to help leverage me over the side.

"Fuck, man, do you know who did this?" Dane asked, acceptin' my cut so I could shrug outta my tee and carefully pull it over Mei to cover her nakedness.

I shrugged back into my cut shirtless and took her back into my arms, cuppin' her head as I cradled her to my chest. Hopin' it was just a bad concussion that knocked her out cold.

"Considerin' the three characters written in Sharpie on her forehead mean *betrayer* or *turncoat* in Chinese, I'm guessin' the motherfuckin' Seven Song triad," I answered grimly as we fell into line, walkin' back to the bikes.

"Shit," Dane cursed.

"What're you gonna do?" Bat asked, starin' at Mei with genuine concern. He'd met her when she was only twelve years old the night Kate died, and she'd been even more beat up than this.

"Take her home and check her out properly. Don't think she needs the emergency room, and if we can keep the pigs outta this, we can deal with it in our own way. I'm done with bringin' them into our shit after the fuckin' mess they made outta The Prophet killings."

"Shouldn't a doctor see to her?" Dane asked.

"I was one, a lifetime ago," I told him even though it was usually somethin' I kept under my hat. No one save Zeus, Bat, and Smoke knew all about my history, and I liked it that way. "I can make sure she'll be okay. But we gotta get her home."

"We'll follow," Bat offered.

"I need one or both of you to teach that fucker at reception a lesson. He saw the triad fucks drag Mei behind the motel and didn't do shit. I get this is a don't ask, don't tell piece of shit motel, but that does not fly when women are involved."

"No shit," Bat hissed, crackin' his knuckles and sharin' a look with Dane, who fished a pair of brass knuckles outta his back pocket. "We got you covered, brother. Get Mei home, and we'll meet you there. I called Nova and Lion. They'll be waitin' for you."

"If it wasn't war before," I said darkly as we round the corner into the parkin' lot, and I saw Bat had the foresight to drive his truck while Dane drove his SUV. I moved to the truck and lay Mei in the back seat, acceptin' the keys from Bat. "It is now."

"But she's not even Fallen," Dane pointed out, not judgin' but curious.

"No," I agreed, swingin' up into the Ford and lookin' back at Mei lyin' prone in the back seat. "But once, she was mine."

CHAPTER THIRTY

Mei

I WOKE UP TO RINGING. IT WAS LIKE A DOZEN BELLS BOUNCING through my skull cavity where my brain should have been, clangin' against bone again and again in such a cacophony that I couldn't think beyond it.

When I tried to clutch my head to still the noise, a long, painful groan wrenched out of my throat at the sharp ache in my ribs and the dull throb in the rest of my torso.

"Don't move."

I'd never been good at the whole obedience thing, so, of course, I jerked in surprise, hissed at the pain, and then tried to shove myself upright against the mountain of pillows cushioning my back because I didn't recognize that voice.

I pried my gluey eyes open and let the spinning room settle for a second before I focused on the woman setting up an IV bag on a metal trolley beside the bed I was laid in. She was the same streaky blonde-haired biker babe who'd arrived the first night I'd spent at Axe-Man's with Cleo. She was beautiful, like a Russian supermodel or, well, a biker babe. There wasn't anything soft in her features or demeanour, just a cool girl edge that made me want to be like her when I grew up even though we had to be close to the same age. I mean, it had to be the middle of the night, and the girl wore a Canadian tuxedo like she'd strolled off the fucking runway.

I remembered her name was Harleigh Rose and thought that was fitting.

"Am I dreaming?" I croaked, and even the words scraping up my throat hurt. "I didn't think I was gay, but I'm wondering if this is the start of some kind of sex dream."

Harleigh Rose stopped what she was doing––checking my pulse against the time on her *Rolex* watch––and blinked at me for a second before that cold expression shattered with belly-laughter.

"Well," she said, still chuckling. "That has to be one of the weirder things a patient has said when wakin' from unconsciousness, but I'll take the compliment."

I smiled, but the movement pulled at a bandage on my lower lip and stung brightly. With a hiss, I tried to relax against the pillows. "There has to be something in the water here. All of you are so hot...and tall."

She laughed again. "You're not the first person to say something like that, actually."

"How bad is it?" I murmured, unable to keep up my normal blasé façade when every inch of my body throbbed like a disco party.

She hesitated, gaze going toward the ajar door. "Bad enough you won't be up for sex in the real world for a while."

"Damn."

She snickered. "Do you remember what happened?"

"Yeah." I swallowed thickly as panic blared through me like feedback on a speaker. The feeling of the Red Pole holding me down while he and his lackeys systematically beat me wouldn't fade for a long time. The feeling of helplessness was somehow even worse than the resulting pain from the assault.

"You better brace. The only reason Cleo and Axe-Man aren't up here is 'cause my dad's downstairs with half the club, and they're fightin' about what to do."

"With me?"

It had always been risky coming to Entrance when I was still loosely affiliated with the triad, but I honestly hadn't thought Axe-Man would let the club run me out of town, let alone that he'd really *want* them to. Though, after a serial killer had put his hands on Cleo, I guess I couldn't blame him for wanting "the most dangerous thing" he'd ever known on the first train out of town.

I just didn't know how I was going to do that. There was no way I could ride my bike in this condition, and...

Harleigh Rose's hand on my leg beneath the covers jerked me out of my spiral. When I looked up at her in surprise, her head was cocked, and her gaze was considering.

"Not with you," she said slowly. "*For* you."

I blinked dumbly at her.

"Listen, I get you're *new* here and everything, but we're The motherfucking Fallen. No one hurts one of ours without serious retribution. Especially when it's one of our women."

"Didn't I overhear you say two weeks ago that you'd happily run me out of town if Axe-Man wanted that?" I asked, my tongue thick and numb in my mouth.

I thought I might've been in shock, not from the attack, but from the mere idea that I might be even loosely enfolded in The Fallen.

No, not The Fallen.

In the family Axe-Man had made here in Entrance.

Her smile was a thin slice, red as blood. She was Zeus Garro's daughter, and she looked it at that moment with violence in her eyes. "You might be the girl who sent Axe-Man to prison, but you gotta understand something. I was the girl who stabbed my now-fiancé in the chest. Bea was the girl with her own stalker psychopath. Loulou was the girl who shot a rival biker in the head." She shrugged as if such things were normal, a rite of passage, and maybe in the biker babe handbook they were. "If Axe-Man forgives you, who are we to hold the past against you?"

"I doubt he forgives me," I muttered, but there wasn't my normal conviction behind it because I was reeling. "I think I have a concussion."

Harleigh Rose nodded. "You do. And he might not forgive you, I dunno. He's a private guy, and he doesn't share much. But if he's throwing down for you, it's for a reason."

"Probably for Cleo. I bet she's freaking out. And...well, he's just a good guy." The *best* guy. My off-white knight. Always and forever the hero, even when it was to his detriment, even when people (like me) didn't deserve it.

"He is," she agreed as voices swelled downstairs. "But trust me, girl, these bikers don't do anythin' they don't wanna do."

"He's protective, and those instincts have to be blaring after what happened to Cleo," I explained. "Trust me, if Axe-Man wasn't such a good guy, he'd probably be wishing the triad had killed me and saved him the trouble."

"You are the human personification of a pain in my fuckin' ass," Axe-Man said as he stepped into the room and crossed to the bed, arms folding across his chest as he studied me with a glower. "But no man who's been to war wishes death on anyone just 'cause they can't stand them."

I looked over his shoulder to shoot Harleigh Rose an I-told-you-so look, but she only ducked her head and smiled.

"It's not just about you, though," he continued, ignoring my impudence like he usually did. "Nova and I got a call from Jae Pil. Seems the triad went after Sara, Chloe, and Jae tonight too. Figure they got lucky seein' me leave your room on their way outta town and thought they'd extend the bloody love letter to the club by writin' you into it."

"Are they okay?" I asked at the same time as Harleigh Rose did.

"Jae's got a broken fuckin' hand that'll take him outta commission at the shop 'til it heals. They roughed up Sara and Chloe, but not as bad as you. Bumps and bruises, mostly. They're at King and Cressida's house with the doc. They'll be okay. Truth is, they targeted the club, but they specifically wanted to piss *me* off by goin' after the civilians workin' at Street Ink."

"Fuckin' cowards," Harleigh Rose hissed.

Axe-Man grunted his agreement, but his eyes were like nails driven through my skull, pinning me back to the pillows. "Why didn't they kill you tonight, Mei?"

I sighed, but the act hurt my ribs so much that I winced and had to take a moment to catch my breath. In that time, Zeus Garro entered the room, his presence taking up all the air in the space that wasn't already occupied with Axe-Man's palpable frustration. He was followed by Axe-Man's friend Bat Stephens and a red-headed man covered in tattoos whose leather vest was festooned in a myriad of patches, one of them reading "Enforcer" and another bearing the shape of the Grim Reaper.

So this was the infamous Priest McKenna.

I'd met a lot of criminals in my twenty-five years, but the dead look in those eyes made a sharp shiver zip my spine up a little straighter.

It was hard to imagine this dead-eyed biker with the pretty blonde Bea, but in some way, it made me relax to do so. Cleo was filled with light, but she'd always been drawn to the dark, and it helped to know she'd still found that in Bea. Helped to know Bea and I had something in common and that Cleo hadn't just...become a new person with new types of friends in my absence.

"I'd like to hear the answer to that question, too," Zeus told me as he took up position at the foot of the bed.

It was a large room—–peaked ceilings, French doors open slightly to let in the breeze of a patio, big enough to fit a California king bed and oversized furniture to fit Axe-Man's Viking warrior size—–but suddenly, it felt too small.

"I can only guess," I said after swallowing thickly, staring down at my hands and noticing the skin and blood under my fingernails from fighting back. I picked at it absently. "Kasper Kuan never liked me after what happened in Calgary eight years ago, but over the years, he got used to me."

"Why?" Axe-Man demanded. His hand clenched and flexed open again and again. I always looked at his hands for his emotional tells. He couldn't keep them from giving away his thoughts.

"Why did he get used to me?" I shrugged, then groaned when pain spiked through my shoulder. "Can I get some more drugs?"

Harleigh Rose nodded, but Axe-Man shook his head. "When you're done answerin' my questions."

"Dad, what the hell is wrong with you?" Cleo asked from the doorway, clearly being held back by Kodiak. "Are you serious right now?"

"We need answers, Cleo," he said without looking at her, without inflection. "She's brought trouble to Entrance, and we need to know how to safeguard against her."

"Don't you mean against *them*?" I asked sweetly.

His brows lowered even further. Another series of hand clenches.

"You're being barbaric," Cleo nearly shouted, ducking awkwardly under Kodiak's arm and crutching into the room.

When she got close enough, she hit her dad in the back of the knee with a crutch and waited for him to turn to her before stating, "Mei's just been beaten up. If you have any decency, you'll save this interrogation until she'd had some painkillers and some sleep."

"It's fine, Glory," I said, but the words were thin because gratefulness was lodged in my throat. "I don't mind."

"Well, I do," she countered.

I hadn't seen her so vivacious since the accident, and clearly, none of the others had either because they all visibly softened in their stances. Even Axe-Man.

He sighed raggedly and reached out to cup Cleo's face. "Just a few more questions, and then we'll let her sleep, Glory. But only if you get your own ass to bed. You need rest to recover, too, and tonight's been a lot."

"I'm fine," she snapped. Kodiak snorted behind her, and she twisted to glare at him. "I *am*."

He lifted one shoulder in a shrug and yawned like he didn't care either way.

"I'll get you some more drugs," Harleigh Rose interjected, already turning to leave. "The good stuff."

"Thank you," I murmured, then to Cleo, "You should sleep, Glory. We have a long day tomorrow of doing nothing but sitting on the couch and watching *Sailor Moon*."

Her mouth flattened as she considered me for a moment, but I could see the tremble of exhaustion in her arms as she braced herself on the crutches. "Okay, but only if it's Super S. I know you like the original season, but Chibiusa rocks."

I laughed even though it opened the split in my lip again. "She's totally why you'd dye your hair pink, isn't she?"

She tossed her head the way she used to when she had long hair, forgetting for a moment that it had been shorn. "She's the daughter of two heroes, and she becomes her own hero. It's very inspiring."

"It's a cartoon," Kodiak muttered.

"It's *anime*," Cleo and I retorted at the same time.

We shared another smile before she whispered, "I'm sorry, Rocky. I know they aren't acting like it now, but the club will find the guys who did this to you and make them pay."

"Because Queen Cleo demands it?" I teased, feeling too many eyes on us, assessing me.

"Because it's the right thing to do," she countered, balancing on one leg to pat my head before she turned to crutch out of the room. Before she left, she turned and pinned each of the men with a look. "Be nice, please. She's my best friend."

"Will do, sweetheart," Zeus promised solemnly even though his eyes were crinkled like they were smiling.

By unspoken agreement, everyone waited until Cleo had left the room before they closed the door behind her and Kodiak, and turned their attention back to me.

"Enough with the lies, Mei," Axe-Man said, pulling up a chair from against the wall. "Tell me everything."

For a moment, I thought about really doing that. Unloading all my secrets, all the things that had happened since I ran from the scene of the crime at Turner Farm that night so many years ago. But I couldn't flay myself alive like that, especially now when my future seemed utterly precarious. Without Seven Song triad's protection, I was officially going up against the Red Dragons alone. Worse than that, if Kasper truly believed I was betraying him and working with The Fallen, this was only a warning.

He'd kill me if I acted against him.

"It was a warning," I told them. "Tonight."

"The triad doesn't give warnings."

"Not usually," I agreed, adjusting on the pillows with a grimace. "But Kasper killed his brother's lover once. I think killing another would be stretching the family loyalty to the breaking point, even for a Chinese family."

"So you are fuckin' him." Even though there was no undulation in Axe-Man's tone, his entire body seemed carefully clenched around a mass of emotions working behind his stormy eyes.

"No," I said, suddenly so tired I couldn't keep my eyes open. "I agreed to be Jiang's beard when I moved to Vancouver. We go out on 'dates' every week or two, and I attend certain functions with him. We don't have a physical relationship, but I guess, after all these years, we're friends of a sort."

Friends the way two stray cats were friends, banding together to hunt mice but wary enough of each other to sleep apart.

"Jiang Kuan is gay?" Bat asked, his black brows raised into his hairline.

I levelled him a cool look. "What, gangsters can't be gay or something? It's the twenty-first century."

"I'm not shocked he's gay," Bat corrected. "I'm shocked his brother allowed him to live for it. Kuan is known for bein' an old-school sonuvabitch."

"Yeah, well, Kasper basically raised Jiang after their parents died. And family is complicated. That's why I'd say I'm alive right now. That, and even though they obviously saw Axe-Man leaving my room, they didn't have enough evidence to support me working with The Fallen. Kasper knows I knew the Axelsens in Calgary. It's feasible I might have run into Axe-Man in town, and he was confronting me."

"Feasible, but not likely," Zeus noted.

"Jiang is valuable, not just as his brother, but to Seven Song," I admitted. "He's the Vanguard, which means he's in charge of operations. Basically, he coordinates most of the triad's big jobs. If Kasper killed me, Jiang might turn on him, so basically, he kills me, he *has* to kill Jiang, just in case."

"You've wedged yourself into quite the position," Axe-Man

drawled. "Only question remainin' is why the fuck you'd do that?"

Exhaustion was knawing at my bones, sucking out the marrow, but I still managed to jut my chin out at Axe-Man and say coolly, "My reasons are my own."

"Not now, they aren't. You're in my house, hangin' around my daughter, causin' trouble in my town, so the reasons are owed to me. Pay up."

"You never used to be so stupid, Axe-Man," I said casually just to watch those big hands fist. "Do you really think *I* brought trouble to Entrance when the mother chapter of the fucking Fallen MC resides here? You don't think the Kuan brothers had their eyes set on you from the moment they expanded to British Columbia? You don't think they still *hate* The Fallen for what Rooster Cavendish did to them in Calgary? I'm one girl, not the destroyer of fucking worlds."

"You destroyed mine once before," he stated through clenched teeth. "I won't let you do it again."

"Fuck you," I tried to hiss, but it came out like a whisper because I felt like I'd been punched in the gut again.

"Axe-Man, step out," Zeus ordered in a quiet, intractable manner.

For a moment, I thought he'd argue, but with a glower in my direction, Axe-Man pushed himself out of the chair and stalked out of the room, shutting the door a little too hard behind him.

I closed my eyes and focused on my breathing so I wouldn't cry like a little girl.

The bed decompressed by my hip, and the scent of leather and a hint of vanilla filled my nostrils. When I opened my eyes, Zeus was sitting beside me. Up close like that, I could see the tan lines in his face, the crow's feet, and rows in his forehead paler than his tanned skin. He was weathered from years of riding on the back of a bike in all elements, and there were some threads of silver in his dark brown, blond-tipped long locks, but all of that only proved to heighten how ruggedly handsome he was.

I blinked, a little dazzled despite myself.

"You gotta excuse Axe-Man. Never seen him treat a woman anythin' but gentle. What happened to Cleo? It's been hard on him, and he's not himself."

When I didn't deign that with a response, he cracked a small smile and chuckled.

"Yeah, you comin' into town didn't help matters much. But you're a smart woman. I bet I don't hafta tell ya that there's a thin fuckin' line between love and hate. He loved ya once, but after eight years and what happened between ya, it's understandable he got a bit turned around. I think he'd be hard-pressed to know himself exactly where he stands next to it."

"Deep beyond the boundaries of hatred," I said dryly.

"But you don't hate him."

I let my lids lower, hiding the extent of it from those astute silver eyes. "No."

"You want to help him and Cleo. That's why you came?"

"Yes," I said slowly, suspiciously.

"So do I," he said easily, opening his scarred hands to show me his palms as if to prove he wasn't hiding anything. "I'm thinkin' we can help each other in that."

"Oh yeah? How's that?" I asked, an edge to my voice I couldn't curb.

His lips twitched in his beard. "You tell me why the hell you'd pretend to date Jiang Kuan—the truth of it—and I'll protect ya from the Seven Song triad even if Axe-Man doesn't like it."

I gaped at him for a moment before I snapped my jaw shut. "Why the hell would you do that?"

Another lip twitch. He tugged on his beard to cover it up. "'Cause I'm a man ruled by my gut, and it's tellin' me you got more goin' on than you're sayin'. It's tellin' me that when a man acts like a bastard after a girl's bein' beat, it's 'cause he's beatin' himself up for lettin' her get that way. You got history with a brother'a mine, which means you got history with me."

"It's bad history," I clarified as if he was a moron.

This time, he straight out laughed. From the belly, head thrown back, tanned throat working. I figured I could understand how Loulou fell in love with him at seventeen. And it wasn't just because he was gorgeous. He was being genuinely kind to me when I hadn't realized how close I was to falling apart. A few nice words were the equivalent of Band-Aids over bullet holes, but at that point, anything helped.

"Only bad 'cause at one point, there was a helluva lotta love there," he surmised. "Honestly? All that's icin'. You're a woman in trouble, and that's reason enough for me and mine to protect ya, yeah?"

I shrugged weakly, both because it hurt to do so and because I felt utterly raw and vulnerable sitting in what must have been Axe-Man's enormous bed, wearing what I was just realizing was one of Axe-Man's old Street Ink tees, being seen by the keen eyes of President Zeus Garro. I felt like all the hurt I'd harboured inside for so many years had been brought to the surface, both literally and figuratively, by the triad's beating. Like I wore the story of my life on my skin, but unlike with my tattoos, I hadn't been the voice telling the story.

"You know about how Axe-Man's wife died?" I asked softly, staring at my hands. There was a long cut through the symbol for *faith* that made it impossible to read.

"Yeah, only Bat and me, but Priest won't breathe a word."

"Then you probably know I tried to get into the Centre Street Crowd in Calgary so I could get information on the people who killed Kate. I'd overheard my grandfather and Axe-Man talking about Seven Song, and I remembered Kate murmuring their name when she was dying. Anyway, after everything happened in Calgary, Jiang found me sometime later and offered me a trade. I pretended to be his girlfriend, and he'd get me information about the real man who'd ordered the hit on Kate."

Bat cursed under his breath, shook his head, and gave in to the urge to say, "Axe-Man would lose his ever-lovin'-fuckin' mind if he knew that shit, Mei. You wanna get killed tryin' to avenge a death that happened over a decade ago? How do you even know Jiang isn't jerkin' you around, and Seven Song *were* the ones to order the hit?"

"I can't know for sure, obviously, but it seems clear Jiang had no knowledge of it if it was Seven Song. Being close to him meant I could snoop around Kasper and the higher-ups without suspicion. Jiang doesn't have any reason to lie to me, not when our arrangement means we trust each other and keep each other's confidences, or we die. Besides, it wasn't just about avenging Kate at that point," I tried to explain, feeling so miserable I was nauseated by it. By myself and my everlasting stupidity. I felt so often like my heart was in the right place, but I could never seem to make the right choices despite that.

I squeezed my eyes shut against the burn of tears and opened them when words burst from my mouth with unnecessary ferocity, "It was about getting redemption for what I'd done to Axe-Man and Cleo and Lin, too."

The silence that followed had texture, a roughness that abraded my sensitive, bruised skin until it made me want to whimper.

Finally, Zeus cleared his throat and rested a paw lightly on my calf. "I get you're a strong woman, so you might not like me sayin' this, but it's gotta be said. Have you ever thought'a askin' for forgiveness instead'a fightin' for it?"

"How can I ask when I haven't earned it yet?" I countered.

Zeus stared at me for a long moment, Bat and Priest quiet

but attentive, reading whatever I was trying desperately to hide beneath my skin.

It was Bat who said, "Not sure I ever met anyone who matched Axe-Man for stubbornness."

"He's stubborn; I'm stubborn. It's always been a little complicated," I admitted.

Zeus and Bat laughed at that, which made my stomach settle a bit. It was just nice to make people laugh, especially in the wake of my confession.

"Please, don't tell him," I asked, even though I doubted they'd agree to it.

I was no one. Axe-Man was their brother.

"I won't," Zeus said immediately, and then, at my startled expression, his lip curled. "For now. But you will, Mei, or I'll do it for ya. Now, tell me what information Jiang's given ya on the Red Dragons."

"Why?"

"I gotta feelin' we can't stop you from carryin' on in your mission unless we lock you in a fuckin' tower, yeah?" When I nodded reluctantly, he grinned. "Well, I got a wife, five kids, and a club to run, so I don't got the time to guard ya like a dragon. Besides, I think Axe-Man's got that role handled. I figure if you're gonna throw yourself into trouble, someone's gotta have your back, so it might as well be the club. You're not the only one who wants to give Axe-Man some fuckin' peace."

"So let me get this straight," I said slowly. "You're not only going to keep my secret from Axe-Man, you're going to actively help me take down the Red Dragons to avenge Kate even though Axe-Man would flip if he knew we were doing this?"

"We're a fuckin' biker club, Mei, not a goddamn nunnery. You think we're opposed to a little good old-fashioned revenge?" Zeus asked with a smile as sharp as a knife's edge.

I looked up at Priest, who stared back at me with those cold eyes and grinned a manic, heart-stopping grin, and then Bat, who cracked his knuckles and pounded a fist over his patch that read "Sergeant at Arms."

"I'll bring the guns," he vowed.

When I laughed, relieved and delighted, they joined in. It was the first time in a long time I felt part of something good.

CHAPTER THIRTY-ONE

Axe-Man

I WAS COMIN' IN FROM MY MORNIN' COLD DIP IN THE LAKE, shakin' water from my hair like a dog before rubbin' a towel over it, when I heard the shatter. Droppin' the cloth from my face, I saw Mei standin' in the mouth of the kitchen, hands open, shards of ceramic and a pool of coffee at her feet.

"What the fuck?" I demanded.

"Sorry," she said instantly, closin' her hands, then starin' at them as if she couldn't remember what she'd been holdin'. "I was...*shit*. I broke your mug. I'll buy you guys a new one."

"Don't give a fuck about the mug, Mei," I muttered, tossin' the towel over an open hook by the door and stalkin' toward her. I still had my unlaced boots on from trekkin' up the stony path from the beach, so I didn't mind the broken pieces as I hauled Mei into my arms despite her squawk of protest and then carried her over to the island. I plunked her down by the sink and glared at her. "I meant, what the fuck are you doin' outta bed? You've got a damn concussion."

She stared at me blankly for so long that I pressed a hand to her forehead to feel if she'd come down with a fever overnight. It was unlikely, but if I'd been wrong about internal bleedin', I'd need to rush her to the hospital.

"You don't feel hot, but you're clearly outta it. You shouldn't be up walkin' around."

"I was hungry," she admitted, gaze fallin' down to my bare chest and back up so quickly I almost missed it.

"Thought you'd be sleepin', so I did my routine in the gym and took a dip, but you could've texted. I'll make you somethin' after I clean this up."

I enjoyed a couple of minutes of silence that clearly meant Mei was still in serious pain from the beatin' and the concussion 'cause she never obeyed so easily. I cleaned up the broken mug and the coffee, then started the machine to brew a fresh pot and got rice, ginger, and chicken stock out to make congee without even thinkin' about it.

"What are you making?" she demanded sharply while I rinsed the rice before addin' it to the pot on the stove.

"What's it look like?"

"Congee."

"Good to see the triad didn't rattle your brain too hard," I said dryly as I added eight cups of chicken stock.

"But you hate congee."

"Good thing I'm havin' a protein shake instead, then. This is for you."

A long pause. Even though I wasn't facin' her, I could imagine the look of confusion drawin' two lines between her brows.

"Why are you making me breakfast?" she asked slowly, suspiciously, like she thought I'd fuckin' poison her or somethin'.

"Jesus, Mei, you were just fucked up by a group of Seven Song thugs last night and left in a fuckin' dumpster. You think I'm above makin' you somethin' comfortin' for breakfast?"

"I think you hate me, and the last thing you said before you rescued me from Purgatory was that I was the most dangerous thing you knew. It's understandable I might be a little confused this morning, especially when you seemed pissed at me even after you brought me back here."

I'd been pissed.

No, not just pissed.

Fuckin' incensed. The kinda anger that was particular to someone I knew and cared about gettin' hurt on my watch. I was a trained fuckin' soldier, a goddamn educated doctor, a motherfuckin' *Fallen brother,* and I still couldn't seem to keep the people around me from harm.

How could I be anythin' but royally pissed with myself?

I'd acted savagely last night. Takin' Mei like she was my enemy then discardin' her without a fuckin' care, leavin' her in a place that wasn't safe even when the door locked with that flimsy fuckin' chain.

I closed my eyes against the current of self-loathin' that threatened to pull me under. I was so busy deep breathin', I didn't hear Mei slide carefully off the counter and walk over to my side. When she touched my back lightly, I acted on instinct, droppin' the wooden spoon I'd been usin' to stir the congee to twist and grab Mei by the wrist.

We both froze. I loomed over her, reminded of how fuckin' slight she was when she always projected such a dangerous, self-contained edge. She looked so fragile this mornin' with one eye painted in purples and blues, her lip puffy and held together with a butterfly bandage, her cheeks swollen beyond their usual steep angle. The damage was horrible, and it made me feel like a fuckin' bastard.

Without thinkin', my hold on her wrist gentled and

dropped, my knuckles skimmin' over the tight skin of her cheek. "Gotta ice this."

She swallowed thickly. "Yeah. But right now, I'm more concerned about the whiplash you're giving me. Why are you being so nice?"

My heart was a heavy carcass in my chest. "You think I'm so different a man now, after prison and all the rest, that I can't treat a woman who's been assaulted with kindness?"

"I'm not just any woman," she corrected with almost a wince.

"No," I agreed, runnin' my thumb down her square jawline so I could pinch her chin and force her to meet my eyes. "You've never been just any woman. We might not be...friends anymore, Mei, but once, you were family. Once, I went to prison happy to think I'd given you a chance at a beautiful life. One I believed to my bones you deserved. Don't know why you stopped talkin' to me, and honest to fuck, I don't wanna know anymore. We don't hafta open up those old wounds. Right now, this mornin', you're a woman I've cared about who needs carin' for, and that's all there is to it."

"How can you forget even for a second?" she whispered thickly, her long, straight lashes casting shadows on her purpled cheeks.

The sight of her so hurt was like a knife thrust into my gut, the pain unrelentin'.

"At this moment, your pain is fresher than mine. I'm not sayin' this changes things between us other than to say you're stayin' here for a while. 'Til you recover enough not to sway like this." I steadied her with two hands on her shoulders, then decided, fuck it, and picked her up by the armpits to carefully place her down on the island again so she'd rest while I made her breakfast. "'Til you find a place that isn't a shithole."

"Purgatory Motel has its own charms," she protested, but it was weak 'cause she was white with nausea.

Quickly, I grabbed a steel bowl from the dryin' rack and moved between her thighs, grabbing most of her hair off her shoulders before she threw up into the bowl. When she was finished, I took the bowl to the sink, wet a cloth, and got a glass of water for Mei, then I took the bowl outside to rinse it at the side of the house.

When I got back, she was chuggin' the water.

"Careful, or you'll make yourself sick again," I warned. "Just sit there and let me finish the congee. You'll feel better with some food in your stomach."

She made a noise of consent without liftin' her gaze to mine, no doubt embarrassed about pukin'.

"I was a doctor, remember," I reminded her as I went back to the stove. "Not my first time holdin' a bowl."

"No, but still..." She sucked in a deep breath. "Thanks."

"Don't mention it."

I cracked open the window beside the sink after checkin' on the pot and then poured us both a new cup of joe. When I handed it over, Mei shivered, freezin' in just my oversized tee. Cursin' under my breath, I went into the laundry room, exchanged my damp bathin' suit and towel for a pair of clean grey sweatpants, and grabbed Mei a fresh zip-up hoodie that was part of the set.

When I returned with it, she blanched a little but didn't protest when I forcibly put the hoodie on her.

"I'm concussed, not paralysed," she said afterward as I handed her the coffee mug again.

"You were cold."

"You're barely wearing anything. You aren't?"

I looked down at my bare chest, absently notin' that the teeth marks Mei'd bitten into my chest were still pink. Cleo hadn't seen me bare-chested this mornin' 'cause Lin had taken her to therapy, but I made a note to put a shirt on before she got home and noticed.

"The cold doesn't bother me, never has."

"I forgot," she said softly. "You used to wear just your Fallen cut when it was snowing out."

I shrugged. "It's the Vikin' blood."

"Where's Cleo this morning?"

"At therapy, should be back soon. I'll give you breakfast and get you back to bed then I gotta get to the shop. Sara, our receptionist, quit 'cause of the assault. Can't blame her, obviously, but now we gotta get a temp and rearrange all of Jae Pil's appointments 'cause of his broken hand. I'm just goin' in for a couple of hours to get shit on track, but I'll be back before dinner. Lin's gonna do up a hot pot for everyone."

"You mean..." She paused delicately. "I'm invited to stay for dinner?"

I resumed stirrin' the thickenin' congee. "That's what I said."

It was almost palpable, her struggle to digest that little bit of news. Sharin' food was a big deal in any culture, but it was especially important to Lin and Mei. Bein' included would mean a lot to her.

The idea of her sittin' at my family table again did funny things to my chest, simultaneously openin' new wounds and soothin' old ones that'd never healed right.

"And what are you going to do about the triad?" she said finally, turnin' to a topic she was more comfortable with, which said a lot about who Mei was as a person.

A fighter ready to take on the world even when she was hurtin'. It was stupid as much as it was admirable as hell.

I shot her a look over my shoulder. "You let me and my brothers worry about that."

"Just because I'm hurt doesn't mean I'm some damsel in distress, Axe-Man. I'm not going to faint if you tell me what you have planned for them."

I laughed, surprised by the warmth that suffused my chest. It'd been a minute since I'd had reason to laugh like that.

"I'm not worried you'll fuckin' faint. I'm worried you'll get on your stupid excuse for a bike and hunt them down yourself. Never thought you were a damsel, Mei Zhen. You've always been a dragon."

Wasn't sure who was more surprised by the words, Mei or me. It brought our shared history rushin' back into the room, the water line risin' 'til it threatened to drown us both in the past. My head reeled with the memories, the good ones, the dinners with Cleo, Lin, and Rocky, the late-night sketch sessions, and the school pick-ups. That last night but before Turner Farm, with Mei in that red dress, smellin' like cherry blossoms and springtime freshness, held in my arms in a dimly lit parkin' lot for her only dance at prom. The feel of her lips on mine, so startlin' and so wrong, I'd never let myself think what it would really be like to kiss her back.

And then last night, when I hadn't kissed her at all, but I'd done more. Suckin' her red-tipped breasts into my mouth, palmin' that high, tight ass, drivin' into the snug heat of that wet pussy. How powerful I'd felt fuckin' a woman with so much of her own wildness, her own power. How she'd matched my ferocity with her own and urged me to give her more.

"Shouldn't'a touched you," I was sayin' before I realized it.

The congee was done, thick and glossy. I ladled it into a bowl and got some chopped scallions and soy sauce, then arranged them on the island beside Mei so she could dress it how she liked.

I was turnin' away when she touched my arm lightly. Her face was more open than I'd ever seen it, eyes wide, dark pools reflectin' myself back at me, lips parted on soft breath.

"Please, don't be."

"You and I both know it was wrong."

"No, we don't." That tone was so familiar, stubborn as a

goat, fiercely convinced of her own opinion. It was and always had been oddly charmin'. "I know it won't happen again. I get you probably regret it, but can we please both agree not to talk about it? I don't think I can stand raking it over the coals."

"'Cause I hurt you?" I asked, ashamed I hadn't really thought about it. I'd assumed all her hurts came from the triad, not my own hands, but I was just as capable of inflictin' pain, and I'd been close to mad with a combination of lust and years of frustration reachin' a boilin' point.

"No," she said again, this time rollin' her eyes. "You didn't hurt me. But it would hurt me if you made what happened into a bad thing. It just...was. I know our relationship is complicated, but having you fuck me like that was the simplest form of pleasure I've had in a long time. So don't ruin the memory for me, yeah?"

Her smile was twisted like hot metal, not right on her face, but her words seemed sincere enough. I'd known, of course, that she'd had a crush on me back in the day, but that was eight years ago. There'd probably been enough men since then to diminish that crush to childish fancy. It should've been a relief to know she was sexually mature enough to write off what happened as an act of madness, but it left me feelin' on edge.

"Right, well, it won't happen again. While you're under my roof, you're safe, yeah? Even from my grumpy ass," I tried to joke, but it fell flat.

Mei only accepted her bowl of congee while I busied myself makin' a quick protein shake.

"I'm headin' up for a shower, but I'll take you back up before I leave so you can rest in my room."

"I can stay down here," she countered immediately.

"No. Cleo and Lin'll be here, and you need to sleep. The guest room is filled with my art shit, but some of the brothers will be over to clear it out for you. 'Til then, you're in my bed restin' even if I have to tie you down to the bed posts."

I caught her fierce shiver from my peripheral vision and tried to tamp down the correspondin' heat in my gut. It was like now that I'd let anger rip away the veil of respectability between us, I couldn't hide from the fact that Mei wasn't seventeen anymore.

She was twenty-five years old, still sixteen years my junior, but it was hard to hold the same prejudices I'd used to have around age gaps when there were so many healthy examples in the club. Zeus and Loulou were nineteen years apart in age, but they'd clearly been made for each other. Even with two newborns, a preteen foster kid, and a club to look after, they acted like newlyweds.

Lila and Nova had twelve years between them, and I bore witness every fuckin' day to the chemistry between those two. Lovin' Li had changed Nova, taken him from somethin' like a caricature to the truest, best version of the man I'd met on my first visit to Entrance when he was just a punk-ass graffiti artist.

King and Cressida were the heart and soul of the club in a lotta ways, always the listenin' ears, the thoughtful friend, and I figured it was 'cause of the bounty of peace their love produced. So much, there was an excess for the rest of us to benefit from.

Even Priest and Bea, night and day, the couple no one hardly saw comin' made a strange and beautiful kinda sense, like the oddly lovely atmosphere of a graveyard at dawn.

Hell, we were gearin' up to celebrate Harleigh Rose and Lion Danner's weddin' next month, and the whole fuckin' town seemed excited about the union between the biker princess and the town's ex-cop, good guy.

If anyone tried to tell me not one of those couples should exist 'cause of somethin' so fuckin' stupid as age, I'd've knocked them back a step so they had better perspective to reconsider.

So it fit wrong, thinkin' of Mei as bein' too young, now.

But she was still dangerous in all the ways she'd always been. Too tempestuous, too reckless and stubborn, too willin' to fall on someone else's sword 'cause she'd never really felt peace, but she wanted that for everyone around her.

And she was dangerous in new ways too.

I watched her as she sucked the congee from the spoon, pink tongue flashin' out to catch the dregs. All that finely honed beauty contrasted by the near-vicious level of lust I now knew she was capable of made my heart pound like the door knocker on a haunted mansion. Urgin' me to revisit old ghosts and exorcise them so I might be able to stay a while, explore this old-new girl with the pretty tits and loyal heart and big brain in ways I'd never dared to before.

Her eyes were fixed on the mark her little teeth had made in my left pec, the pink lines raised and angry even though she'd bitten me through a shirt. Watchin' her expression go soft and dark made me want to storm those few feet between us, force her thighs wide to make space for my body between them, tunnel my hands in all that sleek black hair, and *plunder* her.

"Axe-Man?" she breathed. I had the sense she'd wanted to call me Henning, but hadn't.

For one brief, mad moment, I wanted her to speak my given name. Imagined the breathy catch in her voice over the "H" and the moan over the "i-n-g" like she was gettin' off just on the sound of me between her lips.

Fuck.

I shook my protein shake in my water bottle and turned slightly so the observant minx wouldn't see how my traitorous cock was hardenin' in my grey sweats.

"Holler when you're finished, and I'll help you upstairs," I muttered as I made my way to my bedroom to take a *very* cold fuckin' shower.

CHAPTER THIRTY-TWO

Axe-Man

THE NEXT TEN DAYS WERE PAINFUL, MOSTLY 'CAUSE HAVIN' MEI IN the house again felt good. Even though it'd been years, there was a time when havin' Cleo and Mei underfoot all the time was my life. The sound of their giggles as they both recuperated on the leather couch in the livin' room while they watched anime shows and superhero movies, the sight of them tangled together in silence readin' the same copy of one of Cleo's favourite graphic novels, the small smile on Cleo's face that seemed like a miracle every time Mei brought it to life.

The Fallen family seemed to take Mei's introduction to the household in better stride than I did. Bea was there most days, and even though it surprised me at first, Cleo's two wildly different best friends seemed to get along well enough. I thought it was 'cause Mei was softer than she wanted to seem and Bea was darker than she appeared.

She'd bonded most surprisingly with Curtains and Boner.

She and Curtains could geek out like Mei and I used to over comic books and strange biological facts but also about topics I'd never thought Mei'd have a mind to, like how to launder money through online sports gamblin' and old age pensions.

Boner was easier to understand, and somethin' about watchin' them together made my chest ache. 'Cause Mei might've been the baddest girl I'd ever known, but she fuckin' loved to make her people laugh. When she and Boner got goin' teasin' each other, it pulled the rest of us into their orbit 'til we were all clutchin' our sides laughin' up a lung. That first hot pot dinner with Lin had ended up with nearly half the club around our huge, scarred wood table, and Mei and Boner'd made Cleo laugh so hard, she sprayed broth out her nose. It reminded me of so many dinners with Kate, Lin, Cleo, Mei, and me back in the day that I almost felt my ex-wife was a ghost at the table with us, remindin' me I'd never figured out exactly what happened to her.

The restless dissatisfaction I'd felt since Cleo was attacked and The Prophet was killed by someone other than me had been exacerbated by Mei's reintroduction into our lives. It brought the unjustness of Kate's end into fresh focus and empowered me to search out the last of the answers I needed to lay her memory properly to rest.

Not just for me, but for Cleo, and even Mei.

But havin' Mei in *my* space wasn't just about old memories.

It was also about new ones.

No matter how hard I worked out with Wrath in the gym or how late I stayed up tryin' to drop into a dreamless sleep of exhaustion, thoughts and dreams of Mei Zhen plagued me every single fuckin' day.

In fact, on the fourth night, the same one I moved back into my bedroom after Ransom and Carson'd finished clearin' out the guest bedroom and Cress and Lila had bought some nicer things for it so Mei'd be comfortable, the worse had happened.

I'd given in to the hauntin' temptation to take out those red lace panties I'd stolen from her and wrap them around my cock. It was late, deep in the early mornin' hours, and the house was quiet around me, so I figured I had room to give into my ragin' need to jack off into that sweet-as-hell lace. They still smelled like her, and the idea of my cum mingled with hers had me hard as fuckin' steel.

I was noisy when I jerked myself, but it'd never matter before 'cause Cleo's bedroom was on the main floor at the back of the house. Only, in my lustful delirium, I'd forgotten Mei was just down the hall.

I'd discounted the first creak in the hall as the wind whistlin' with a spring storm outside the window, tossin' leaves and blossoms against the pane, but the second creak got my notice.

I tried to stop, but I was so close to comin' imaginin' Mei ridin' my big cock with that lace thong pushed to the side, the bunch of fabric rubbin' hard against her clit, enough to make her come hard all over me.

Seconds away from comin' myself, gruntin' like a beast, I lurched into a half crunch when my bedroom door creaked up slightly, and Mei appeared in the crack. The night light in the hall was enough to cast her in a yellow glow, my own body naked on the bed and clearly outlined by moonlight. For a second, I thought she'd retreat.

I should've known better.

Instead, she leaned comfortably against the doorframe and watched me come hard into the cloth. My eyes shut as the climax thundered through me, but she'd still been there when I finished. I collapsed to the pillows, chest heavin' and sweaty, waitin' for what she would do.

After a moment, she pushed off the frame and moved across the room on silent feet to my side. I tensed as she slid a finger in the coolin' spunk on my abs and brought it to her mouth, suckin' on it with an audible *pop* and a little kittenish moan.

Then she grabbed her cum-soaked panties, where they lay loosely in my curled palm, and backed away to the door.

"Next time," she said in a low, velvety purr. "Don't waste that cum on my underwear. I can think of better places for it."

I'd avoided her as much as I could for three days.

Lucky for me, there was a fuck ton to do.

We were all hands on fuckin' deck doin' recon on the Seven Song, and we quickly sussed out their system.

They funnelled money into the country with foreign nationals from China who handed off suitcases and briefcases full of cash to straw men who'd take it to one of the casinos in Vancouver or, unfortunately for us and the T-Bird Squad, the Indigenous-owned casino, Lake Edge, to "wash it" at the tables. They'd bet a little and cash out the rest, exchangin' their dirty money with fresh casino cash.

They also used their dirty funds to invest in real estate and failin' businesses, or in the case of Stella's Diner and Honey Bear Café, businesses that were good fronts for money launderin'.

It was brilliant but fuckin' *bold*. The provincial gamin' commission was on to them, which was why they'd hightailed it up to the rez to funnel money through Lake Edge Casino.

Still, it worked.

And the cops didn't have Curtains' hackin' skills to link it all back to one little commercial space in Vancouver's Chinatown.

The Golden Door Inn.

If it sounded familiar, it was 'cause it was the same name as the front of the Seven Song triad in Calgary, where I'd once had a meet with Jiang.

We got to work shorin' up weaknesses in local businesses, startin' with Loulou reachin' out to her old high school boyfriend, Reece Ross, to offer him a loan from the club so he wouldn't sell to the triads and followin' up with Curtains installin' security in some of the storefronts that'd been targeted.

Street Ink Tattoo Parlour was also fucked-up levels of busy now that Jae Pil was out with a broken hand. We'd brought in a buddy from a shop in Vancouver we trusted to pick up some of the slack, but we already had a six-month waitin' list, and it was just gettin' longer. Not to mention, without Sara, we had a temp runnin' the front desk and doin' it in a way that made it clear he was drownin'.

I was complainin' about it with Nova where we sat loungin' in a black velvet booth at the Wet Lotus Strip Club we owned in town, ostensibly celebratin' Lionel Danner's bachelor party after a day of ridin' bikes up the Sea to Sky for lunch at a steakhouse in Whistler and then an afternoon of some of us ridin' horses out at his ranch. It was the perfect end of the day, accordin' to most of the chapter, only Lion was facin' *away* from the stage, playin' poker with Wrath, Lysander, Buck, and Zeus. It wasn't that H.R. would've been pissed with him for appreciatin' the girls undulatin' their bodies on stage––she was born and raised a biker chick, and she was cool as shit about that kinda thing––but Lion didn't give a fuck about anyone save her.

And for the first time in my life, I got him.

The woman twirlin' from the pole five feet from our table was as relevant to me as a muted TV in the background. Even though I was shootin' the shit with Nova, King, Bat, and Dane, all I could see was Mei.

She'd infiltrated my life like a fuckin' disease, and I was gettin' worried there wasn't a damn antidote.

The truth was, no matter how hard I tried, she was always the first thing I noticed when I entered the room. It wasn't that she was beautiful, even though her sheer loveliness was blatant, almost glarin'. It was that no matter where Mei was or what she was doin', she did it with confidence. With purpose.

She'd drawn the eye by sheer force of her magnetic personality. Once, if Mei'd told me she would do somethin', however outlandish, I would've believed her 'cause she was just that powerful, that capable, even at seventeen. Now that she was grown, it was even more palpable.

I caught her watchin' me too much, but I couldn't even snap at her 'cause the only reason I'd noticed was 'cause I was watchin' her right back.

"Mei mentioned to Lila that she'd be happy to fill in," Nova was sayin', and even though I'd been zonin' out, Mei's name brought everythin' back into focus.

"Not a bad idea," Bat mused. "Girl's got enough tatts. She's gotta know a decent amount about the art'a tattooin'."

"That's what I figured."

"Hell no," I barked, shocked that they were even havin' this discussion. "I'm not havin' Mei Zhen in the shop every day."

Nova rolled his eyes at my high drama, probably 'cause that was usually his fuckin' role. "It'd just be 'til we find someone actually fuckin' qualified. That idiot today made an appointment for sixty minutes when we needed three *hours* to do the back piece my client wanted. He's worse than useless."

I sucked back a swig of beer as I tried to fight through the auto-response anger and rationalise why it was such a piss-poor idea to have Mei in the shop.

It didn't work.

"I already got the girl in my town, in my goddamn home sleepin' down the hall. You think I want her at work too?"

"What's the big deal?" King asked, too innocent, wide-eyed like some kinda kid when he'd been a man since he was a preteen and his dad went down the first time. "She's just your daughter's kid best friend. It's not like she's...distractin', right?"

"She's the human version of a nightmare," I retorted.

Nova snorted. "Yeah, a nightmare you want to fuck."

Wasn't that the fuck of it?

Still, I hadn't realized I was so fuckin' obvious.

"Yeah, brother," Nova said with faux sympathy, pattin' my hand. "It's that fuckin' obvious."

I forcibly unclenched my fist. "Fuck."

"What's the problem, exactly?" Dane asked. "She's gorgeous, she's clearly into you, and I gotta think, with the way Cleo loves both of you, she wouldn't care if you guys started somethin'."

"Started somethin'?" I scoffed a little too hard. "Thinkin' Mei's...fuck, sexier than I got any right to think is one thing. I don't wanna, what, make her my Old Lady?"

I waited for everyone to chime in on my behalf, but for outlaw bikers, these fuckers believed way too fuckin' much in romance.

Hell, King literally called his woman his Queen and wrote her poetry.

Nova'd secreted love notes into Lila's tattoos years before he even admitted he was into her.

I was fucked.

I looked at Bat and Dane, but they only shared a little smile and then shook their heads at me.

"You're all fucked," I declared.

They laughed at me.

"Feels good to see someone else struggle," Nova admitted. "I'm the one with all the wisdom now."

Bat, Dane, and I all scoffed, but he only shrugged smugly. "Hey, I'm the one goin' home to a smokin'-hot woman who'd do anythin' for me."

Somethin' about those words tunnelled under my nails like bamboo.

Do anythin' for me.

Once, I'd thought Mei would do anythin' for Lin, Cleo, and me, and then she'd fuckin' disappeared after that night at Turner Farm. None of us saw her, even fuckin' heard from her, for eighteen months. I'd sat there in that cage goin' over every moment we'd had together, wonderin' where I'd misjudged.

It was one of the qualities I'd always thought we'd shared.

A willingness to do anythin' for our loved ones. For each other.

"She's here, man," Bat said, leanin' close to my side, murmurin' as the others joked around. "Take it from a man who knows, sometimes showin' up for someone is the biggest act of love there is."

"Mei doesn't love me," I told him. "Not anymore, if she ever really did. She was a fuckin' kid, and I was the only adult after Kate died aside from her grandfather who ever made any time for her. It was puppy love, at best. She's here for Cleo."

"You sure that's totally true?" he pushed. "Listen, I'm not a fuckin' therapist, and I'm in no place to give advice about successful relationships. Amelia was basically a foreign creature to me after years'a marriage and you know, we only got hitched 'cause she ended up pregnant with the boys. But I do know loyalty, and I do get family. That girl dropped everythin' in her life to be in Entrance for Cleo, even knowin' you hated her."

"She loves Cleo that much," I admitted, 'cause I'd always known that.

Even when Mei'd disappeared and returned, I'd never asked Cleo if they were in touch 'cause part of me didn't want confirmation they *were*. If Mei was dead to me, I needed her not to exist at fuckin' all.

"Yeah, or maybe she loves you enough to brave your hatred if it means bein' close to you again?" he suggested. "Either way, stop tiptoein' around it, man. You want her. You know what's between you. It isn't like you to be a coward. Just fuckin' *ask* her what happened."

"You know, I've never liked you much," I grumbled, but my

oldest friend only laughed and slung an arm around my shoulders to tug me close.

"Yeah, yeah, I love you, too, fucker."

The lights dimmed suddenly, and a spotlight trained on the side of the main stage. All twenty-odd men in the club quieted instantly, wonderin' what kinda special show they had in store for the groom.

Most of us roared with laughter when Harleigh Rose herself sashayed onto the stage in cowboy boots, fishnets, tiny denim shorts, and a matching denim bra with her big hair all over the place.

"There's been a change of plan, boys," she purred into the microphone as she stalked toward centre stage. "The groom is ending the night with a private show from his *favourite* stripper. Unfortunately, it's private, so you'll all have to get lost." There was a chorus of groans, but she held a hand up to ask for silence, which she immediately received. "Thankfully, I'm a gracious bride, so all of you have lovely ladies waiting in private rooms for you. Those of you with Old Ladies might just find somethin' sexy and familiar inside of yours."

Nova whooped, already standin' up and makin' his way to the back of the club. "Which one's my Flower Child in?"

Harleigh Rose laughed. "Name's are on the doors. Happy dancin', boys. Now make yourself scarce."

"Fuckin' wait 'til I get outta 'ere," Zeus shouted as he covered his eyes and made his way through the tables. When the music swelled, "Born to Be Wild" blarin' through the speakers, he cursed and hightailed it outta there.

Lion laughed, his face broke open with joy as he got up to take a seat closer to the stage. It made somethin' fuckin' ache in my chest seein' that connection, knowin' it was one I'd never had 'cause Kate and I had saved each other, but we'd never been *in* love.

Not like the love that transfixed Lion to Harleigh Rose movin' for him on that stage.

Moved by somethin' I didn't want to explain, I didn't go into the back rooms lookin' for one of the pretty Lotus flowers to entertain me.

I got on the back of my bike and rode up the mountain roads to my house on Lake Mead.

CHAPTER THIRTY-THREE

Mei

All The Fallen brothers and their women were occupied that night with Lion's bachelor party, but Cleo wasn't up to something like that, so we stayed in the cabin with Lin for a girls' night. We did Korean facemasks, Lin braided Cleo's hair, I drew funny caricatures of them both just to hear them giggle and exclaim over how bad they looked, and we feasted on ice cream mochi and sour gummies. It was the kind of night I hadn't had in years, even toward the end of my time in Calgary because I'd been so busy helping Old Dragon take care of Mum and then visiting her in hospice that I hadn't made much time for fun.

As the old fortune teller Madame Cheung had told me, I'd been too focused on death and the dark.

Those things would always occupy a part of my mental landscape because revenge and justice were integral to who I was, but being back with the Axelsens in Entrance reminded me how important it was to prioritize joy too.

When was the last time I'd snuggled up on a comfy couch with a best friend, too many snacks, and a marathon of *Avatar: The Last Airbender* episodes to binge?

"Do you miss Daiyu?" Cleo asked me at one point, tucked under a cream blanket she'd knit out of chunky wool.

Her feet were in my lap, and I absentmindedly cracked her toes, making her squirm.

"Every day," I said baldly.

Lin had gone home, and Cleo was basically half asleep, the room dark around us but for the flickering lights of the television. It made everything seem womb-like, Cleo and I sisters in a safe place.

"Yeah," she whispered back. "I miss Mum every day, too."

"I'm glad you have The Fallen," I told her, not for the first time. "It's cool that you have this huge family who really cares about you."

Her lips twisted, then softened. "No, you're right. I've been feeling a little smothered lately, but I can't imagine my life without every single one of them. Even brothers like Skell, who's kind of a jerk, or Lab-Rat, who's always high. It's like no matter how bad life gets, we all know we will keep each other safe."

I swallowed thickly before I could find my voice. That was all I'd ever wanted.

Seeing something in my face that gave me away, Cleo made a soothing noise in the back of her throat and pushed her toes under my thigh. "You're here, now. You can be part of all of this, too."

"I'll only stay until you're back on your feet."

"But don't you get it? You don't have to. I know you came for me. And for Lin. And Dad, no matter what's happened between you, but there are even more reasons to stay. I guess I didn't realize until the past couple of weeks how alone you've been, Rocky. How come no one is ever texting you to check in? Where are your friends calling you to arrange a visit? Why do I get the sense you've been in some kind of self-imposed isolation since you left us last?"

Because I deserved it, I wanted to say, but didn't because even thinking the words hurt. Because I let down the only family I ever had.

Daiyu, in her last moments.

Axe-Man and therefore Cleo and Lin.

Even Florent, who I hadn't spoken to in years and never would again, had been so fucking disappointed in me.

"Oh Mei," Cleo breathed, shifting awkwardly so she sat beside me, resting the whole length of her side against mine, her casted leg propped up on the coffee table. She rested her head on my shoulder and grabbed my hand. "Will you ever stop beating yourself up about what happened?"

"I don't think so. I think I'll be sorry forever."

"Even if the people you wronged don't want you to be sorry any longer?"

I paused, breath shivering in my lungs. "Maybe especially then."

"For what it's worth, I forgive you. In my mind, there wasn't even anything *to* forgive. You and Dad made your choices that night, and even though neither of you told me exactly what went down, I know you both well enough to know your motivations were always pure."

I snorted. "Pure stupidity, maybe."

"Maybe," she agreed. "I know a little something about making dumb choices. I think I'll hate myself for being so stupid for the rest of my life, but do you want to know the little truth that makes it possible for me to live with myself every day? I know I'm a good person. I know I might have acted foolishly, but my reasons for doing so came from a good place. A loving place. S-Seth Linley tried to take my goodness from me, but I know..." She sucked in a wavering breath, and I squeezed her hand tightly. "I know he could never do that. He took a lot from me, but he can't have that. So I might be scarred and broken and so fucking scared, Rocky, all the time, but I refuse to believe that I'm not worthy of love and happiness. It's hard to believe sometimes, but even on days when I want to die, I cling to that knowledge. I deserve happiness, no matter what's happened to me. No matter the choices I made. And so do you."

"Glory," I whispered through my too-tight throat. "You can hardly equate our circumstances."

"No," she agreed. "But I can equate our hearts. I know you, and I see you, and I love you, okay? I needed you here with me because I've never had to hide from you. Not the good, the bad, or the ugly, and it's because I know you'd rather die than see me unhappy for even a second. It's because I know even when I'm at my worst, you think it's some kind of privilege I've shared that with you."

I couldn't breathe, so I tucked my nose into her hair and held her closer. "Yeah."

"Yeah," she agreed. "Well, I feel the same way about you. So try, for me, to connect a little? To open your heart and see what you could build here if you gave it a real chance. The people here are more like you than you realize. All these characters society has deemed mad, bad, and dangerous to know? Well, they'd all die for each other, too."

"What does that say about us, huh? That we measure love by our willingness to die for each other?" I teased.

Cleo blinked those huge green-grey eyes solemnly. "I think it means we've been through hell, and we know what it's like to die inside, so we know exactly what price we'd pay for the people we care about."

"Damn, you're wise," I said, half joking and half in awe.

She wrinkled her nose, her freckles stark against her pallour. "I think I've spent too much time with the Garros. Seriously, they have crazy biker wisdom."

We giggled.

"You know, I never wonder about who my bio dad was," Cleo mused as she traced the Chinese *fung wong* phoenix tattoo on my forearm. "Mum never spoke about him, and I was pretty young when Henning entered the picture and completely changed our lives. I couldn't imagine––wouldn't want to imagine––my life without him.

"Dad's given me a good life," she admitted. "Sometimes, I wish he could see that. He takes everything on his shoulders, and he's a man, not a titan. He deserves some peace and happiness of his own. A-and, well, he was always more settled when you were around back in the day."

My laughter burst out of me unbidden. "You're kidding, right? I think I only ever heard him raise his voice around me, even back then."

"Yeah, but he usually keeps everything inside. It's good for him to get it out, you know? Even now, I think he was slowly driving himself mad with guilt over what happened to me. You've been a good distraction." When I snorted, she tugged at my hand until I looked at her. "I think he's being mean to you as some kind of test. Like if he can drive you away, it means he was right, and you were never worth the trouble. But if you stay...if you stay, Mei, I think we could all be happy again. I think you could make a home here with us."

She hesitated, biting her plump lower lip, her gaze falling to my throat. Though my bruises had basically faded and the pain in my ribs was only a dull throb if I moved too fast the wrong way, I knew she imagined the dark marks I'd had there. There had been hickeys from Axe-Man's savage mouth, but they'd been kind of disguised by the ring of finger mark bruises around my throat, too. Or so I'd thought. By the way Cleo was staring at me now with those sad, astute eyes, I wondered if I was only fooling myself.

My heart started hammering into my rib cage, rattling the

breath in my lungs. Cleo had never known how I felt about her dad. It had never been an appropriate crush, let alone a realistic one, so I hadn't wanted to burden our relationship with it. Now, I wondered if I hadn't been wrong to talk about my feelings with her. She'd always been so much smarter than me in the ways of the heart.

"I think you could make each other happy," she finished with a little shrug like she was frustrated by her own words. "I've thought so for a long time."

"Glory..."

"No, let's not get into it. I don't know what's between you, what was or what is now, but I know what I *see*. And you don't hurt the way you and Dad have been hurting for eight years without a whole lot of love missing from your life. I just wanted to mention it because, well, because if he ever forgives you, forgives himself, then nothing would make me happier, you understand?"

I could feel my blood rushing hot and hard through my veins, frenzied by the hope her words had stirred in the bottom of my gut where I thought I'd lain those childish fantasies to rest. Even though I didn't respond, not with a word or a nod, Cleo seemed satisfied by my paralysis as if it was answer enough. She settled against the cushions again and sighed with a little smile as she closed her eyes.

Well, it was nice she could be so fucking Zen about the whole thing.

I guess she didn't understand that, to me, the idea that Axe-Man might actually forgive me was even more detrimental to my mental health than maintaining the status quo of his hatred. Because if I actually had a shot at meaning something to him, I didn't think I could survive ever losing it again. And given my history of unluckiness in love, I thought it might be easier not to try.

After the last episode finished, I helped a very sleepy Cleo to her room, staying long enough to stroke her hair back and watch as she immediately fell into a deep sleep. Later, I might wake up to the sound of horrific screaming and sobs, Cleo woken by the past staking her through nightmares. I'd lie awake and listen to Axe-Man's feet thump softly across the second-story hallway and down the stairs. Sometimes I went to the top of the case so I could listen to the low murmur of his voice as he soothed his daughter by choice back to sleep.

Tonight, I thought she might sleep through, though. She'd actually eaten most of the dinner Lin made and enough snacks to put a grown man into a deep coma. I'd noticed too she seemed to sleep better when Kodiak took her for their "nature adventures." She told me they didn't speak much on those outings, but she always returned with actual colour in her cheeks, and her manic movements were usually more subdued.

So I wasn't expecting any drama for the evening. Not with Cleo asleep and Axe-Man out at The Fallen owned strip club, The Wet Lotus. I was planning to try my hand at drawing a new storyboard for the next novel I was writing and turning in only when exhaustion forced me under.

But when I opened the door to the guest room, Axe-Man was sitting on the edge of the bed with my handpainted Chinese jewellery box open on the floor beside him, the contents spilled across the carpet, and one held in his four-fingered left hand.

I froze as the blood fell down the elevator shaft of my body to crash into the soles of my feet. Wooziness descended so quickly, I thought I'd faint.

Axe-Man had found the letters.

Not just letters, really, though I kept those unopened with the "return to sender" stamp across the front in the box, too, along with print-outs of the emails I'd sent and postcards I'd mailed. I carried the box with me where ever I moved as a reminder of all that I'd lost.

All the detritus of my bald longing on the floor at his feet.

"What are you doing?" I whispered before clearing my throat and trying again. "You're supposed to be at The Wet Lotus."

"What the fuck are these, Mei Zhen?" His voice was a low rumble like thunder on the horizon, promising the kind of storm you immediately took shelter from.

Only my shelter was his home, and he was currently sitting on my bed.

I bit my lip as I tried to think about a feasible lie, and then, failing that, I shrugged. "Isn't it obvious? I tried to write you."

"'I miss you," he started to read, voice tight, and my knees almost gave out so I braced myself against the wall. "'In Chinese or English, there are no words to properly express just how much missing you eats at me. It's like your absence is a rabid animal, taking huge chunks out of me whenever I'm vulnerable, nipping at my heels just when I think I might be getting too close to some kind of new okay.'"

He looked up, piercing me with that gorgeous blue-green

eyed stare. I opened my mouth, closed it, and tried again. "I wasn't trying to hide it that I missed you."

"From day one," he noted, shaking the letter in his hand as if it was a live thing he wanted to strangle. "Why the fuck didn't you send them?"

"I *did*," I gritted out between clenched teeth. "Notice the 'return to sender'?"

"You didn't send shit for a year and a half," he retorted. "Why didn't you send these right away? Why weren't you *there* visitin' me? You fuckin' disappeared on us!"

"It doesn't matter now," I murmured, so weary I felt ancient.

"Of course, it fuckin' matters now," he roared, standing up to toss the letter to the floor with the others. His fist thumped against his chest over his heart as he glowered at me. "You think that Kang's side was the only one you cut into that night at Turner Farm? I still fuckin' bleed from that wound. It never healed right, and the moment I saw you in the hospital again, it was like bein' cut open all over again. You got the means to heal that hurt, and you're tellin' me you won't?"

"Are you actually telling me that knowing why I abandoned you would clean all that bad blood away?" I asked with a skeptical scoff. "You're a stubborn old tiger, and you know how to hold a mean grudge."

"When it's deserved," he retorted, stalking forward slowly, his big body rolling and clenching sensuously beneath his thin tee and worn jeans like the gait of a jungle cat.

I sucked in a quick, quivering breath as he gripped my chin and curled his back to bring his gaze down to mine.

"You tellin' me, the fierce Mei Zhen is too cowardly to confess her sins?"

"Fuck you," I spat, backed into a corner and feral.

It was too much being confronted with this after I was already raw from my conversation with Cleo. His anger confused my body, made my nipples bead and thighs clench because it reminded me of the animal savagery he'd fucked me with in the motel. Suddenly, I was panting, and my hands were forming claws to rake over his pectorals, over the teeth marks I'd already left behind in his flesh. A warning and a dare.

Come at me, everything in me screamed, *you want my penance, then fucking take it from me.*

I shouldn't have been surprised when he read that in me because Axe-Man had always been good with languages and the vocabulary of Mei was no exception.

"Do I need to threaten to turn you over my knee again to get some honesty from you?" he practically purred, crowding me against the wall beside the door. Without breaking my gaze, he reached out with one hand and carefully closed it around my throat. "You want me to fuck the truth outta you, don't you?"

"I thought you weren't going to touch me again?" I taunted even though I knew I was playing with fire. As if that wasn't enough, I lunged up on my tiptoes to snap at his lower lip, biting it sharply enough to rend the thin skin. A little bead of blood welled like a garnet gemstone on his mouth, and without thinking, I lapped it up and hummed at the sweet metallic taste of him on my tongue. "I thought you couldn't stand the sight of me."

The truth was, I ached for the burn, for the danger of all that strength and ferocity under my hands and mouth again. Something about his viciousness was honest and made me feel cared for in a way that was elemental. He wanted me despite everything between us, and it made me feel *powerful.*

Axe-Man's eyes were black with lust as he ran his rough thumb up and down the column of my throat where my pulse thrummed. His body was a looming threat curved over mine, our noses almost touching, but I vibrated with something more than anger and fear.

"I can't. Even though you stabbed me through the fuckin' heart, it can't fuckin' forget how to care about you. Even with my blood on your teeth, I can't fight the mad urge to kiss you. Maybe especially with my blood on your teeth, your little claws in my chest. I've always had the bad habit of wantin' what wasn't good for me."

"I wouldn't hurt you. Not again," I amended breathlessly.

"You're still a fuckin' liar with a mouth full of sharp teeth and secrets. I hate you, Mei, but I got this madness in me that wants you anyway. This anger I got wants to take pieces outta you with my words and my teeth. Bruises you 'cause I want you to hurt and mark you 'cause some damn dumb part of me remembers what it was like when you were mine."

"I was never yours like this," I countered. "You didn't want me."

"You were too young," he countered, scraping his teeth across my throat over the grip of his hand there. He smelled like cedar and pine forest and clean, cool fog rolling over mossy ground. His long, silky hair tickled my collarbone. "But you're not a kid anymore, and I wanna fuck 'til you forget all the goddamn lies. I wanna punish your tight cunt with my cock and all this pretty skin with my teeth. I wanna destroy you like you destroyed me."

"So do it," I dared, baring my teeth at him, his blood still stuck in the grooves. "Show me how much you hate me. I can take it."

On a ragged groan, he closed his teeth over my neck just beneath my ear and sucked hard at my pulse point. "You can't fuckin' handle what I wanna do to you."

"Try me. It's been almost two weeks since I was hurt. I can take whatever you give me." I shoved my hands up between us and pushed him back with the leverage of the door at my back. He only moved back a few inches, but it was enough to dart out from the corner and into the middle of the room.

He looked fearsome as he turned to face me, his muscles coiled like heavy rope beneath his skin, his chest heaving with heavy breaths as he fought for control. My eyes skimmed his torso to the obvious bulge in his jeans, the way that thick cock lay hard down one thigh. As I watched, he squeezed his length in one big palm.

"You wanna fuck me?" he asked, his voice cold, so arctic it shot shivers across my skin. "You wanna prove you can handle me? Take off your clothes and do it nice and slow."

My hand trembled as I reached for the waistband of my black sweatpants, but not from nerves. I felt electrified with wanting, with the reality of the moment, standing there in front of the man I'd wanted for half my life, undressing for him.

It was sexy as hell, vulnerable yet empowering.

Axe-Man didn't even blink as I slowly pushed the waistband of my sweatpants over my hip bones and the swell of my ass until they fell in a puddle at my feet. I bent in half to push my feet out of the fabric, twisting slightly so he could see the round curve of my bottom in the tiny black thong I wore. His hiss of anguished hunger made my toes curl into the carpet.

When I stood again, I pulled the hem of my cropped black tank over my head and flung it at his face.

Axe-Man caught the cotton before it made contact, his gaze still unnervingly focused on my near nudity. His mouth was a pressed line in his thick beard, his cheeks ruddy and flushed.

My nipples beaded in the cool air, the only spot of colour among the dozen of black-inked tattoos on my torso. I could feel Axe-Man tracing the designs—*his* designs—with his gaze. Over the cobwebs and chain link looped beneath my breasts, the koi fish swimming around my naval, the huge Chinese tiger prowling down my left thigh, and a pair of female hands forming a heart shape on my side. There were countless tattoos all over my body, barely a few inches without ink, but this was the first time he'd been able to study them. I always tried to cover up around him so he wouldn't notice the way I'd stolen more than two years of his life, I'd also stolen his art.

He stalked forward with a low, ragged growl, his eyes on my body a physical touch, a warmth close to uncomfortable. When he was within reach, he clamped a hand over my hip and traced the Chinese characters he'd once drawn of my name now inked on the outside of my rib cage.

"You little thief," he snarled, tracing another design up to the lower curve of my small breast before he harshly pinched my nipple and toppled me to the bed. "You have me all fuckin' over you."

My body was still bouncing against the mattress when Axe-Man pinned me down with a hand to my upper chest, the other making deft work of his belt. I lay there gasping, not in fear but dizzying, brilliant anticipation.

My mouth went completely dry when he tugged his belt through the loops with a slick *slap* and folded it together in that one palm.

Before he could do anything else, though, I pressed back on my shoulders and wrapped my legs around his neck, twisting until he was forced to fall to the bed beside me. As soon as he landed, I was on him, my knees pinning his arms to the bed by the biceps, one hand on the centre of his chest and the other pressed to his throat. His pulse thrummed beneath my fingertips, his throat working on a hard swallow beneath my palm.

"I hope you didn't think I'd just roll over so you could spank me," I taunted in his ear. "You'll have to try harder if you want me to submit to that." I was dangerously high on our contact, like I was floating above reality, and the consequences of my daring couldn't touch me. So it wasn't surprising that I bent even closer and tugged his earlobe sharply with my teeth. "If you want me to submit to *you*."

Axe-Man grunted as he wrenched first one arm and then the other out from under my knees. Freed, he slapped his palm against my ass with a resounding *smack*. Heat exploded under his touch and sank roots deep into my groin, lighting me up from the inside out. A gasp fell from my lips, and without thinking, I rocked back, chasing his hand as it drew back.

He let out a cruel, rough chuckle that felt like a caress directly to my pussy and then *again*. A loud *crack* as his palm connected with my ass cheek, and the pain tunnelled through my entire body until I felt hollow, aching to be filled up.

A full-body shiver rolled through me as he palmed my stinging left cheek and squeezed it, massaging the hurt deeper into the flesh. I canted my hips back, searching for more contact, and then slid my groin south, searching for the iron ridge of his erection beneath the denim. Finding it, I ground down on his length, tossing my head back with a loud moan.

Axe-Man cursed under his breath as he used my lack of awareness to flip me to my back on the bed again. I didn't fight it. Instead, I lay there panting as he recovered his belt and used it to bind my hands together tightly. Done with that, he pinned my belted hands in one of his own and raised them above my head, pressing them into the pillow.

"Enough," he declared, leaning back so he sat heavily on my hips. His eyes burned with satisfaction as they took in the sight of me prone beneath him, bound and still. "Now if only you'd shut the fuck up."

"Make me," I bit out, but I was too breathless to taunt him.

In fact, I was panting so much, it drew Axe-Man's intense gaze. His eyes raked over my breasts, and then he traced the spider's web design with the short nail of his index finger until red scratch marks outlined the black ink. The effect was strangely erotic, and I could tell by the way his breathing deepened that he thought so too.

"Don't wanna hurt you," he admitted in a gruff voice. "You're still recoverin'—"

"Aw, afraid little ole me will make you lose control, Axe-Man? Because I can handle this. I *want* it," I dared. "If you can't handle a girl half your size—"

My words cut off with a truncated groan as he wrapped his hand finger by finger around my throat and squeezed slightly. Simultaneously, his other hand slipped behind him and between my legs, bullying them wider until he could cup my shamefully damp groin in his palm.

"Is this what you want?" he asked, his words hard but frayed at the edges with desire he couldn't mask. "You don't want my forgiveness, but you want my rage and my cock? What, Jiang's not doin' it for you?"

"You're such a fucking jerk," I spat, bucking to throw him off me. "I'm not sleeping with Jiang. I never have, and I never would. Not least of all because he's *gay*. You know that. Why, are you jealous?"

His laugh was a dark cough. He watched my face with stern intensity as he ground the heel of his hand into my clit.

"Why are you so hungry for a good, hard fuck then, huh?"

"I'm not," I ground out even as I squirmed into his touch, my back arching slightly off the bed.

The cruel little smile on his mouth shouldn't have sent a shivery pulse of desire through me, but I almost gasped at the sight. When he moved his hand from my throat to one of my nipples and twisted it *hard*, my eyes started to cross.

"Oh, I think you're eager as hell," he argued, whispering to me in that husky drawl I'd always loved. "You don't want to be spanked; you want to be fucked until you can't remember your own goddamn name. 'Til you forget every single inch of yourself and all the bad things you've done."

"Yes," I admitted on a sob as he began plucking at each nipple, back and forth, back and forth the way a musician picked music from guitar strings. "God, *yes*."

"You might be able to forget, but you should know, I never will."

"Please," I said, mindless now, only the tension in my chest and the mounting warmth between my thighs. I didn't know what I was pleading for exactly—a release, maybe. Not just physical but from my grief, from the mountain of self-hatred I'd buried myself beneath. "Please, Henning."

He looked wild over me, a predator watching his prey in its death throes, his eyes manic with primal delight. There was still a hardness in his expression, a cruelness in the twist of his lips over his teeth, a wolf ready to devour.

"This doesn't change a fuckin' thing," he swore, already bending, teeth bared, for my throat. "I still fuckin' hate you."

"I don't care," I said because at that moment, I would have said anything to get those teeth in me. Hate was better than apathy.

Axe-Man made a rough noise of approval in the back of his throat, latched his teeth onto the curve between my shoulder and neck, palmed my entire pussy in one hand, and then *ripped* off my thong with one fierce jerk. When my wet folds were bared to his touch, he palmed me again, not rubbing or fucking, not even moving. Just holding my pussy like he had a right to it.

It was bone-quakingly hot.

Meanwhile, he sucked hickeys on my shoulders and collarbones, a necklace of vampire kisses, a wreath of bruises that I'd watch turn from one jewel tone to another. Garnet, ruby, amethyst, hints of sapphire and tourmaline and citrine. Even as he bit into my flesh and pressed his mark into my skin, I started to mourn the loss of those notes. They were written in hate, but after years of my letters being returned to sender unopened, it felt good to get a response.

Even though I wasn't normally an obedient girl, I kept my hands pinned above my head.

By the time his ruthless mouth reached my nipples, I was panting like an animal, arching into him.

"Axe-Man, come on, yes, there, *please*," I babbled.

His hot breath ghosted over my left nipple but didn't connect.

"Fuck, do you need a road map?" I demanded.

"You want me to fuck you into the bed?" he snarled, his brows tangled, eyes flashing lightning bright.

My womb quivered, but I jutted my chin up. "Sometime in the next century, yes."

With a glower, he pulled off me completely, standing on his knees so I didn't even have the weight of him.

"Wait," I started to protest, but the rest of my sentence died as I watched him thumb open his jeans and tug the zipper down, revealing grey boxer briefs that were damp at his tip with spilled precum.

My mouth dried up in an instant.

I watched with my heart beating so hard in my throat I thought I'd choke as Axe-Man slid his hand into the waistband and pulled out a thick, veiny cock.

My mouth flooded in an instant.

The sight of that big cock, long but hefty like a fucking club and so veiny I could spend hours tracing them all with my tongue, did devastating things to my body. I thought, desperately, honestly, I might do anything to play with that dick.

But I didn't have to beg or plea.

Because Axe-Man chuckled low at the expression on my face, the way a villain might before revealing an evil plan, and he knee walked up my body until he settled on my chest.

And that cock was right in my face, inches from my open, drooling mouth.

The smell of him rocked me. Musk and salt and that dark, drugging scent of man.

"If you won't be quiet," he murmured, fisting the root of his erection and slowly thrusting forward to smear his precum over my parted lips. "I'll shut you up myself."

He punctuated the last word by sliding his cock smoothly

over my tongue straight into the back of my throat. I choked, but he only retreated slightly before pressing in again. The feel of his girth rubbing over the roof of my mouth and the back of my tongue was sexy as hell. I loved the struggle to take him in my throat, canting my head slightly so he could wedge himself deeper. I held my breath as he pressed closer and closer until the rough texture of his pubic hair scratched my chin.

He'd braced a fist on the wall and the other on the pillow beside my head, his hair a tangle of gold around his face as he stared at my lips split wide around his flesh.

For a single moment, we locked eyes, and I felt a frisson of connection, something deeper than sex.

Axe-Man thrust even deeper until I gagged, and I watched vicious desire contort his features before he pulled out.

Again and again, he fucked my face. It should have felt demeaning maybe, but the sight of him using me, driving in and out of my throat, over my highly sensitized tongue was so hot, I'd leaked down my thighs onto the bedspread below.

A stiff breeze could have pushed me over the edge, and when Axe-Man lightly wrapped his hand around my neck, feeling his cock move in and out of that tight enclosure, I closed my eyes and moaned so long I could barely breathe.

Light-headed, overwhelmed by desire and the reality of Axe-Man touching me like this, I rubbed my thighs together wantonly.

"No, no," he grunted when he noticed my attempts to get off. "You wanna come, you do it on my cock."

When he pulled out of my mouth, a thick web of saliva linked my lips to his cock. I licked at it, my mouth wet and open and used. With a groan, Axe-Man thrust two fingers over my tongue, hard back and forth. He tasted like salt and vaguely of me from palming my wet pussy earlier.

"You drenched for me?" he demanded, already using his other hand to reach back and check for himself. He bared his teeth in a grimace as his fingers encountered my sopping wet pussy. "Fuck, you liked that."

He sounded slightly surprised. If he'd been intending to punish me with that brutal throat fucking, he was with the wrong woman.

"Yeah," I agreed because I was out of sass at the moment.

My voice was wrecked from his dick, but if the precum beading on Axe-Man's blunt weapon of a cock was any indication, he liked hearing it. He stared at me for a long second lying there, mouth wet and ruined, nipples damp and pebbled, neck wreathed in bruises from his teeth. It was like watching a play the way emotions moved quicksilver over his face: lust, violence, anger, desperation, sadness, anger again, and finally resolve.

His jaw clenched hard, he moved to my side fluidly and then stood at the end of the bed. I watched riveted as he tongued the side of his mouth while he stared at my pussy for a long, almost enraptured moment.

Then, he shook himself like a horse ridding itself of a pesky fly and retrieved a condom from his pocket. When I made a little, unbidden noise of protest, he grinned at me meanly.

"You want my bare cock, my cum inside you, you gotta earn it, Mei. You won't tell me shit, you don't get me fuckin' you raw. You don't deserve my cum." He rolled the condom onto his fat dick as he spoke, and I tried not to drool.

I gasped, though, when he tugged me by the ankles to the end of the bed before flipping me over easily and yanking up my hips. He groaned as he ran a thumb down my wet slit and then slapped my bare ass before he grabbed me by the hip. Only then did he lean over my back, grab my ponytail, and wind the hair around his fist. My head canted back to ease the sting in my scalp, my throat bared to him, my pussy convulsing at his delicious cruelty.

"Ask nicely, and I'll fuck you 'til you forget everythin' but the sound of my name in this sweet mouth," he whispered against my neck before fixing his teeth there.

He held me down as I shuddered violently and then notched the hot head of his sheathed cock at my entrance, pulsing slightly so he almost entered me but didn't.

"Fuck," I cursed through my teeth, trembling with the need to be filled. "Fuck you."

He tugged a little at my ponytail, making me hiss and then shiver with pleasure. "Oh, I plan to fuck you into the mattress, but only after you *beg* me for it. Tell me, Mei. Wanna hear you say you want my cock."

"Oh God," I gasped, my neck suddenly unable to hold my head up. "Oh God. *Yes*. Fuck. Axe-Man, please fuck me. I need you to stretch me open on your cock."

"Jesus," he hissed.

And then he slid inside me in one heavy thrust. It took him a second to open me up enough to take all of him, but I panted and ground my hips back into him until I could feel his balls pressed against me.

"Yes," I murmured, dizzy with pleasure and the knowledge that this was Axe-Man inside me. The fantasy was nothing compared to the reality, even when he was hate-fucking me. "Don't hold back. I like it rough."

"Fuuuck," he groaned, tugging on my ponytail again as he brought his body over mine and whispered into my ear, "A rebel on the street and a good girl in the sheets. Who would've thought."

"Are you complaining?"

"Not at all." He nipped my ear and then leaned back on his heels to drag his heavy cock nearly all the way out of me, staring at our connection. "But remember, you asked for this."

I opened my mouth to say something sassy, but he impaled me again, forcing the air from my body on a long, wailing moan. With someone else, I might've been embarrassed by the noises he pulled from me as he worked me back and forth on his cock, but Axe-Man was a vocal lover, praising me for taking him so good and for having such a pretty, greedy pussy. He grunted and growled, slapping my ass to watch it jiggle and eventually reaching beneath me to pinch cruelly at my throbbing clit.

I came the first time so quickly, it almost scared me. I gasped and shuddered like our connection was electrocuting me. Axe-Man fucked me through it, unrelenting, almost pitilessly driving me higher and higher until I thought I understood why the French called orgasms the "little death."

The second time, he coaxed it out of me, urging my limp body up so I sat impaled on his dick. He gripped my hips and shuttled me up and down on his length, his teeth fixed to my neck when he wasn't grunting encouragement into my ear.

"I'm going to come," I nearly sobbed, dropping my head back to his shoulder, reaching back to grip his hair in my hand so tightly he grunted. "God, no, I-I don't think I can do this."

His chuckle was mean and sexy, a side of him I'd never known that I knew now I'd be addicted to forever. "Take what I give you. You asked for this."

Fuck, but I did, and the strain of taking him in my swollen pussy was the same unbearable pleasure-pain of loving him and longing for him. Unbidden, tears burned at the backs of my eyes. I didn't want this to end because I didn't know if I'd ever have him like this again.

"Tell me you want me," I whispered as my cunt clenched down on him, and I quivered on the edge of release. "Please."

He didn't ask why I needed to hear it. Instead, he moved one hand up to cup my throat and turn my head so he could speak against my parted, panting mouth. "Goddamn you, but yeah, I want you. Never want to stop fuckin' this pretty, perfect cunt. You're so fuckin' dangerous 'cause you make me so fuckin' weak, Rocky."

It was that.

The sound of my old name in his mouth.

I broke open on a scream he quickly muffled with his hand. He fucked me as I writhed in his arms, caught up like Thetis shape-changing to escape in Peleus's stronghold. Only, Axe-Man wouldn't let me go, wouldn't let me pretend I was anyone else but Mei Zhen Marchand. The girl who'd loved him too young and abandoned him when it mattered. The girl who'd come back but wasn't forgiven. The girl he wanted, but wouldn't let himself like.

But none of that mattered when he called me Rocky as I came and then again, a moment later, when I milked his cock with my climax and felt the kick of his orgasm inside me, and he moaned his name for me again in my ear.

Because in the end, if he was fucking Rocky, it meant there was hope he could love me again even after everything I'd done.

And that rocked me just as much as the orgasm that swept through me and turned my mind to static.

CHAPTER THIRTY-FOUR

Mei

"What happened that night?"

It was dark now. Axe-Man had turned the lights off with a thump of his fist when he returned from the bathroom with a wet cloth to clean between my legs. I wasn't sure if he'd wanted the pitch dark to hide the care he took with me, the fact that he returned at all let alone to tend to me, or if it was because he sensed I needed the shield of darkness after what we'd just shared.

I thought for sure he'd leave after cleaning me, but he'd only tossed the cloth to the floor, jerked off his unzipped jeans, and lay down on the bed beside me. We weren't touching, but I could feel the vibration between the long line of his body and my own, like our attraction had its own frequency. He didn't speak for such a long time, I'd wondered if he'd fallen asleep, but I didn't want to do anything to disturb this odd peace between us.

Instead, I relished the slight aches and twinges in my body from the rough fucking. Nothing really hurt, which was a happy indicator I was ready to go back to the gym for training, but the throb in my nipples and pussy was pleasant enough to lull me into a kind of meditative state. Nothing existed for me in that dark room but Axe-Man, me, and the knowledge that we'd fucked, and this time, it had been about more than just anger and hate no matter what he'd said before.

I didn't know what it meant, and later, I'd probably agonize over it, but for once in my life, I had what I wanted, and I was going to savour it for a moment.

So I wasn't prepared for Axe-Man's question like a monster looming in the dark.

For a second, I thought I'd imagined him saying those words because I'd both feared and yearned for him to ask so many times over the last few weeks.

What happened that night?

Such an easy, obvious question with such a complicated, horrible response.

I bit my lip so hard the skin broke, and blood blossomed in my mouth.

"Rocky," he said softly into the dark.

It made it better I couldn't see him. Only the hot, hard line of his body against mine, like a mountain pressed to the horizon. Even though my heart had started racing the moment I realized he'd actually spoken, it calmed me to feel him there. He'd always been a special kind of gravity to me, something to keep me grounded, something I felt on every inch of me, in every molecule in a way that was both natural and profound.

"I need to know," he continued.

I was grateful there was no antagonism in his voice, just a weary kind of supplication. He had so many demons, many of which I'd given him myself, and he deserved to have some––this one––laid to rest.

I cleared my throat, my open eyes fixed on the inky blackness in front of me, my hands opening and closing on the sheets.

"Cedar took me home."

The house had been dark, but that wasn't surprising. My parents had never been home, and since Daiyu moved into hospice, no one spent much time at the house. We were always with her, waiting, waiting, waiting without even hope to keep us buoyant. The house felt like a dug-out grave waiting for a body, and I shivered when I unlocked the door and pushed inside.

"There was blood all over me, but I guess I'd forgotten because when the lights suddenly turned on, my first thought was why would anyone be home? Not, holy shit, I should hide before someone sees me looking like something from *The Walking Dead*."

"It was Florent," Axe-Man said, not a question.

"It was Florent."

I could still remember the look on his face, brows knitted fiercely over dark eyes, skin flushed with fury, lips a pale line. He'd never seemed so...big before. Not because he was an especially tall man, nothing compared to Axe-Man, but because his rage inflated him, made him grotesque.

"I won't ask where you were," he said in this low, vibrating bass, his Quebecois accent more distinct than ever. "I don't have to. I know you were with Henning Axelsen. Whatever trouble you're clearly in was his doing."

"No," the word hurt my throat as I coughed it up. "No! Henning saved me tonight. H-he..." I choked on a sob and then sucked in a sharp breath through my teeth. "No. I wouldn't be here right now if it wasn't for him. And because of me...I think Henning might go to jail."

"Oh." Silky tone rich with satisfaction. "I'll make sure of it, Mei. You will never see that man again. Are we clear?"

I didn't hear his words because it occurred to me that Florent was home when he should have been with Daiyu.

"Why aren't you at the hospital?" I demanded.

And then Old Dragon appeared in the mouth of the dark hallway looking so old, older than I'd ever seen him before. Pale and drawn like a ghost floating in the shadows.

And I knew.

"No," I whispered, and whatever was left of my heart, of my sanity broke with a great, echoing crack, and I dropped hard to my knees on the marble, not even feeling the pain. "NO!" I screamed. "No, please, no, no, no."

I couldn't seem to stop, not even when Old Dragon collected me carefully in his arms, pulling me slightly into his lap over his crossed legs. He tried to hush me and soothe me even as I was distantly aware of his own tears splashing to my fevered skin.

I paused in my storytelling because Axe-Man was touching me suddenly. Without realizing it, I'd sat up in bed, curling around my bent knees with my arms locked around them. His hand, the hefty weight of it, slid under my hair to wrap around the back of my neck and hold firm. It was oddly comforting, and after swallowing hard a few times, I tried to continue my story.

"I don't know how you felt the moment you knew Kate was dead, but for me, at that moment, after losing you in a way just an hour before, I couldn't express my grief even in my own head. There were no words or even thoughts, just pain. Throbbing between my temples. In the balls of my feet, in the space between each rib. I just felt stripped of my skin and set on fire, every inch of me in excruciating pain." I sucked in a shuddery breath and slowly let it out. "I'm not telling you this to, I don't know, make you pity me or anything."

"I don't pity you," he assured me in that low voice, but his hand flexed on my neck in a way that translated to comfort.

"I don't know how long he let me cry for, but I don't think it was long. Or, maybe, he was laying into me the whole time and

I just didn't recognize it. But finally, Florent lost his cool completely."

"You will listen to me," Florent hissed, suddenly in front of me, his fingers sliding off my wet, snotty chin as he tried to grasp it. "That man made you miss the last moments with your mother. Do you recognize that? Can your pea-sized intellect realize that he's a monster, and I've been remiss in letting you fixate on him. On that criminal, pathetic *family?"*

My only response was a shivery wail that echoed in our large foyer. Old Dragon clasped me closer to his chest and said something about not now.

But Florent didn't listen.

He gripped my chin harder and forced me to look up into his ravaged face, and he promised me low, cold, "Hear me on this, Mei Zhen Marchand. You will never see the Axelsens again."

The word finally penetrated, a fresh wound, a mortal wound breaking through the haze of pain.

"What?" I whispered.

"I think," I told Axe-Man in the dark, curling even tighter so my knees cracked and my shoulders pulled in their sockets. "I mean, it sounds dramatic, but I really wasn't human in those moments. It's like the horror of everything just overloaded my circuit and everything after was just...instinct. Like an animal."

"An animal cornered and afraid," he muttered darkly.

I coughed, but it was supposed to be a chuckle of agreement.

"I don't remember exactly how it happened, but suddenly, I was lunging at him. At Florent. At my dad, only he wasn't my dad by then. He wasn't even someone I knew. I don't even think I saw him as a person. He was worse than a monster or the devil whatever personification of hate and fear people give to things. He was the axe cleaving me in two, and I thought if I could just get my hands on him, the pain would stop."

"You attacked him?" he sounded surprised, which kind of

amazed me. If anyone knew how intense I could be, how foolish and violent and *dumb*, it was Axe-Man..

"Yeah. I tried to scratch his eyes out. It didn't work, but I think he probably still has scars on his cheeks. I've always had strong nails, and I dug deep. Days later, I still had his flesh under my nails."

I thought he'd condemn me, then. Call me crazy or something because, yeah, that would have been fair.

But instead, he shifted until he sat behind me, his bent legs splayed open but bracketing my hips. He wasn't touching me, and I don't think he could bring himself to give me that much comfort, but the heat and strength of his body at my back, a parenthesis around my waist, was more than enough.

Over the past eight years, I'd developed a habit of not breathing. Just holding my breath without conscious thought until suddenly I was gasping for air.

I wasn't doing that as much now, living in Entrance.

And here in the dark womb of a room with Axe-Man, all I could sense, I felt like I could breathe freely for the first time in almost a decade.

"What did he do?" he finally asked.

When I didn't answer immediately, he moved his legs a little closer, the crisp hair on his thick thighs and strong calves tickling my skin.

I sighed and released the rest of the poison.

"The neighbours, Dean and Tiffany Straith, heard the commotion and came over to make sure everything was okay. When I came to, Florent and Dean had me pinned on the floor, but I was still thrashing and shouting and sobbing. I remember my throat was in agony from the screaming, and I couldn't seem to get enough air. The cops came, and paramedics sedated me."

I trembled all over, unable to stop even when I dug my fingernails into my calves, trying to anchor myself with the pain. Only when Axe-Man leaned forward to press his chest against me like a warm, heavy blanket could I find the strength to carry on.

"When I woke up, Old Dragon wasn't there a-and obviously, Daiyu––Mum––wasn't there. It was just this horrible white and blue room with beeping machines and Florent standing beside my bed like he'd never sat down. The scratch marks on his cheek looked *black,* and the sight of them brought everything back. I started to cry. When I lifted my hand to wipe away a tear, I realized…" I sucked in such a large breath it ached in my lungs, burning. "I was handcuffed to the bed. Florent told me he was pressing charges against me for assault. T-that he was having me committed to a correctional facility."

"It's over."

Dad's voice echoed in my mind, trapped like a ball in a pinball machine, pinging off the walls of my skull.

It's over.

Meaning my life as I knew it.

He had me committed.

In Canada, the only way to commit someone involuntarily was by authority of a doctor. Unfortunately, Florent Marchand donated to Rockyview Hospital every year and had been doing so for a decade.

So three days after Henning Axelsen was hauled away for murder and intent to distribute, I was getting out of the car at Ryerson Adolescent Correctional Facility.

In the dark of Axe-Man's beautiful, homey lake cabin, tears rolled down my cheeks and dripped down my knees.

But my voice was clear when I continued, "I had my eighteenth birthday there. I wasn't allowed contact with anyone outside, and no one could visit unless they were on the approved list. Obviously, Florent didn't allow any, so I was alone."

My shudder was so violent it threw Axe-Man off my back.

He pressed closer, wrapped those quilted arms around me, one across my belly and the other diagonally over my chest like a seat belt. It was a secure hold. I felt pinned to him, but not in a threatening way. More pinned like a barnacle to a rock, seeking stability and safe harbour from the crashing waves.

I took a moment to focus on the feel of him breathing and matched my tempo to his. Slowly, my muscles relaxed until I sagged against him.

"How long?" he finally rasped, but I couldn't read anything in his tone.

"I got out that fall. Jiang found me and paid the doctors off to release me without Florent's permission under the condition we would work together moving forward. Old Dragon contacted him through some old friends and arranged the whole thing, because he didn't have enough pull on his own to get me out. I enrolled at the University of British Columbia that January. Daiyu left me money, or else I wouldn't have managed. Old Dragon was the one who picked me up, and we drove west together. I never spoke to Florent again."

"I'm shocked he allowed that."

"Yeah, well..." I tried to shrug, but he held me too tightly. "I registered under Mei Zhen Lung, and it took him a while to find me. I don't know if you remember, but I wanted to go to U of T, so when he wanted to find me, he started on the East Coast. He showed up once." A grey day because there were lots of grey days in the Pacific Northwest. He'd forgotten an umbrella, and rain dripped from his nose and lashes. I'd had the startling thought that we actually did look alike in the shape of the mouth and the square jaw. "He was contrite, a bit. Not enough. But he tried to make it seem like I owed it to him to accept his logic. He tried to make it seem like I graduated at the top of my class because he'd separated me from my vices."

"From me."

"Yes."

He made a noise like a grunt, and his usual lack of eloquence made me smile despite the hard conversation. That was his magic, after all, making everything better.

"It wasn't the reason," I added, just in case he might've agreed with Florent's fucked-up rationale even though he hated him. He was like that, Axe-Man. Always willing to self-flagellate. "I'm smart, so there's that. But also, I didn't have any friends so nothing distracted me from schoolwork."

"Why didn't you try to make friends...date, try on the normal young adult schtick for a while."

The words stuck in my throat, but I forced them onto my tongue because Axe-Man deserved the truth, and it felt better than I'd thought it would to purge all the dust and gunk of my history. "Honestly, I didn't even think about it. What happened to you, how I left you like that in the field, how I missed Mum's passing, how Florent...betrayed me. It was all just too much. I didn't trust myself, and I didn't trust anyone else. And..." I sucked in a deep breath for courage. "Even after years passed, you and Cleo were still so elemental to me that it felt impossible that anyone could know me without knowing you. My love for you has always been the cipher needed to decode me."

"You were never really in love with me, Mei," he said, scrubbing a hand over his face. "You'd just had so little real affection 'til you met Kate, Cleo, and me that you thought we were better than we really were. Really are," he corrected.

"I lived eight years without that affection and I still think you're the best." Admitting that was so vulnerable, like laying down willingly on an autopsy slab and cutting open my own chest. *Here*, I wanted to say, *look at the way my loneliness has corroded my internal organs.*

His heavy sigh stirred the hair over my shoulder, tickling my ear. I wasn't sure what he would do with my confession, but the fact that he hadn't recoiled with me seemed positive.

After a long moment, he asked, almost reluctantly, "What did you study?"

I smiled into the dark. "Not medicine."

I waited for him to ask for more. What was my major? What kind of career had I made for myself? But it seemed Axe-Man had reached the end of his patience with himself and was finding a way to tap back into his resentment of me.

When he spoke next, his voice was deeper, clipped. "Well, it's no wonder you made the mistakes you did with Florent for a fuckin' father."

I flinched, but he caught me in it, stilling me with his rough hands cupping my shoulders. It was like he wanted me to absorb the full blow of his words. The absolute insult of being anything like my father.

I shivered, but stilled. How funny that I'd always considered myself a rebel, yet I obeyed Axe-Man without thought, even to my own detriment. It went beyond atonement for my sins to something deeper that lived in my blood and bones, in the hardwiring of my circuitry. I'd rarely obeyed anyone my whole life, even when it was prudent, but I *liked* listening to Axe-Man. And I realized it was because he was one of the only people in my life not to give me a reason to distrust him. Even in his hatred, I knew he would never hurt me.

"Did you really think I'd just...disappear on you?" I found the courage to ask because even though his dark mood spilled through the room, he was still sitting there behind me, holding me in an approximation of a hug from behind.

Another bear-like huff. He rolled the tension from his shoulders, letting his hot palms slide down my arms to rest on my thighs. Each palm was nearly the width of the meatiest part of my leg, and I worked out. It always made my mouth dry to see the size difference between us. To know, now tangibly, how easy it would be for him to bend and shape me into position for his pleasure. It didn't help that I was naked, and he still wore his tee and boxer briefs.

"Not at first," he admitted. "But one month into two, then three, then six and a year had passed. On the outside, maybe it wouldn't've been so bad. Maybe if I'd been at home with Cleo on Cleary Street when you'd vanished, I would've understood... Nah." He shook his head hard, hair flying, then laying with mine against my shoulders. I wished it was light enough to see the gold and black shine together. "I would've gone lookin' for you. Fuckin' what-ifs've always driven me mad. Doesn't matter now. Back then, imprisoned and betrayed by my brothers in the club, I was fertile ground for believin' the worst in people."

My head dipped between my shoulders as I imagined him in that place. He would've been too big for the regulation bed, feet hanging off the end, and he already had trouble sleeping under the best of circumstances. Separated from Lin and Cleo, his women who were his life's purpose. Suffering the consequences of betrayal from The Fallen, but also, however unintentionally, from me.

He would've waited for me every visiting hour. Looked for me in every letter received. Been alarmed and worried at first, then increasingly hurt until it tipped the scale into the kind of hatred I could still feel even now beating at my back.

"I'm so sorry, Henning," I whispered into the bracket between my kneecaps, like hands cupped around a mouth whispering a secret. "I don't think you'll ever be able to know how sorry I am. How much the things I've done have haunted me and haunt me still."

"I know a lot about hauntin'," he muttered, moving away to lean back against the headboard. For a second, I was aggrieved, thinking he was pulling away from me, back behind his iron shield. But then he reached for me, by the hips, fingertips in my belly to pull me back against him. My relief was so acute that for one embarrassing moment, I thought I might actually *cry*.

His rings caught the moonlight and glimmered like the flashing silver bellies of fish in a dark stream as he curled them over my thighs again. "He came to visit me."

"Florent?!"

"Mm. I realize now, he came to gloat. Reminded me that he'd warned me what would happen if I got you into trouble again after Kate died. That he wouldn't be so forgivin'. He was the reason I didn't get bail. Guess the CEO of Barrington Grouse Oil's got some contacts in high places."

"Fuck," I hissed, curling my nails into my palms until they broke the skin. "What a fucking *asshole*. God, I wish I had properly gouged his eyes out."

Axe-Man's bark of laughter surprised me so much I jumped a little. He just curled me closer, burying his face in my hair to laugh against my neck.

It felt even better than the orgasms he'd given me.

"Fuck, I forget how fuckin' bloodthirsty you can be," he said, his voice still warm with humour. "You're a dragon, all right. Teeth and fuckin' claws."

"I'm no dragon," I whispered because it felt wrong to make light of something I'd wanted, a symbol I'd revered for my entire life.

It was the only design Axe-Man drew in my sketchbook that I didn't have on my body because I didn't think I'd earned it yet.

"Well, you sure as fuck got your teeth and claws in me," he muttered, and I knew he was referring to the bite mark on his chest and the scratch marks I'd cut into his shoulders.

"Sorry," I said, but I didn't sound it.

To my intense delight, he chuckled again. "Left my fair share of marks on you tonight, so I can't complain."

"Is this where you tell me this won't ever happen again?" I ventured, thinking it would be easier to just rip it off like a Band-Aid and get the hurt over with now.

Axe-Man was quiet for a long moment, his finger tracing

the vaguely visible outline of the tiger tattoo on my thigh. I wondered if he knew I got it for him and figured he did. I'd never been good at hiding from him, and my tattoos were the most honest thing about me.

"You got your claws in me," he repeated, so low I had to strain to hear him even though I was pressed to his front.

I opened my mouth to ask for clarification, but suddenly, he was moving, shifting out from behind me with more grace than just a big man should be able to muster. I sat there mutely, watching as he stepped into his jeans and made for the door.

My heart dropped into my stomach and fizzed like a Mentos in a shaken soda bottle. I thought I'd vomit, but I gripped the sheets tight enough to ground myself.

Just when I thought he'd leave me naked and yearning again, without a word of comfort, he turned to face me, a wedge of light spilling through the cracked open door to illuminate his handsome face and turn his eyes to blue glass.

"No feelin' is immutable, Mei," Axe-Man said, and I could feel the intensity of his stare on the side of my face. "No feelin' lasts forever. Not even love, sometimes. Not even hate."

CHAPTER THIRTY-FIVE

Mei

I WONDERED IF I'D ALWAYS BEEN A MASOCHIST OR IF SOME strange alchemy had occurred in the empty recesses in my chest where a heart used to pound after losing Kate and Ma that made me yearn for any kind of feeling.

Even if it was pain.

Because sitting at the receptionist desk of Street Ink Tattoo was the worst kind of torture imaginable. Nova was too soft a touch to treat me poorly, but the rest of them were loyal to Axe-Man and they spoke to me only with work orders or barely concealed suspiciousness.

They hated me for him.

Ironically, I loved that he had that. A community of people to take his back without question.

Once, I'd had that too. In him and in Cleo.

Now, I had Jiang and Old Dragon. Only, Old Dragon was lost in the mire of his dissolving memories. Most of the time, he couldn't remember my name. My friendship with Jiang was complicated by our semi-opposing mission statements, but I thought we had a tacit kind of understanding that transcended our deal. Though, I hadn't heard from him since Seven Song threw me in the dumpster behind Purgatory Motel. It was understandable he was keeping a low profile, for his sake and mine, but a part of me was a little hurt he didn't reach out to check on me.

At least I had Cleo again, though I had years of absence to make up for.

I watched from behind an open ink catalogue as Axe-Man prepared his station for his next client. He was fastidious, but then again, he always had been. It was in his nature but had also been finely honed by years in the military and medical school. He did nothing by half.

My mind took us back to the Sunday brunches he'd made for Cleo and I after Kate died. It was a new ritual, one that was meant to take our minds off the tragedy for a few hours. For a man who didn't know how to cook up until that point, he'd learned quickly and thoroughly. Pancake boards piled high with steaming hotcakes and littered with fun, delicious items to decorate them with. Fruit platters cut into shapes until the whole board seemed like a painting with dinosaurs and fairy tales brought to life in watermelon wedges and blueberries. When Cleo and I bought him an apron for his birthday one year that read "Flippin' Fantastic", he'd worn it every Sunday brunch after that even though the huge, burly blond looked faintly ridiculous in it.

"You gotta stop it," Nova murmured from my left, leaning against the reception desk the way he did sometimes to shoot the shit with me. "It's not good for anyone."

I shrugged, but the movement was too sharp. It gave away my guilt and shame like a fucking beacon. "You're right, I really don't know anything about ordering ink."

Nova gave me a slow, curling half smile. On anyone else, I would have begrudged him the pitying expression, but he was just so dang pretty it was hard to be irritated with him for anything.

Besides, he was kinda, sorta my only ally at Street Ink Tatttoo Parlour.

"That I can teach ya," he said pointedly, his thick lashed gaze sliding over my shoulder to Axe-Man. "I've known that man for near on a decade, Blossom, and he is one'a the biggest mysteries in this town. That said, he's also one'a the kindest motherfuckers I've met. Haven't *ever* seen him look at a person the way he looks at you, and it's not rainbows and violin quartets, you get me?"

I got him.

Oh, he didn't have any idea how much I. Got. Him.

Henning had never been an angry guy. Even after Kate was ripped away from him, he'd kept his head high, his heart warm and open.

He wasn't like me, prone to bitterness and rage.

He was good.

So fucking good.

My off-white knight.

And I'd done the worst thing you ever could to a man like that.

I'd broken his heart and his trust.

We might have reached a kind of truce, but it was obvious by the way he continued to glare at me from across the shop that he was still struggling with my reappearance in his life.

"Yeah, I get you."

"I don't think you do. Otherwise, you wouldn't have a hickey right there on your neck," he quipped with a roguish grin.

I tried not to immediately cover up my neck with the curtain of my hair. Instead, I levelled him with my coolest look.

"I know I've only been filling in for three days, but I've decided you're my least favourite Fallen brother."

Nova laughed loudly, drawing Axe-Man's attention to us. I could feel his scowly gaze on the side of my face, but I refused to look over at him guiltily. I was allowed to laugh. It was a free fucking country. And I was trying to take Cleo's advice to heart. See if I could have some kind of...community here after all.

"I'm gatherin' you're a lotta complicated things, girl. But don't make one'a them a liar," Nova teased.

"Shouldn't you be working, not gossiping with the staff?" I quipped.

"Nah, them's the perks of bein' the boss." He leaned farther over the counter to peek at the sketchbook I had open on the counter. "What's that you got there?"

"I'm an artist myself," I admitted, curling the pencil over the curve of Knight's wind-swept hair. The image depicted him on the back of a huge white motorcycle on a deserted road, travelling to his next destination.

"No shit. No one told me that." He moved around the desk to look properly at the sketch over my shoulder. "Comic books?"

"Graphic novels."

His brown eyes narrowed as he took the sketchbook from me without permission and started flipping through my rough story boarding for the next Off-White Knight story.

"Hey, Axe-Man, you know Blossom here is an artist?" he shouted.

I dropped my head to the desk on a groan. "Jesus, Nova, discreet much?"

I heard the telltale thud of Axe-Man's boots moving over to the counter.

"Don't call her Blossom," he ordered Nova for the tenth time, after Nova'd decided on the nickname for the tiny pink cherry blossoms I had down both arms in memory of my ma.

Her favourite movie, *In The Mood For Love*, had originally been called "the age of blossoms" as a tribute to the fleetingness of youth and time. It seemed a fitting tribute for Daiyu, who was taken too early.

"And no," Axe-Man said quietly. "I didn't have a fuckin' clue."

I straightened at the hint of hurt in his tone, needing to validate it with my vision. He was holding the sketchbook now, frowning down at a sketch of Knight fighting off a ninja in an alleyway.

When he looked up at me, a question was burned into his expression.

I sighed. "I'm a graphic novelist."

"Oh good," Cressida Garro said as she pushed into the shop with her incredibly handsome husband, King, and their baby, Prince, on her hip. "The cat's out of the bag! I was hoping to ask you to agree to a little signing at Paradise Found. What do you think? We have the full Off-White Knight series. People come in all the time asking when book seven will come out."

"Well, if these idiots left me alone between clients, I might have an answer for you." I was used to acting tough, but inside my chest, my heart ran a race for its life. "How long have you known?"

She winked at me. "I've been reading the series since book one. The pieces clicked together when I heard Cleo call you Rocky. I always thought Knight looked like Axe-Man."

"Is that why you were nice to me at Lin's shop? Because you wanted me to sign at your store?" I couldn't help but be suspicious.

She laughed. "I was nice to you because life is messy, and I have no clue what happened with you guys back in the day, but *no one* writes a series about someone without loving them through to their core. So I figured, if you were in town, you were here for good reasons. Was I wrong?"

"No," I admitted, before sneaking a peek at Axe-Man who was tracing an image of Knight shouting at his frenemy Rocky, who was constantly pulling him into dangerous situations.

"It's us," he murmured before looking over to me for confirmation.

I bit my lip.

"Everyone wants Knight and Rocky to end up together," Cressida added helpfully, handing the baby off to King so she could fish through her leather messenger bag and hand over a copy of The Off-White Knight: Nightmare Circus. "There's even fanfic about them."

King grinned at Axe-Man, enjoying this entirely too much. "Cress told me their couple name is "Rocight", like *rocket*. Cute right, Axe-Man?"

"You're basically famous, brother." Nova laughed, slapping a hand on Axe-Man's back.

"No, no. People don't know, I mean, I've never said Knight is inspired by someone in real life," I assured him quickly. "And I write under MZ Lung, so it's not obvious or anything."

Axe-Man swept his gaze over my exposed arms and neck. I was helping out at a tattoo shop, and he'd officially already seen the extent of his designs on my skin last night, so I'd ditched my jacket and worn one of my signature black cropped tanks. A living bulletin for Axe-Man's work.

He was probably wondering what I'd steal from him next.

Two years of his life.

His art inked on my skin.

Now, his face popularized in my seriously well-known graphic novel series.

Cressida seemed to sense the energy crackling between us and hustled to push her husband over to Nova's station, talking loudly about the ink he was getting in honour of their son. Nova followed and the rest of the shop, curiously silent, resumed its hum of chatter.

"Little thief," Axe-Man accused finally, but he didn't sound angry exactly.

More like resigned, only I didn't know to what.

I shrugged one shoulder, itching to take my sketchbook back from him. "I became kind of obsessed with *wuxia*--martial artists heroes--after watching *In The Mood For Love* with Daiyu so many times. Jiang noticed my drawings one day. He helped me pitch a literary agent friend of his, and the rest was history. I never thought I'd be a writer or an artist, but it's kind of a dream."

"I can see it," he murmured, rubbing a thumb over the Knight's four-fingered hand curled into a fist to punch his adversary. "It suits you. Always had a vivid imagination."

"If it makes you feel any better, Old Dragon is a character as well. And the first book starts with the Off-White Knight going on a crusade to save his daughter, Gloria."

His lips twitched in his beard. "Not very original."

"Sometimes life is stranger than fiction," I retorted. "You're not mad?"

He sighed so hard it ruffled the pages. "Fuck, don't think I gotta lotta anger left in me. It's fuckin' exhaustin' tryin' to stay mad at you."

"Even when I steal from you?"

When he locked eyes with me, he was wearing that special smile he used to have just for me. A curling of his ruddy mouth, a softening around his eyes. Like something about me warmed him from the inside out.

I hadn't seen that expression in such a long time, it momentarily took my breath away.

"Especially then."

My brows shot into my hairline. "Seriously?"

"Fuck yeah." His voice went gruff as he stepped closer, placing the sketchbook on the counter and one hand on the side of my neck over the little axe tattooed there. It matched the bigger one he had inked on the back of his right shoulder. "How can I stay mad when it's obvious you kept Cleo and me with you in every way you could over the last eight years?"

I couldn't breathe properly with his hand on me, his thumb tracing his design, his eyes another caress along my exposed chest mapping the stylized Band-Aid over an anatomical heart on the upper swell of my left breast and the lunar cycle along the ridge of one collarbone.

"You got every one of my designs from your sketchbook on this pretty skin?" he asked, husky and low.

I shook my head, trying to find my voice, trying to understand what was going on. "A-all but one."

"Which?"

"The dragon."

He frowned. "Would've thought that's the first one you'd get."

Another shrug. His hand swept down my throat over my collarbone to the naked skin on my right shoulder.

"I didn't think I deserved it," I admitted unwittingly, so caught up in his hands on me, in the energy between us that I was more honest than I'd intended.

His eyebrows jumped a little, but he only hummed and traced the uninked skin of my shoulder around to my back. "It'd look good startin' on your back and curlin' over your arm just here. A dragon needs space to fly free."

"Yeah, I left it clean for the design."

"You should get it," he said, a little too firmly. A little too loud.

The shop went quiet again around us.

"What?" I whispered.

"You should get it. Complete the set," he said casually, but I could see his pulse throb in the side of his neck and his gaze was too intent on mine.

There was nothing was casual about anointing myself with the last of Axe-Man's designs. It felt...final in good ways and bad. I hadn't realized until that moment that I was waiting for Axe-Man's validation to get it. If I'd never returned to Entrance, it was probable I'd have gone without that final and most important tattoo for my entire life. The last big blank space on my skin an empty frame.

"I'll do it, Blossom," Nova called out from his station, where he was applying a stencil to King's naked and very impressive torso. "After work tonight if you stay late."

I couldn't seem to break eye contact with Axe-Man, who'd stiffened and glowered at Nova's suggestion.

"Uh, okay, Nova, thanks," I called back weakly.

Axe-Man pulled away from my skin like I'd burned him and abruptly turned on his boot to stalk back to his station. When I opened my mouth to call him back, his next appointment came through the doors and called out to him.

When I looked a little helplessly back over at Nova, King, and Cressida, all of them were grinning a little madly at me. Nova even winked.

It wasn't reassuring at all.

It was dark beyond the one-way screened windows of Street Ink Tattoo Parlour, but the lights of the other businesses on Main Street glowed prettily, highlighting couples walking to dinner and friends out for an after-work beer.

I watched them from the front desk, wondering what it might be like to go on a date with Axe-Man one day. Where we would go and what we'd do. It was a pretty harmless fantasy, but I blushed when Nova waved a hand in front of me like he'd been trying to get my attention for a while.

"You ready?"

I nodded, getting out of the wheely chair to move toward his station at the back left of the shop.

"Nah," he corrected, grabbing my hand to lead me to the right front station. "Let's do it here."

I glared at him, digging in my heels. "That's Axe-Man's station."

"You don't say," he said, unperturbed, still tugging me forward until I reluctantly followed him. "It's better lightin' over here."

"It's nighttime."

"Right." He stroked a hand over his chin. "Comfier chair?"

I shook my head on a snort. "You're trouble. Has anyone ever told you that?"

His grin was wildly beautiful. "My fiancée does all the fuckin' time."

I'd met Lila for the first time two days ago when she'd come into the shop to pick up Cleo for lunch at Stella's Diner. She was just as glamourously beautiful as Nova, a Latina with long dark hair and exaggerated curves inked all over with gorgeous floral tattoos. She'd been Nova's muse long before they were even a couple, and I thought there was something so beautiful about that.

"Take off your shirt and get comfortable on your stomach while I get everythin' set up," he offered.

Everyone had gone home for the night, even Axe-Man had taken off without a single word or glance in my direction half an hour ago. Even though a tattoo artist in Vancouver had inked Axe-Man's designs into my skin over the past eight years, it felt wrong to be getting his Chinese dragon inked onto me in his own tattoo shop by someone else.

There was an ache in my throat I couldn't swallow down, something like hope gone wrong. I guessed a little part of me had hoped Axe-Man might want to finish my canvas himself.

But just because we'd been getting along better, just because we'd hate fucked twice, didn't mean everything was forgiven. Of course, he wouldn't want to put his own mark on my body. There was something utterly possessive about it, an act of ownership.

And he didn't want to own me.

No matter how much I longed for it.

It was even worse now that I knew how deliciously dominant he was in bed. How good it felt to be bent and shaped by him, to take his blunt weapon of a cock in my throat and my cunt.

I shivered a little just thinking of it as I took off my shirt and settled on my stomach over the comfortable chair.

It embarrassed me a bit to admit I always got aroused when I was tattooed. Something about the low-grade buzz of pain, the sharp bite on tender skin arrowed straight to my sex. It was probably a good thing Axe-Man wasn't doing the honours or else I might have actually jumped him before he could finish.

Heavy motorcycle boots thudded across the floor as Nova came back from the thermal printer and sat on the rolling stool at my side. I listened with my eyes closed as he adjusted his wheely table of supplies within reach and began to prep the area of my back and shoulder for the tattoo. Music played on low in the background, the only noise in the quiet shop other than the odd metallic rattle of tools on the tray and the rumble of wheels over the floor as Nova moved around the space. The familiarity of the process lulled me into a kind of trance not unlike the meditative space I occupied when Axe-Man bossed me around in the bedroom.

Thoughts drained from my brain and left me empty and at peace.

The first bite of the tattoo gun was almost welcome.

I was a bit surprised Nova didn't keep up conversation, because he seemed like a charming character, but I was pleased by the silence. It made it easier to get lost in the process.

He probably worked silently on me for three hours outlining the huge, undulating dragon from my lower left back diagonally across my spine and up around my right shoulder. I'd have to come back in for at least one other session for the shading and colouring.

I stirred a little when he pulled the top of my leggings down a little over the upper curve of my ass, exposing the top of my left butt cheek.

"What're you doing?" I almost slurred, so deeply relaxed I was almost drugged.

He didn't answer.

Instead, rough fingers prepped a small area on my ass and pressed a stencil to the skin.

"Nova, seriously?" I said, squirming a little because those rough hands felt a little too good on the tender skin of my ass. "The tattoo shouldn't extend that far."

A grunt, but otherwise no comment.

It was the grunt that made me pause though.

Not only because Nova didn't seem like the kind of heathen to use sounds instead of words. But because I would recognize that rough grumble anywhere.

"Axe-Man?" I squawked, trying to push up to turn and look at him.

A firm hand on my other ass cheek kept me pressed down.

"Axe-Man, what the fuck are you doing?" I demanded,

twisting my head awkwardly so I could see him now, bent over my ass with the tattoo gun posed in one gloved hand.

He shot me a dismissive glance and started the machine, pressing the buzzing gun to my skin.

I hissed at the tenderness on the thin skin, at the new knowledge that it was *Axe-Man* tattooing me and not Nova. That it was Axe-Man who'd put the final finish on my canvas of his artwork. That I'd wear his art done by his hand for the rest of my life.

I bit my lip to stop the shudder that threatened to roll through me and then groaned a little when he palmed my opposite ass cheek and growled, "Be still, Mei."

"What are you doing?" I asked again, breathy with arousal.

I could feel my pulse move between my thighs where it grew steadily stronger, a drumline of arousal beating through my core.

"You don't stay still, you won't find out," he warned in a harsh growl.

Fuck, that was hot.

Being pinned down by his big hands while he inked whatever he wanted into my skin.

Like he owned me.

Like I was his to do what he wanted with.

A little sigh escaped my parted lips, and I realized I was panting.

Axe-Man cursed. "Fuck, this is turnin' you on, isn't it?"

When I didn't answer other than to cant my hips up a little, he growled.

"I can smell how wet you are," he told me darkly as he turned off the gun, placed it on the rolling table, and took my waistband in both hands.

I shivered as he slowly peeled my leggings farther down my thighs until they were caught around my knees. He ran his knuckles along the underside of my ass and down one thigh, then back up the other, repeating the process until I shivered.

"I touch your pretty pussy, you gonna be wet from this?" he questioned casually as if he wasn't torturing me.

I choked on a groan and nodded, hiding my face in the crook of my arm.

"From the pain or from the fact I was the one givin' it to you?"

Another shiver rattled my spine and made the tenderness of my newly tattooed skin flare up. "You," I admitted.

"Yeah," he agreed on a long growl, finally sliding his knuckles into the narrow lane between my thighs and up into my wet pussy. "Jesus, soakin' wet."

He coated his knuckles in my slick, back and forth, before shocking me by smoothly sinking two fingers deep inside me. I whimpered at the stretch and then gasped as he twisted those thick digits so they rubbed against that bundle of nerves inside me.

"Stay still while I fuck you," he reprimanded when I automatically started gyrating on his hand. "Show me you can be a good girl."

I cursed as I pushed my ass back into him. "More, please."

"Greedy," he accused, but he didn't sound angry.

He sounded pleased.

Just two fingers fucking inside me while I lay prone on a tattoo chair, but I was already close to coming for him.

"Still," he ordered, pressing down on opposite butt cheek from the new tattoo. "Or do I need to tie you down?"

A shiver ripped through me on a keening noise I maybe should have been embarrassed by. But with Axe-Man, I felt no shame, only the kind of desire that raged through me like an out of control wildfire.

"Yeah," he agreed, and I pulled my face out of my arm just

in time to watch him pull his tee over his head by the back of the neck.

His huge torso was densely packed with muscles that had been developed over a life time, bulky and heavy. I wanted to bite into every ridge of his abs, test the strength of his bulging biceps with my teeth, press my fingers into those lats until they bore my fingertip bruises. The colourful tattoos stamped over nearly every inch of that beautiful canvas had been added to over the years, and I was hungry to catalogue each and every one.

He moved around to the front of the chair and squatted down, his gaze burning into mine.

"Give me your hands, Rocky," he ordered.

I would've done it anyway, but calling me Rocky was the magic word. Soundlessly, I offered him my wrists and watched as he bound them securely in his tee under the chair back. His grin was wicked when he tested them and realized I was pinned and at his mercy.

"I'm gonna play with your sweet cunt for a while," he told me, almost conversationally. "Work you open so you can take my cock. Then I'm gonna use you to make myself come and when I do it, I'm gonna blow just under this sweet new tatt I've given you."

"Yes," I hissed. "I have an IUD, and I'm clean. I want to feel every inch of your naked cock filling me up."

Axe-Man pressed his thumb to my parted mouth, tracing the shape of it with the rough pad before he straightened. His groin was at my eye level as he slowly undid his belt, flicked open the button on his jeans, and slid down the zipper. I was panting by the time he peeled open the denim to reveal the thick length of his cock behind the black cotton. When he stepped forward to press himself to my face, I groaned as I breathed in his scent through the fabric and mouthed at the ridge of his dick.

"As much as I'd like to come down your throat," he told me as he pulled away and moved around behind me. "I need to feel your tight pussy around me."

I leveraged my hips up as much as I could, spreading my thighs until they strained against the material of my leggings around my knees. I felt trussed up and on display for him and it was the sexiest I'd ever been.

"Fuck, you're a vision," he praised as he got on the big chair and straddled my legs, sliding his naked dick between my wet thighs. "Better than any fantasy."

The praise was almost too much. I whimpered as he teased us both by sliding in the hot crevice of my pressed thighs and then yelped when he smoothly slid inside me on one strong thrust. He was too big to press in all the way on the first drive, but I loved the delicious sensation of him working me open. I loved the struggle of taking his girth deep inside me. It might have been my imagination, but he felt so much better ungloved, a hot imprint on my insides.

He held me by the hips as he fit himself inside me, careful not to disturb my freshly tattooed back, shoulder, and upper left butt cheek.

"Love seein' my ink on you," he admitted on a groan as he tunneled in and out. "Love it way too fuckin' much I got carried away puttin' my mark on you."

"I want whatever mark you want to give me," I confessed as I pushed back with every thrust, mindless enough with pleasure to be honest. "With your tattoo gun, your teeth, your tongue, your cock. I've always wanted to be your canvas."

"You'd even wear my cum with pride, wouldn't you?" he taunted through gritted teeth, reaching beneath me to slap lightly at my pussy each time he ground deep inside me. "You wanna feel my warm cum runnin' down your thighs?"

"Yes," I gasped, neck straining, legs trembling as I fought off the tidal wave threatening to take me under and rob me of this exquisite tension. "Fuck, yes, please, Henning."

"You might hate me when you see what I marked you as," he admitted, voice tight, hands even tighter on my hips as he drove harder and harder into my clenching heat. "But I don't fuckin' care. You got your teeth and claws in me, it's only fair I got my ink on you. Even when I hate you, you're mine."

I came.

So hard I screamed, my body convulsing in shock waves on the chair. So hard I almost threw Axe-Man off the chair. He adjusted his weight to thrust down into me, keeping me still as he chased his own climax. I was still breaking into smaller and smaller pieces when I felt him growl viciously and pull out of my spasming pussy. The sound of my softening groans and the hard *thwap* of his hand shuttling over his cock, slick with my cum, echoed in the empty shop. A moment later, he let out a savage shout that sent another current of pleasure pulsing through me, and he came all over my right ass cheek and thigh. The hot splash of his seed felt like a baptism, like acceptance after years of praying for absolution.

And when he rubbed his big, rough palm over my cheek, smearing his cum into my skin, I was as close to bliss as I had ever been before.

"My cum and ink look fuckin' beautiful on you," he told me, quiet and rough as gravel. There was a captivated quality to his tone that told me how genuine those words were. "You were just a girl before, and the moment you came to town and I saw you were a woman, you awoke this fuckin' beast in me."

I shivered as he ran a thumb under my newly inked ass cheek, studying it.

"But you like it," he murmured, not a question.

Still, I nodded, a melted puddle of pleasure on his chair. "That's an understatement."

"Don't know what I'm doin' with you," he admitted, patting

my cheeks until they jiggled. "But I can't seem to fuckin' stop. Lovin' you feels like a curse, so why don't I want it to end?"

It wasn't a question I could answer. I knew he wasn't *in* love with me the way I'd loved him for years, but it felt like enough that he was admitting he still cared for me or cared for me again. I wanted him to release me from my makeshift tie, roll me over and collect every inch of me into his big, strong hold, but I knew that was taking the dream too far.

Having him like this was more than I'd ever thought I'd have, and even though I knew it wouldn't last, I was resolved to enjoy him like this until the very last second.

It was strange the way he made me feel. The sex we had was hard, almost primal. He was taking, and I was giving in a very true sense. Nearly taking too much, but not quite. Nearly giving too much––everything––but not quite. But the way he touched me didn't feel like taking, not at its core. It felt like, with every bite of strong square teeth and lash of his tongue, wth every stroke and spank and bruising grip, he shaped me like clay. Bringing the raw, real me to the surface, refining and pulling and positioning until the climax fired me into being, and in the aftermath, I felt different. Not other. Not new. Seen. Always seen with Axe-Man, even when I tried to hide behind the hate fucking. Even when he tried to pretend he was disgusted by his desire for me. His hands were honest, always. It was why he was such an incredible artist on canvas or flesh. On me. Because he spoke more with his actions than he'd ever been capable of with his words. The fact that he'd deigned to tattoo his art onto me himself spoke volumes. It made me...ache with hope. Stupid, wonderful, dangerous hope.

So I pretended I was fine when he carefully taped up my new ink and helped me right my clothes, gently pulling up my leggings and putting my tank over my bandaged back himself. I didn't cry when he tenderly rubbed the circulation back into my wrists or when he raked his fingers through my messy hair.

I didn't beg him to kiss me because I'd had his cock in my mouth and my pussy but not the simple profound pleasure of his tongue in my mouth. I ached for it more than I'd ever ached for anything else.

I even followed him back to Lake Mead on my own bike, laughing into the wind as I coaxed him into racing with me through the dark back roads to the cabin as if I hadn't been fundamentally changed by experiencing his tenderness and possessiveness in the shop.

As if "even when I hate you, you're mine" wasn't on repeat in the back of my mind.

And I didn't hunt him down to make him explain himself when later that night, after a late dinner with Cleo and Axe-Man and then a game of Texas Hold 'Em that we both let Cleo win, I went upstairs for bed and checked beneath the gauze on my ass to see what note he'd written into my skin.

Property of the Off-White Knight in the same small black, gothic writing of the tattoos *love* and *loss* on his knuckles.

CHAPTER THIRTY-SIX

Axe-Man

The human heart was a sadistic thing. Somehow, the same woman I'd hated had become the only woman my battered heart felt whole and enlivened by. I watched her chat with Boner and Curtains in the corner of the clubhouse, perched on the arm of a leather couch while she debated somethin' animatedly with her hands flyin' through the air. The sight of her was like a fist punched through my chest, stranglin' my heart. It felt good and bad at the same time, like I couldn't breathe, but also, I didn't want to 'cause I wanted to arrest this time when she was back in my life forever.

I'd never felt this electrified by a person in my entire life. It was unnervin' to be so possessed, so overrun by feelings when I'd been a fairly calm and rational man my entire fuckin' life. It felt like I was two men at war, my head and my gut brutalizin' each other over what my heart should do about the question of Mei Zhen Marchand.

The mess of emotions fightin' inside was impossible to ignore. Too complicated, too raw. I was angry, sad, bewildered... but above all, the reason I was currently brittle with rage, I was bitterly disappointed in my sense of self-preservation. 'Cause almost from the moment I saw Mei Zhen Marchand standin' in my home, a long-buried but vital part of me'd wanted to open my arms and receive her warmly. Say "it's been too long" and "my heart never stopped thinkin' about you," but to do so was to open all the windows and doors of a house in the face of an oncomin' storm. More than hazardous, it was a death wish.

And Mei had already killed one of my lives stone dead. I wasn't a fuckin' cat, and I couldn't afford to take a risk with what I had left. Not for me and sure as fuck not for Cleo.

So why did I want to?

Why did I want to step into the brutal wind of the storm and hold her tight so the shape of her small form would stamp itself on me like a notice of return to sender?

"Oh fuck," Wrath grunted as he slid onto the stool beside me at the bar. "I know that fuckin' look."

"Eagerness?" I countered. "Been waitin' eight years to get my hands on the man who ordered Kate's murder."

"I don't doubt it, brother. But this...eagerness is 'bout sex, not violence." He shot me a sidelong glance as he began loadin' his gun with the bullets we had lined up on the bar.

I shrugged it off. "Never realized before now there seems to be a thin line between hate and sex."

Wrath's perpetually unsmilin' mouth twitched into somethin' like a grin. "The quote's 'a thin line between hate and *love,*' man."

"Lovin' Mei would be the stupidest move I ever made."

"Why?"

I snorted, frustrated by myself, by Wrath, by the fact that

this club was a group of noisy fuckin' meddlers. "'Cause she broke my heart eight years ago in a way I'm still not fuckin' over. I'd be sentencin' myself to a shit ton more pain if I actually fell for her this time around."

It was crazy that I was even at this point when a couple weeks ago I'd been sure I never wanted to see her face again. Now, that very sentiment made me want to punch my fist through a fuckin' wall.

Even though I tried not to examine the reason I'd tattooed "Property of the Off-White Knight" on Mei's sweet ass, I knew some of the reason lay with my fear of her leavin' us again. This way, even if she abandoned us, she'd always carry a piece of me around with her.

It was overly possessive and totally fucked in the head.

But I couldn't deny even thinkin' about my mark on her skin gave me some kinda primal satisfaction as she stood across the room from me. Settled somethin' in me that'd been seethin' for eight years.

Wrath was quiet for a minute, loadin' his Taurus and then his backup Glock. I'd finished gearin' up already, a bulletproof vest over my tee and beneath my cut, my axe freshly sharpened, my own handgun loaded and ready in its shoulder holster, extra clips attached to my belt. Around us, the other brothers were preppin' for the showdown, too.

It was finally the night we were ambushin' the White Snake of the Red Dragon triad.

After Mei relayed the information Jiang Kuan had given her, Curtains went to work on verifyin' it and expandin' on the idea of ambushin' his convoy on their way up to Whistler to check on distribution up there. The kid was a grade A hacker, but he'd been thrown for a loop when Mei told him her friend, Obsidian Swan, could lend a hand, too.

Apparently, they'd known each other at some point, but

whatever their history, they succeeded in gettin' us exactly the information we needed.

The White Snake would be travellin' in a three-car convoy for Whistler leavin' from Vancouver at one thirty in the mornin'. It'd take them about an hour to hit the most deserted stretch of the Sea to Sky Highway just north of Entrance, where a group of brothers would be waitin' to take them out. Another group would come up from behind, cagin' them in. Curtains would be in a car trailin' so he could work on hackin' the systems, but the rest of us would be on our bikes.

We'd done similar manoeuvres before, but the Red Dragons were notoriously hard to pin down, and we needed to be ready for shit to hit the fan.

"'S been years since I lost Kylie," Wrath said abruptly, jarrin' me 'cause the man never talked about the lost love of his life. "Seems like a long time and such a fuckin' short one simultaneously. I can tell you straight up, brother, the only reason I could get up every mornin' after that was 'cause I knew when I had her, I relished every fuckin' moment'a lovin' her. And when she was at risk, I twisted myself into knots tryin' to protect her. In the end, it wasn't enough," he admitted on a broken sigh, lookin' at his empty hands like they were to blame. "But at least I tried, ya know? Even though you could argue it was stupid to love her when it was so fuckin' unlikely we'd ever find peace together, I was brave enough to try."

He looked me dead in the eye then, his blue eyes more animated than I usually saw them. "Sometimes, sayin' somethin's stupid is just a cowardly way outta takin' a chance on bein' brave."

My fist spasmed on the bar as I struggled to digest his words. I got him, I did, but our situations were totally fuckin' different.

"Kylie never hurt you," I noted, tryin' to stay calm when I felt like climbin' outta my skin. "Mei had her reasons, and she's explained them, so I get why she did what she did, but it's more than that." I closed my eyes for a second, thought of the knock-out fight we'd had just that mornin' when she'd fuckin' insisted on comin' with the club for the ambush 'cause it was *her* fuckin' mission and her fuckin' intel. I'd lost my shit. There was no way she was puttin' herself in danger two weeks after taking a beatin' from Seven Song triad. There wasn't even a fuckin' need to 'cause we had it covered.

But she'd yelled at me 'til she was blue in the face, sayin' she'd do it herself if she had to 'cause she'd made an oath to avenge Kate and hadn't spent the last five years fake datin' a Chinese crime lord just so a misogynistic asshole could sweep in and save the day.

"You have a white knight complex," she'd accused. "Why the hell do you think I based a character called the Off-White Knight after you? I don't need saving. In fact, maybe I should be there to save *your* ass in case you need backup."

I'd given in, but not gracefully.

"I know you're not used to followin' any rules, but you gotta know, Mei, you wanna stay alive, you follow *mine*."

In response, she'd tried to turn on her heel and storm out, but I caught her by the wrist and wrenched her into my chest so I could punctuate my orders with the stamp of a bruisin' kiss.

Now, I sighed heavily and scrubbed a hand over my face before turning to face Wrath fully. "My wife kept secrets, and she was murdered for them. My daughter..." I paused to swallow the angst that rose in my throat like bile. "Kept secrets and was very nearly murdered. You think I got it in me to love another woman who's as reckless as they come, who'd martyr herself in a fuckin' *second* if it meant savin' someone she loved, someone she just thought deserved to live more than she did, and she's got a fuckin' *low* opinion of herself, you're wrong. Maybe it makes me a coward, or maybe it makes me smart.

Either way, I don't got it in me to take that risk. Life's taught me not to."

Wrath made a noise in the back of his throat before he nodded slowly and clamped a hand on my shoulder. "Yeah, man, okay. My bad. I was wrong. Thought I recognized that look on your face."

"From what?"

"From the one I saw in the mirror every time I was around Kylie," he admitted. "I thought for a second Mei was the love'a your life, but if you don't feel the full-body fuckin' compulsion to be with her no matter the madness, then I was wrong."

I blinked at him as he slid off the stool and holstered his weapons. His gaze was pinned over my shoulder where I knew Mei was geared up and chattin' with Boner and Curtains still. I could hear her laughin'.

"For her sake, then, you should put a stop to the games you're playin'," Wrath murmured. "'Cause I might'a been wrong 'bout the look on your face, but anyone with eyes can see she lives for you, and she'd die for you in a second."

He turned and stomped away to where Zeus and Bat were porin' over a map of the highway, leavin' me shell-shocked and irritated.

"Fuckin' bikers," I muttered.

I WAS IN THE CONVOY THAT TAILED WHITE SNAKE ALL THE WAY from Vancouver, keepin' far enough back he couldn't see us, and the only reason we could track him was 'cause Curtains had hacked into his car system while we waited parked down the street from his company's skyscraper on Burrard.

"ETA ten minutes," Curtains relayed into my earpiece as I drove beside Dane and Bat along the curvin' Sea to Sky corridor into the mountains. "Zeus and the guys will take out the front car. Axe-Man, Bat, and Dane, you got the last car. I'll stop White Snake's."

I checked over my shoulder to make sure Mei was still with us, sandwiched between us at the front and Curtain driven in an unmarked SUV by Boner at her back. She looked sweet on the back of the Kawasaki decked out in a leather bodysuit and it'd taken everythin' in me not to kiss the fuck outta her when I'd seen her come outta the clubhouse bathroom ready to roll out with us. 'Cause even though a part of me didn't want her in danger, another part was turned on by her competency, and the fact she could ride with us, fight with us, and hold her own.

Bat revvin' his engine beside me alerted me to the fact we were catchin' up to the convoy, the last black SUV visible just disappearin' around the bend a few dozen yards ahead of us.

Adrenaline surged through my blood, carbonated and heady. This was what I loved about the life, ridin' on a bike, doin' shit in our own way on our own terms after a lifetime of military directives and medical rules.

Ride free or die hard, The Fallen MC motto.

I gunned my Harley-Davidson Softail and sped forward, Bat and Dane flankin' me as we raced through the dark night toward danger, reckless and wild.

We timed it just right, comin' up on the SUV right after a curve in the road so they didn't see us comin' and have time to escape. Bat took one side and Dane the other, shootin' out the tires while I stayed on their tail.

Up ahead, there was a screech of tires on asphalt and then a metallic crash as Zeus flashed his head beams from the side of the road, startling the driver to swerve into the waitin' row of spikes we'd placed across the asphalt. A plume of smoke unfurled into the air from the crash site at the side of the mountain road.

The car in front of us lost control as it tried to race ahead on the rims of their shot-out wheels. It was drizzlin', the rain makin' the roads slick beneath our bikes but also the SUV. The crash obstructed the road and the two cars were forced to slow down as they strategized what to do about their predicament. Finally, Curtains worked his magic and the front SUV rolled to a stop, lights off, engine dead.

That was the problem with new cars. They were fuckin' easy to hack.

I slowed down with the car, gettin' ready to surround the last car with my brothers. Only, the sound of a revvin' engine behind me alerted me to the fact Mei fuckin' Zhen had a different plan.

I started to turn just as she gunned past me on her sleek crotch rocket, a blur of black swervin' around the SUV in front of us, Bat at its side, and up to the car housin' White Snake. My heart leapt into my fuckin' throat as she gained speed inside of slowin' down on approach. I opened my mouth to fuckin' yell at her when she steadied her feet on the bike seat and carefully got into a crouch. A moment before impact, she lurched into the air, flyin' at the SUV just as her bike slammed into its rear.

She landed with a hard *smack* on the top roof, scramblin' to get purchase so she wouldn't fall right off the front. I watched in horror as she held up her hand, a signal to Curtains, and the sunroof slowly opened.

Shots fired so fuckin' quickly, I couldn't see what the fuck was happenin'. It prompted the Red Dragons in the last car to try their luck while we were caught out. They opened their windows and started firin' at Bat and Dane.

Fear for Mei burned through me, leavin' scorched earth in its wake. My imagination, forever fixated on the worst outcome after what'd happened to Cleo, envisioned Mei with a bullet between the eyes, elegant body slumped over the roof, cloaked in her own blood. Bile rose into my mouth, and my heart clenched so hard, I wondered if it'd ever beat again. Only the thought of gettin' to her, savin' her no matter what I had to do, prompted me forward.

I crouched, runnin' around the side of the car beneath the triad shooter's eyeline and firin' off a shot into the window while Bat hit the fuckin' deck to get outta Dodge. There was a curse inside the car as the shooter recoiled. I jumped up and slammed my body to the side of the vehicle beside the window, aimin' my gun inside to fire off four more rounds.

Silence.

"You good, Demon?" Bat called out Dane's club name.

"Just a graze," he shouted back.

I risked a peek into the back seat, found the two men there dead and the driver twisted to face me, gun raised. He got a shot off, but the angle was bad and the bullet hit me in the vest over my upper chest. I took a step back from the impact, cursin' but already squeezin' off another shot. It didn't hit him.

"On me," I grunted to Bat before crouchin' and makin' my way to the front door. I unclipped my axe and swung it into the door handle, usin' the wooden grip to open the broken door wide.

Bat fired three shots into the interior. I heard the thud of the body hit the dash.

"Clear," he called out to our brothers dealin' with the middle car.

"You got this?" I barked.

Bat nodded, but I was already movin' toward the second car to check on Mei's status.

Zeus and Priest had just finished tradin' shots with two triad men hangin' out the back windows and were movin' in on them. I charged by them, slammed my axe into the front passenger door and wrenched it open, droppin' out of range with my gun leveled at whoever sat within.

Mei sat there in the lap of a tall white man in a black suit. Her knees were bent into a crouch on either side of his thighs, her chopper blade raised and pressed beneath his chin, cuttin' into his throat just enough to release a thin line of blood.

Relief swooped through me hard enough I almost lost my fuckin' balance.

'Til I noticed the silver, enamel enlaid gun pressed up under her rib cage, the gangster's hand steady on the trigger.

"Hello, Axe-Man," White Snake said calmly, even though he kept his gaze fixed on Mei above him.

I didn't react to his knowledge of my name. A good enemy knew who his rivals were.

"Drop the gun," I ordered from my own crouch, levelin' my own weapon at his temple.

"I don't think so," he countered. "I believe I can get a shot off before you do. Before, even, this *siu lung* can slit my throat."

He'd called Mei "little dragon."

That, more than the sound of my name in Kate's killer's mouth made rage surge through me blood-hot.

"You've been watching us," Mei murmured, studyin' him with narrowed eyes.

"Of course," White Snake agreed.

"Not because we're your enemy," she continued in a strange, choked voice.

I tensed, my heart beatin' in my throat even though I could feel my brothers takin' my back. Somethin' wasn't right, Mei was suddenly pale as a corpse, her knife wobblin' under his chin.

Fear flooded the fires of rage inside me, and I tightened my grip on my gun, ready to shoot his fuckin' brains out. Nothin' was goin' to harm Mei. Not on my watch. Not ever fuckin' again if I had anythin' to do with it.

"You don't drop the fuckin' gun, I'll shoot you through the head," I barked out, and when he didn't immediately obey, I signaled to Priest through the window where he stood at the driver's door.

He shot through the glass into the dead body in the driver's seat.

It provided the distraction I needed to shoot White Snake through the hand holdin' the gun to Mei's side.

And my girl?

She didn't fuckin' hesitate, rollin' outta the car as White Snake shouted in pain, movin' to cradle the neat round wound pulsin' blood through his wrist. She hit the ground on a smooth roll and jumped to her feet behind me, her own small gun raised and ready to shoot at White Snake.

Pride clamped itself around my throat, and inappropriately timed lust tightened my gut.

Fuck, she was magnificent.

Mei safe, I pressed my still smokin' gun up under his chin where Mei'd left her blade's mark.

"You killed my wife, and you just threatened my woman," I growled, pressin' hard into the axe and the gun so he choked and spluttered, gone white with pain. "Tell me the reason you murdered Kate Kay and I might not blow your brains out right here on the side of the road."

"I'll do better," he growled, turnin' his head so I got a look at his face in the dim light of the bikes' headlights for the first time. My breath got stuck in my throat as I suddenly understood the reason Mei'd balked before. Other than his wide brown eyes, he was a male version of my daughter. "I'll tell you the reason Katherine Kay was murdered, and I'll give you reason not to kill me. Cleo's already lost her mother, do you think, after all she's been through, she deserves to lose her father, too?"

CHAPTER THIRTY-SEVEN

Axe-Man

MAXWELL DUTTON, OTHERWISE KNOWN AS WHITE SNAKE, Dragon Head of the Red Dragon triad, was bound to a metal chair in one of the closed garage bays of Hephaestus Auto at The Fallen MC compound. He was middle-aged but not much older than me, with silver at his temples and in his goatee, lines beside his dark, shrewd gaze, and a mouth that was the same shape as Cleo's.

It was almost unbelievable how much they looked alike.

Father and daughter.

Cleo had Kate's beautiful grey-green eyes, but otherwise, she was a female replica of Maxwell.

Kate'd never told me who Cleo's biological father was, and I'd never cared to ask. What did it matter, especially when it was probable the sperm donor had been one of her many johns back in her days of prostitution? What did it matter when I loved Cleo and considered her, almost from the first moment I'd decided to help them both, as my own?

So, it hit me hard, lookin' at Maxwell from the corner of the room, knowin' he'd fathered a woman so precious to me and knowin' he didn't deserve to be called anythin' close to Father. He'd abandoned them both to misery and tragedy. And however he was plannin' to spin his fuckin' tale, I knew he had somethin' to do with Kate's death either directly or indirectly.

I'd been fightin' a battle with the tumult of emotions this revelation had wrenched up inside me the whole ride back to the clubhouse with Maxwell tied up in the back of Boner's SUV. The bodies from the last two cars were piled up on a tarp in the trunk while Carson, Ransom, and Dane stayed behind to drive the two SUVs that hadn't crashed up into the mountains to disappear. We left the one that'd slammed into the side of the mountain pass. It looked like enough of an accident to pass with the law when someone finally called it in.

We'd dispose of the bodies later, but for now, the majority of the club was here, waitin' for me to take the lead. Zeus was at my shoulder, a solid presence, a comfort. He'd given me the floor 'cause this was my life, and he knew better than most, a man needed to take the lead in vanquishin' his own monsters.

The one that'd been hidin' under my bed for the last twenty years was finally before me.

I wanted to kill him worse than I'd wanted almost anythin' in my life.

But Cleo deserved to know what happened to her mother.

Mei deserved to have answers after pursuin' them for us for near on her entire life.

I wanted death, and a small selfish part of me felt I deserved it too after all the shit life'd piled on me. But I was good at blockin' out that voice.

And when the door to the garage swung open, and Mei walked in as if she had a right to be involved in Fallen business 'cause it was *my* business and I was hers in a way I realized now

I'd always be, it soothed the last of the violence inside me that had me frozen on the sidelines.

She walked right up to me, looked up into my face as she grabbed my left hand, and smoothed her fingers over the place where my pinky finger'd once been.

"You got this," she whispered, so soft it was almost soundless. A statement of trust meant just for me. "We get our answers, you can finally put the past to rest."

A sound of loss rose in my throat, but I swallowed it down painfully as I squeezed her small hand in mine.

"I wanna kill him," I admitted, duckin' down a bit to speak into her ear. "Wanna rip him apart with my bare hands and set the pieces on fire."

"Yeah," she agreed without hesitation. "Me too. If he doesn't have the right answers, we *will*. But let's make sure Cleo's sperm donor is a real piece of shit before we take the option of knowing him from her forever."

I grunted 'cause she was right.

Even though I had all my brothers supportin' me in this, it settled me to have Mei there even though club business was usually closed to outsiders. It surprised me a little that I wanted to extend her this trust, but then again, maybe it shouldn't have. Mei was on my team long before I'd even met most of my brothers in Entrance. She knew me, knew this situation, in a way they never could.

With one last look into those dark eyes to fill me with resolve, I stepped around Mei and stalked toward White Snake. I grabbed a metal chair as I went, draggin' the legs against the polished concrete with an ear-splittin' screech that made Maxwell Dutton flinch. When I was close enough, I spun the chair back and straddled it, casual, like we were just havin' a little chat.

Retrievin' the knife I kept in my boot, I lifted the wicked blade between us so it caught the light. It blinded Maxwell, made his eyes water and blink. Then I took his bound hands where they lay chained together on his lap and raised them to the chair back, loopin' the metal through the bars before securin' them to the chair with my knife stabbed between the links.

"I'm gonna ask you some questions," I told him in a voice I didn't hardly recognize, somethin' dead and cold like I'd heard from Priest or Wrath when they interrogated men for the club. I felt like that now, like a corpse reanimated by somethin' dark and evil, as I stared into the eyes of the reason Kate was taken from us. "And if I don't like the answers, if I feel like you're lyin' to me, I'm gonna take a finger from you. And if I run outta fingers, I'm gonna start on your toes. If you're stupid enough to keep it up, what do ya think? Maybe I'll move on to your ears next and then your tongue."

Maxwell stared at me for a long moment before sayin', "I never took you for a man who'd enjoy torture."

"Not torture if it's deserved," I countered.

"You'd really do anythin' for the Kays," he muttered, a little awed, a little puzzled. Somethin' robotic confused over the depth of human emotion. "Even now Kate's dead."

"Just doin' what *you* shoulda done as her lover, as Cleo's father," I ground out. "Now, start at the beginnin' and don't leave anythin' out."

It was a short story, love cut off by tragedy.

Maxwell Dutton met Katherine Kay when his buddies hired her for his twenty-first birthday party. She was sixteen, but he didn't know that at the time. She was beautiful, and she moved like a dream, ethereal, otherworldly almost, like a fae dressed in tacky pleather. He could see through it, he told me, to the soft spirit beneath the body glitter and eyelash glue.

He sent his buddies away, and they catcalled, jeered at him for fuckin' the prostitute.

But he didn't.

They stayed up all night talkin'.

He became obsessed with her.

His life wasn't soft or easy, but his affection for Kate was.

I got him, 'cause even though our love'd never been romantic, I'd felt the same way about her.

Even though he hated the lifestyle she was forced into by poverty, by circumstance, he wasn't in a position to get her out. He couldn't even get himself out.

Maxwell was a 49er for the Seven Song triad, a lowly foot soldier desperate to climb the ladder.

When I asked him how he became a white member of a Chinese gang, he'd smiled thinly. "Wrong place, right time. Kasper Kuan was still establishing his foothold in Calgary, and a group of rednecks caught him outside a bar where he was doing business. They were beating him to death in the back alley where I was bartending. I saw them when I took out the trash and chased them away."

"Kasper owed you his life."

"He would never admit that, even to himself. But he did bring me into his fold after that. There was a kind of...softness he had for me, and he was not a soft man. He brought me into his protection detail, and I worked myself up from there. By the time Kate got pregnant later that year, I was ready to marry her. Take her out of one life and into my own. It wasn't safe exactly, but it was safer."

"But you abandoned her."

"No," he said, fierce and stone cold, piercin' me with his eyes. "If I did, it was only as Mei abandoned you."

"Keep her name out of your mouth," I growled, openin' my hand.

Priest stepped forward and placed a pair of pliers in my palm. Without hesitation, I clamped them around Maxwell's pinky finger on his left hand.

"You lost that finger saving her," he told me, and when I shot my gaze up to his, he had that same thin smile on his face. "I know everything about you, Henning Axelsen. Did you think I wouldn't keep an eye on the man raising my daughter?"

"If that was true, if you're implyin' you've been watchin' over Cleo, then why the hell didn't you step in when she needed help the most?" I seethed.

He flinched, just slightly, a tiny recoil in his throat. "I didn't see that coming."

I snorted.

"You didn't either."

Without remorse, I pressed the pliers together, cuttin' into his finger until he hissed.

"I didn't see what was happening back then either," he admitted, raisin' burnin' eyes to me. "I became so obsessed with Kate, my friends in the triad started to take notice. So did Kasper. Maybe he was just curious. Maybe he wanted a bead on me as I started to make a name for myself in the crime world. Either way, he started to visit Kate."

He swallowed thickly, and I found myself doin' the same.

The idea of Kasper's hands on Kate made me physically ill. A sense of portentous doom dug roots into my belly.

"He fell in love with her, if you can call it love," Maxwell continued, but it clearly pained him to do so. "I didn't realize it, but he started keeping her from me. Paid her pimp Jimmie Page for exclusive access. But Kate was pregnant, and I was in love with her. I couldn't let it go. One night, I followed Jimmie to find out where he was keeping her and found her in a swanky hotel. I waited for Jimmie to leave and then broke down the door. Kasper was inside."

He looked wane, as if he'd vomit any minute.

"I lost it," he admitted. "There were bruises all over Kate, and he was...touching her, and I went ballistic. I still don't remember the cops coming, prying me off his body. I beat him so badly, I heard later he lost partial vision in his right eye."

"He had you locked up," I surmised.

He nodded. "Locked up with attempts on my life every day for the first six months of my stay. He knew a lot of people inside, and others would do anything for the money."

"Clearly, you survived."

He grinned. "I thrived. When I got out ten years later, I had enough of a reputation to mean something in the province, but it was too late. Kasper wasn't using Kate the same way anymore. He thought her having my kid was a betrayal, and he shunned her until someone told him she was doing real estate. He figured he could blackmail her into doing deals for the triad, laundering money through the sales with cash purchases."

I swore viciously. "Why the fuck wouldn't she've told me?"

"He threatened Cleo."

Despair strangled my throat so hard, I struggled to get air into my lungs for a full minute.

"When I got out," he continued, "I went to her immediately, but she was already married to you. She was...happy and safe except for this deal with Kasper. I should've been enough, but I wanted to help her. If I couldn't have her, I could make her safer...I offered to get Kasper off her back."

"And he found out," I deadpanned.

He nodded. "He found out. The triad system doesn't allow for disloyalty. When you take the oath, you agree that the price for betrayal is to be killed by the five thunderbolts; death by metal, wood, water, heat, or burial. Weapons, beating, drowning, burning, or being buried alive. They chose the first, obviously for Kate, with *lingchi*."

"Kate wouldn't have been sworn into the triad, though."

"No, but she was working for them as a Blue Lantern. The uninitiated but affiliated are still held to the same standards."

"So, it was Kasper who ordered the hit," I surmised in that same voice I didn't recognize. Honestly, at that moment, I didn't recognize myself. A mystery that had haunted me for thirteen years was finally solved, yet I felt no relief. "But it was 'cause of you."

Maxwell lifted his chin. "It was."

"I should fuckin' end you for lettin' her swing out there alone. She'd already been through so fuckin' much, and for her to die like that..." I swallowed the thick tangle of rancid emotions chokin' the back of my throat. "You deserve to die for this even though you didn't call the hit."

"Maybe," he agreed with surprisin' calm. "I've often wondered the same."

I stared at his fingers caught between the metal teeth of the pliers and imagined all the ways I could disassemble him. Carve him up and parse him out under the earth, never to be found.

Oh, I wanted to end him. For touchin' Kate, for lurin' her into that fucked-up situation and then for bein' stupid enough to leave her unprotected and at the mercy of a man like Kuan.

But he was Cleo's *father*.

Who was I to take that away from her when my girl had already lost so much?

It had to be her choice, not mine.

And the girl she was, the girl *I'd* raised, would never condemn someone to death.

So, I raised my head and declared, "Not gonna kill my girl's sperm donor. I'll leave it up to her how she wants to deal with you. But tell me, why the fuck haven't you tried to contact her if you've been watchin' her all these years?"

"I got her mother killed. And, until The Prophet, she was happy and thriving without me. I disturbed the life of someone I loved once before to tragic ends. I wasn't about to do it again."

"Only you have," Mei said from behind me, her voice a whip through the air crackin' against Maxwell's cheek so hard he flinched again. "This war with the Seven Song, it's because Kasper hates you, still. And he's coming to Entrance to threaten The Fallen MC because he knows Cleo is your daughter. Will he come after her directly?"

Rage burned through me so cleanly, it erased any understandin' I might have harboured for the man tied to the chair in front of me. I reared up and grabbed him by the front of his shirt, wrenchin' him into the air.

"Is she in danger?" I roared in his face, the pliers split over my fist like makeshift bronze knuckles. When I brought it down on his face, I felt the crack of bone under the impact. Blood poured from his nose down his fancy-ass dress shirt and tie. It wasn't nearly enough, so I grabbed my axe from its holster and pressed its edge against the thin skin of his neck. "If you put her in danger, I'll skip the fingers and toes and go straight for your fuckin' head."

"She's not," he assured me quickly, but there was fear in the tight lines of his face. "I've been watching, and Kasper hasn't made any moves toward her. Why would he when I've shown no interest?"

"I watched that motherfucker put a bullet through the skull of his own brother's lover without hesitation. Now, I know he ordered men to slice up Kate for the transgression of what?

Talkin' to you? Movin' on without him? If you think he isn't searchin' for a way to take the both of us out at the knees, you're a fuckin' dumb fuck who doesn't deserve to live."

My breath steamed through the billows of my chest, and my heart thundered so hard it threatened to crack a rib.

"I could end this right now by killin' you and deliverin' you like a mid-spring festival present to Kasper. Then, he'd know not to fuck with us, and he wouldn't care as much to try with you outta the picture."

"You wouldn't do that to Cleo."

"She doesn't even know you exist, and she doesn't have to," I barked, but he was right, and it cut through me like a hot blade.

"Might I suggest, instead of killing me, we collaborate?" Maxwell offered, his voice choked off by the pressure of his collar pulled tight around his throat and the axe cuttin' just so into his neck. "I've been working toward taking down Kasper for years. I've got a stake in taking them down same as you. More than you. All I want in return is a chance to meet Cleo."

"Abso-fuckin'-lutely not," I snapped. "After everythin' she's been through, she doesn't need a new father to deal with."

"I just want to know her," he said, soft like he was an innocent, like he hadn't been a part of makin' her an almost-orphan at twelve years old. "She'd be in charge of how much or how little we interacted."

I scowled at him, heart beating like a fist on the inside of my rib cage. It killed me, but there was no way I had a right to keep this from my daughter. I wouldn't lie to her, and she deserved to know where she came from, even if that person was a pile of steamin' dog shit.

"I'll tell her about you," I muttered begrudgingly. "'Cause it's the right thing to do for Cleo. Not for you. And I'll do it when the time is right, after all this shit is finally put to bed."

Maxwell brightened, and it irritated me that he was sittin' there surrounded by outlaws with his finger in the vice of pliers, and he looked as comfortable as if he was sharin' a beer with me at the local pub. Then again, a man didn't become the leader of a criminal syndicate by showin' fear in the face of adversity.

"So, we'll work together?" he confirmed, and there was a bloodthirsty hunger there I could recognize.

I wanted to work with White Snake like I wanted a bullet through the head. Fury was still pumpin' through me, takin' me as close as I'd ever been to killin' the true reason for Kate's tragedy. As far as I was concerned, Maxwell's negligence was just as much to blame as Kasper's will to murder her.

I was paralyzed by the internal battle of what was right and what felt right in that moment.

'Til a small hand pressed itself into my back, a heated brand that sank through cloth and flesh straight into bone. Through the fog of hate and fury, Mei's presence cut like a *dao* sword.

"Axe-Man," she said, but she said it the way she would say Henning. Like it was made of magic, like it could open doors and move worlds.

Like she had unshakeable faith in me and everythin' I represented.

Hearin' it now grounded me unlike anythin' else could've.

"He used Jiang to manipulate me," Mei murmured. "To keep me from finding the truth and to help him take out the Red Dragons. Everything you're feeling right now, Kasper deserves to have rained down on him."

"Doesn't mean this motherfucker doesn't deserve some of the same," I countered.

"You're right," Mei said, and her voice was a slitherin' thing, curlin' like a snake around my neck to hiss at Maxwell. "So, take what you want from him. White Snake owes you a finger or two for the pain he's put you through, but when you're done, wash your hands and let's work on a plan."

It was an odd moment to realize Mei Zhen's ironclad hold

over me. But somethin' like love surged through me at those wicked, cruel words. It was the sensation of bein' seen at your very worst and not bein' found wantin'. No, it was the exact opposite. It was bein' seein' at your worst, on the precipe of burnin' down the whole world for selfish reasons, and bein' encouraged to take your fill.

No one had ever seen the darkness in me and *enjoyed* it. Not like Mei.

It made that part of me easier to accept, easier to relish when I secretly longed to indulge the sinful side of my nature that called for bloodshed, more than just an eye for an eye. That howled for rough touches and bite marks like stamps of ownership on flesh. That failed at bein' a soldier and a doctor but thrived at bein' this outlaw, 1%er biker.

Mei saw it all, the bad and the ugly, and she *still* thought I was good.

She always had.

Something fundamental shifted in my rib cage, tectonic plates grindin' painfully to make room for somethin' new, a mountain range of her unshakeable belief that spanned the entire length of my spine and made it easier to hold up my world.

Filled with resolve, I grinned at White Snake with all the predatory instinct inside me bared between my sharp teeth. "I think it's only fair, before we get down to business, that I take payment like Rocky said. What do you think, Maxwell, two fingers or three?"

CHAPTER THIRTY-EIGHT

Axe-Man

THE LAKE WAS A SHEET OF RIPPLIN' BLACK VELVET NEAR THE shore and shimmerin' silver under the full bellied moon overhead at its depths where I rowed the small boat holdin' Mei and the four dead bodies of the Red Dragon triad we'd killed earlier that night.

It was hours later. After I'd taken two of White Snake's fingers, which he'd stoically endured with the kinda martyred acceptance I recognized all too well. He felt he deserved it, at the very least, for what had happened to Kate and to his daughter as a result. I was glad we were on the same fuckin' page 'cause there was no way I could move on to strategy without purgin' some of the violence ragin' inside me.

After, when I'd washed up and Maxwell's three-fingered right hand and shot-through wrist was bandaged by Bat, we'd gathered in church to vote on workin' with the Red Dragons to take down Seven Song.

Not one brother had objected.

The Red Dragons had once caused problems for a rival MC, the Berkserkers, but they'd never done shit to The Fallen. While the Seven Song had helped the Calgary chapter betray me, nearly taken out Curtains when he'd tried to help their hacker, Obsidian Swan, escape her cage, and finally, they'd threatened our entire club if we didn't act like obedient fuckin' dogs and haul their product for them.

As Wrath said, they deserved to burn for one transgression, let alone all three.

In our world, three strikes were two too many.

So, Zeus called the meetin', and we'd gone back to the garage where the prospects assembled a makeshift war table, and we'd bent heads with White Snake to plan the ultimate revenge against Kasper Kuan.

The whole time there'd been something buzzin' under my skin. This awareness of Mei that transmuted the physical space between us. There was a Chinese concept of the red thread of fate, a string that connected souls that was unbreakable, one that could stretch through time and distance without falterin'. It was hard not to apply the theory to my relationship with Mei when I'd felt linked to her inextricably, undefinably for years, even after an eight-year separation. I'd never healed around the wound of her absence, I realized now that she was back in my life and lodged under my ribs like a second heart. I'd just learned to breathe through the pain. I hadn't been in love with her before, but there'd been somethin' there and I could see that now. This awareness like the thread between us was just beginnin' to take shape.

When I pulled her into my lap to pore over the plan, she hadn't protested. No, not my Rocky. She'd thrown herself into the strategizin' like *Hua Mulan*, like she'd been born to the seedy underbelly of this world, like she thrived in this darkness as much as me.

We didn't speak on the drive back to the house in the club's unmarked SUV, the bodies wrapped neatly in the back for us to dispose of. With the Seven Song triad lookin' at land beside Angelwood Farm, we didn't want to take the risk of buryin' the bodies on the property, so we were doin' it like the Vegas mob used to. Rowin' them to the middle of the deep waters in Lake Mead to drop them, laden with stones, to the murky depths. Priest'd offered to come with me, but Mei had assured him a little too happily that she'd be there to help with the cleanup.

There was only the not-quite-silence of the night-filled forest around us, the rustle of creatures just as nocturnal as we were navigatin' the underbrush. The sharp scent of pine and sap cut by the cool dampness of lake water. The gentle slap of the oars as I churned them through the smooth surface to propel us forward.

It should have been peaceful, and in some ways, it was. For the first time in my life, I was close to wipin' the slate clean. Collectin' answers and dolin' out punishments.

But a deeper part of me was vibratin' like a struck tunin' fork waitin' for somethin' to join me in harmony.

I stopped rowin', and Mei immediately went to work as if this wasn't her first time disposin' of bodies. Maybe it wasn't. There were still so many questions to fill the gaps of our eight-year estrangement, but for the first time since she'd arrived, I was excited to ask them.

I let myself watch her for a few moments, her efficient movements as she worked methodically to heft one body up onto the side lip of the boat without rockin' it and then another on the other side to balance the weight. She was still in that black leather bodysuit, the supple fabric outlinin' every smooth curve and slight dip of her form in the bright moonlight. Her ethereal beauty was enhanced by the silver beams and oddly, magnificently highlighted by the macabre nature of her task. She looked like an angel of death, something dangerous and capable, someone whose very kiss might be lethal.

And it was.

Lethal to my willpower.

Destructive to every single wall I'd constructed around my heart over the hard years of my life.

I wanted her to burn me down to ash and raise me up like a phoenix, reborn in the fires of her all-consumin' love.

It was reckless to be loved like that and love like that in return.

And I'd made myself into a calculated man. One based in the head, not the heart or the gut. But for once in my life, I wanted to take a risk for *myself*. I wanted to be selfish and fuck the consequences.

I wanted Mei, and I didn't care about anythin' else.

She didn't say a word as I sat there in silence without helpin' her. There was a loud splash as she tipped first one body and then another into the ink-dark lake.

She smiled slightly as she worked, enjoyin' this task, maybe, or bein' in on it with me. It occurred to me this scene was like somethin' outta her books—Rocky and her Off-White Knight cleanin' up a crime scene.

"Rocky," I said finally, and the word sounded scraped out of my throat, dredged up hard from the pit of my stomach.

It lay bloody and raw between us.

She stilled on her knees in the belly of the boat and braced her hands slowly on the rails like she was bein' rocked by more than the gentle waves.

"You put yourself in danger tonight," I said, and it wasn't a good start. I watched her face get tight, the stubbornness comin' out in the jut of that little chin. "Throwin' yourself at the car. You put yourself in danger thirteen years ago to try to save Kate. You did it a-fuckin'-gain eight years ago dealin' for the Centre

Street Crowd to try to get answers for why Kate died and then to try to save me from a fate Rooster and Kasper Kuan tried to pin me to."

"I'd do it again," she snapped, defensive and righteous. "And it's about more than just trying to right the wrongs I made with you."

"You don't have to right shit," I argued. "You explained your reasons for bein' gone."

She scoffed. "You're still holding it against me like a knife pressed to my throat."

I blinked 'cause she was right in a way. I'd been usin' it to keep her and all those emotions she brought to life in me at bay. If I couldn't forgive her, I could still give in to this new temptation for her body without puttin' my heart at risk. I could enjoy havin' her around without acceptin' we were somethin' more than just old friends turned enemies now.

We were, and always had been, somethin' more.

Partners in crime, at the very least.

And we could be more, I thought, if I had the balls to risk it all on Mei one more time.

My heart fuckin' leapt in my chest, tryin' to get closer to her. Urgin' me to wrench her into my arms and smother her smart mouth with mine.

I wasn't much of a talker, nothin' like King with his poetry or Nova with his charm. But these words needed to be said. I owed her them even though she'd never think to ask.

"I did," I agreed, lowerin' myself to my knees in the boat, two bodies and a bench seat between us, but at least we were more on level. "Your love language is throwin' yourself in the face of danger to save your loved ones from somethin' so slight as a paper cut."

"Murder and revenge are a hell of a lot more serious than a paper cut," she retorted, and I was still gettin' it wrong 'cause I meant that as a compliment. "Doing anything for the people you love isn't just something I hold in theory, Axe-Man. You and Cleo deserve action."

"So do you," I told her solemnly as I took her face in my hands. There was still blood caught between the grooves on my fingers. "I'm tryin' to give you words, but I've never been much good at that. Maybe, you'll understand what I'm tryin' to tell you better like this."

Her skin was soft against the calluses of my fingertips, her mouth a dark bud unfurlin' at the centre of her luminous, moon-kissed face. I watched her eyes widen almost comically as I bent closer, and she realized what I was plannin' to do.

But she didn't stop me.

No, instead, the moment my lips touched hers, she loosed a soft sigh like a silk ribbon unspoolin' between us. I caged it between our mouths when my lips closed on hers and then, with one slick slide of my tongue between her teeth, I fed my own groan back to her.

Cherry blossom in my nose, sweetness like cool water in my mouth, the smoothness of unblemished skin on my palms, satin hair under my fingertips. My senses were filled with her 'til I felt like I was drownin', six feet beneath the waters lappin' at the side of the boat.

It would've been a happy death, submerged in the depths of Mei Zhen Marchand.

I slid my hand over her cheekbone into her hair to cup the back of her skull and tilt her so I could take the kiss deeper, plunder into her mouth just to feel her whimper.

Why had I waited so long to fuckin' kiss her?

'Cause now that I had, I knew I'd never wanna stop.

When I pulled away, she chased after my lips, fistin' her hands into my shirt to keep me close. I chuckled low and pressed my forehead to hers so those big obsidian eyes took up my entire world view.

"I forgive you," I told her. "In case that wasn't clear. In case it wasn't obvious that there's nothin' to forgive you for. In case you still needed to hear it."

She breathed softly as she stared into my eyes, lickin' her lips nervously like she didn't believe me.

I'd given her a fuck ton of reasons not to.

"I don't hate you, Rocky," I said, and the words were too simple, a contradiction of the cruel ways I'd treated her, of the promises I'd made to hate her forever.

But they felt like more than that.

I don't hate you 'cause I love you.

Only I wasn't ready to say those words 'cause I was worried I didn't know what the fuck they meant anymore.

I wanted to be her friend like before. I wanted to be her lover like we were now.

But there was somethin' in me screamin' for more.

Screamin' for everythin'.

The same instinct that had encouraged me to ink my possession into the sweet skin of her ass. The same instinct that urged me to mark her up with my tongue and teeth so anyone lookin' at all her beauty would know it belonged to me.

And I couldn't bring myself to accept that. Not after life had taught me love was a built-in tragedy. Not when it showed me through Kate and Cleo what happened to the human heart when it was foolish enough to wish for the fantasy of some kinda happily ever after.

Not when Mei'd left us once before and had no plans to stay.

With Cleo recoverin', the triad at our doorstep, and Kate's death so close to avenged, I couldn't focus on somethin' so selfish and risky as my own feelings.

Even more than that, though, a part of me knew if Mei left again, or if, fuck, life saw fit to take another woman from me, I'd never recover.

Mei's eyes were glazed with tears as she looked at me. Her fingers uncurled from my shirt and shifted up into my beard and then the hair over my ears. She studied every plane and angle of my face, a face she'd have to have memorized after spendin' years drawin' it for the Off-White Knight.

That she'd made a hero outta me that way still burned in me like I'd swallowed starlight right outta the sky.

"You loved me once," I murmured 'cause the space between us called for sacred whispers. "Can you forgive me now for bein' a hurt bastard?"

She laughed a little, but it was waterlogged. "The memory of what I did to you is like a knife in my chest, and every time I think about what happened, it twists brutally into my heart. I'm the one who needs forgiveness, not you."

"How about we're both forgiven?" I suggested, brushin' my thumbs over her sharp cheekbones. "I think at this point we can agree, we're more than enemies."

She smiled, and I didn't resist the urge to press my thumb into the divot of her one-sided dimple. "Enemies with benefits, I hope?"

"No," I growled, leanin' forward to nip her bottom lip. "We were never enemies, Rocky. I've loved you before, and I was foolin' myself thinkin' I ever stopped."

She bit her lip, lookin' skeptically up at me through her lashes.

"I loved you," I repeated firmly.

"No, not the way I wanted to be loved. Not like loving me was the only choice you ever could have made. Not like it was love me or die for not having me."

Her longin' was so palpable I could feel it echoed through that link that anchored us together against all odds. I thought of her over the last near-decade, mostly alone, with only Old Dragon to love her and Jiang to keep her a perverse kinda company, and I ached for the both of us. Despite havin' Cleo and the club, I'd been a special kinda lonely without her, too. I wasn't one to give much of my inner self to people unprompted and Mei was the only one determined to break down my walls anyway. It made me feel seen and worthy that she'd always gone to that much effort to know me.

"Let's get this done," I decided, pullin' away to deal with the last two bodies 'cause there was somethin' I wanted to show her, and I knew if I didn't do it *now,* I'd lose my fuckin' nerve.

Mei hesitated, bitin' her lip like she wanted to say more, but eventually, she helped me toss the last body over the edge and then waited quietly as I rowed us back to shore.

After I tied up the boat to the dock, I took her hand and led her up the ramp to the house. It was quiet inside, empty, 'cause Cleo was stayin' over at Bea and Priest's. I didn't bother to turn on the lights as I led Mei through the dark into the garage off the side of the house. Only when I closed the door behind us did I let her go and flip on the light.

This was my studio space.

My safe place.

Cleo and Lin didn't come in unless I invited them, and mostly, I didn't.

It was for that part of my brain that needed to express itself in pen and paint 'cause words never seemed to do.

I surveyed the huge room with floor-to-ceilin' windows along two sides showin' the dense forest at the back of the property and then turned to take in Mei's reaction.

Her pink mouth was dropped open in a little comical "O" of shock.

I got her.

It was shockin', even for me havin' been the one to paint them.

I'd been possessed to create the way I always was, blackin'

out as I dragged acrylic over canvas, pen over dense, textured art paper. For the last six weeks Mei'd been in my life again, all I'd been able to create was her.

The many faces of Mei Zhen Marchard stared back at us where they were propped against the wall, against each other, restin' on easels half finished. Mei on the day I'd seen her in the hospital, curled up with Cleo like the yin to her yang. Mei naked and sprawled on the pink bed of Purgatory Motel with her tiny red thong caught around one ankle lookin' entirely debauched in the wave of destruction from my mouth and cock. Mei in one of her martial arts poses, ready for a fight, limbs loose but ready, weight on the balls of her feet, slick hair caught up in a bun on top of her head.

Mei was everywhere in the studio 'cause she was everywhere I looked inside my own head.

I preferred to paint landscapes, and I'd only dabbled in a couple of portraits of Cleo and Lin, a paintin' of Angel and Monster for Loulou, and another of Prince for Cressida and King. Nova'd asked me to do one of Lila for her birthday, too. But the ones of Mei, they were the best I'd ever done.

She didn't look at me or move an inch off the landin' in front of the door as she whispered, "What is this?"

"I told you once eight years ago that I loved you, and you implied it wasn't enough." I moved toward her again, takin' her limp hand to lead her into the middle of the concrete floor. "I asked what the fuck I had to do to show you how much you were loved." I swallowed the burn in my throat. "How much I loved you."

Back then, it'd been obvious that the ultimate expression of love and possessiveness would be for me to have her tattooed on my skin like I did with Cleo, Kate, and Lin, but that hadn't been possible then. I hadn't remembered that 'til now, and gettin' ink for her didn't seem wrong anymore. It seemed almost wrong I *didn't* have her inked onto me when she was so clearly a part of my fate in this life.

It was somethin' to think about for another time when I could see beyond the next minute with her.

For now, I hoped this would be enough to prove to her the sheer fuckin' enormity of my feelings for her.

"Is this enough?" I asked, voice rough with disuse 'cause I wasn't used to voicin' the things written in ink on the inside of my chest. "'Cause I haven't been able to get you outta my head since the moment I saw you again at the hospital. I told you, you got your teeth and claws in me, Rocky. And the fuck of it is, even when I wanted so fuckin' much to hate you, it was *me* I hated, for lovin' you still and for wantin' you now in this new way that rocks me."

I gestured to the pieces of one paintin' I'd taken my knife to in a fit of fury after I'd found out she was still workin' with the triad. They were piled on the floor,'cause even furious as I was, I couldn't bring myself to throw them in the trash.

I bent my knees to bring me closer to her level and cupped her gorgeous face in my hands once more. "You knock the wind outta me, Mei. Every fuckin' time I lay eyes on you. And I only get it back when we touch, and the relief is a sweet, sharp ache in my goddamn chest."

"Axe-Man," she whispered, reachin' up to clutch my wrists tight, as if she was afraid I'd disappear. "Don't play games with me. Not when you have to know how long I've wanted you just like this."

"No games," I swore. "And no promises, either. I don't got any answers but this. No matter what happens in this life, you mean somethin' to me. I made the mistake of tryin' to regret that and the truth is, I never could. Better or worse, you're mine and I'm yours. This attraction might fade. A...relationship seems impossible with every-fuckin'-thing between us and in front of us. I gotta focus on Cleo, not to mention shit that's constantly goin' down with the club. It's dangerous, and after we put Kate's killers to bed, I want you *safe*. But I will always be the Off-White Knight to your Rocky. That's an oath I'll swear in blood, and if I ever break it again, I give you leave to kill me by metal, wood, fire, water, or earth."

Tears glazed Mei's eyes, catchin' in those thick lashes. But she didn't let them fall, my Rocky, 'cause she was a fighter not a crier. Not even now in the safest place there was for her between my arms.

"I feel like I'm dreaming and it hurts because I know I'm going to wake up," she whispered in a choked-off voice.

I made a noise low in my throat in response to that pain and decided to do somethin' about it. I'd bought the stuff for a photo shoot Nova'd done with Lila, but I still had some of the paints lyin' around ready to use.

Steppin' away, I went to the work table in one corner and collected what I needed as I ordered her, "Get naked."

There was a pulse of surprise in the air as she hesitated.

I looked over my shoulder with a raised brow and growled, "Now, Rocky."

She bit her lip then slowly dragged the zipper of that tight leather bodysuit down between her breasts. Beneath it, she wore a flimsy lace bra in black and red and below that, unveiled with teasin' gradualness, a matchin' set of panties.

My hands flexed against the handles of the paint cans as I ignored the impulse to ravage her right then and there. Instead, I placed my items beside her as she continued to undress and then lay out a massive drop cloth and transferred everythin' back onto that. Next, the canvas, a huge forty-eight by sixty inch spread I'd been savin' for a landscape of Lake Mead.

It was better served for this.

I squatted to lift the lid of the red paint with my pocket

knife, then the black, and white as I spoke. “Gonna show you just how fuckin’ beautiful you are to me. How worthy.”

She flinched, and I knew I’d hit home with that word.

My girl had a low fuckin’ opinion of herself, thanks to her fuckwad father, Florent, and the loss of so many people in her life. Me included.

My throat burned again, like my heart was on fire, and the only way to put it out was to make this fiercely beautiful woman feel seen.

“It’s body paint,” I muttered as I shucked my shoes and my shirt, decidin’ the jeans could be wrecked, and I didn’t give a shit. “It’ll wash off in water.”

I took Mei’s boots and leathers to the work table and then stalked back toward her, watchin’ the flush seep into her cheeks and spill down her torso.

“Gonna paint you,” I told her. “Then I’m gonna fuck you like I shoulda the first time.”

Before she could say a word, I was haulin’ her up into my arms, cuppin’ her sweet ass in my hands. She automatically wound her legs around my waist and drove her fingers into my hair. Her mouth was open, pantin’, waitin’ for me to claim it.

So I did.

And fuck, but how had I fucked her before without takin’ this sweet, lush mouth.

I ate at her, suckin’ the moans off her tongue, bitin’ into that lower lip ’til it was swollen and poutin’.

Only when she was thrashin’, a wild thing in my arms seekin’ more, did I drop carefully to my knees and lay her back on the drop-clothed floor, her hips still hooked over my lap. Arranged like that, black hair like the halo of a dark angel around her delicate face, I felt my heart come to a complete fuckin’ stop.

She lay there, chest heavin’, tongue trapped between her teeth as I reached for a thick brush and dipped it generously in the red paint. The moment the cool tip touched her skin, she gasped and squirmed.

I pinned a palm on her chest and growled, "Be still."

She froze, only the quickness of her breath and those blown-wide pupils denotin' her struggle.

"Good girl," I practically purred as I traced the brush down over the inside of her left thigh all the way back to her foot, where I painted her toes one by one 'til they curled. "Be still while I worship you."

She shivered hard, bitin' into her lip 'til it bled. I watched her lick it off then decided it wasn't enough, leanin' forward to lick the rent lip with my own tongue.

"Fuckin' delicious," I told her as I pulled away from her chasin' mouth.

She moaned. "You're trying to kill me. You really do still hate me."

I laughed deep in my belly as I traced the inside of her other thigh and down to the opposite foot. "Be good for me, Rocky, and I'll take you as close to death as pleasure can get ya."

Paintin' her was unlike anythin' I'd done before. The livin' canvas of her flawless, pale skin pulled tight over supple muscles and subtle curves. She was perfectly formed right down to the hands I pulled in my lap, the fingers I sucked into my mouth 'til they glistened before I painted those too in red paint. It was harder and harder for her to stay still and obedient as I traced the curves of her waist and the divot of her naval, the swell of her small, sweet tits, round and round in smaller and smaller circles 'til I sucked the peaks into my mouth and finished them off with a dollop of white paint.

At some point, I abandoned the brushes, dippin' my fingers into the paints until they blurred, white and red makin' pinks that streaked the knobs of her spine when I turned her onto her hands and knees before me. Avoidin' her healin' tattoos, I patterned colour over each bone in her rib cage so it looked like

I could see straight through to her heart. A darker colour for the handprints I fixed over the globes of her plump ass before fillin' them in all over with paint. I left one handprint though in carmine red over her throat, my thumbprint at her rapidly beatin' pulse.

Only then did I lean carefully over her back so I didn't smudge the paint and whisper, "Every inch of you is fuckin' gorgeous. Inside. Out. Covered in paint. Covered in cum. Covered every day in my ink like a livin' breathin' fantasy. All of it, any which way, *is mine*. You get that, little dragon?"

Her breath hitched as she realized why I'd painted her all in red and white, makin' her into the red dragon I'd once won for her at the Calgary fair, showin' her what I'd seen beneath her skin all along.

She was a dragon, fierce and beautiful, and I wanted every fuckin' inch of her, even her sharp teeth and hooked claws.

"Yes," she panted as I pressed her carefully to the canvas, her front splayed across the textured, treated cloth. "Your dragon."

She let me manipulate her and that was sexy as fuck too, her obedience and pliancy 'cause she saved those just for me.

Only after I gently peeled her away from the canvas did she surprise me by pushin' me with two painted hands onto my back on the drop cloth. I didn't try to get away as she clambered on top of me, straddlin' my hips with those red and white streaked thighs. When she leaned over me, her hair curtained our faces, tipped at the ends with red, pink, and white.

"If I'm yours, though," she murmured, pausin' to bite my lower lip. "You're mine."

She ground down on the hardness beneath my jeans 'til I hissed and grabbed her hips. Only then, face wreathed in a wicked, gorgeous grin, did she set to work paintin' me too.

She didn't bother with the brushes.

Her clever little fingers dipped in black and white paint to trace the boxed muscles in my abdomen, the long splay of tendons in my neck and thighs. They dragged my jeans off and then my boxers so I was naked beneath her, and then she painted every inch of my front except for my face and groin.

"Mei," I rasped, fistin' her hair, uncarin' about the paint on my hands. "You got two seconds before I got no control left. Use them well."

She grinned and settled between my thighs to lick once, twice, kittenish at the head of my weepin' cock.

And I broke.

I surged to my knees and pressed her to the paint-smeared cloth beneath us. She laughed as I did, tryin' to scramble away, but I held her slick body still and growled at her as I pinned her hips with mine.

"No runnin' now," I warned her. "Not again."

"No," she agreed. "I'm home again."

I tongued the seam of her mouth at the same time my cock caught on the entrance of her wet little cunt, and I thrust inside both simultaneously. Her pussy pulsed around me as I started workin' her open, and her tongue fought mine like the little dragon she was. Nothin' in my life had ever felt as right as havin' her claws in my shoulders and her teeth at my mouth, nibblin' and bitin' like she wanted to eat me whole.

I'd let her, I realized, as I fucked her with long, powerful strokes that rubbed the coarse hair at the root of my dick into her clit. I'd let her chew me into pieces or swallow me whole as long as she stayed with me forever.

"You're mine," I told her, and I wanted it to be an order, but somethin' in me was howlin' and roarin' to hear her say it back.

"Yours," she agreed.

I pinned her hands above her head, leanin' back slightly to watch her tits bounce as I fucked her ever harder.

"You take my cock so fuckin' well," I praised her, watchin' as the words made her shiver and drove her higher. "Always knew you were made to fight, but God, were you made to fuck, too."

My fighter liked to be called a good girl, a pretty little thing.

So I showered her with praised as I reached down with my other hand to play and pluck at her clit. She shuddered harder and harder as my grip grew more unforgivin', my thrusts so powerful she keened on each deep stroke.

"Come all over my cock," I told her. "Let me watch you break apart around me. So fuckin' pretty when you come hard on my dick, Rocky."

Tears squeezed out the corners of her closed eyes as she wrenched her head back on a silent scream and started milkin' me with her convulsions.

"Oh yeah," I grunted, drivin' in to take her higher and higher. "Never seen anythin' more glorious than you takin' every inch of me and lovin' it like this."

"Please," she cried out, still comin', but spiralin' softly back to earth like a feather caught up in a current. "Want to feel you come. Paint me with it."

Lightnin' raced down my spine so hard, I almost blacked out as her words filtered into my brain. My balls tightened, my gut clenched, and seconds later on a groan that was torn from my fuckin' soul, I pulled outta her warm, wet pussy and spilled my seed all over it.

She twitched and moan as each hot splash striped her sensitive folds and when I was finally done, squeezin' out the last drop and smearin' it with my cock head over her clit, she reached down to collect my cum on one finger and brought it to her mouth. She hummed as she licked it off, and even though I'd just spent myself, my cock twitch in a valiant effort to harden again so I could fuck her there too.

Instead, I sat back on my heels, lifted her hips onto my thighs and watched up close as I rubbed my cum into her folds, paintin' her there like I'd painted the rest of her.

When I was done, I leaned over to plant my forearms beside her head and stamped a kiss on her warm, pliant mouth. "There," I proclaimed. "Now, every inch of you is mine."

"In case it wasn't clear, I always was," she said through a smile that was more at peace and lovelier than any expression I'd ever seen before on that exquisite face. "I'd be yours forever, if you asked. Even if you never do, I already am."

CHAPTER THIRTY-NINE

Mei

I LIKED THE PLAN TO TAKE DOWN THE SEVEN SONG TRIAD.

Mostly because I was heavily involved.

It started with Jiang Kuan.

A week after we'd made a deal with White Snake, I used a burner phone to make plans to meet Jiang at our usual spot outside of downtown Vancouver.

Capilano Suspension Bridge Park was the perfect place for a rendezvous because it was always packed with tourists and locals alike. It was in the middle of a swathe of temperant rain forest, the treed canopy dense, second-growth forest with a swift-moving river cutting through it. Over the rushing water, they'd constructed the famous suspension bridge, a narrow ribbon of wood planks and webbed railing that only tempted brave hearts to cross.

I met Jiang, as I always did, smack dab in the middle.

He waited for me, leaning against the railing over the edge

that dropped 230 feet to the Capilano River. I sidled close to him, resting my forearms on the railing to lean over it.

"You don't look scarred from the experience," he started blandly.

But then, that was his way.

That he'd mentioned the beating at all meant he'd been more than concerned about me.

"It could have been worse," I allowed. "They got the jump on me when I was in a deep sleep."

"Ashes Li has scratch marks on his cheek. I believe those *will* scar."

"Good," I said with a little smile that Jiang echoed.

We didn't look at each other, just two people enjoying the expansive view.

"You didn't get in touch. I was worried The Fallen had done something to you," he confessed.

"I told you before, Axe-Man and Cleo wouldn't let them do that."

"Mmm. You told me Cleo wouldn't, but you didn't have such unshakeable belief in Henning Axelsen last time I saw you."

I shrugged one shoulder, but my heart still felt swollen and too large in my chest, suffused as it was with Axe-Man's forgiveness and attention. The last week had passed in an almost drugged state. Days spent with Cleo, mornings at Box n' Burn so Axe-Man and I could start to teach her the basics of self-defence now that her cast was removed, afternoons curled up at the cabin with an assortment of The Fallen babes, playing games, drinking and chatting like we were some kinda sisterhood. Late evenings when Axe-Man came home from work, and all of us would make dinner, sometimes with Lin, too, then watch Cleo's favourite black and white movies together on the hand-drawn leather couch. And the nights. Seven long, wild nights of being Axe-Man's lover.

The best seven nights of my life, bar none.

We'd moved beyond hate-fucking, but there was still a rough edge to the way we came together each night. A kind of desperation like we were making up for lost time or we were running out of it. He seemed insatiably hungry for me now that he'd had a taste, devouring my pussy with his talented mouth for over an hour last night until my cum had soaked the bed and his beard, fucking me so hard I had a patina of bruises, fresh and fading, to add to his inked art on my skin.

I'd never felt so wholly possessed in my lifetime, so seen and desired.

It was everything I'd ever wanted.

So, I didn't even care about the sneaking around.

It made sense to keep our tryst from Cleo. She had so much going on, and it wasn't like her dad and I were...dating.

We were just enjoying an extended reunion now that we were friends again. Exploring the lust years of yearning had turned into needle-point sharpness and Axe-Man's new, gluttonous appreciation for me in his bed.

If it had been more...

If I'd believed he ever could have fallen *in* love with me, maybe I would have told her. Maybe I would have fantasized about it.

But already, this new reality felt too good to be true, more than I'd ever really hoped for. It felt like bad luck to be greedy for more when, for eight years, I'd believed I'd never have anything at all.

Besides, even though Axe-Man had said he'd forgiven me, even so far as to say there was nothing to forgive, I knew in my bones I'd never be worthy of his love that way. Both because I'd hurt him so badly before, and because he'd loved before, a woman much better than me, and I knew I could never replace her.

So, I was happy with him, with her, with the impending

takedown of the Seven Song after years of Kasper hiding in plain sight before me.

And Jiang, frenemy that he was, seemed to sense that.

"I've never seen you like this," he murmured, eyeing me sidelong.

"Hmm?"

"You seem so settled in your skin. Where is the bitter knife of Mei Zhen pressed to my throat?"

I laughed. "I was never that combative, was I?"

He raised a brow in answer.

"Okay, I was. I still am, only now, I'm in a place where I want to believe the best in the people I've chosen to care about."

"Axe-Man and your Cleo."

"Yes, and The Fallen MC as a group. They're good people. They...they're a family. A criminal one, yeah, but I like their values. They'd burn down the world for each other."

"Ah, and you'd burn down the world for your Axelsens."

"Yes, and maybe for you. If you'd ask," I said honestly, twisting to face him, the wind moving the hair off my face so I could see him clearly. He was so beautiful, long and lean and cut into hard angles like the ridges of a sword. "Would you ask me, though, *dai lo*?"

Jiang considered me before flipping over to lean his back and elbows on the bridge railing. "Maybe."

"And if I asked for the same?"

He pursed his lips slightly, looking into the forest as if it held answers. The rushing of the river helped conceal our words, the packs of tourists drifting over the swaying bridge obscured our purpose, but I could see him very clearly in that moment. Alone even in his own triad, kept separate by something that shouldn't have ostracized him. I ached a little for him, as I always did, and hoped fervently that he'd make the right choice today.

"I told Kasper you were loyal," he said eventually. "He didn't seem to believe me, but he said a ring would make him feel more comfortable."

I watched, stricken, as he fished into his pocket for a black velvet jewelry box and flipped it out to reveal a huge emerald-cut diamond ring.

Unbidden, I laughed. "Jesus, Jiang, put that away before you blind someone."

Or worse, Axe-Man saw it from his hiding spot on the other end of the bridge and came storming over. A little part of me thrilled to see a potential display of jealousy, but I knew it couldn't happen or it would blow up our whole plan.

Jiang frowned at me but pocketed the ring. "Is the idea of marrying me so unpalatable?" he asked stiffly.

"Yes," I said, but my mouth softened. "You're gay, and for better or worse, I've been in love with Axe-Man my whole life. We are not a good match, and you know it."

He scowled but didn't argue.

"Save a proposal for someone you love, Jiang."

He scoffed as if finding that someone was an impossibility.

"Aren't you sick of this? This inaction, this dishonesty? I know I am. I want to change things for both of us. I want the chance for us both to find peace. If I had a way to do that, would you help me, big brother?"

His gaze shifted over a passing crowd of high school students before he answered. "If I could. But I live in the real world, Mei, and sometimes, you do not."

"I'm going to kill Kasper," I told him baldly and watched him flinch like the words were throwing stars aimed at his face. "I'm going to kill him because, whether you knew it or not, and I believe you didn't, he ordered the hit on Kate. He did it because he loved her, and I think after she betrayed him by loving White Snake instead, he started his vendetta against White Snake. It was the reason he moved to Vancouver to fight with the Red Dragons, the reason, maybe, behind his general prejudice against white people. Does the timing sound right for that?"

I watched Jiang's eyes shutter.

"I think he killed Eero because if he couldn't have happiness, he didn't want you to have it. Misery bonds people, and even though you lost your love to Kasper, it still brought you closer to him. You've had nothing to live for ever since, but him. What if I could give you something of your own and the only price you had to pay was giving him up?"

"Don't speak to me of this," he muttered, making to move away.

I snagged the sleeve of his cashmere jacket. "Speaking of it won't change it. I'm going to take my pound of flesh because I deserve it, Axe-Man and Cleo deserve it, Kate deserves it, and I believe, so do you and Eero."

"Don't speak of him, either," he whispered, his voice raw, hand trembling as he fished a cigarette out of the pack in his pocket.

"I'm sorry, J, I'm so sorry for what happened. Let me help make it right. If you help us, you could step into the vaccum and take over Seven Song."

He tried to light his cancer stick three times before it caught. "No. You think he doesn't care about me, but he spared you, didn't he? If you meant less to me, he would have killed you that night at Purgatory."

"It wasn't because you loved me. It was because if he killed me, he'd probably have to kill you so you wouldn't flip on him. Taking two lovers from someone doesn't exactly inspire loyalty. Don't be loyal to a fault now, Jiang. Let us help each other like we always said we would."

"No," he said slowly, like he didn't want to. "I can't. He's my brother. He loves me, I know it, and I love him. He's all the family I have here."

"Sometimes, you get to choose your family," I said, sliding

my fingers down his sleeve into his hand to twine them together. "I thought I'd be alone the rest of my life after my ma died and Florent kept me from the Axelsens. Then you showed up, and now, I might have a chance to be part of a family that defines what it means to have each other's backs."

"I sought you out for selfish reasons," he reminded me.

I shrugged. "It led to the same result, though, didn't it?"

He squeezed my hand before letting me go. "If you go after him, just know I will not take sides."

"You won't leave here and go straight to him?"

He sighed, turning to me fully for the first time. I let him take my arms in a firm grip and shake me slightly. "You are my *meimei*. My little sister as he is my big brother. I won't hurt either of you. Do what you will, what I always have known you will do and what I *want* you to do even if I cannot help. I won't stop you. Besides, you know revenge isn't frowned upon in China the way it is here. Confucius himself said 'One should not live under the same Heaven with the enemy.' Kasper has made himself your enemy, and you must do what you think is right. The woman you are, I always knew this day would come."

"So, you did know he'd killed Kate?" I asked, trying to hide the ache of betrayal in my voice as I recoiled.

"No, of course not. But I wondered it was only a matter of time before he went after The Fallen again and you'd not let any harm come to the Axelsens."

"That's fair," I said, reaching up to pat his cheek. "I can respect where you're coming from, even if I wish you'd help me. For both our sakes. Unfortunately, I can't take the risk. I'm sorry, J, but you'll have to come with me."

I glimpsed his startled expression for only a moment before he turned his head to look at one end of the bridge and then the other. Axe-Man stood sentry at the left and Wrath at the right.

When he looked back at me, I already had the syringe raised and pressed it into the thin skin of his neck.

"I love you," I told him in Cantonese as he swayed and fell into the railing. I tossed his arm over my shoulder like he was my boyfriend and we were shuffling along in a romantic stroll toward Axe-Man. "I promise, when I'm done, both our worlds will be a better place."

WE USED JIANG'S PHONE, ENCRYPTED TO A FACIAL SCAN, TO SET up the meet at a laundromat with a businessman who ran an import export business between China and Canada. We knew this was the concept both because The Fallen had been running surveillance on the triad and because Curtains was a real genius with tech, and he hacked into Jiang's phone when we brought him back to the compound.

Axe-Man didn't like it, but I had to go alone. The meet always took place in a deserted parking lot either early in the morning or late at night and the two contacts were alone. The fact that I was a woman could be a problem, because the triad was traditionally an all-male syndicate, but I knew Jiang had changed that in recent years, inducting more females into the fold. Also, one of the most famous American triad members in recent years was Sister Ping, a Snakehead who'd smuggled hundreds of people through Manhattan's Chinatown.

Hopefully, my contact would raise an eyebrow, but let it be.

I dressed the part, too.

This, Axe-Man liked and didn't like in equal turn.

When I'd walked into the living room before we left for the clubhouse, he'd taken one look at me and scowled. Cleo had laughed in delight and clapped her hands as she took me in.

"You look amazing," she crowed.

I tugged at the short hem of the black sheath dress one of the Fallen babes, Tayline, had lent me because we were the same size. It was classy, made of rich velvet with a little belt to highlight my waist. Paired with black Louboutins I usually wore out with Jiang and big hair Lin had taken half an hour to tease into place, I looked like someone who might frequent the beautiful Lake Edge Casino near Entrance.

The second we got into Axe-Man's Jeep, he'd clamped a hand around my thigh and tugged me across the console into his lap so he could lay claim to my mouth. By the time we pulled apart, my lipstick was eaten off, my hair was irrevocably tousled by his big hands and there was a hickey high on my neck under my ear. Axe-Man pressed the burgeoning bruise with his thumb and grunted in satisfaction.

"Heathen," I'd teased, but fuck if it didn't feel good to experience him like this.

"Your heathen," he growled, nipping at my bottom lip. "Don't let any of those motherfuckers get too close or you put them down, yeah?"

"Oh yeah," I agreed, playing with the ridiculously soft hair in his beard just because I was allowed the intimacy, and holy shit, did that feel amazing.

"And when you get done with this shit, I'm gonna eat you out while you sit on my face in this dress."

"Aye aye, sir," I said, a little breathy because, well, I'd always wondered but never could have known Axe-Man would be so deliciously filthy.

Now, we were a block away from the meet parked in front of a Subway. I was in a black van with "Angelwood Produce" embossed on the outside. Within, Curtains sat on an overturned bucket, fingers flying on the keyboard as he enabled the tracking devices they'd put in the duffle bag of cash I was given.

"You're sure they'll only speak Cantonese?" Bat asked from beside him.

The two of them, Axe-Man, Zeus, and Priest were all crowded into the tiny space going over the final details. The rest of the brothers were at the clubhouse waiting for orders to roll out.

"Seven Song is almost purely a Cantonese gang," I told him as I adjusted the thigh holster for my knife. "And there are a lot of second, and third generation members, too, who might only speak English. It isn't like the old days."

"We've been watchin' 'em, and they mostly speak Cantonese," Curtains confirmed, running a hand through his copper hair so it stood on end. "Your contact's name is Wang Wei, does that mean anything to you?"

"One of the most famous poets in Chinese history. It just means they're using famous Chinese people or maybe literary references as code names," I mused. "I'll go in as Wu Zetian."

Axe-Man grinned at me. "Fittin'."

I shrugged and batted my lashes.

"Who's that?" Curtains asked.

"The only woman to ever rule China as a lone Empress. The original badass," Axe-Man responded.

Zeus chuckled. "Well, you got the run'a this show, Blossom. You meet the mark, exchange the money, and see if he'll take you into Lake Edge. Don't push too hard. He objects, we got the trackers in the bundles of twenties, and we can track 'im and the cash once he leaves. No use puttin' yourself in danger or blowin' the whole thing by bein' too pushy."

"Oh, he'll want her company," Axe-Man muttered darkly, arms crossed and eyes scouring my form.

"Not gonna take that bet," Bat murmured.

"You ready?" Zeus asked, handing over the hockey bag filled with one million dollars in cash.

I didn't ask where he'd gotten his hands on that much money. They were an outlaw biker gang that dominated the marijuana industry in North America and ran guns in a country with strict laws that made it hard to obtain them legally. I had no doubt they were rich as hell and didn't keep all their ill-begotten gains in a bank like normal civilians.

I hefted the heavy strap over my shoulder and went to the door, Priest pulling it open for me.

"You so much as flinch, I'll be there," he promised quietly, much to my surprise.

I looked into his face and saw the almost joyful anticipation there. He wanted the mark to come at me just for a chance to exact violence on him. A little shiver tore down my spine, and I thought, not for the first time, that Bea was much more of a badass than me if she'd somehow won the heart of Priest McKenna and survived his brand of affection.

I nodded back at him in thanks and hopped out of the van.

Axe-Man caught my hand before I could walk over to the unmarked SUV I was borrowing for the meet.

"First sign of trouble, you're outta there," he ordered, his face creased with troubled thoughts he didn't try to hide from me. "Last time we tried to corner these fuckers, they took two years of my life and a finger from me. Won't let them have you, ya hear?"

We'd had another rip-roaring fight about my involvement last night, but in the end, Axe-Man had given in at the reminder that I had just as much skin in this game as he did.

And I wasn't some damsel in distress like Kate had been. I'd been training in martial arts my whole life to hone myself into a weapon, and I'd spent the last eight years on the fringe of the triad.

I could handle myself.

It didn't mean I was immune to his concern. In fact, it felt like a direct hit of sunshine to know he was near beside himself with worry.

I wrapped my fingers around his and squeezed. "Trust me."

He swallowed thickly. "I do."

"This time, we've got each other's backs. Today is the day we put the motherfucking Seven Song triad six feet beneath the earth. And Axe-Man? I've got *vigorous* plans to celebrate afterward."

His expression softened into that tiny smile he had just for me. "I look forward to it."

Before I could turn to go, he was tugging on my hand again, fixing something around my wrist I couldn't see until it was secured there. A golden bracelet shaped like a dragon winked at me in the yellow light of the streetlamps in the parking lot.

I looked up at Axe-Man with my heart beating too hard in my throat.

"It's a tracker," he explained, voice rough with emotion that also shone from his turquoise eyes. "Not losin' you again."

Then ask me to stay, I wanted to say, *ask me to be your Old Lady, and I won't let anything in the world take me from your side again.*

But he didn't ask, and I didn't beg.

For now, this symbol and his concern were enough to satisfy my voracious heart.

With one last smile, I let go of his hand and walked to the car to get the show on the road.

I wasn't nervous as I drove the last block to meet the mark. I was *excited*, vibrating with anticipation that thrummed through every molecule.

People who said they were above revenge were incomprehensible to me. Nothing was more satisfying than working hard to right the wrongs done to you and yours. It was the sweetest kind of effort and reward.

And today, I'd finally taste it.

I parked in front of the dilapidated laundromat and turned off the ignition. It only took two minutes for a car, a nondescript black sedan, to pull up beside me.

Sucking in a deep breath, I opened the door, grabbed the bag of Fallen cash, and rounded my vehicle to meet the mark halfway.

I didn't recognize him, but then, I wasn't expecting to. He was someone who did business in Vancouver and didn't run in my circles.

What did surprise me was his greeting.

He didn't speak.

Instead, he raised his right hand and formed it into a series of gestures.

Adrenaline burst through my veins and thundered through my heart.

It was a series of *mudras*, originally Buddhist hand signals that Chinese crime syndicates had claimed and bastardized for their own purposes decades ago. I wasn't a master of them, by any means, but I had seen Jiang do that exact series of movements a few times before.

It was the way to identify a fellow 49er if you were worried someone might be wired.

I lifted my right hand and mimicked his gestures.

The small gentleman grinned at me, revealing one gold tooth in his wide mouth. "How much?"

"One million." I lifted the bag between us, but before I could hand it over, movement in my periphery stalled me.

The thud of motorcycle boots walking toward me and the jangle of a wallet chain. I turned my head to see a weathered biker stalk toward us from behind a truck and lost my breath as surprise shot through me.

Because I knew this biker and he wasn't one of The Fallen.

Or, at least, he hadn't been in eight years.

"My security," my contact introduced with a wave of his hand. "He follows me to the casino so there are no problems."

I blinked dumbly at Johnny "Cedar" Hopper as my heart lodged in my throat and threatened to suffocate me. Would he give me up? Did he even know my relationship to the triad? Before or after Kasper had labelled me a traitor?

And what the *fuck* was he doing here now playing security for Seven Song triad?

Last I'd known, the mother chapter of The Fallen had purged the Calgary chapter of everyone involved in Axe-Man's betrayal and put the club under new leadership. The old members had been stripped of their Fallen tatts and sent packing.

Cedar, for his part, did not seem surprised to me. He didn't seem fazed by anything about the situation.

"I was hoping," I said after a moment, deciding to focus on the mark again, "to accompany you to the casino. It's my first time funneling this much money, and if I'm to bring this much regularly, I'd like to make sure it's in good hands."

He hesitated, sharing a look with Cedar.

"The Vanguard himself assured me it would be possible," I pressed, name-dropping Jiang, who was currently being held at The Fallen compound.

Wang Wei narrowed his gaze at me then watched as I bounced the bag in my grip, illustrating the weight of the cash inside.

"Fine," he decided finally. "You may come with me."

I tried not to grin too hard and also to ignore the way Cedar studied me.

"Lead the way."

Lake Edge Casino was basically brand new. The government had given the local Indigenous people permission to build and operate a casino five years ago, and two years of fast-track construction and permits later, Lake Edge was born. It was built all in native timber—huge beams and entire treated logs made it look like an enormous, elevated cabin.

I'd never been inside, but I could see immediately it was popular.

Wang Wei had divided the cash into two, taking five hundred thousand in cash into the casino with plans to launder the rest through other avenues.

We were greeted at the door by the pit boss, a man of Asian descent who spoke to us in flawless Cantonese. He led us to a high roller poker table in the back of the huge main floor, leaving us for a moment only to return with glasses of champagne.

Clearly, he was on the take.

Cedar stood behind my chair when I sat beside Wang Wei at the table. It made unease crawl down my spine like a collection of tiny spiders.

"You are my lucky lady," Wang declared to the table and then proceeded to lose about fifty thousand dollars of my money.

"Don't tense," Cedar whispered into my arm after a particularly alarming loss. "This is how it works. He loses so he doesn't arouse much suspicion at the table or with the dealers and managers who aren't on Seven Song's take."

"How do you know this?" I murmured back, pretending to fix my earring so I could tuck my chin to my shoulder away from Wang.

A little, bitter chuckle. "A man's gotta make his way in the world somehow, Mei Zhen. Not everyone lands on their feet like Axe."

"So you work for the triad now?"

He paused, then said, "Contract work."

That was curious and definitely demanded answers, but he was keeping my secret so I decided not to press. Obviously, he knew Axe-Man was a member of the Entrance chapter, too, and he hadn't made any moves against him. Maybe he wasn't driven by revenge like me.

"Wasn't Axe-Man who did this," Cedar muttered, angling his body to pull up his shirt sleeve and show me the warped, melted skin over his delt where, presumably, his Fallen MC tattoo had been burnt off. "I made my bed, I'm lyin' in it."

"You're not going to blow the whistle on me?" I whispered, then moaned loudly with Wang when he lost ten grand in one hand.

"You're not my enemy," he said, but he did it in a way that implied he had one and I might even know them.

I hummed in response and turned my attention back to the game.

Wang cashed out after losing way too much money, but no one batted an eye at handing over four hundred and fifty thousand dollars of casino washed cash to a man with a fake ID who had a history of performing this exact same thing multiple times a quarter.

The pit boss jerked his chin up at Wang as we left.

"Well," he said, a happy little smile on his face as we went back to his car in the lot. "I assume you are pleased with our protocol?"

"Oh," I purred as I followed him into the back seat and slid close to him, moving my hand to his thigh to trail it up his torso to his cheek like I was going to kiss him. His eyes were wide and black with surprise and desire. "I like it *very* much, Mr. Wang Wei."

I leaned closer, whispering my lips over his soft jawline as Cedar started the car and pulled into the street.

"But I'm surprised you don't know 'poverty begins with the pursuit of greed,'" I whispered an inch above his open, panting mouth, quoting Wang Wei himself.

He made a noise of confusion a moment before I was on him, my legs locked around his torso and my arms in a lock around his neck. He scrambled desperately, kicking out his legs, scratching at my arms unsuccessfully through my coat. I held tight, stronger than I looked, much stronger than this small, doughy money pusher.

It only took ten seconds to knock him out in the sleeper choke.

Cedar met my gaze in the rearview mirror without blinking. "What's your plan now?"

I pulled the knife from my thigh holster below his eyeline and then lunged forward like the strike of a snake to lodge the blade under his throat.

"Be a doll and take me to the drop-off, won't you, Cedar?"

CHAPTER FORTY

Axe-Man

We followed Mei's tracker to Vancouver's thrivin' Chinatown to the door of a place I'd never frequented before, but knew of intimately from another time.

A laugh like a cough. "Fuck me."

The building was called the Golden Door, just as the Inn in Calgary's Chinatown had been named where I once met Jiang to discuss partnerin' against our more corrupt leaders.

"You ready for this?" Bat asked me as he adjusted the straps on his flak vest tighter. "Mei's the point of the spear on this."

"You think she isn't capable, then you don't know her," I informed him calmly, even though fear lodged like splinters beneath my nails. "Watched her near cut a man in half when she was seventeen. I'm sure eight years has taught her to do much worse."

"Not what I meant," Bat corrected. "This is the culmination of years of anger and bloodlust for you. You think you can handle takin' them down without implicatin' yourself? You need jail time like you need a bullet in the head."

"Hey!" Boner protested, knockin' on wood to null the jinx.

"I'll be good," I promised, but I got where he was comin' from.

I was excited like an Olympic athlete before their event, years of trainin' and eagerness about to culminate in an episode that would mean either success or failure. Adrenaline burned through me like premium fuel, and I was reminded of myself at eighteen, gettin' ready to leave the outpost to patrol the local village where insurgents often lay in wait. It was anticipation that made your teeth ache, but if you knew how to harness it, it was powerful as fuck.

Across the street at the red-painted door of the Golden Door Inn, Mei appeared comin' outta the back seat of a black sedan holdin' a Louis Vuitton duffle I assumed was filled with clean cash from the casino.

Seconds later, a familiar figure got outta the driver's seat and strolled around to join Mei on the pavement.

"Fuck me," I cursed, shocked to see Cedar standin' there.

Bat stilled beside me like he'd been frozen atom by atom.

"You good?" Dane murmured to him, but Bat didn't bat an eye.

"What the fuck is he doin' with the triad?" Zeus asked rhetorically. "Fuck, he hasn't blown her cover yet."

"He was my best friend once," I said slowly, tryin' to work it out. "It's possible he'd protect Mei like he did even after he betrayed me back in Calgary."

"You still wanna go through with this, now?" Z asked, givin' me lead to make the decision 'cause it was my girl on the line.

I swallowed thickly. "Let's give her ten minutes. If she can get people outta the building, we head in as planned."

Curtains had pulled up the plans for the building on his tablet so we'd have an overview of what we were walkin' into even though we knew they would've made extensive changes. This was, after all, one of the biggest criminal banks in the province and not the quaint, run-down Chinatown inn it appeared to be on the outside.

We waited for what felt like hours after Mei and Cedar entered the building. My pulse was poundin' so hard, it was like a percussion played against my skull. I had faith in my Rocky to handle herself, but sendin' her into enemy territory with a fuckin' turncoat was more than my blood pressure could stand.

Finally, the distant sound of a fire alarm started to blare.

Zeus and I shared a wolfish grin.

The doors burst open, and the business-attired lobby personnel flooded out into the street with smoke curlin' around their bodies, dissipatin' in the fierce spring wind. We waited a minute more, and the bees from deeper in the hive emerged, men in dark suits with guns and swords on their hips.

"Ready, brothers?" Zeus asked, vicious excitement in his tone.

A chorus of grunts in agreement and we opened the slidin' door of the van to pour out into the brick alleyway across the street. Behind the Inn, another group of brothers were gettin' off their bikes and headin' in around the back.

We weren't wearin' our cuts, clad in generic black clothes so we fit in well with the crowd of panicked employees. It was easy to slip inside against the tide of people fleein'.

Mei'd managed to set a real blaze inside, usin' a match to set fire to the curtains along the side wall of the lobby. The air was already dark and acrid with smoke, so I pulled my black bandana over my mouth and nose and lowered the rim of my toque farther over my eyes. Bat, Dane, Zeus, and I were the tip of the spear, headin' toward the back of the lobby without falterin' while King, Wrath, and Priest secured the lobby.

We found the staircase beside the elevator and hustled down the stairs. The smoke hadn't made it through the fire door, which meant the level below us would probably be unaware of the panic above them.

Especially because the stairwell was soundproof with only the *thwack* of our motorcycle boots echoin' off the white walls.

When we reached the bottom, two flights down, a keypad was beside the door.

We'd figured as much, so we weren't deterred.

I covered my ears as Zeus shot a round of bullets into the wall beside the door.

Seconds later, it swung open with a mechanical whir, and two men stepped swiftly into the stairwell.

Bat shot one of them in the head, and the man collapsed soundless to the ground.

I kicked the other in the side of the knee. The crack of bone was loud in the muffled silence as was his ensuin' scream. I used the butt of my axe handle to hit him in the temple.

He fell with a *splat* to the ground beside his buddy.

Zeus waited for us with his fingers just wedged inside the open door and then grinned as he shoved it open. Bat held it from between the wall and the door while Zeus pressed himself to the wall on the opposite side of the door.

I slid to the ground with my gun raised, ready to fire inside.

Only no one was there to greet us.

Instead, the vast underground warehouse was filled with men and women in their underclothes sittin' at rows of plastic tables countin' money in electronic counters and dividin' it into laundry bags placed in huge rollin' baskets bein' shuttled to the back of the room where an enormous door to a safe was closed, but ready to receive the illicit money bein' handled by, most likely, illegal immigrants smuggled into the country and indebted to the triad.

No one seemed to realize they'd been breached.

A few 49ers patrolled the outside of the room on the right and left, and the entrances at those walls, but other than the two soliders we'd taken out, we had free entry to the inner workings of the bank.

Z, Bat, and I shared an incredulous look and moved slowly into the room, guns at the ready. Bat stayed near the door, holdin' it for the brothers I could just hear thuddin' down the stairs after us.

Across the room, I spotted Nova's dark head appear at the mouth of another entrance.

Above the vault in a glass room that overlooked the workers, I recognized the face of Ashes Li, Kang Li's little brother, and the Red Pole of the triad. The same man who'd taken his fists to Mei in her room at Purgatory Motel. Even from a distance, I could see the healing scratch marks left over from Mei's struggle.

Just as we were about to move farther into the room, I noticed a flash of black near the stairs to the room and saw Mei slink up the metal treads to the room filled with upper level triad members.

"Fuck," I cursed, drawin' Z's attention. "To Mei," I said with a jerk of my chin.

His brow lowered on a fierce scowl and he *moved.*

I was reminded that even though Zeus had never been to war, he knew how to move like a fuckin' ghost, big body fluid and light as he swept low between the tables on his way to the patrolman on the left side of the room.

I went the other way round, creepin' up on a 49er flirtin' with a girl in a sweat-damp undershirt. I held my finger to my mouth as I stood to my full height behind him, bettin' she wouldn't breathe a word, and then I snapped his neck.

I helped him to the floor so he didn't make a noise.

"Thank you," the girl, not more than fifteen at most, whispered to me.

I nodded and moved along.

Zeus had already taken out the other man in this section without drawin' notice, but across the room, Wrath had engaged in a fistfight with someone, knockin' him into one of the tables. Cash went flyin', and the workers screamed, fleein' the brutality of the fight.

Nova was there in a second to help, but Zeus and I kept movin' forward, runnin' straight out to the room above the vault, when a gunshot rang out through the space. I looked up to see a body hit the glass, smearin' blood across the pane as it fell to the ground.

Fear rose in my throat, but I swallowed it down.

A young woman threw herself at me, cryin' out for help in Cantonese. I gently wrenched her off me, assurin' her we'd help.

But first I had to get to Rocky.

She'd gone up the opposite staircase, and I hadn't seen her, or Cedar, since.

I took the steps two at a time, already swingin' my axe at the door before I'd even hit the landin'. Zeus was at my back as I yanked it open by the handle, firin' over my shoulder at a 49er who leveled his gun at me. He fell to the ground with a yelp, shot through the shoulder, his gun dropped uselessly to the ground.

We stepped into the room, and I took out the man I recognized as the old White Paper Fan from Calgary. The bullet to the belly didn't stop him from firin' at me, but I dropped to my knees and took out one of his with another bullet. He collapsed to the ground with a shriek, gun skitterin' across the floor. I picked it up and shoved it into my waistband before whirlin' around to face the rest of the room.

Zeus was breakin' the arm of a man who'd tried to stab him, and at the other entrance, Priest burst through the door, usin' a dead body as a shield.

Mei was movin' in a flurry at the front of the room, but before I could go to her, someone rushed me in my periphery. I lunged outta the way, the blade aimed at my gut, glancin' off my flak vest and thinly slicin' my forearm.

I spun around to face Ashes Li and grinned, my teeth bared. "I was hopin' you'd be here. Remember me? I killed your brother 'cause he murdered my wife."

He cursed at me in Cantonese as he came at me in a flurry of martial art moves, swift and fierce. I was too big for that kinda movement, but I used the long handle of my axe to block his strikes until he exhausted himself. He got few hits in, but the flak vest blocked the worst of the impact.

"I was there, too," he taunted me. "I delivered the final blow and watched as the blood left her body."

He was hopin' I'd make a mistake in my rage. But I was forty years old and a vet, not some wet-behind-the-ears prospect who could be goaded into gettin' himself killed.

I waited until Ashes pulled back to make another cut with his *dao* sword and then lifted my gun in my non-dominant hand. He tried to dodge the implied bullet just like I thought he would. His feint to the left cost him his life. 'Cause in an instant, I dropped my gun and fisted my left hand around the axe in my right, swingin' it with all my might at Ashes.

The thud of connection vibrated down my arms almost painfully.

The blade had connected in that tender junction between neck and shoulder where I most loved to bite my mark in to Mei. Ashes swayed, caught by the momentum of the strike, in shock and uncomprehendin' of the life-endin' blow I'd dealt him.

If I'd been a different kinda man––a better one––I would've wrenched the axe out and let him bleed out all over the floor. A slow but relatively painless death.

He didn't deserve that.

Not after Kate.

Not after he'd taken his hands to Mei.

So I stalked forward, kicked out his legs so he sank to the floor, and then I caught him by the handle of the axe so he stayed upright on his knees. Then, I planted a foot in his sternum, pried the blade from his neck with a bloody, squelchin' *suck*, and brought it down again on the same spot.

The axe was too small for a proper beheadin', but I didn't care about that. The next swing killed Ashes in one decisive fell, levelin' him broken like a damaged toy on the ground.

"For Kate, you motherfucker," I cursed as I pulled my axe free again.

The chaos had stilled around us, and I looked up suddenly, searchin' for Mei amid the carnage.

When I found her, I let out a bark of shocked laughter.

She was sittin' on the table the triad members had been meetin' at, sippin' from a glass of leftover sake with two dead bodies on either side of her, both their necks obviously broken.

"A little messy," she noted dryly, takin' in my blood-splattered body and drippin' axe with a small smile. "But now I know why they call you Axe-Man."

I laughed again, shocked to find myself enjoyin' a moment with Rocky in the aftermath of battle even though I shouldn't've been.

This was my fighter, my Rocky girl.

I caught sight of Priest up noddin' at her in respect as he cleaned his wicked knife on his tee and fought the inappropriate urge not to laugh again.

Instead, I stalked over the bodies to Mei and caught her up in my arms, kissin' that smug smile off her mouth. "You're somethin' else, little dragon."

She grinned back at me, wipin' a droplet of blood off my cheek with a little wrinkle in her nose. "You get home and cleaned up, I'll show you just what I am."

CHAPTER FORTY-ONE

Mei

THERE WERE ONE HUNDRED AND ELEVEN ILLEGAL IMMIGRANTS being kept in the underground facility of the Golden Door Inn. Some of them were as young as eleven, some as old as their late eighties. All smuggled from China with the promise of some kind of Canadian dream. Only, they hadn't had enough money to pay the premium prices of the Seven Song triad, so they'd been indentured by the syndicate into working in their underground bank.

I tried my best to deal with them, speaking rapid-fire Cantonese as I sought to soothe and reassure them, while the club dealt with all the rest.

King, Nova, and Dane were in charge of the front of the house. They'd put out the fire and reassured the workers before the fire trucks came. While they dealt with upstairs, below stairs, unbeknownst to the cops and firefighters, the most notorious MC in the country were at work cleaning their weapons, tending to their few cuts and scrapes, and figuring out the best way to steal half of the Seven Song triad's illegal money.

"We can't take it out on the back of our fuckin' bikes," Wrath grunted. "C'mon, be real, Boner."

"I am," he countered. "We got saddlebags, backpacks, pockets." He put both hands in his hoodie pocket and bulged it out in an approximation of how much money he could fit in it. "I could get ten grand in here alone."

Before Wrath could growl something at him, Axe-Man stepped in calmly. "It's not the worst idea"—he held up a hand to stop Wrath—"'cause it's our only fuckin' option. We don't have time to figure somethin' better out. Kasper wasn't fuckin' here, and he's gonna get wind of this eventually, even though we took care of the affiliated members. You think the girls workin' upstairs don't know who they work for? They'll call it in any minute if they haven't already."

"He's right," Zeus verified. "We wanna take a cut, we gotta get a move on."

"Especially 'cause we don't know where that motherfucker Cedar went," Axe-Man muttered, still brooding over why Cedar would've helped me and why he would've contracted with the triad.

It seemed pretty obvious to me that Cedar had no other option but to help Seven Song after he'd been excommunicated from The Fallen, but I knew Axe-Man wouldn't let it go until he had more concrete answers.

"It's gonna bring what's left of the triad down on our fuckin' heads," Bat argued. "You wanna buy that trouble?"

"What triad?" Priest deadpanned, his cold gaze shifting over the dead gangsters they'd sat in seats at the table like a macabre meeting of the dead. They'd all had numbers of executive members of the triad inked into their necks.

The only two missing were Jiang, who was secured at the clubhouse, and Kasper, whereabouts unknown, unfortunately.

"This kinda outfit doesn't just disappear," Dane said, backing Bat up.

"That's true," I said, stepping into their little grouping even though I had no real right to. "That's why we took Jiang. He didn't want an active part in hurting his syndicate or his brother, but his brother killed his lover and threatened to do the same to him just for his sexuality. And he's loyal to me. I think, if we let him take charge of what's left, we could get the triad out of Entrance and make a kind of truce."

Axe-Man slung an arm around my shoulders and tucked me into his side. It was a physical show of support and pride that warmed me through to my bones.

"Even if we take half this cash?" Kodiak asked with brows raised.

"Even then," I said. "Your cut for killing the king and installing the prince."

"We haven't killed the king yet," Axe-Man growled.

"We will," I promised.

He grinned at me, a wide, wolfish expression full of teeth that should have been frightening but was wildly thrilling instead.

I couldn't wait to get home and take out the rest of the adrenaline buzzing through my veins on him.

"Okay, get movin'," Zeus ordered. "Take as much as you can carry and fill a few bags. Not too many, we don't need anyone wonderin' what the fuck is in the laundry bags. Curtains, can you check for security cams in the area and corrupt the footage?"

"I'll see. If it's a closed circuit, we might need to get in there personally."

"Not a problem." Dane grinned.

"And what about them?" I asked Zeus as the brothers

started mobilizing. "We can't just leave them here to keep working for the triad."

Zeus cut his silver gaze over the terrified groups of immigrants and sighed. "Fuck, havin' a heart's a fuckin' nuisance."

Axe-Man grunted his agreement but smiled down at me in secret comradery.

I loved him then so much it was hard not to shout down the basement with it.

"We'll call in an anonymous tip after we're clear."

"That won't work. We don't want the RCMP trollin' this place for prints and takin' the rest of the triad money under control if we don't want bad blood," Axe-Man pointed out.

"I have an idea," I suggested with a pleasant smile.

Zeus and Axe-Man both sighed.

Two hours later, long after The Fallen MC had vacated the premises, two of the women working the front desk opened the fire door to the stairwell and let one hundred and eleven Chinese immigrants file through the late-night lobby into two waiting school buses Curtains and Boner had appropriated from a local lot for a few hours. They were waiting outside of the Vancouver Central Legal Aid office when it opened at nine o'clock the next morning.

"FUCKIN' MAGNIFICENT," AXE-MAN GROWLED AS HE CARRIED ME into his bedroom and shut the door with his foot before pressing me up against the wall to bite and kiss at my neck. "You're fuckin' glorious, Rocky."

"And you need a shower," I pointed out even as I canted my neck to give him better access and fisted my hands in his tangled waves.

"You don't like me dirty?" he rumbled, and the vibration against my throat made my toes curl. "'Cause I've unlocked a new fuckin' kink apparently."

"Oh yeah?" I asked breathlessly as he carried me into the adjoining bathroom and straight into the shower.

I squealed when he turned on the water without moving us out of the spray, both of us still in our clothes straight down to our socks.

"Yeah," he said against my mouth before biting at my lower lip then soothing the sting with a swipe of his tongue. "You in a little dress kickin' ass."

My laughter turned into a moan as he slid his mouth down my chin and neck, licking up the water droplets until he reached the ruined wet velvet of my dress. He dropped me so suddenly, I almost lost my balance, but he caught me before I could falter, pressing me up against the cold shower wall, so I hissed. The zipper was loud in the tiled shower as he undid it, trailing a finger down my spine as it was exposed inch by inch.

"Axe-Man," I said on a shiver. "Don't tease me right now."

"Call me Henning," he demanded. "And I'm gonna fuckin' devour you, Rocky. Don't worry."

The lust that had lain coiled in my gut since I'd seen him dispatch men with the casual competency of a seasoned warrior surged through me. Maybe I was a different kind of girl, but knowing I had a predator dropping to his knees behind me, ready to turn that big body into a tool for my pleasure, was the headiest thing I'd ever experienced.

The dress fell with a wet smack to the tiles. A moment later, Axe-Man's hands were on my ass, plumping the cheeks, slapping one and then the other.

"What're you doing?" I asked even though I didn't really care.

As far as I was concerned, he could do anything he wanted to me, and I'd probably love it.

"Admirin'," he said a moment before he spread my cheeks and licked me from my pussy to my asshole.

I shivered and groaned, throwing my head back as I canted my hips.

"That's a girl," he murmured before diving in like a starving man at feast.

He was ravenous, sucking at my pussy lips, fucking me with his tongue, circling my rim again and again before piercing it with his tongue in a way that made my knees give out. Thankfully, his big hands propped me up, and he only growled into my pussy, eating me with even more vigor. I was muttering his name over and over as he added one finger and then two into my achingly empty channel. I reached back to clutch at his hair and haul him tighter to my folds, loving the scrape of his beard on my inner thighs in contrast to his soft, wet, wicked tongue and lips.

Just when I thought I would spiral into the abysses, Axe-Man bit the inside of my thigh and circled his thumb once over my asshole before sinking it smoothly inside.

"Henning," I shouted, slamming the tiled wall with my fist as I came apart around his tongue and fingers, sliding on the wet floor as my knees gave way, and he was forced to pin me to the wall as he fucked me through my orgasm.

"Holy shit," I panted when I found my voice again.

Axe-Man surged to his feet, absolutely drenched, his tee

plastered to every defined, bulky, and delicious inch of him, his hair gone to flaxen gold in the wet.

He was like something from ancient times, a Viking marauder come to plunder me. And I was only too willing to surrender.

I leapt into his arms the moment he stepped toward me, locking my legs around his waist so I could have my hands to wrench his tee over his head. Axe-Man held him, shucking it to the ground behind us. I reached between us to undo his zipper and pull his thick cock out from the gap in his boxers.

"Need you in me now, Henning," I demanded against his mouth.

"Can't get enough of you." He pressed me to the now warm tile wall by a hand in my sternum, the other cradled under my ass as he watched himself notch his cock against my cunt and slowly push inside.

Once he was rooted deep, he ground closer and sealed my mouth in a wet, filthy kiss that stole my breath from me.

"Gonna fuck you hard, Rocky," he promised darkly, pulling out to his tip and then shuttling back inside me so hard my vision exploded in sparks and pinwheels of pleasure.

"Please," I begged, curling my fingers into his shoulders, scraping with my nails because I knew he liked a little pain too.

He drilled me into the wall, the warm rain shower creating a soft symphony in the close, dark enclosure of the shower, punctuated by his lavish praise of my sweet tits, my pretty pussy, my hot, lush mouth. For a man who didn't talk that much, he was vocal as hell and so fucking filthy with his words when he was inside me.

I could not complain.

Instead, I groaned and whimpered as he gripped my ass and pulled me on and off his cock, arms corded and bulging with the effort, abs contracting in a way that made my mouth dry despite the water all around me.

An orgasm barreled down on me almost viciously, panic curling around the pleasure.

"I can't, I can't..." I panted, struggling against the dark tide.

"You can and you will," Axe-Man growled, before fixing his teeth to the junction of my neck and shoulder to bite into me *hard*.

I broke apart under that hold, thrashing on his cock, trying to escape the feral beauty of the climax, but he wouldn't let me go, pumping me full of his thick cock again and again until he came with a muted roar, his hot seed flooding me and spilling out down my thighs.

"Better than I ever could have dreamed," I whispered as I floated in the giddy aftermath, wet and plastered to him.

"Better than I deserve," he whispered back, smoothing a big hand down my hair as he turned off the shower and hauled me out into the bathroom with a grunt. "But I've never been afraid of hard work, and I'll work to deserve you."

"Henning."

"Rocky," he countered, setting me on the counter to grab a towel.

He proceeded to dry every inch of me like I was precious. My feet and between my toes, my legs and my swollen pussy, my belly and the divot of my naval, even my hair he bundled gently into the towel to squeeze dry.

"I know you got a low opinion of yourself," he told me when he was done drying me and tossed the towel into the other sink so he could cup my face in his rough hands. "But your brain goes there, you gotta remember that there's never been a moment, even when I thought I hated you, that I didn't admire your spirit. You're the most loyal, lovin', and sacrificin' person I know, and your beauty and worth have got everythin' to do with that and nothin' to do with your exquisite fuckin' face. But that doesn't hurt either."

I laughed a little wetly and let him drag me back into his

arms, tossing me over his shoulder and slapping my ass as he stalked into his bedroom.

"Henning!" I protested. "You're still soaking wet."

"You can lick me off with your tongue for round two," he declared before tossing me on the bed.

I was still laughing when he crawled between my thighs and ate it out of my mouth.

CHAPTER FORTY-TWO

Axe-Man

THE SATURDAY AFTER WE SYSTEMATICALLY DISMANTLED SEVEN Song's Golden Door Inn Bank, I woke up in my bed at Lake Mead and saw Mei lyin' beside me. Just the sight of her, tangled and naked in my sheets, hand outstretched as if reachin' for me even in sleep, sent a wave of physical reactions through me. My heart started thrummin', my gut swooped the way it did when you dropped with turbulence in an airplane, my mouth watered and my hand spasmed with the instant impulse to reach out for that hand and bring her closer.

She was inside me now. Lodged under my rib cage, beatin' like a second heart. Or maybe, she'd always been there, hidin' in the dark recesses of my chest, waitin' for me to recognize her for what she was and give her the light she needed to thrive within me.

Such a long, messy history filled with mistakes on both

sides, it seemed wildly unlikely that we could've ended up here in this bed together in this home I'd made in Entrance.

But in little ways, it made sense.

This madness had lain dormant inside me for years, not 'cause I hadn't met the person I was born to love but 'cause I had, and we just hadn't been ready to go there. So, for eight years I'd been in this holdin' pattern, livin' but not for myself, goin' through the motions.

And it was only when Mei arrived back on my doorstep that I woke up again.

After all the battles I'd fought in my life, it should've occurred to me fate would give me a fighter to stand at my side and have my back. Someone as fierce as she was lovely.

I traced my thumb over the Chinese symbols for *love, faith,* and *honour* on her hand 'cause I couldn't resist the urge to touch her, but I didn't wake her up.

It was beyond time for me to do somethin' I'd been putting off.

Cleo was already in the kitchen when I padded down the stairs barefoot in old sweats and a Hephaestus Auto tee. Sittin' at a stool with her chin propped on one knee, eatin' cereal and readin' one of Mei's Off-White Knight books while she listened to Taylor Swift.

"You know this Gloria character is kind of badass," she told me as I came into the room and poured a coffee before goin' over to top hers off.

I kissed her forehead as I did. "Fittin' seein' as she's based on my badass daughter."

She smiled at me, and I felt it like a hit to my chest. Those grins were startin' to come easier now that Mei was back, now she had her casts off and more of a routine set. She was excited to get to Box n' Burn every day to learn self-defence and she was writin' again, somethin' private in a pink diary Bea'd given her, but it was better than nothin'.

"You doin' okay, Glory?" I asked her, leanin' a hip against the counter and smoothin' her hair back with one hand 'cause she liked the contact. It was growin' now, startin' to curl prettily around her face. "Tell me honestly."

"Yeah, Dad," she murmured, tippin' her head back to look up at me with those Kay sage-green eyes that were so fuckin' beautiful. "I'm getting there every day. Sometimes it's hard, but I think it'll be hard the rest of my life. My mum and dad taught me to be tough, so I can handle it when things go dark."

"She'd be so fuckin' proud of ya." I had to swallow the lump that rose in my throat, but my voice was still hoarse. "But no way anyone could be as proud of you as me. You know that?"

Tears sprang to her eyes, but she didn't try to dash them away. Instead, she leaned over to rest herself against my torso. "There's this thing online about 'lucky girl syndrome.' Bea and I were talking about it, joking that I had 'unlucky girl syndrome.' But then I thought about it. The truth is, I am the luckiest because God took Mum from me, but He set the scales right when He gave me to you." She looked up at me with her cheek pressed to my gut, and her eyes were wide with gratitude. "I don't think I'd be alive today without you, Dad. Mei was right when she made you into the Off-White Knight, because you don't wear armour, but you're the best hero I ever could've had."

My gut churned with emotion, heat and pressure behind my eyes I hadn't had to deal with since Cleo was found near dead in a fuckin' field.

These tears were good ones, though, and I was man enough to let my daughter see the way her words moved me.

"Glory of the father," I muttered the definition of Cleo's name and the reason I'd always called her Glory. "Always, sweetheart. You and me against the fuckin' world."

"You and me and Mei," she corrected and when I blinked,

caught out 'cause there was somethin' in her voice I hadn't been expectin'. She laughed. "Right?"

"Right," I drawled, takin' a sip of joe to collect my thoughts. "Fuck it, you know, then?"

She laughed again and it was bright and loud and long. I wondered if it would wake Mei up and decided even if it did, there could be no better alarm.

"Um, *yeah*, Dad. You and Mei've never exactly been subtle."

"Um, hate to break it to ya, kid, but there was no *me and Mei* before the last couple of weeks."

"Sure, Dad."

"I'm serious."

She rolled her eyes playfully and then sighed like I was the kid and she was the parent. "Dad, you think after watching some of the most epic romances in *history* play out in front of my eyes the last five years, I don't recognize soul mates when I see them? Whether you want to admit it or not, I've been quietly rooting for you and Mei since I was seventeen."

"No shit." The back of my neck was hot with somethin' like embarrassment. "Was I the only one blind to Mei's crush?"

She shrugged, sippin' her coffee. "There was a lot to hide behind. She was your daughter's best friend, seventeen years old, from the right side of the tracks when we were decidedly from the *wrong* side even if Mei liked slumming with us there. It wasn't the right time." She peered at me from under curly lashes. "Is the time right now?"

"Well, believe it or not, I was comin' down here to tell you about Mei this mornin', but you beat me to it. Not sure I expected you to take it so well, honey."

Cleo put her mug down and swiveled on the stool in her oversized pink knit sweater to plant both her hands on my chest and smile up at me. "We've always been a family. And I've been through too much to ever be, I don't know, jealous about the way you love each other. You and Mei have the biggest hearts I know; there's room enough for all types of people and all types of love between us."

"How'd I get so lucky to have you for my daughter?" I asked her, honest as fuck overwhelmed by her sheer goodness and angry still, deep in my gut, that some fuck had tried to take that from her.

Even after exactin' retribution for Kate's murder by dismantlin' the Seven Song triad, a part of me would always rage I hadn't been the one to murder The Prophet instead of Priest.

"You saved Mum and me," she reminded me flippantly. "I think you deserve it."

I wrapped her up in a big hug, pressed my nose into her fragrant hair, and just let myself feel awe and gratitude and sweet as fuck relief that she was still here with me. That The Prophet hadn't succeeded in robbin' me or the world of Cleo's loveliness and magic.

"So what does this mean, then?" Cleo asked, muffled against my chest before I pulled away. "Will she stay here with us?"

My chest tightened. "I dunno, Glory. We haven't talked about it."

"You are dating, though," she pressed. "She's going to be your Old Lady?"

I ground my teeth together and shrugged one shoulder.

"Men," she muttered.

"Hey, it's not like Rocky loves to talk about her feelings either," I protested.

"What happens when a dragon fights a tiger?" she asked, paraphrasin' a Cantonese sayin'. "A freaking stalemate. Just, don't fuck around here, Dad. For all our sakes. You guys deserve to be happy, and you both have a bad habit of forgetting that."

I grunted as I moved away to take stuff outta the fridge to make us pancakes.

"You did ask her to Harleigh Rose and Lion's wedding today, right?"

I paused with my head in the fridge as I grabbed the bacon then carefully pulled it out to place it on the counter by the stove, not facin' Cleo.

She made a noise of exasperation. "Bikers, seriously, you guys are ridiculous. You're all lucky women dig a guy in leather."

I was still bustin' a gut laughin' when Mei trailed down the stairs and into the kitchen. She'd put on a pair of black sweatpants and a cropped black tee that showcased the taut, tattooed expanse of her belly and lower back.

My mouth went dry, and I'd had her twice only eight hours ago.

"Close your mouth, Dad," Cleo teased under her breath.

I shot her an unamused glance, but she was already openin' her arms for Mei, who walked right into the embrace and kissed her hair.

"No nightmares last night?" she murmured.

"No," Cleo confirmed, pullin' away to smile softly. "I slept like a baby knowing you guys were out taking down Kasper Kuan."

Mei winced, slidin' her gaze my way. "Uh, we didn't actually get Kasper."

Cleo frowned. "Kodiak told me you guys took out the bank."

"We did, but Kasper wasn't there," I said, steppin' in to fill in the blanks. Usually, I kept club business from my kid, but she was too caught up in this shit to be left outta the loop. "Curtains had him buyin' a first class ticket to Hong Kong a couple hours after we took down Golden Door. He's fleein'."

A thundercloud rolled over her face and for a second there, she didn't look a thing like a girl who loved pink and knittin' thick, fluffy fuckin' blankets curled up on the couch to watch classic movies or anime shows. She looked like a woman scorned who wouldn't rest 'til vengeance was exacted on those who'd wronged her.

It was a look I'd seen in the mirror a thousand times, on Mei, too. On my brothers in the club and some of their women, even the softer ones like Cressida after King was shot.

But never on Cleo.

It was as beautiful as it was terrifyin'.

"Don't worry, sweetheart," I told her, voice a little guttural with raw, violent promise. "He's a walkin' dead man."

"Promise?" she asked in that same sweet voice, expression dark as night.

Mei blinked at her then glanced at me with comically wide eyes.

I swallowed my laugh. "Swear it."

"Well then," she said, shruggin' off the mood. "That's good news."

"You know," Mei told her, tuggin' on a short lock of Cleo's hair. "I think I'm starting to wear off on you. You're pretty scary, Glory."

She laughed. "You are who you spend time with I guess. It's a miracle I've lasted this long without some bloodlust." Her gaze went distant for a moment, returnin' to that fallow field we'd found her in, maybe. "It's a good change, I think."

"Me too," Mei agreed softly, smilin' at her friend with that earnest affection she only ever showed Cleo, Lin, Old Dragon, and me.

It seemed like a mornin' for sharin' truths so even though I'd fully intended to keep the truth about Maxwell Dutton from Cleo for the foreseeable future, faced with her now, I couldn't stay the course. She wasn't the same shy girl who'd hidden behind a certain naivete for years to keep out the bad things in life.

She was forever changed by what The Prophet fuck had done to her, and it didn't have to be all bad. She was fightin' at the gym, hungerin' for revenge and searchin' for a new kinda independence.

Kate wasn't here and she hadn't been here to offer me advice in over a decade, but I had to believe she'd want her daughter to know the truth and be strong enough to make the decision about how to handle it on her own.

"Glory," I started, movin' to lean on the island across from my girls. There must've been somethin' in my eyes 'cause Mei made to take Cleo's hand. "We learned some shit when we were after the Red Dragons that you should know, too.

Cleo blinked at me. "You don't usually share stuff about the club with me."

"Yeah, and I'm not gonna lie, I thought about doin' the same here, but it wouldn't be right." I reached over to take her free hand in both of mine. "The reasons Kasper went after your mum, wasn't 'cause of the real estate deals she was doin' for him. Not exactly. She was workin' with him, 'cause years before, he'd been one of her clients and he'd fallen for her."

"Oh," she breathed, hand spasmin' in mine.

"You want me to continue?"

She nodded, but there was a wary distance in her eyes that said she was ready to shut down if she couldn't handle this shit.

"Problem was, your mum was in love with a different man. A guy they call White Snake, 'cause he was a white man in a triad. When Kasper found out about them, he arranged White Snake to go to prison, leavin' your mum heartbroken...and pregnant."

My daughter blinked slow, once, twice. "I thought this might have been where you were going."

"His name's Maxwell Dutton, and, he's not the one who killed your mum. He seemed to honest to God love her. But she was killed 'cause of her relationship with him. In the end, Kasper couldn't take the jealousy."

"He's a fucking psychopath," Mei muttered darkly. "That's why he killed her."

There was a long silence as we both let Cleo digest the news. She was a thoughtful woman, takin' time to arrive at conclusions Mei and I could rush toward. I wondered how it had to feel for her, knowin' she and her mum had both been attacked by a psychopath and only Cleo had made it out alive.

"Why did he tell you this?" she asked eventually, looking out at the window at the sparklin' lake. "What did he want out of it?"

"He wants to meet you," I confessed. "But I told him fuck no, if you don't want to. Or 'til you're ready. It's all on your terms, Glory. You get me?"

She stared at her hands in Mei's and mine for a while, worryin' her lower lip between her teeth before she looked up into my eyes. Her expression was unusually fierce.

"I don't give a fuck," she decreed, shockin' the hell outta me by swearin'. "He's nothing but the man who contributed half of my DNA. My real dad is and always will be *you*. The man who quit his dream job to take care of me. Who went to jail to keep my best friend safe and free. Who created a home for mum and me for the first time in our lives. How can you ever think I'd care to meet a man who didn't protect us when the dad I ended up with has proven again and again he'd give his life for me? No," she bit out. "No fucking way do I want to meet this guy."

"Okay, honey," I agreed immediately, ignorin' the way my heart throbbed with an excess of love for her. "I hear ya. But you hear me on this, if you ever change your mind, you come to me and I'll set up a meet. The door's never closed unless you want it to be."

"I do."

"Okay, but you might change your mind after you've had some time to think about it," I soothed.

"It's true, Glory," Mei murmured.

"Whatever. I'm glad you told me," she added, a little gentler. "It feels good you felt I was strong enough to hear this. But for now? I want to pretend Maxwell Dutton doesn't exist and my family is right *here*. You two and Lin and every single person in The Fallen."

"Yeah," I agreed roughly, haulin' my weight up on my hands planted on the counter to kiss Cleo's forehead. "Whatever you want, Cleo. Always."

"Always," Mei agreed, pressin' her own kiss to my daughter's cheek.

Cleo shut her eyes for a moment, breathin' in a way I knew she was doin' my 4-7-8 technique. When she finished, she opened her eyes and smiled a little.

"You okay?" Mei asked.

"Yes," she declared. "I'm too excited about the wedding to let this news ruin my day. Only good thoughts today for Lion and H.R."

"I'm glad. It'll be good for you to celebrate some love and happiness."

"I got some other great news this morning, too," she added impishly. "That nothing could diminish." Cleo stared at me over her back with raised brows, waitin' for me to step up.

I sighed, drawin' Mei's attention. Draggin' a hand through my hair, I tried to find the simple words to ask a complicated girl on our first date after years of shared history.

"Come here, Rocky," I started.

She blinked at me then shifted her gaze toward Cleo, a subtle reminder we weren't alone.

"Came down to tell Glory this mornin', but she beat me to the punch," I admitted. "Seems my daughter is smarter than both of us 'cause she knew this was inevitable."

Mei looked at her best friend, who smiled so widely it brightened the whole fuckin' room.

"Told ya so," she said, cheeky and proud.

Mei startled into a burst of laughter. "Are you serious? You knew, and I mean, you're okay with it?"

Cleo rolled her eyes. "*Yes*. I know I told you it was hard watching everyone fall in love around me and not having that for myself, but honestly, I'm not open to love right now. Maybe I won't be ever again. That doesn't mean I'm not over the moon the two most deserving people I know have found it in each other. Just as long as you don't make out in front of me, I can definitely rubber stamp this union."

Mei laughed then, collapsin' into giggles that sounded like pure joy and relief. Cleo caught her up in her arms, laughin' too, and they shared a hug filled with the kinda comradery they'd had since they were girls.

I hadn't allowed myself to think much about revealin' our relationship to Cleo until I'd decided to do it this mornin', but thinkin' on it now, it was obvious Cleo'd only ever be happy for us. The kinda friendship those girls shared was somethin' sacred, without jealousy or bitterness or regret to bog it down.

And my girl loved me as much as I loved her.

We wanted the moon and the stars and the sky for each other.

She'd even realized before me that I had that already in Mei.

When they broke apart, Mei looked at me hesitantly.

"Come here, Rocky," I repeated from where I leaned against the counter, openin' my arms for her.

The smile that slowly broke open her face was like seein' the sun after years of darkness. She came to me then, a skippin' graceful lope that gained speed until she was crashin' into me. I closed my arms around her and imprinted her shape into my body, bendin' my head to kiss her hair.

"You wanna go to the weddin' with me today?" I murmured there. "Not the most romantic first date after years of waitin', but I want my girl at my side while two of my favourite people tie the knot."

Mei pulled back to look up at me, rockin' up to her toes so she could press a kiss to my bearded chin. "Then, I'll be there."

I grabbed her chin and held her still so I could taste the happiness in her smile with my tongue.

"Okay, okay," Cleo protested in a laughin' shout when I took the kiss a little deeper. Somethin' soft hit the side of my head, and I realized she'd thrown a tea towel at us. "Keep it PG-13 for the kids, please!"

Mei broke away from the kiss with a laugh and spun like a ballerina to face Cleo, already launchin' into a conversation about what to wear to the weddin'. I rested against the counter and watched my two girls shootin' the shit in the house I'd made myself, and I wondered if it was possible I'd finally bought some peace for myself.

Of course, I should've known better.

CHAPTER FORTY-THREE

Mei

EVEN THOUGH THE FALLEN BABES HAD WARMED UP TO ME OVER the last few weeks, I was still honoured to be invited to get ready with Harleigh Rose and her bridesmaids. Lila was her maid of honour, and Loulou, Cressida, Cleo, and Bea were her bridesmaids, but it seemed like all The Fallen women were crowded into H.R.'s sprawling ranch house that morning. Most of the men were at the clubhouse until the ceremony started, but Boner and the three prospects––Ransom, a wildly handsome teenager; Pigeon, a skinhead with eerily pale eyes; and Carson, a good-looking jock-type who was best friends with King and Cress––were on guard duty stationed around the property while planners set up for the ceremony. It was Carson who stayed inside with us, his boyfriend, Benny, cuddled comfortably in his lap because he was one of the gang, too.

"Okay, *please*, I am dying to know," Tayline gushed dramatically as she sprawled on the couch beside me in the living/dining room where they'd set up beauty stations. "What's Axe-Man like in bed?"

"Tay!" Cleo shouted. "Please don't be gross."

"Welcome to my world, babe," Harleigh Rose drawled, waving at Cress and Loulou. "I've had to put up with these two talking about fucking my dad and brother for *years*. It's about time someone else felt my pain."

Loulou and Cressida grinned unabashedly, but to my surprise, it was the former who winked conspiratorially at me. "Hot dads for the win, am I right, Blossom?"

It seemed Nova's nickname for me had taken hold with the rest of the club, and I wasn't mad about it.

Not even a little.

"Definitely," I agreed with a sly smile. "Sorry, Glory, but really, I've got to defend Axe-Man's reputation here."

"Oh my God," she groaned, putting her hands over her ears as she started to hum loudly to drown out what I intended to say.

I started by slipping the thick strap of my black satin dress off my shoulder to reveal the little love bites that peppered my upper breast. Tayline clapped in delight, and Lila laughed so hard, there were tears in her eyes.

"I waited years to get my hands on him, and let's just say, it was well worth the wait," I divulged to more laughter.

"It's always the quiet ones," Harleigh Rose said sagely. "I loved Lion for years before we got together, and I never could've known what a bossy sex god he'd be in the sack."

"Maybe all bikers are good in bed," Lila mused. "Because Nova seriously took his time with me this morning, and I'm telling you, I'm still weak in the knees. I'm worried about walking down the aisle without falling."

"Trust me," Hannah, the most experienced of us, said dryly, "they aren't."

Everyone laughed, including Cleo who'd lowered her

hands to participate again. She looked happy and pretty sitting in the chair getting her makeup done by Lila. Her hair had grown out enough to curl around her ears, and she'd gained a little, though not enough, weight. Even though we'd bought pink hair dye, she said she wasn't ready to reinvent herself quite yet.

"So, are you officially Axe-Man's Old Lady, then?" Cressida asked, getting up to grab a bottle of tequila from the sideboard. "Because this deserves a toast, if so."

I bit my lower lip and shared a look with Cleo. "I think we're taking it once step at a time. It's...casual right now."

Lila rolled her eyes. "C'mon, babe. Nova told me what Axe-Man inked onto you without your permission. You still want to tell me it's casual?"

"Oh! What did he do?" Tayline leaned forward with huge brown eyes.

I stole a glance at Cleo who sighed heavily, even though her eyes sparkled. "You better tell us, Rocky, before Tay tackles you and searches you herself."

I stood up, pulling the silky fabric of my dress up over my ass cheek, exposed by my underwear. The words were a rich black in thick gothic script: *Property of the Off-White Knight.*

"Jesus," Maja, Buck's Old Lady, gasped, waving a hand to cool herself. "I think I just had a hot flash."

I blushed as I dropped the fabric and sat down.

"You okay he marked you like that?" Cressida asked softly. "Men like ours can get a little...territorial. Still, he should've asked you before making it permanent."

"It's always been true," I admitted with a shrug, feeling that truth keenly. "He just inked it into the surface. I'm not mad."

I was elated, to be honest.

When I lay in Axe-Man's arms at night, overfull with love, so close to bursting I thought I'd split apart atom by atom and die if I didn't confess how much I wholly and ardently loved him, I comforted myself with the reminder of those words on my skin.

He had to feel more for me than friendship and lust if he'd branded me with his name, right? And this morning, when he'd told Cleo about us, I'd felt hope take up permanent address inside my chest.

Loulou studied me with pursed lips, Angel asleep in her lap, her hand carding gently through her daughter's abundance of golden curls. "You know, sometimes the things we love the most, we also fear the most. It requires a lot of trust to admit to a vulnerability. Especially for men like The Fallen who think they need to be unconquerable. Especially for a man like Axe-Man who's already lost so much."

"You're being nice," I said because I almost couldn't bear to hear those words.

Hope could be lethal in the wrong dosage, and I was dangerously close to my max consumption.

Loulou's lips twisted into a wry smile. "I'm being honest."

"It's my wedding day," Harleigh Rose interjected, sitting in a white lacy nightgown even as Hannah did her makeup dramatic and bold, the contrast somehow suiting her to a T. "So let me give you some of my honesty, too. To be the best kind of lover, you have to be a fighter. Don't stop fighting for him if you love him. I fought and literally almost died for Lion, and I'd do it again today, tomorrow, and any day following."

"Let's hope there's no fighting today," I quipped because I couldn't handle any more of this.

This...sisterhood. This group of women in all shapes and sizes and ages who sat together like a family, teasing and supporting and loving so blatantly the room seemed filled with magic.

I'd never had this on such a scale.

With Kate and Cleo and Lin, yeah.

Sometimes, when Daiyu was alive and made time for me after long hours of work, with my ma.

Never like this.

You could make a home here with us, Cleo's voice rang in my mind, and I looked over to see her watching me with a sad little smile like she knew just what I was thinking.

That I didn't deserve this like she and Axe-Man did, but I was so fucking happy to share in it with them for a while.

"I'm going to get some fresh air," I murmured as the conversation moved on around me.

Cressida shot me a worried look, and Harleigh Rose brushed my arm as I passed by her, but no one followed me, and I was grateful.

It was a gorgeous April day, the sun a bright gold coin in an unblemished blue sky. It was still cool, a breeze ruffling the long grass over the meadow beside the house, and the manes of the three horses grazing in the paddock beyond that. I rubbed my arms as I leaned against the balustrade and took in a few deep, long breaths with my eyes closed to settle my fragile spirit.

"Blossom," Boner called, but it wasn't his usual charming tone.

I opened my eyes to see him standing in front of me, scowling.

Scowling because Kasper Kuan was at his back holding a gun to his temple.

My first bizarre thought was that it was the same gun he'd used to kill Jiang's lover, Eero.

My second was pure, undistilled fear.

"Kasper," I greeted calmly even though I was reeling. Fourteen people were inside, one of them a bride on her long-awaited, much-earned wedding day.

What the fuck was I going to do?

"I don't believe you have an invitation to the event," I continued blandly.

I had a knife in my thigh holster, light enough to throw, but Kasper was too hidden behind Boner. There was no way I could hit him cleanly.

"Two of my men have the other Fallen brothers at gunpoint, too," Kasper warned, jerking his head to the left.

A second later, Pigeon and Ransom shuffled into view with gunmen at their backs.

"What do you want?" I reiterated, this time with grit in my tone.

I cursed myself for not even bringing my phone outside. If I screamed, would they have time to shoot all three bikers dead? Who inside the house was armed?

Cleo was in there.

Cleo.

I closed my eyes and took another deep breath.

"I'm only going to ask one more time, Kasper, what do you want?"

"You pathetic *tou zoi zi*," he spat, cursing at me. "You think you can come for me and actually succeed in taking out a Dragon Head when you are nothing? Some whore Jiang has entertained himself with and then tossed aside only to be picked up by biker white trash?"

"So what, you came here to kill me?" I asked, opening my arms. "Go ahead then, but leave the others out of it."

He laughed, and even that was a dull, droning monotone. It was wrong to see his short, soft body threatening someone as big and strong and capable as Boner. I wondered how he got a bead on him and then remembered he'd been Dragon Head of the Seven Song for long enough to have accrued a myriad of offensive tactics.

Inside Hozier's voice rose as someone turned up the volume

on the music. I was glad. Hopefully that meant no one would hear us outside.

"You think one death is enough?" he hissed. "One life isn't enough. Do you know how much you *fucked* me with Golden Door Bank?" he snarled. "It wasn't just the triad's own bank, you *wu lei zing*! The fucking cartels used our bank."

Boner laughed. "Oh boy, Javier Ventura is gonna fuck you up for losin' him money."

"Shut up," Kasper ordered, and quick as a flash, he buried a small knife into Boner's side.

"Fuck," I whispered, moving forward to get to them.

Boner grunted, his knees threatening to give out, hands going to the knife in his gut.

"Stay where you are, Mei Zhen," Kasper demanded. "I don't just want your death. I want your white man to *suffer*. I want Maxwell Dutton to know he will never be free of me. I will stalk him and his until he has no one left."

His gaze darted to the door. "Is his daughter in there right now?"

"No," I said, forcing my body to stay loose. I rolled my eyes for added effect and hoped it wasn't too much. "She isn't well enough to attend the wedding. She's being guarded at the clubhouse with the men."

He glowered at me, but Ransom barked, "It's true, asshole. You think they'd bring her to a wedding after what happened to her?"

"You're welcome to check," I offered. "But there are armed men inside so it's your risk."

"Fine," Kasper said. Fat drops of sweat beaded on his forehead, rolling into his eyes so he had to blink hard through the salt sting. "It doesn't matter. You'll do. Get down here, Mei Zhen, you're coming with me."

I swallowed, warring with my flight-or-fight response.

There was nothing for me to fight *with* other than my body

and a knife against three gunmen. If it was only me, and not Ransom, Boner, and Pigeon at risk, I might have risked it. But they'd be dead on the ground before I could even get close enough to engage the 49ers.

And I couldn't flee.

There was no way I'd expose Cleo to more harm.

No way I could let violence into the house at my back filled with sisterhood and happiness and soon-to-be-wedded bliss.

No *fucking* way.

So, I sucked in a deep breath and tried to channel Axe-Man's strength. "Okay."

"Fuck *no*, Blossom," Boner grunted, voice strained from the pain of his wound. Blood pooled between his fingers and trickled down his wrists.

I ignored him and then Ransom and Pigeon as they started to struggle in their captive's holds.

Kasper waited until I reached him and then recoiled the gun at Boner's temple so he could bring it down hard on the back of his head. Boner collapsed instantly, eyes rolled up into the back of his skull.

I swallowed my whimper of distress as Kasper left him on the ground and gripped me hard around the bicep, dragging me toward the path that led to the back of the property where they must have parked.

"Ransom, Pigeon," I called out as I stumbled after Kasper. "Tell Axe-Man—" I had to swallow a hopeless sob as it rose into my mouth. "Tell Axe-Man I love him, and I hope he forgives me for leaving him again. But I'm not sorry for doing it. He told me once he'd pay any price for me. It's my turn to pay the price for him."

Ransom elbowed the gangster at his back in the belly and wrenched out of his hold, turning to fight him at close quarters.

Kasper started running, pulling me behind him. We were almost at the car I could see through the trees when I heard the gun go off behind us. I swallowed another sob and prayed it wasn't Ransom who'd been shot.

It occurred to me as we reached the car and another gangster started the engine as Kasper shoved me into the trunk, that I probably wouldn't live to find out either way.

The trunk slammed shut and darkness descended.

I closed my eyes as the tears came and terror claimed every nerve in my body, but even then, in the dark driving toward my death, I couldn't be sorry I was the one paying for our revenge instead of Axe-Man or Cleo or the rest of the club I'd unwittingly started to think of as my home, too.

CHAPTER FORTY-FOUR

Axe-Man

"LOOKS GOOD, MAN," I TOLD NOVA AS I STUDIED MY NEW INK IN the mirror at the clubhouse before gettin' dressed for the weddin'. "Thanks for takin' the time this mornin'."

Nova clapped me on the back, his smile wide in the reflection behind mine. "Anytime, brother, you know that. Especially when the piece has got a message as good as this."

The left side of my mouth curled up as I traced the design inked into my left pec; five stylized slash marks with dragon's talons peekin' through at the ragged ends, like I'd been cut open by one.

And I had.

I'd already told Mei she had her teeth and claws in me, and I wanted to tell her the rest of it. That I was so in love with her, I felt mad with it. That I wanted her to stay here in Entrance with me forever. That I wanted to tie us together with more than just ink and paint and words. I wanted ceremony and legal papers with our names on them. I wanted decades of adventures as the Off-White Knight and his Rocky.

I was almost forty-one years old, and I'd only just found the love of my life after years of strife and loneliness. I wanted to start our life together right this fuckin' minute.

But I'd never been much good with words, and I couldn't seem to find the right ones to explain to her the magnitude of how I felt.

So I'd reverted to action. Somethin' I knew would mean the fuckin' world to her as she meant the world to me, 'cause she'd told me so at seventeen.

I got her tattooed into my skin forever, right over the heart she owned in my chest.

"Good to see you happy, man," Nova muttered, pullin' me around into a back-slappin' hug, careful not to press into the fresh ink. "Didn't realize 'til Mei came to town that I only ever really saw you smile around Cleo."

I grunted my acknowledgment 'cause hearin' those words from a man who was a brother and a best friend to me, as well as a trusted business partner, was every-fuckin'-thing.

"You guys about ready to head over?" Lion asked, comin' into the main room of the clubhouse decked out in an emerald-green suit with a white rose in the lapel.

"Eager?" Nova teased.

Lion leveled him a solemn look. "Damn eager. Can't wait to make Harleigh Rose Danner my wife."

Zeus scowled as he joined our group. "Still think she should keep her maiden name. This is the twenty-first fuckin' century."

King knocked into his dad with a laugh. "Sure, old man. You couldn't even wait for Lou to graduate high school before you made her Mrs. Garro, so shut up about it."

"I think we oughta propose a toast to the groom," Bat announced as he brought over a bottle of Patrón tequila, Dane and Wrath followin' with two trays of shot glasses. "The man who gave up his sterlin' reputation with the law to come over to the dark side with his lady love and her Fallen family."

Lion laughed good-naturedly as Bat filled the shot glasses, and Dane and Wrath handed them out.

"It wasn't just for my Rebel Rose," he admitted, hoistin' the glass into the air to address the club as we gathered around him. "Found a home and a family with her and hers, and I'll be grateful to you all for that forever."

"Are you cryin'?" King asked Curtains who was dashin' somethin' from his cheek.

Curtains scowled. "Fuck off, you're the one who writes poetry."

"Yeah, but you don't see me cryin' over Danny's lame-ass toast," he quipped.

I laughed as I fished my vibratin' phone outta the pocket of my black jeans--as good as my formal wear got, given I didn't have to stand up with Lion at the altar.

"What's up, honey?" I asked Cleo, surprised she'd be callin' me when she was enjoyin' her sisterhood over at the Danner ranch.

"Dad." Her voice trembled and instantly my blood turned to ice in my veins. "Dad, the triad came to the house. M-Mei was outside, and I guess she made a deal with them. Her for our safety. They...they took her. They stabbed Boner and shot Ransom, but by the time we got outside, they'd driven off with Mei."

When Cleo had disappeared with a serial killer on the loose, I'd gone mad with panic and fear. So mad, I'd wondered in an absent kinda way if I'd ever return to sanity. It'd seemed unlikely, even after Priest and Kodiak found her near dead in a fallow field, even after she'd come out the other side of seven surgeries, even when she was back at home but clearly flounderin'. I'd been frozen from the inside out, fear splinterin' off in shards inside my blood stream so hurt it hurt just to live, just to breathe.

Hearin' now that Kasper'd taken Mei when last we'd heard he'd fled the country to take refuge in China, wasn't like that.

After losin' Kate, after witnessin' the horrors unleashed on Cleo, I'd never fully regained that stability I'd once prided myself on.

So there was nothin' to stop me from goin' berserk like my Vikin' ancestors.

The wooden stool at the bar beside me was up in my hands before I could blink, then sailin' into the wall with a crash that brought the entire fuckin' room to a standstill.

"What the fuck, Axe-Man?" Buck groused.

But Zeus's phone was ringin', Nova's, Priest's, and King's too.

Their women were callin'.

Callin' to tell them the triad had takin' my Rocky.

"Curtains," I growled so rough the word tore up my throat comin' out. "They took her."

My brother stared at me for a long second before his mouth fell open and the colour leeched out his already pale skin. Without a word, he hightailed it outta the room, hopefully to get his gear to get a lock on where they took her.

"They got Mei," Zeus was tellin' Bat with his cell to his ear.

I couldn't hear them properly over the rush of blood in my ears.

"They'll kill her," I said to myself, gut clenchin' so fiercely I thought I'd vomit. "They'll kill her in the car or soon after."

"We got time, brother," Bat tried to reassure me, movin' close to clamp his hand on my shoulder.

I didn't even feel the touch.

"No, this is the Seven Song. They'll kill her, and they'll do it brutal. They'll film it or leave her for me to find."

I knew how these fuckers worked.

They strung up Kate at a fuckin' carnival as a message to me, to everyone who read the paper or watched the news that you did *not* fuck with the Seven Song triad.

And Kasper had loved Kate. He'd given her a chance to "earn" his forgiveness by forcin' her to work for him. He hadn't *wanted* to hurt her, but still, he had 'cause she'd betrayed him.

The man had killed his own brother's lover for bein' a man or white or just 'cause he was miserable without Kate and wanted Jiang to be miserable too.

He would work hard to give Mei the worst death imaginable.

Metal, wood, water, fire, or earth. Which one would they choose for my girl?

I shuddered so violently, Bat's hand fell off me. Without thinkin', I pulled the glass from the bar top and threw that into the wall too with a loud roar that ripped up my lungs.

"Brother," Zeus shouted, gettin' in my space. "Brother, hear me. Take a deep fuckin' breath and let's figure out how to get your woman back."

I shoved him away, but Bat was there pullin' my arms back. I shook him off, but Wrath was in his place, wrenchin' me still with the help of Dane.

It was Smoke, our oldest member and one plagued with hideous asthma, who stepped up with his rollin' oxygen tank and slapped me across the face. "Get it together, man."

My body shook like a horse riddin' itself of fleas as I fought for control.

It was the sight of Curtains comin' back into the room that grounded me slightly.

"Her bracelet," I ground out as Curtains, ignorin' my quiverin' rage, jumped up onto the stool beside me and flipped open his laptop. "She left the house wearin' it."

"I can get a lock on it," he promised, fingers already flyin' over the keys.

"King, Nova, Priest, take some brothers and get the fuck over to the ranch. Make sure Boner and Ransom are gonna be okay and soothe the women."

"I'm sorry, man," I told Lion, realizin' through the fog that it was his fuckin' wedding day. "I gotta find her."

He stepped forward and grabbed my shoulder, jerkin' it a little. "Harleigh Rose and I can get married any day. We'll get you Mei back, Axe-Man. That's a fuckin' promise."

"I got it," Curtains howled, shovin' the screen to show me a movin' dot on the Sea to Sky Highway headin' down to Vancouver. "I can track it on my phone. Let's move out, see if we can catch them before they stop."

'Cause the moment they stopped, they'd end her.

End the life of a girl who'd do any-fuckin'-thing for the people she loved. A girl whose love language was throwin' herself on a sword meant for someone else's side.

Fuck, but why had I fucked around in claimin' her? Why the fuck had I let her outta my goddamn sight for one second?

"Let's move out," I demanded, movin' in the crowd of my brothers toward the door to grab our buckets, our boots, and the extra weapons we'd planned to leave at the clubhouse for the duration of the weddin'.

"We'll get her, brother," Bat swore to me. "I refuse to watch you live out another fuckin' tragedy."

"Pigeon told Cress," King said, stalkin' out the door beside me. "That she told him to tell you she was sorry to leave ya, but that she was happy to do it. It was her turn to pay any price for you."

Fury and terror blinded me for a full second, robbin' me of everythin' but the colour red.

"We'll find her," I agreed, swearin' it to myself and to Mei, where ever she was.

This was not how our love story was endin'.

We were on the Sea to Sky Highway, a column of riders two by two, twelve men in total with the rest of the brothers at Danner's ranch to deal with things there when Curtains held up a hand to signal for us to pull over.

We moved in practiced tandem, pullin' off to one shoulder, so close to Vancouver, where I knew without a doubt they were takin' Rocky.

The second Curtains took off his sunglasses to look me in the eye, I knew what he'd say.

"Sorry, man," he whispered brokenly. "They must've stripped her or done a pass with a wand. We lost the signal."

The roar that tore outta me left the taste of blood on the back of my tongue. Despair throttled me, but I tried to breathe through the panic and fuckin' *think*.

What recourse did we have?

"Where was the last place you had her?"

"South Vancouver."

As if summoned by my furious roar, the full-bellied skies opened up and unleashed a torrent of rain. It was dangerous to drive the windin' highway on a bike in this kinda weather, but not a single brother made a move to leave.

"We head there," I decided. "I'll make a call on the way and see if I can't get more information."

Curtains nodded, and we moved as a unit back onto the rain-slick street.

The phone rang six times before the motherfucker picked up.

"How did you get this number?" Jiang demanded.

"Your brother's got Mei," I said and felt the frisson of shock over the phone line. "Where would he take her?"

Jiang swore vividly in Cantonese. "How long has he had her?"

"They were in a movin' car for forty minutes. Last we had a bead on them, they were in South Van. Any idea where he'd take her?"

He was silent for too long.

"Jesus fuckin' Christ, Jiang, this is Mei Zhen. The girl who kept you safe by pretendin' to be your girlfriend for half a decade. You fuckin' *know* she'd throw herself in front of a bullet for you, so don't you fuckin' hesitate to tell me where the fuck she could be!"

"Like she's throwing herself in front of his bullet for you?" he countered furiously. "You think she was taken because of me? It's *you* who raided and destroyed Golden Door Bank. It's *you* who married Kate Kay. This is because of *you*, Henning Axelsen."

"You don't think I know that?" I shouted over the rippin' wind and cry flyin' into my face as I took a hard turn and righted the bike beneath me. "You don't think I know she's payin' the price *I* should be payin'. You don't think I'd kill myself before I let her be killed for me?"

Heavy breathin', both of us.

"I'll see what I can find out, but the triad is in tatters. Whoever was working with Kasper is loyal to *him*, not me."

"You wanna be the Dragon Head of Seven Song, it starts now with you figurin' out where my girl is," I demanded before hangin' up.

As we rode, I tried to think of what could be in South Van that'd attracted Kasper.

If he was gonna kill her by the five thunderbolts, he'd be lookin' for a river or beach to drown her, and the Fraser River cut through the area. I doubted he'd have the patience to find somewhere to burn her alive, so drownin' or death by weapon seemed the most likely.

'Til I remembered that one of the city's biggest Chinese graveyards was in South Van.

I called Curtains over the Bluetooth.

"Six men head to Marine Way along Fraser River to check out the beaches," I told him. "Five with me to check out Ocean View Cemetery."

Curtains lifted his fist where he rode beside me, and when we reached the crossroads twenty minutes later, he took five men to the left while I kept to the right.

Bat, Dane, Wrath, Kodiak, and Lysander were with me, even though the latter wasn't a part of the club. Lion'd sent him with us 'cause he worked with him at his PI firm, and he had skills we could use.

Ocean View Cemetery was semi-famous for bein' the site of mass burial graves from some of the first immigrants to British Columbia. I knew Seven Song still smuggled people into the country and used the method of mass graves to dispose of the bodies that didn't make the horrific journey across the ocean on freighters with little food or water.

It stood to reason this might be where they'd kill her and dump her in one such grave.

I was so fuckin' cold, and it had nothin' to do with the lashin' rain as we got off our bikes and crowded together in the parkin' lot.

"The rains gonna turn everythin' to slop, but look for any fresh graves," I told my brothers. "He might've buried her alive."

Fury filled the space between us, the faces of my brothers filled with violence.

My phone vibrated once before it was at my ear. "Talk to me, Jiang."

"He buried her alive."

My heart topped dead in my chest.

"Ocean View?" I managed to get out.

"Yeah. I don't know where, Henning, I swear to you. Kasper handed her over to a crew waiting there and took off. He's on the way to a private air strip to fly to Hong Kong." He paused, breath loud and rattling. "You can get to him. I have the address and flight number. Or you can try to find Mei."

Pain split my body in two. The part of me desperate to murder the man who'd killed Kate, who'd buried Mei alive, with the part that simply could not fuckin' live without Mei. The need to put my past to bed permanently or pursue a future that felt like the biggest gamble I'd ever made on the other.

It wasn't even a choice.

"I'll find her," I swore. "Don't think Kasper's off the fuckin' hook. He's a dead man. I don't care how long it fuckin' takes me to end him."

"Right," Jiang whispered. "I'm on my way. I'll help you dig."

I hung up and moved between the grave stones, notin' that Wrath was already on his knees at an unmarked grave, diggin' into the wet soil with his bare hands.

"She has four hours give or take, if they buried her alive," Bat told me as I passed him. "We've got time."

Not enough of it.

The six brothers I'd sent to the Fraser River joined us after half an hour of searchin' and then Jiang arrived with three men loyal to him, clad in suits that were destroyed the second they sank their knees into wet soil.

One hour.

Two.

Three.

We had a system, but there were too many fresh graves and the unrelentin' rain had turned everythin' to brown soup. I was startin' to have trouble breathin', chokin' on the terror that was risin' like lava inside, burnin' me up from the inside out.

'Til I saw the gravestone.

Hai Lung 1937-1989.

The same name as Old Dragon's wife who'd passed away not long after they'd immigrated to Canada.

I didn't believe in coincidences, but the ground seemed undisturbed, the grass brilliant green and wet with dew.

Still, I couldn't move on. Droppin' into a crouch, I fingered the grass as I tried to figure out where the fuck that monster would've buried my girl.

It was then I noticed it, the demarcation in the grass at the edge of the tombstone. I followed it with my finger, walkin' back on my knees to trace the rectangular shape. My mud-caked fingers dug into the edge and *wrenched*.

The grass came up in a neat fuckin' rectangle and beneath it, freshly churned earth.

I tossed the grass and started diggin', vaguely aware I was yellin' out for my brothers as I buried my hands in the earth. Dirt rained over my shoulder, beside my knees as I dug and dug, my nails breakin' on stones, skin peelin' back over rock and roots. They started to bleed, but I didn't notice.

"Rocky, Rocky." I wasn't even aware I was yellin' as Wrath and Dane dropped to their knees beside me and dug too. "Rocky, come on, love, please be here for me."

I started to fuckin' despair as we dug out three feet then four, 'til finally, my finger stabbed into wood.

A plain coffin, the wood still bright yellow and new.

A roar rose in my throat as I dug faster, Bat with us now and

Curtains, Kodiak, Lysander. My brothers diggin' into the edges of the coffin so we could lift the lid.

When enough dirt was cleared, I could hear the dull thud of impact behind the lid.

"ROCKY!" I bellowed, workin' hard, finally able to try to pry the lid off.

When it wouldn't budge, even with Bat and Dane tryin' to help me, boots slidin' in the mud, fingers slippin' on the wet wood, I took out my axe.

I could hurt her, if I wasn't careful, but it'd been too long with her in that box buried in the fuckin' earth, and they could've hurt her, too.

So I swung, wedgin' the axe in the foot of the coffin, breakin' it open with the first crack of the blade. Another hit, mud flyin', my boot givin' way to mud so I fell to my knees.

But it was enough.

Usin' my hands, I splintered the wood apart from the hole I'd made 'til the lid finally gave way from the base and popped open. I grunted, my brothers at my side, as we shoved the lid off the coffin.

And there she was.

My Mei.

My Rocky.

Blood splattered over her face and caked around her fingernails and knuckles from tryin' to pry at the lid from the inside. Dressed in her black satin gown like a funeral shroud.

But she wasn't dead.

She was breathin', and she was mine.

I fell into the coffin, hittin' my hip hard on the wood beside her in my haste to gather her in my arms and wrap my entire fuckin' body around her like a shield. Like we were still under attack and only my body could save her.

She was sobbin', great heavin' sobs that wracked her whole body into convulsions. I held her too tight and peppered her wet face in kisses, whisperin' how much I loved her, how fuckin' necessary she was to me, how grateful I was that she was alive, alive, alive.

"Are Boner aa-and Ransom okay?" she almost yelled in her haste to ask. It made my heart, already threatenin' to break outta my chest, swell larger with love. "Are the girls okay?"

"Boner's in the hospital, but he's gonna be okay. Ransom was only skimmed with the bullet. He's patched up, and the girls are good," Bat assured her 'cause I was too busy kissin' Mei's gorgeous fuckin' face.

"I knew you'd find me," she cried, clutchin' me hard, nails diggin' into my wet, ruined shirt. "I knew it!"

"Always," I swore. "Always, little dragon. But swear to me right fuckin' now, you won't pull this sacrificial shit again. Swear to me!"

"I swear," she said instantly, shudderin' against me, pullin' and clawin' to get me closer as if she wanted to crawl beneath my skin. "I was s-so scared," she admitted, diggin' her little hands into my hair so tight it burned, pullin' my head outta her neck so she could stare at me with those gorgeous, wet black eyes. "I was so scared, but I knew you'd come. You were made to keep me alive."

"Rocky," I murmured, smoothin' her wet hair away from her face so I could press a kiss to her forehead. "You're the one who keeps savin' me."

"No," she swore fiercely. "It's you. Because in all the darkest moments of my life, even lying in a fucking grave, the possibility of seeing you again was what I lived and fought for."

With a groan of achin' relief, I took her wet, tremblin' mouth with my own, feedin' her all the love bubblin' up from my overfull soul.

When we broke apart, I kept her clasped to me and made a private vow I wouldn't go another fuckin' day without Mei Zhen Marchand by my side.

"I love you," I confessed, reachin' between our bodies to wrench open the button-up, poppin' buttons 'til I could reveal the fresh tattoo I'd got for her. "You got your teeth and claws in me, and I'm never lettin' you go, you hear me? I've been a fool for most of my life, but I know how fuckin' lucky I am to have the love of a woman as fierce and fuckin' perfect as you. You hear me? I'll scream it from the fuckin' roof. I love you," I ended on a roar.

"Henning," she whispered, the tears still comin' but softer now, and there was a new kinda fear in her eyes. "I don't know if I deserve that."

"You deserve everythin', and I'm gonna be the one to give it to you," I swore, kissin' her again 'cause she was *alive,* and she was mine.

"There is blood on these hands," she whispered roughly, small fingers curled tightly, the skin so pale in the milky moon they seemed luminescent. "I know better than anyone it can't be washed off. I killed one of the men before they could get me in the grave. Shot him in the throat with his own pistol."

That explained the blood on her face. Laughter blossomed in the dark place in my belly reservered for violence and venegence and wrongs that felt so fuckin' right.

I used one'a my thick, calloused fingers to peel back each of hers gingerly, like petals on a flower reluctant to bloom. She resisted only for a moment even though I could see in her eyes a fragile kinda hope she was afraid to voice. Those black eyes watched me carefully as I brought her hand up before my face and slowly pulled her bleedin' index finger into my mouth, suckin' it down to the base. Her nostrils flared, cheeks darkenin'. A hiccough of breath caught in her throat along with her flutterin' pulse.

I slid my tongue over her digit as I pulled off, then repeated the movement with the next finger and the next. On the third, she shivered so violently I heard her spine crack.

"I happen to like the taste of blood," I reminded her in a voice thick with remembered lust. "And I don't give a fuck about anythin' in your past or mine anymore, you hear me? I would wade through a lake of blood for you. I would dig 'til the bowels of hell opened under my raw, stingin' hands. I would cut out my own heart and barter with Satan himself if it meant keepin' you safe. You're mine if you'll say I'm yours, and I'm keepin' you forever."

Mei clung to me even tighter, flippin' me so I was on my back in a coffin six feet in the earth, and all I could see was my girl hoverin' over me like the angel of death, ready to kiss me into heaven. "Then," she promised, "I'm yours."

EPILOGUE

Mei

"Wake up, sleepy dragon."

The familiar voice wove like a velvet ribbon around my dreamscape self and tugged me gently back into wakefulness. When I blinked my eyes open, Axe-Man was bent over my body in the bed, one hand stroking back my hair and the other propped on the mattress.

My first thought, still heavy with sleep, was that he was some kind of heathen angel, a fallen warrior made celestial because of his good heart.

"Sleepy," I murmured as I curled into the pillow I was cuddling. I'd stayed up late the night before finishing my final draft of the next Off-White Knight novel and then when I'd come to bed, Axe-Man had convinced me with one searing kiss to stay up a little later.

His chuckle was low and warm. "Need you to stop that so I can show you somethin'."

"Show me in my dreams?" I suggested as I closed my eyes again.

"I wanna show you one of my dreams, you give me the chance and wake up."

I sighed, but my lips were already curling into a grin as I peeked one eye open again. "Is it a passable waking hour or before dawn?"

"It's seven o'clock, lazy girl," he teased, taking my hand to play with my fingers idly as he waited for me to rouse myself.

"Too early."

"Early for a reason," he amended, losing his patience. I kept my body loose just to make it harder for him when he pushed back the warm covers and collected me into his arms. He was so much bigger than me I knew even lifting my dead weight into the air would be no hard task for him. "You're gonna wanna thank me for my surprise and if we do that we need at least an hour for you to properly show your gratitude before I hafta get to work."

"Oh I am?" I murmured, nuzzling into his neck, the pine in the beard oil he used rich in my nose as I curled around his torso. "Because right now, I was thinking more punishment than reward."

His chuckle reverberated through me, keeping me warm even though I was only wearing a cropped black tee and cheeky underwear. He carried me down the stairs straight through to his garage studio. The temperature was cranked up in there, a cozy, turpentine-scented space.

I only had a moment to miss Cleo's presence in the house, because she'd declared last month that she was moving out, that she needed independence. Of course, Axe-Man and Kodiak had colluded so that the little bungalow they'd found her off Main Street was actually owned by Kodiak and occupied the lot beside his own house.

Cleo hadn't been happy about that when she found out.

But it gave all of us peace of mind, so she'd gritted her teeth and seemed to be bearing it with relative grace even if she called me frequently to complain about "The Bear" and his grumpy, bossy ways.

Axe-Man's palm cupped the back of my head, fingers threading through my hair to tug me out of his neck. I went willingly, easing into the kiss that waited for me and moaning at the now-familiar taste of my Old Man on my tongue.

Okay, so being woken up early wasn't so bad when it meant being carried like a damsel by my off-white knight and kissed like we'd reached the end of our fairy tale.

When he finally pulled away, there was that private little smile in his beard as his eyes scoured my face. A happiness in those aquamarine eyes that made my heart turn over in my chest and then restart a little too fast.

"My whole life I was searchin' for somethin'," he murmured as he walked us into the middle of the room and sank down onto one of the huge knit blankets Cleo had made. I frowned at it before Axe-Man's voice drew my gaze back to his. "I joined the army to save people and then, when that failed, I became a doctor to do the same. Married Kate to save her and Cleo. I did it all 'cause I wanted to be a good man, but more, 'cause I was tryin' to fill this ache for belongin' inside me that was gnawin' through flesh and bone. That hunger didn't ease 'til you showed up in my life again, the same but different in all the ways that mattered 'cause those eight years meant I could finally see you. See you and know what you were always meant to be to me. My saviour. The dragon at the base of the tower willin' to protect the few precious loved ones she's got inside. I'd never had someone fight for me before and it knocked the wind outta me. The sense too or I would've done this a long time ago."

Done what? I mouthed, my voice lost in the rush of blood roaring through my body, ricocheting off my bones.

He stared at me then, his golden brows furrowed, mouth a firm line. It was an expression that said he'd go to battle to get what he wanted and I knew what he wanted was me.

Even after three months of being his, it was knowledge that pierced me straight through the soul. I was his. So, what more could he want?

"We don't have the easiest love story," he said with a wry twist of the mouth as he shifted, moving me from my straddle over his hips with our torsos pressed together to my ass in the cradle of his lap facing the wall I hadn't been able to see behind his head. I gasped at the sight of the huge canvas propped against the wall, tears springing to my eyes, my hand flying up to cover my dropped open mouth. "But all those mistakes were pieces in the puzzle that brought us here, to this moment, and there is nothin' more beautiful to me than this. You and me. This love I got for you that fills my lungs like air, pumps my blood through my body like you own every beat of my heart."

A little hiccough sob escaped my mouth and I pressed my trembling lips together in a bid to hold myself together.

Axe-Man propped his chin on my head and wrapped his arms around me the same way he had when I'd confessed what Florent had done to me, how he had kept me from him all those years ago. "Each piece of that torn paintin' is a chapter in our lives that one or both of us fucked up 'cause of recklessness or pride or just bad fuckin' timin', but look how goddamn beautiful they are bound together by gold. By love."

I swallowed convulsively, trying not to sob, trying to say something half as beautiful as Axe-Man's words as I stared at the painting of me he'd once torn apart in a fit of rage and now mended together with thick gold paint. I knew the Japanese art of kintsugi well. It was the practice of taking what was broken and repairing it with gold to show that scars have their own beauty.

"I wouldn't change a single second," I whispered thinly through the lump in my throat as I clutched at the muscled arms holding me tight. I slid my hand down his forearm until I could hold that beloved four-fingered hand. "Not one second of pain for what we have now."

"Yeah," he agreed gruffly, pressing a kiss to the side of my head. "Like I said, nothin' more beautiful than the story we got. We fought and we overcame and now we're here about to live out one of my dreams."

"Mmm?" I asked without asking because my throat was aching with the poignancy of that gorgeous painting and this gorgeous moment.

He shifted, moving one of his arms away to fish in his pocket. With his other hand, he lifted my left fingers to his mouth and pressed a kiss to each of the Chinese symbols on the back of my palm: love, faith, and honour. When he lowered it, the other hand was there, something shiny winking in the gold light of an late summer morning spilling through the wide windows.

I sucked in a breath as cool metal pressed around my ring finger, the rough pads of Axe-Man's fingertips pushing it into place at the base of my knuckle. When he pulled his hand away, I caught sight of the golden spiral of a diamond frosted dragon with ruby eyes nestled in its new home on my left hand.

"We paid the price of this love, Rocky," he murmured into my hair, holding me close again so his entire torso was flattened to my back and curled around me, a human shield. "And I wanna spend the rest of our lives reapin' the rewards of our labour. I'm not gonna ask, 'cause I got the feelin' you'd scoff and I'm tryin' to make this romantic. So, I'll just say, I wanna marry you. Not next year, not in six months. Soon. Fuckin' tomorrow.

'Cause I'm nearly forty-one years old and I finally got the love of my damn life and I don't wanna waste another second. Marriage, babies, if you'll have them with me. A dog, a cat, whatever the fuck. Any and everythin' with you 'cause there's nothin' I wouldn't give you if you asked."

"Henning." The word burst from between my lips, an explosive sob that felt ripped straight from my soul. I twisted in his arms, launching myself at him as much as I could so he had to brace himself on a hand in the blanket even as the other came up to palm the side of my face. I dug one of my hands into his beard and the other into the hair over his ear, holding the most precious being in the whole world between my palms. "All I've wanted since I was seventeen was you. If you think for one second, I won't marry you and have your beautiful babies and watch you get older and hotter every day for the rest of forever, you're an idiot."

The smile that cracked open that serious face was like a lightning strike in a storm-filled sky, so beautiful it was almost blinding, an electric current straight to the heart.

He laughed, then, and hauled me closer to do it into my mouth, slot it between my teeth with the hot swipe of his tongue.

"Told ya you'd wanna express your gratitude," he teased, nipping the bottom curve of my mouth before tipping me over onto my back to press his big body over mine on the blanket.

"You're lucky I love you or I'd smack you for that," I said, but it was faux severity in my tone because I couldn't be anything but happy knowing I had Henning's ring on my finger and a shared future rolled out ahead of us.

"Don't I know it," he joked before sealing our mouths. "Luckiest man alive."

"I think it's perfect," Cleo gushed from the kitchen, undeterred by the fact I'd slipped down the hall into the guest bathroom a few minutes ago. Her enthusiasm for wedding planning wouldn't have surprised me before her attack, but it did now. She came alive anytime Axe-Man or I asked for her opinion so we'd made a tacit agreement to let her spearhead the whole thing.

It was beautiful to watch organized, inquisitive Cleo flex her muscles after months of depression. We'd only been engaged a few weeks and she already had so much planned.

"It is," I called back through the crack in the door over the roar of the bathroom faucet turned to full blast. I was hoping it had masked the disgusting sounds of my upchucking my breakfast.

After splashing water on my face and patting it dry, I joined my best friend in the kitchen where she and Lin were pouring over Cleo's Pinterest board for the event.

"Dr. Sun Yat-Sen Classical Chinese Gardens are so gorgeous," Lin agreed as she rolled dumplings deftly in her small hands and added them to trays already lining every counter in the kitchen. It was Henning's birthday dinner that night and we were throwing a huge party for him at the house. "Your ma would be proud you are honouring your heritage by getting married there, Rocky."

I hummed as I slid onto a stool beside Cleo, because I'd had the same thought. "I'd like to do the traditional tea ceremony before the reception starts, too. With you and Old Dragon, if that's okay with you?"

Lin froze mid-dumpling roll and blinked at me. Her mouth opened, but she seemed unable to find any words. I'd never seen Lin speechless before and I almost joined Cleo in her giggles at the sight.

Lin scowled at her granddaughter then dropped her gaze back to the dumplings as if she was completely unaffected, but I noticed the slight tremble in her hands as she worked.

"That would be fine," she told me primly.

Cleo nudged me with her elbow and grinned.

I grinned back. "Thanks, Lin. I know it would mean a lot to Henning. He always says you're the best mum he could ever have."

Her throat worked as she tried to swallow down the emotion, but finally, she gave me a curt nod that was meant to end the conversation.

"Soooo," Cleo drawled, drawing my attention to the screen where she had everything laid out neatly in spreadsheets and documents. "The earliest they can fit us in is ten months, but I figure that's perfect so we can get everything right down to the last detail."

I stared unseeing at the screen as I worried my lower lip. "What if they had an earlier cancellation?"

Cleo frowned. "They have a waitlist for those and we'd be pretty low down. I think it's better to book the date as soon as we can, but I wanted to talk to you before I agreed to anything because I know numerology is important."

"Nothing with a four," Lin said immediately. "Eights are best."

"Um, guys..." I started to say, my palms sweating so much they slid off the butcher block counter top.

"Eight would be nice," Cleo agreed. "They were apart for eight years. There's something poetic there."

"I don't think––"

"June is always cold in Vancouver," Lin mused. "July is better."

"That's true," Cleo hummed, tapping away at the keyboard. "July 8th is a Saturday, I think."

"Perfect."

"Guys!" I shouted, too frazzled by my burgeoning panic to modulate my voice. "That's not going to work."

Lin merely blinked at me, like I was overreacting, which I was. But Cleo blushed and ducked her head.

"I'm sorry," she said quietly. "I'm being totally...overbearing. I'm just excited that my best friend and my dad are getting married. But it's your day, not mine, and I'm totally embarrassed that I've taken over."

"Glory, no," I stressed, swivelling on the stool to take both of her hands in mine. "Absolutely not. That isn't why we can't get married next July. I'm beyond thrilled you're helping us with this, and so is Axe-Man. Honestly, I think we're relieved because we aren't the wedding planning types."

Cleo's crumpled brow smoothed with relief. "Well, yeah, that makes sense. Dad said the only thing he cares about is you and him being legally bound forever."

I couldn't help the grin that claimed my face despite that latent panic and nausea swirling in my gut. "Fuck, he's great."

Cleo smiled back at me. "Exactly. The two best people I know are getting married to each other! It's not every day that happens. And you know I love weddings. Bea said she and Priest aren't the marrying types, which, yeah, Priest as a groom is just a weird thought. So this is the only time I'll get to be a maid of honour. I'm sorry if it's a bit much."

"I promise, Glory, it's not," I said emphatically.

"Then what's the problem?"

I debated what to do with Cleo and Lin's eyes hot on my face, searing through skin into the layers below, trying to search out my secrets. This secret wasn't one I could keep indefinitely and even though I'd wanted to tell Axe-Man first, there was something to be said for checking in with Cleo.

She'd lost so much to The Prophet, including her womb. From the earliest years of our friendship, I could remember Cleo playing house with her dolls, dreaming of her future family. It seemed somewhat cruel now, to be pregnant when we hadn't even been trying, when I was actually on birth control.

I didn't want her to ever think she could be replaced in my heart or Axe-Man's when that could never be the case.

I clasped her hands tighter in my sweaty palms and sighed deeply before dragging in a bracing breath to say, "Because I'm pregnant and it might be old-fashioned, but I'd like to marry Henning before we have our baby."

I noticed out of the corner of my eyes as Lin dropped the dumpling she'd been making to the counter with a dull splat, but my focus was on my best friend.

For a moment, she seemed frozen as if in amber, perfectly preserved, expression blank. And then suddenly, her beautiful grey-green eyes widened almost comically, her mouth dropped open, and a sob burst forth. I was so startled by the sudden onslaught of tears, I could only brace myself awkwardly beneath her weight as she collapsed against my torso, her wet face shoved into my neck, and she clung to me.

"Glory?" I asked tentatively over the wracking sobs, making eye contact with Lin who seemed equally and unusually unsure of what to do. "Are these sad tears? Because you have to know, no matter what happens, you will always be irreplaceable to both of us. And this baby, God, this baby will be so lucky to have a big sister like you to inspire them in life."

A wail pierced the air as Cleo started to cry even harder.

I winced, rubbing her back with one hand and stroking her

hair with the other. Maybe keeping my mouth shut was a better course of action.

It took a while, at least ten minutes, before Cleo's sobs turned to soft weeping and her hands had softened from claws in my back to the gentle press of her palms. My shirt, really one of Henning's I'd stolen because I loved the Hephaestus Auto logo so much, was drenched through from left shoulder to breast, but I didn't complain at all as Cleo finally moved away from my neck trailing a string of snot.

Lin handed her a square of paper towel and Cleo blew her nose loudly before sucking in a few deep breaths. Even then, she didn't take one hand from me, sliding it from my shoulder down my arm to link with my hand.

I figured that had to be a good sense, but I still couldn't breathe properly through the apprehension strangling my throat and it wasn't helping dull the pre-existing nausea.

"Sorry," Cleo whispered raggedly, accepting a glass of water Lin had at the ready and taking a few eager sips. "Wow, talk about an overreaction."

"Don't worry about that," I urged her. "I just want to make sure I haven't...hurt you with this. Maybe I should have waited to tell Axe-Man so he could be the one to tell you."

"No." The word was a fierce snap like a whip against the countertop. "No, I'm glad you told me. I-I think it was best coming from you."

"Okay..." I waited, but when she didn't fill in the blank, I asked, "What are you feeling, honey?"

She laughed, face splotchy and red and wet with tears and snot, but so pretty she made my heart ache. The noise was free and bright, a clear ringing of celebratory bells. When she finished, her mouth stayed hooked in a smile, eyes bright and sparkling as they locked on mine.

"Oh, Rocky," she exclaimed softly, like she was in some kind of awe. "I don't think I've ever been happier in my life."

"Seriously?" I asked, the word punched out of me as I gripped her hands again, a little too tight.

"Seriously," she said with a firm nod and that gorgeous, wide smile. "I thought the wedding was exciting, but that's only like a day. This is a gift that will last forever!"

Tears pushed at the backs of my eyes and I didn't try to curb them as they slipped down my cheeks. "I'm scared, Glory."

"Well, yeah," she agreed. "Being a mother...that's a lot. But Dad's already the best dad in the whole world and you have me and Lin, and the entire club to help you when you need it. But really, you won't. You're a fighter, a dragon. The girl who took down a freaking Chinese triad because they caused mum's death. I think raising a mini Mei or Henning Axelsen might pale in comparison to that."

"Maybe not if they're a mini Mei," Lin muttered.

Cleo and I laughed, a little too loudly and a little too long, collapsing against each other as we did until we were just hugging and we did that for a while too.

"I love our family," Cleo said with a happy little sigh.

"Me too," I choked out, trying not to lose it completely because my fiancé's birthday party was in a few hours and there was still so much to do. "You want to help me with my surprise for Axe-Man?"

Cleo beamed as she pulled away to smile at me. "Absolutely."

Axe-Man

Forty-One.

Fuck.

If I wasn't fit as hell, with a gorgeous young fiancée who couldn't seem to get enough of me, and a beautiful family who were all well and happy around me, I could've spent the day a little maudlin.

Forty-one felt old, for some reason, in a way that forty hadn't.

Zeus and Bat, a year older than me, had both laughed in my face at my grumblin', but Buck and Smoke, our oldest members by a longshot, had both clapped my shoulder in comradery. That, and sharin' a bottle of Barrell Seagrass Gold Label 20 year old rye whiskey with those four men, Nova, Wrath, Kodiak, and Dane at the clubhouse before the party at the house had put me in a decent mood by the time I reached home.

Still, Mei had laughed when she saw us enter the kitchen. She was in there shootin' the shit with the Fallen babes who'd spent hours settin' up decorations––includin' a life-size cutout of Mei's Off-White Knight––and makin' food for everyone. Seein' her there, even before she noticed me, wearin' low-waisted black jeans that clung to the blades of her hipbones and a tiny shirt that was really only a black bandana tied around her tits, I was hit with joy. A rush of it like inhalin' drug from a pipe only so much fuckin' better 'cause it was clean, and pure, and lastin'.

And then she'd turned, taken one look at my face, and

laughed like she could read every thought I'd had that day and thought I was stupid but lovable for havin' them.

Good fuckin' Christ I loved that woman.

"Fuckin' love you," I told her, voice pitched over the swell of music and voices fillin' the house so everyone and Mei could hear me. "So goddamn much, Rocky."

The way she'd smiled at me then, like I was somethin' prophesied she'd been waitin' her whole life for. It made my heart stop for a full second in my chest, arrested by her beauty.

That was all it took for this birthday to be the best damn one I'd ever had.

It was more, too.

Mei was livin' in my house, sleepin' beside me every night in my bed, makin' both of those things ours. She'd agreed to be my wife and if it wouldn't've bummed Cleo, I'd have eloped with Mei the day after I proposed. I wanted her to be my wife, to be whatever word or symbol that had ever existed as long as it signified her as mine and me as hers.

It was the brothers, too. Crowded in my house drinkin' beer, talkin' too loudly, Priest startin' a game like darts that involved knives, and Wrath, Mei, Harleigh Rose, and Skell throwin' them at a corkboard they'd dragged out from Mei's office; Boner and Curtains startin' a round of karaoke that turned into a rap battle against King and Carson, and Nova and Lila. Cressida and Benny threw popcorn at them as they egged them on, and Zeus and Lou sat in the one huge chair, her between his legs, Monster asleep in the big curve of his dad's arm, Angel laughin' softly as Loulou played with her where she lay on her propped-up knees. Cyclops and Tayline had lit the firepit outside and roasted marshmallows they smeared against each other's mouths, eatin' off the sticky sugar like there wasn't a crowd of people watchin'.

It was chaos.

Fuckin' gorgeous chaos.

A group of people who'd been through the fuckin' ringer and knew now how to milk the last drop of joy out of every moment of their lives. Knew it was the people and the laughter and the adventure of life and lovin' that made it all so fuckin' worth fightin' for.

I sat at the scarred dinin' room table with Lion and Bat and Dane playin' poker when everyone seemed to flood inside at some unspoken command, crowdin' around the table, pullin' out chairs, draggin' over stools, standin' where there was room to stand.

I leaned back in the high-backed wood chair and watched my woman move in the kitchen, a secret little smile on her face as she pulled a white frosted cake from the fridge. My daughter was there too, gigglin' like she did when she was young and carefree, whisperin' in Mei's ear as they pushed candles into the spongy cake top.

"Fuckin' beautiful family, brother," Bat murmured to me, knockin' his fist against mine. "Don't know many men more deservin' of it."

"Maybe you," I countered, but my gaze stayed fixed on my girls in the kitchen, on Mei as she lit the candles and the flame did pretty things to her pretty face in the play of light and shadow.

Someone turned off the lights and the room was plunged into darkness, only the bright silver light of the moon floodin' the lake reflectin' inside. Enough to see Mei by the light of the candles as she started to sing "Happy Birthday" while she walked toward me.

Everyone's voices rose to join her, but in those moments, nothin' existed for me but her. My Rocky. My dragon. My girl.

The second she was within reach, I tugged her around the waist and hauled her into my lap. She laughed, adjustin' the weight of the cake deftly in her arms so she didn't spill it when I jerked her, and then carefully placed it before me. One of her hands found the back of my neck under my hair, rubbin' her thumb over my pulse point.

She pressed into me, breath warm on my ear as she whispered, "Happy birthday, Daddy."

A little chuckle emerged from my belly at her teasin' before I got a look at the cake she'd made me. Shaped like a heart, frosted in white icin', punctuated with black straws, it had my birthday present written in black on the top.

DILF (again) est. 2023.

I blinked at the cake, the chuckle lodged in my throat.

A buzzin' filled my ears, somethin' indecipherable that I was pretty sure, if I listened close enough, would have sounded like my inner self roarin' fuck yeah again and again and again.

'Cause fuck yeah.

This was it. Right now. In this moment.

Pure, unfiltered happiness the kinds of which I'd never experienced before.

On my forty-first birthday, I finally had every single thing I'd ever wanted, ever even dreamed about.

I looked at Mei, her face illuminated by the light of the moon and candle flames, and I found I had no fuckin' words to express that kinda joy.

So, I kissed her.

The kinda kiss that could swallow you whole. The kinda kiss you felt in your toes, the warmth of it meltin' your spine and burnin' through your throat 'til you felt like you were on fuckin' fire.

"I love you," I whispered fiercely against her mouth, vaguely aware of people murmurin', wonderin' why I hadn't blown out the candles. "Love you so fuckin' much, Rocky. You and this baby. Cleo and Lin and this family we make together."

"Me too," she whispered back, clutchin' at me so tightly, her nails cut crescent wounds into my shoulders even through my tee. "So fucking much, Henning."

I kissed her again, hands in her hair holdin' her to me like someone might try to pry her away. The lights snapped back on, but I didn't pay them any notice. Voices rose, but I ignored them. So did Rocky.

'Cause all that existed in that moment was us and the news of the baby we'd made together.

"I'm going to be a big sister!" Cleo's happy shout cut through the fog and I pulled away from Mei in time to see her throw her arms in the air and squeal.

Bea threw her arms around her as much as she could given her hugely pregnant belly, and one of the brothers set their fists thumpin' on the table in a chorus of joy.

I stood up, my arm still banded around my woman, and together we moved to Cleo so I could take her from Bea and hug her tight.

"You're happy?" I murmured into her hair. "You're good, Glory?"

"The best," she whispered back, squeezin' me with all her might. "I haven't even met the baby yet and I love them with my whole soul."

"Just the way I love you," I told her, holdin' the back of her head for a minute to let that sink in.

"Just that way," she agreed softly.

When we pulled apart, I saw Mei receivin' hugs from Lila and Cressida, before Boner pushed through and lifted her into the air to spin her around.

"I'll be Uncle Boner, right?" he asked her.

Mei laughed, shovin' him in the shoulder as he dropped her to the ground lightly. "Uncle Bones, maybe, but I think they might have to call you Aaron or it'll be a little creepy."

"Oh c'mon, like this gang doesn't love an age gap," he argued with a waggle of his dark brows.

I shoved him harder than Mei had, pushin' him into the wall with a semi-serious snarl. "Watch yourself."

He lifted his hands in the air, but there was a shit eatin' grin on his face. "Just happy for you, man."

"Good, then you'll all be happy that I'm gonna take my woman upstairs for a bit to celebrate properly," I declared, bendin' to shove my shoulder gently into Mei's belly so I could sling her over my shoulder.

She shrieked in protest, but I swatted her ass and stalked out of the dinin' room past the kitchen to the stairs.

There were hollers of approval from downstairs and someone, probably Cleo, turned up the music again to drown out the sounds of our celebration. When I got to our bedroom and shut the door behind us, I dropped Mei to the mattress and watched her bounce, ready for her to try to escape back to the party on claims of bein' good hosts.

When she didn't, only spreadin' her arms and legs for me, I carefully lowered myself to the mattress and placed my head on her tattooed stomach.

"Best gift ever, Rocky," I murmured, tracin' the black ink of the koi fish around her naval beside where my cheek was pressed. "Not sure how I managed it, but I think I might be the luckiest man alive."

"You're my off-white knight, Hen," she murmured back, shiftin' her hands through my hair. "I know how you got here. You earned it. We both did."

BONUS EPILOGUE

Axe-Man

TWO MONTHS LATER

I HADN'T SPENT A SINGLE NIGHT AWAY FROM HER IN MONTHS, BUT it still didn't explain the vicious acuteness of the pain in my chest as I waited for her to arrive. To distract myself, I stared down at my hands, the silver rings on every finger but missin' pinky and my left ring finger where in just a handful of minutes, Mei would place a new ring.

She'd picked it out herself without my input, an impish grin on her face when she returned home with a small jewelry bag.

"Something unique," she'd murmured. "I'll know it when I see it."

I believed her.

I'd felt the same way when I'd found the gold ring in the heart of Vancouver's Chinatown, the dragon's body an undulatin' circle with a head frosted by small diamonds and eyes a vibrant ruby red. The sight'a that ring on Mei's slim finger, the expression on her face when I'd slipped it on without askin' the question 'cause I was a stubborn old Tiger, but I'd learned after all this fuckin' time that the answer for Mei would always be *yes*, would stay in my mind forever. Pure euphoria, the kind that comes not from a drug but from the realization of a dream long dreamt. The diamond bright joy undercut by a sliver of shock, like she couldn't believe after all these years and all our struggles that she might finally be a real, legal part of her favourite family.

And today, in our backyard surrounded by the family we'd found in Entrance, we were finally tyin' the knot.

"Never seen ya like this," Bat said on a growly rumble of laughter as he slapped a hand over my shoulder and squeezed.

"Scared shitless?"

"Nah, you're not scared at all," he countered. "You just seem fuckin'...*alive*. Like Mei was the electric current you needed to start breathin' again."

"Yeah," I agreed, rubbin' at the echo of an ache in my chest I'd felt for near on a decade. "Eight years is a long time not to breathe, brother. Take it from me. You find happiness, grab it with both hands, and never fuckin' let go."

"Even when it tries to buck you off?" he joked.

"Especially then."

We stared at each other for a moment before I clapped a hand on his shoulder so we were a closed circuit.

"Wouldn't be here without you," I murmured, tippin' forward to butt my forehead against his. "Wouldn't wanna be here without you, either."

Bat squeezed my shoulder hard. "Right back atcha, brother. Love ya."

"Love ya," I agreed, swallowin' the thickness in my throat as I separated from him.

"Aw," Cleo cooed from behind us, walkin' up the aisle in a long-sleeved pink dress the colour of fresh cherry blossoms. "I do adore a bromance."

Bat laughed, but I couldn't find it in me to try.

"You look like an angel," I told her, tryin' not to choke up for the second time in less than two minutes. Fuck, old age and happiness were makin' me soft.

I opened my arms for her and closed them when she walked right into my embrace and snuggled close. My lids fell shut automatically as I held my daughter against my chest, restin' my chin against the top of her silky pink hair. It'd grown out to her shoulders in the past few months, and we'd celebrated her dyin' it pink with a full-on party at the cabin to reveal the "new" version of Cleopatra Axelsen. She smelled the same she always did, that perfume I bought her every year for Christmas, and she felt good in my arms, more substantial than she had in months. She was gettin' better, slowly, so fuckin' slowly, but it was a sure thing now Mei was back in our lives.

Even if I didn't love Rocky with every single breath I took, I'd be forever grateful, forever and gratefully in her debt for helpin' bring Cleo back to herself, back to me.

"I'm so happy the two best people I know finally got their heads out of their butts and realized they were meant to be," Cleo teased as she pulled away enough to smile up into my face.

I knocked a fist gently to the bottom of her chin. "Wiseass."

She laughed, that beautiful, chime-like music I was hearin' more and more these days. "If you wanted an officiant who would gloss over the hard stuff, you should've hired a priest."

I snorted. "Like a priest would agree to marry Mei and me. Especially when she's already knocked up."

We laughed together, but I dragged my knuckles over Cleo's cheek. "No one better to marry us than the woman we love better than anyone else."

Tears glossed her eyes instantly. "Dad, do *not* make me cry before the ceremony starts."

"Yeah, cut it out," Bea called out as Priest helped her down the aisle to her seat, their baby boy Azrael's brilliant red hair shinin' in the sun. "I worked hard on her makeup."

I looked out over the garden as it filled up with all our loved ones with my daughter tucked into the crook of my arm and my best friend by my side, the same man who'd been beside me through so much of my life, and I felt overwhelmed with gratitude.

How did a guy born to a violent asshole, a guy who'd killed people at home and abroad, who'd done so many bad things and made so many fuckin' mistakes deserve to marry the love of his life?

I thought about a line from one of Mei's Off-White Knight novels, "A knight is just a person who always tries to be better and do their best, even if they don't always succeed. The goodness of a soul should be determined by the attempts it makes to do right just as much as for its successes."

I'd tried my entire life to be better than the man who raised me and then better than my past selves. For Mei, that meant I was some kinda hero. To me, it felt like I'd been failin' my whole life. But standin' there with dozens of loved ones smilin' at me, happy for me, a daughter I'd fought for and raised and loved who thought I was the shit at my side, I thought I might've known what Mei was talkin' about.

Sometimes, tryin' to be good was more than good enough.

And I'd spend the rest of my life tryin' to be the best for Rocky 'cause fuck me, my girl deserved only the very fuckin' best. I'd already done the dad thing with Cleo so I had experience, but Rocky made me want to be even better, not just for our new little dragon, but for Cleo, too.

Lion took up a seat to the side of our cherry blossom-strewn archway with his blue guitar in his hands, plugged into speakers hidden around the yard and started playing "Bitter Sweet Symphony." He and Harleigh Rose had married each other the day after I'd dug Mei outta the ground, keepin' the flowers in water in their house, the whole Entrance chapter movin' out to set up everythin' for the ceremony again that next day. Lila and Nova'd tied the knot a couple months ago too, and now, thank fuck, it was our turn.

Cleo tugged me down and raised up on her toes to kiss my cheek, her eyes shinin' bright. "Good luck, Dad."

I squeezed her hand before she stepped behind me, gettin' into place to officiate. Bat thumped me on the back, my only attendant. Lin stood across from me, in a place of honour as Mei's only attendant. She hadn't wanted to walk down the aisle, but Mei refused to let her off the hook entirely.

Even Jiang was there, sittin' in the back row a little stiffly 'cause he was surrounded by bikers who were not his brethren. But we were on good terms with the new Dragon Head of the Seven Song even though we'd run his brother outta the country and disassembled their criminal bankin' enterprise. He was focused on Vancouver again, not Entrance, and we collaborated sometimes when it was worth it for both entities. Not that any of that mattered, in the end.

He was here for Mei just as he'd proved always would be after helpin' dig her outta the earth that day in the graveyard.

Mei'd wanted our small family as involved in the proceedings as possible.

Which was why, when Mei appeared around the bend of the house I'd built as a haven on the side of Lake Mead, she was walkin' beside Old Dragon in a motorized red scooter, her hand restin' on his shoulder as they made their way down the path toward me.

"Fuck me." The words punched outta me at the sight of her, eyes wet, chest heavin'.

I shouldn't've been surprised. If I'd thought about what she might've worn to our weddin', it would've occurred to me that Mei'd never wear white even though it was the colour she'd made me wear that day, a white button-up beneath my cut and tailored white dress pants.

No, on the day my Rocky married me, only one colour would suit her.

Red.

For a second, I thought it might've even been the same dress she'd worn all those years ago at her prom when I'd danced with her in the parkin' lot, but as she got closer, I noticed it was a take on a traditional Chinese Cheongsam. The red brocade silk was stamped with a dragon pattern that shimmered in the light, the neck high and closed with gold buttons at her throat while the narrow skirt split open from ankle to high thigh to reveal a glimpse of her toned, pale legs and the tattoo of the tiger zodiac she'd gotten to represent *me*. A golden dragon was embroidered on the torso in the very same design as the one I'd once drawn in Mei's sketchbook, the same one she had tattooed around her back and right arm.

She had that slippery, silky black hair pinned up in a bun at the crown on her head with red chopsticks danglin' with gold dragon charms, but the wind was already catchin' at the strands, sendin' waves tumblin' around her achingly beautiful face.

It seemed to take a fuckin' age for her to reach me, but I waited patiently 'cause it was nothin' compared to the years we'd taken to get here.

Old Dragon stopped his scooter at the end of the aisle and lifted his tremblin' hand to Mei's in order to offer it to me.

Even though his body and mind were frail most days, his dark eyes were keen and bright on mine as he whispered in Cantonese, "No one is more deserving of my precious gift than you. Take care of each other well."

I thanked him with a small bow over his hand and then pulled Mei's warm fingers into my own to lead her the last few steps to the weddin' altar.

"You have never been more beautiful," I told her, unsurprised by the gravel in my voice. I blinked once, twice, 'cause lookin' at her like this, in my hands, at this altar, about to be my fuckin' *wife* was like lookin' into the sun after years of livin' underground.

And then she smiled, this broken open expression of pure, unrestricted joy, and I had to close my eyes for a second to absorb the beauty of it.

"Hey," she said, waitin' for me to open my eyes before she grinned impishly. "I'm still just your Rocky. I've got a knife strapped to my thigh beneath the garter Cleo insisted I wear, and I'm wearin' black lingerie, not white."

I laughed, the sound ringin' out across the lake and echoin' back like the ripples over the clear blue waters. And 'cause I'd been a stupid, stubborn man for too long, and I didn't feel like waitin' anymore, I tugged my future wife into my arms and kissed her with laughter still rumblin' across my tongue to her.

When I pulled away just slightly, she bit my lower lip playfully and whispered, "Did you ever think we'd make it here?"

"Might not've known it, but everythin' that's happened in my life led me to you. Never wanted to believe in fate 'cause I thought it meant I'd end up like my dad, poor and mean and full of hate. If I'd known the red thread of fate had a face and heart like yours, I'd've embraced it a long time ago."

Her dark eyes twinkled, constellations of stars shinin' like my entire galaxy before me. "You're saying you would've fallen in love with me when I was seventeen and begging you to love me back? Even though I was jailbait, even though I was your daughter's best friend."

I smoothed my hand over her cheek into her hair and tugged out the chopsticks so all that gorgeous hair fell around her shoulders and into my palm. "I'm sayin' my soul recognized yours a long fuckin' time ago, and no matter the time between us and the mistakes we've made, I wouldn't change a fuckin' thing 'cause it meant we could be here today about to be husband and wife."

"If you're about done, we could make that happen," Cleo quipped lightly, the microphone taped to her dress amplifyin' the comment so the entire audience laughed.

Only Mei and I didn't, starin' at each other, still too close for propriety, grinnin' like fuckin' fools in love. And we stayed like that while we said our written vows and when I tied a red thread around Mei's finger, she did the same to me, a physical representation of our soul mate bond, before we exchanged rings. Then my daughter pronounced us legally bound and I kissed Mei Zhen Axelsen for the millionth time, but for the first time as my wife, and all I knew was peace.

Three Weeks Later

Temple Street Market in Hong Kong was the largest night market in the city, so even at two in the morning, the street was crowded with both locals and tourists alike. There was much to entertain. Stalls were filled with designer knock-offs, cheap electronics, and kitschy Chinese souvenirs for tourists. Street performers tucked into doorways and food carts wafting with mysterious umami aromas that made the mouth water.

Amongst it all, a girl visited a tiny stall tucked into the shadows between a purse merchant and hot pot stand. An old woman with folds of silken skin sat within a cocoon of silk robes folded in the same loose, drapery style. Her dark eyes were cloudy, rheumy, and her knuckles gnarled in her little hands like the roots of a very old tree. The table she sat before was clothed in red and littered with tarot cards and a glass orb that was strictly there for tourists.

The girl didn't ask for a card reading or for her future to be sought within the glass orb.

She sat down across from the woman and offered her hands, palms open.

The woman stared at the girl as if looking through her for a long, silent moment and then cupped the palms in each of her small, dexterous hands and bent over them.

"Such a long love line, broken not once, but twice, but scandal," she murmured in breathy Cantonese. Her nail traced the lines on the girl's palm.

After a moment, she stilled, her breath heavy in the tent. The girl remained still even when the woman raised her hands to examine her face with cold, soft fingers.

"Rivers and mountains," she murmured. "I've seen this curious face before."

"You have," the girl agreed. "You told me once I was too focused on death and the dark. You warned me it would make me unlucky."

"Well," she demanded, "was I right?"

The girl smiled, a curl of ribbon beneath the blade of a knife. "I guess that depends on your definition of luck. I lost two mothers, went to an adolescent rehabilitation clinic, lost most of my family for eight years, and nearly died a few times."

"Mmm," the woman hummed with a satisfied smile, but narrowed eyes. "And?"

"And now, I'm married to the love of my life, and I have more family than I know what to do with. So, I guess, in the end, you were right about one thing. I needed to find the balance."

"Between light and dark."

The girl shrugged. "Between being too afraid to be the girl I wanted to be and being too stubborn to evolve."

"Rivers and mountains," the woman murmured.

"Rivers and mountains," the girl agreed.

"Is this why you came to me? To tell me the outcome?"

"No," the girl leaned across the table and planted a red-lipsticked kiss on the woman's papery cheek. "I came to tell you it took years, but I figured out who spoke outside your tent that day, and I came here to kill him."

The woman froze, and when she recovered enough to press, the girl was gone, the red flap of her tent waving as if in goodbye.

A FEW BLOCKS AWAY, AT A BUSY EATERY OVERLOOKED BY TOURISTS but frequented by locals who loved fresh, hot seafood prepared traditionally, an older man sat at a small table drinking tea and reading the paper. It wasn't a Chinese paper, but the *Canadian Globe and Mail* because though he hadn't been back to that country in months, most of his business dealings took place there. He was reading an article about the trial of four high-profile Chinese triad members who were being indicted for fraud and money laundering through a private bank in Vancouver. His hand shook as he turned the page and then reached for his tea. The porcelain was hot against his fingers, the tea too strong and a little bitter as he slurped it back.

The paper told him what he already knew, Seven Song triad as he'd once known it was done. His brother, Jiang Kuan, ran things on Canadian soil now, and Kasper himself had been forcibly retired. He wasn't the kind of man who retired. He was the kind of man who took back what was his. He was the kind of man to...

The burn in his mouth from the hot tea had traveled down his throat and curdled in his belly, a tight heat that made sudden nausea bloom viciously behind his teeth.

He opened his mouth to beckon the server for some water, but a sharp pain in his chest stole his breath. And then another, sharper still, like a blade puncturing a lung, slipped just so between two ribs.

His face contorted with the awful pain, hand pressed to his chest like he could stop the bleeding, only there was no blood. Just pain, pain, pain, flashing through every inch of him until even his tongue ached.

In the moments before that pain overtook him, Kasper Kuan's head fell to the table, mouth gaping and closing, a fish out of water, glossy eyes pinned unseeing out the window into the busy Hong Kong street.

If he hadn't been so focused on dying, he might have noticed a thin slip of a young woman with streaming dark hair and a hulking blond man sitting at a café across the road. He would have noticed them, first because of the size of the foreigner and then because of the beauty of the girl. Then he would have noticed they weren't eating or drinking a thing. Perhaps he would have recognized them, the girl he'd once condemned to death and the man he'd indirectly sent to prison. In the end, it didn't matter anyway because he died, not fifteen minutes after sitting down. The server noticed when he went to deliver Mr. Kuan his hot pot, and he called the ambulance, but it was too late.

By the time the lights reflected off the windows on the street, Kasper was dead and the couple across the street had moved on, catching a plane to Singapore to carry on with the rest of their honeymoon now that business and vengeance were served.

They might have been living their happily ever after, but they were still Rocky and the Off-White Knight, Mei Zhen and Henning "Axe-Man" Axelsen, and necessary deaths would always be a part of their lives. Mei would say later on the plane, holding her husband's four-fingered hand, that it was all about balance.

The End.

Thank you for reading ***Caution to the Wind***!
If you want to stay in the loop you can sign up for my newsletter here!

Need to vent?

Join the **Caution to the Wind Spoiler Group**!

Curious about what happens next for The Fallen?
A Fallen Men novella, *AT*, is coming early 2024, can you guess who it may be about?

If you want to stay up to date on news about new releases and bonus content like extended epilogues join my reader's group, **Giana's Darlings** on Facebook!

Curious about where Cedar disappeared to and what happened to the rest of the old Calgary chapter of The Fallen MC?
Stay tuned for *The Fallen Men, #8.*

If you loved Axe-Man and Mei's age gap romance, check out Zeus and Loulou's forbidden love story in *Welcome to the Dark Side.*

"Taboo, breathtaking, and scorching hot! I freaking loved WELCOME TO THE DARK SIDE."—*Skye Warren, New York Times bestselling author*

Read all of The Fallen Men and want more Giana Darling dark and angsty goodness? Check out the Lombardi family books and pick up *The Affair* about the mysterious Frenchman Giselle Lombardi meets on vacation in Mexico.

Welcome to the Dark Side (The Fallen Men, Book #2) Excerpt

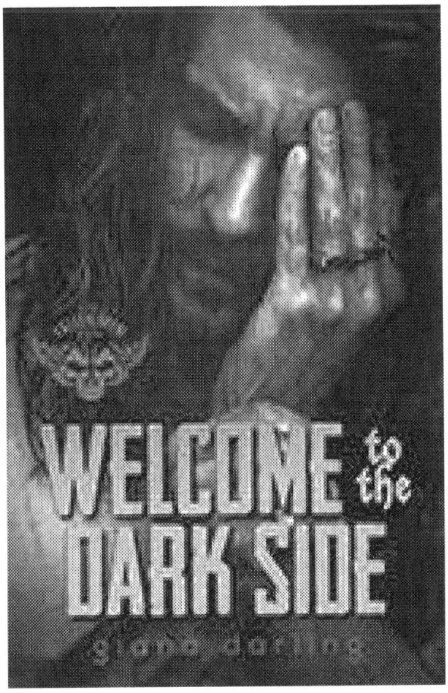

I was a good girl.

I ate my vegetables, volunteered at the local autism centre and sat in the front pew of church every Sunday.

Then, I got cancer.

What the hell kind of reward was that for a boring life well lived?

I was a seventeen-year-old paradigm of virtue and I was tired of it.

So, when I finally ran into the man I'd been writing to since he saved my life as a little girl and he offered to show me the dark side of life before I left it for good, I said yes.

Only, I didn't know that Zeus Garro was the President of The Fallen MC and when you made a deal with a man who is worse than the devil, there was no going back...

A standalone in The Fallen Men Series.

Prologue.

Welcome to the Dark Side Excerpt

I was too young to realize what the *pop* meant.

It sounded to my childish ears like a giant popping a massive wad of bubble gum.

Not like a bullet releasing from a chamber, heralding the sharp burst of pain that would follow when it smacked and then ripped through my shoulder.

Also, I was in the parking lot of First Light Church. It was my haven not only because it was a church and that was the original purpose of such places, but also because my grandpa was the pastor, my grandmother ran the after-school programs, and my father was the mayor so it was just as much his stage as his parents'.

A seven-year-old girl just does not expect to be shot in the parking lot of a church, holding the hand of her mother on one side and her father on the other, her grandparents waving from the open door as parents picked up their young children from after-school care.

Besides, I was unusually mesmerized by the sight of a man driving slowly by the entrance to the church parking lot. He rode a great growling beast that was so enormous it looked at my childish eyes like a silver and black backed dragon. Only the man wasn't wearing shining armour the way I thought he should have been. Instead, he wore a tight long-sleeved shirt under a heavy leather vest with a big picture of a fiery skull and tattered wings on the back of it. What kind of knight rode a mechanical dragon in a leather vest?

My little girl brain was too young to comprehend the complexities of the answer but my heart, though small, knew without context what kind of brotherhood that man would be in and it yearned for him.

Even at seven, I harboured a black rebel soul bound in velvet bows and Bible verse.

As if sensing my gaze, my thoughts, the biker turned to look at me, his face cruel with anger. I shivered and as his gaze settled on mine those shots rang out in a staccato beat that perfectly matched the cadence of my suddenly overworked heart.

Pop. Pop. Pop.

Everything from there happened as it did in action movies, with rapid bursts of sound and movement that swirled into a violent cacophony. I remembered only three things from the shooting that would go down in history as one of the worst incidents of gang violence in the town and province's history.

One.

My father flying to the ground quick as a flash, his hand wrenched from mine so that he could cover his own head. My mother screaming like a howler monkey but frozen to the spot, her hand paralyzed over mine.

Useless.

Two.

Men in black leather vests flooded the concrete like a murder of ravens, their hands filled with smoking metal that rattled off round after round of *pop, pop, pop*. Some of them rode bikes like my mystery biker but most of them were on foot, suddenly appearing from behind cars, around buildings.

More of them came roaring down the road behind the man I'd been watching, flying blurs of silver, green and black.

They were everywhere.

But these first two observations were merely vague impressions because I had eyes for only one person.

The third thing I remembered was him, Zeus Garro, locking eyes with me across the parking lot a split second before chaos erupted. Our gazes collided like the meeting of two planets, the ensuing bedlam a natural offshoot of the collision. It was only because I was watching him that I saw the horror distort his features and knew something bad was going to happen.

Someone grabbed me from behind, hauled me into the air with their hands under my pits. They were tall because I remember dangling like an ornament from his hold, small but significant with meaning. He was using me and even then, I knew it.

I twisted to try to kick him in the torso with the hard heel of my Mary Jane's and he must have assumed I'd be frozen in fright because my little shoe connected with a soft place that immediately loosened his grip.

Before I could fully drop to the ground, I was running and I was running toward him. The man on the great silver and black beast who had somehow heralded the massacre going down in blood and smoke all around me.

His bike lay discarded on its side behind him and he was standing straight and so tall he seemed to my young mind like a great giant, a beast from another planet or the deep jungle, something that killed for sport as well as survival. And he was doing it now, killing men like it was nothing but one of those awful, violent video games my cousin Clyde liked to play. In one hand he held a wicked curved blade already lacquered with blood from the two men who lay fallen at his feet while the other held a smoking gun that, under other circumstances, I might have thought was a pretty toy.

I took this in as I ran toward him, focused on him so I wouldn't notice the *pop*, the screams and wet slaps of bodies hitting the pavement. So I wouldn't taste the metallic residue of gun powder on my tongue or feel the splatter of blood that rained down on me as I passed one man being gutted savagely by another.

Somehow, if I could just get to *him*, everything would be okay.

He watched me come to him. Not with his eyes, because he was busy killing bad guys and shouting short, gruff orders to the guys wearing the same uniform as him but there was something in the way his great big body leaned toward me, shifted on his feet so that he was always orientated my way, that made me feel sure he was looking out for me even as I came for him.

He was just a stone's throw away, but it seemed to take forever for my short legs to move me across the asphalt and when I was only halfway there, his expression changed.

I knew without knowing that the man I'd kicked in his soft place was up again and probably angry. The hairs on the back of my neck stood on end and a fierce shiver ripped down my spine like tearing Velcro. I didn't realize it at the time, but I started to scream just as the police sirens started to wail a few blocks away.

My biker man roared, a violent noise that rent the air in two and made some of the people closest to him pause even in the middle of fighting. Then he was moving, and I remember thinking that for such a tall man, he moved *fast* because within the span of a breath, he was in front of me reaching out a hand to pull me closer...

A moment too late.

Because in that second when his tattooed hands clutched me to his chest and he tried to throw us to the ground, spiraling in a desperate attempt to act as human body armour to my tiny form, a *POP* so much louder than the rest exploded on the air and excruciating pain tore through my left shoulder, just inches from my adrenaline-filled heart.

We landed, and the agonizing pain burned brighter as my shoulder hit the pavement and my biker man rolled fully on top of me with a pained grunt.

I blinked through the tears welling up in my eyes, trying to breathe, trying to *live* through the pain radiating like a nuclear blast site through my chest. All I saw was him. His arm covered my head, one hand over my ear as he pulled back just enough to look down into my face.

That was what I remember most, that third thing, Zeus Garro's silver eyes as they stared down at me in a church parking lot filled with blood and smoke, screams and whimpers, but those eyes an oasis of calm that lulled my flagging heart into a steadier beat.

"I got you, little girl," he said in a voice as rough and deep as any monster's, while he held me as if he were a guardian angel. "I got you."

I clutched a tiny fist into his blood-soaked shirt and stared into the eyes of my guardian monster until I lost consciousness.

Sometimes now, I wonder if I would have done anything differently even if I had known how that bullet would tear through my small body, breaking bones and tender young flesh, irrevocably changing the course of my life forever.

Always, the answer is no.

Because it brought me to him.

Or rather, him to me.

Get it now for FREE on Kindle Unlimited!

THANKS ETC.

First of all, thank you to everyone who waited so patiently for Mei and Axe-Man to release! Losing my social media to a hacker was pretty damn awful and I missed interacting with my readers so much. A lot of personal life stuff kept me from coming back even sooner, but I can honestly say, it feels marvellous to be back. I have so much to share with you all because my forced year of solitude produced a *lot* of words. I wrote six books that are ready to release, with the next one coming in January!

Axe-Man and Mei are special to me for the same reason. They were both born with enormous hearts and over the course of their lives they had to learn to shield and protect them from the horrors of reality. Mei learned to rely only on herself, putting up barbed wire and cutting witticisms to keep people ten feet away. Axe-Man started to hide behind his loved ones, catering to their needs before his own and often letting them speak so he wouldn't have to. Words make us vulnerable, which means that he will always prefer to be a man of action instead of eloquence. It's a beautiful thing to be born with such a giving, loving heart, but it also makes life *painful* sometimes.

Learning how to endure that pain is a part of evolving and at the end of the day, this isn't just a love story, it's a tale about learning to trust yourself to take chances. Only when Axe-Man and Mei throw caution to the wind do they have any hope of achieving their happily ever after.

I hope you enjoyed my Off-White Knight and his Rocky. Writing Mei and her Chinese culture was so incredibly rewarding. It was also a *lot* of work so I will start off by thanking Professors Sharon Kwok and Wing Lo for sharing their dissertations and research with me on Chinese crime syndicates. It was oddly difficult to find resources on this subject matter and their help proved invaluable. If you are interested in other books on the subject, I recommend *Blood Brothers: The Criminal Underworld of Asia, The Snakehead: An Epic Tale of the Chinatown Underworld and the American Dream, The Chinese Triads, Wilful Blindness: How a Criminal Network of Narcos and Chinese Communist Agents Infiltrated the West, The Dragon Syndicates: The Global Phenomenon of the Triads, Claws of the Panda: Beijing's Campaign of Influence and Intimidation in Canada.* I also read some delightful biographies and autobiographies written by Chinese, Chinese-American, and Chinese-Canadian authors such as *Year of the Tiger: An Activist's Life* by Alice Wong, *Minor Feelings* by Cathy Park Hong, *We Were Dreamers: An Immigrant Superhero Origin Story* by Simu Liu, *How to American: An Immigrant's Guide to Disappointing Your Parents* by Jimmy O. Yang.

Now on to the team of people who keep me sane and so very loved.

First and arguably most important of all, my Annette. You kept my online world afloat while I was adrift, fielding questions and criticisms and stress with the ease and grace of a master. To say I am forever grateful for you as my assistant is an understatement that is only underscored by my gratefulness for you as my dearest friend. Having you at my wedding was only appropriate as you are my family and I will never go a day for the rest of my life without loving you.

Nina Grinstead, my PR guru and one of my most beloved friends in the world. Thank you for always been Team Giana, for always bringing positivity, humour, and love to every single interaction we have. I will love you forever and through anything. Meeting you and loving you has enriched my life.

Valentine, my Baby Darling. Sometimes you meet people in life and it's like you've been struck by lightning. There's this immediate sense that you've connected yet you know it's only the beginning. From the moment I met you I was captivated by your energy and as I've had the privilege of getting to know you, I've only fallen deeper in love with you. You're such an incredible woman and you inspire me. Thank you for being a ride or die <3

Jenny, you are a dream. I appreciate what you do for my words and how fluidly you fit me into your schedule!

Erica, thank you for being so incredibly good at your job and so invested in helping me produce the best, cleanest work I can. You mean so much to me both as an editor and a friend. Quite simply, you are invaluable to me.

Najla and Nada Qamber, thank you for turning my vision into beautiful covers and graphics. I've worked with you from the very start and I know I will forever.

Becca, the Serena to my Blair, the Cinderella to my Jasmine, the friend I am so lucky to love. You are a constant light in my life and a source of support and love I will never take for granted. I know if I ever needed you like Cleo needed Mei, you'd be there no matter what and vice versa, and how beautiful is that?

Sarah Gooch, I wish I had the words to describe how much you mean to me. You're my creative sounding board, the source of perfectly curated reels on IG, and a friend I feel as if I've known my whole life. You're stuck with me forever, sorry not sorry.

Giana's Darlings, I often say I have the best readers in the world, and in truth, I feel this is 100% accurate. I know many of you were as frustrated as I was with my extended absence, but whenever I saw you in person or got emails from you, they were filled with love, support, and light. You buoy me during the hard times and inspire me to create all the worlds that live inside my head. Thank you from the bottom of my heart for making my dreams come true. You are all my fairy godmothers.

My ARC team, who are my ride or dies and deserve all the love and thanks in my heart. You are the backbone of my marketing apparatus and I am beyond grateful for each and every one of you. Thank you for all you do for me.

Thank you to my sensitivity readers—Carina, Mika, Jenn, Lacey, and Sarah—for making sure that Chinese culture and Mei were represented respectfully and fully in this book. I couldn't have written it without you.

To my friend, Kandi, whose light brightens my world. Even when I was offline, you always checked in on me and maintained our friendship. I feel so lucky to know and love you.

Brittany, you gorgeous, fabulous woman. Your friendship, insight, and sass are invaluable to me. I love you forever.

Emilie, from @fansofgianadarling, for being such a loyal and caring friend and ambassador of my fans.

Jess, from PeaceLoveBooksxo, for being a ride or die fan and friend.

Tori, for being the loveliest reader and supporter.

Tish, for your friendship and support.

Fiona, Lauren, Bridget, Madison, and Lisa for being my real-life equivalent of the biker girl gang. The older I get, the more I value my female friendships and the depth of wisdom and love we share together. Thank you for being my cheerleaders and besties.

Armie, as always, you deserve your own little paragraph, because without your support on our long road trips and European travels, I never would have started The Fallen Men series. Even when we are apart, I think of you and love you every single day.

Gracie, the best sister in the world, who is the only person in my family to ever believe in me unconditionally. If only Mei had a sister like you to help her along the way.

To my boys, who have been with me since middle school. Someone pointed out to me that I often have groups of men in my books--The Fallen MC, the Gentlemen in the Dark Dream Duet, Dante's associates in the Anti-Heroes in Love Duet--and it makes sense. The lot of you changed my life for the better and continue to support, love, and protect me. You taught me the meaning of found family and I'll always be so honoured and grateful for our friendships.

And finally, for the first time in my acknowledgements I can say thank you to my *husband*. Your love is my inspiration. What a remarkable thing it is to wake up beside the same man every day and feel each morning like the near miraculous gift that it is. I am so lucky to have found my soul mate when I was fifteen and there isn't a moment of our lives together that I take for granted. Thank you for being my paradise.

ABOUT GIANA DARLING

Giana Darling is a USA Today, Wall Street Journal, Top 40 Best Selling Canadian romance writer who specializes in the taboo and angsty side of love and romance. She currently lives in beautiful British Columbia where she spends time riding on the back of her husband's bike, baking pies, and reading snuggled up with her dog, Romeo, and her cat, Persephone.

Join my Reader's Group
Subscribe to my Newsletter
Follow me on IG
Like me on Facebook
Follow me on Goodreads
Follow me on BookBub
Follow me on Pinterest

OTHER BOOKS BY GIANA DARLING

The Fallen Men Series

The Fallen Men are a series of interconnected, standalone, erotic MC romances that each feature age gap love stories between dirty-talking, Alpha males and the strong, sassy women who win their hearts.

Lessons in Corruption

Welcome to the Dark Side

Good Gone Bad

Fallen Son (A Short Story)

After the Fall

Inked in Lies

Fallen King (A Short Story)

Dead Man Walking

Caution to the Wind

A Fallen Men Companion Book of Poetry:

King of Iron Hearts

The Evolution of Sin Trilogy

Giselle Moore is running away from her past in France for a new life in America, but before she moves to New York City, she takes a holiday on the beaches of Mexico and meets a sinful, enigmatic French businessman, Sinclair, who awakens submissive desires and changes her life forever.

The Affair

The Secret

The Consequence

The Evolution Of Sin Trilogy Boxset

The Enslaved Duet

The Enslaved Duet is a dark romance duology about an eighteen-year old Italian fashion model, Cosima Lombardi, who is sold by her indebted father to a British Earl who's nefarious plans for her include more than just sexual slavery... Their epic tale spans across Italy, England, Scotland, and the USA across a five-year period that sees them endure murder, separation, and a web of infinite lies.

Enthralled (The Enslaved Duet #1)

Enamoured (The Enslaved Duet, #2)

The Enslaved Duet Boxset

Anti-Heroes in Love Duet

Elena Lombardi is an ice cold, broken-hearted criminal lawyer with a distaste for anything untoward, but when her sister begs her to represent New York City's most infamous mafioso on trial for murder, she can't refuse and soon, she finds herself unable to resist the dangerous charms of Dante Salvatore.

When Heroes Fall

When Villains Rise

Anti-Heroes in Love Duet Boxset

The Dark Dream Duet

The Dark Dream duology is a guardian/ward, enemies to lovers romance about the dangerous, scarred black sheep of the Morelli family, Tiernan, and the innocent Bianca Belcante. After Bianca's mother dies, Tiernan becomes the guardian to both her and her little brother. But Tiernan doesn't do anything out of the goodness of his heart, and soon Bianca is thrust into the wealthy elite of Bishop's Landing and the dark secrets that lurk beneath its glittering surface.

Bad Dream (Dark Dream Duet, #0.5) is FREE

Dangerous Temptation (Dark Dream Duet, #1)

Beautiful Nightmare (Dark Dream Duet, #2)

Wildest Dreams Boxset

The Elite Seven Series

Sloth (The Elite Seven Series, #7)

Coming Soon

Serpentine Valentine

AT (A Fallen Men Novella)

Sebastian Lombardi's Trilogy

Made in the USA
Columbia, SC
07 February 2024

31618327R00346